THE PIRATE DANCED AND THE AUTOMAT DIED

THE CELWYN SERIES BOOK 4

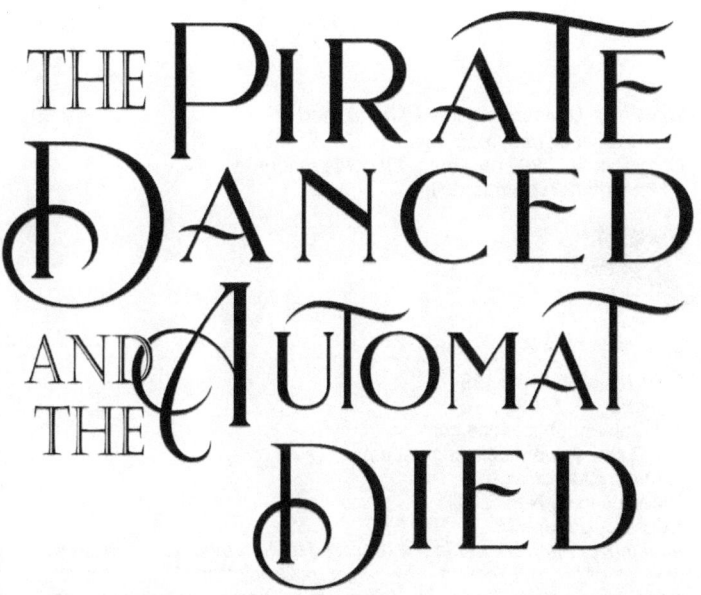

THE PIRATE DANCED AND THE AUTOMAT DIED

LOU KEMP

4 Horsemen
Publications, Inc.

The Pirate Danced and the Automat Died
The Celwyn Series Book 4
Copyright © 2023 Lou Kemp. All rights reserved.
4 Horsemen Publications, Inc.

4 Horsemen
Publications, Inc.

1497 Main St. Suite 169
Dunedin, FL 34698
4horsemenpublications.com
info@4horsemenpublications.com
Cover by J.Kotick
Typesetting by Niki Tantillo
Edited by Joseph M.

Library of Congress Control Number: 2023935229
Paperback ISBN-13: 978-1-64450-949-4
Hardcover ISBN-13: 978-1-64450-950-0
Audiobook ISBN-13: 978-1-64450-952-4
Ebook ISBN-13: 978-1-64450-951-7

Table of Contents

Acknowledgements

MANY THANKS AND LOVE TO MY daughter, Charmaine, who has supported me no matter what, even when I got a third cat. Thank you to friends for their help and feedback: Nikki, Debbie, Peggy, and Karen. To authors and bloggers who have done their best to help me: Anita Dickason, Sue Costner, Gina Ray Mitchell, Norm Backstrom, Benjamin X. Wretlind, and Bob Van Laerhoven. Thank you to John Helfers of Stonehenge Editorial and Jenny Rosenblum for the original editing of this book. Also, well-deserved praise to Joseph Mistretta for the final editing.

Cast of Characters

Jonas Celwyn: mortal magician and provocateur

Professor Xiau Kang: Automat, medical man, skeptic, and scientist

Bartholomew: Widower from Juba, colleague, and friend to Kang and Celwyn

Qing: Mechanical bird & lover of all things shiny and wonderful

Annabelle Pearse Edmunds: Heiress and ward of Uncle Celwyn

Captain Patrick Swayne: Friend to Celwyn, loves Annabelle

Mrs. Elizabeth Kang: Tolerant and beautiful wife of Kang

Zander and Otto: Orphans and now brothers living at Tellyhouse

Tara McFein: Good witch and good vampire

Simone Redifer: Good vampire

Valentine Soriano: Uncle to Tara & Simone, head of their family

Captain Nemo: Captain of the *Nautilus*

Jules Verne: Author aboard the *Nautilus* and part of the adventures

Granger: Nemo's Lieutenant

The Wessex Club: The cream of the Victorian literary world: Thomas Hardy, Oscar Wilde, Henry James, William Butler Yeats, George Bernard Shaw.

Aldonis Pompero: Supreme spymaster, answering only to the Queen

Captain Emilio Dearing: Pirate king and confederate of Talos

Mercury: Friend and confidant of the vampires

Talos: Professor Kang's brother and automat who wasn't as dead as they thought.

Sir John Cecil Winterset: Vampire hunter and ally of Dearing

Ginnie Ford: The witch in league with the warlock, Duncan.

Gibson: American traitor

Prelude

1868
In the waters off the coast of Trabzon, Turkey

THE GONGS IN THE BELLY OF THE *Nautilus* echoed, signaling the time had come to return to Nemo's compound and find answers. They couldn't wait any longer. But before anyone could move, a commotion in the corridor drew their attention as a hatless crewman in torn and dirty clothes stumbled into the study of the submarine. At this late hour, it wasn't a surprise; they had been expecting him days ago.

"Ah, Valdez," Captain Nemo stood and greeted him. "It is good that you have returned."

The man inhaled deeply, swayed, and would have fallen if Captain Nemo hadn't caught his arm and guided him to a chair. In a voice they could barely hear, Valdez began talking fast, as if he would lose his nerve if he didn't. Even before he spoke, the magician felt the cold hand of dread weighing upon him.

"Everyone dead—all of them. Even Mrs. Sogun." Valdez inhaled again. "Their necks were broken."

The automat, Professor Xiau Kang, passed the Captain a whiskey, and Nemo handed it to the man. "Drink that."

It was an order. When the crewman began speaking again, he sounded stronger but no less frightened.

"It was a tremendous fight—the blonde woman was gone and—Dr. Maeler ... he died differently. His throat cut." Valdez slashed a hand across his own throat. As he finished his drink, Nemo handed him another. "Then, I heard a scream. I ran to the last building. The big one." Valdez started shaking.

Bartholomew kept his voice calm. "Take your time."

"I ran in. The man..." he hesitated and stared at Jonas Celwyn, "who was with us—"

"My brother," Celwyn said gently and nodded at him to continue.

Valdez dropped his glass and shook his head when offered more. With another look at Celwyn, he said, "Mr. Pelaez, he ... he pointed at the big yellow machine, and flames burned over it. Then he laughed. And ... and laughed." Sweat poured off the crewman's pale cheeks. "He saw me when I tried to run, and then I couldn't." He pleaded with them. "I couldn't *move*."

Captain Nemo patted his shoulder. "It's all right." He motioned to the guard by the door.

Valdez shot a tortured glance at the magician. "Your brother, he walked right up to me and said I was 'late.'" Valdez switched to Captain Nemo. "H-he said to give this to you, Sir, when I returned here." He fished in his jacket and produced an envelope. As he passed it over, he said, "There was a pig there, a big pig, staring at me." The crewman trembled. "Then he put me in a closet ... with a body. It was Mr. Sogun—his head was turned backward." Valdez waved away Kang's hand as he tried to comfort him. "I was tied up—with so many ropes. The man ... that Pelaez, he left me a knife—he put it under the body. Made sure I saw it."

"So, it would take you a while to free yourself?" Bartholomew asked. The others nodded in agreement.

"When I finally got out, my horse and the rest of the horses were gone."

Bartholomew said, "And you walked all the way back here."

"Yes."

"Pelaez has several days' head start. Damn!" Kang stamped his foot.

Captain Nemo ripped the envelope open and read aloud.

My dear Captain Nemo:

> *As I write this, you should know that I enjoyed your hospitality very much.*

You may think I have abused your good-will, and I apologize, but the greater good must prevail. The "flying machine," as you call it, must not succeed.

It will be used for war.

The horrors of war envelop the air we breathe. Each invention of war bloodies our souls. It must be stopped. I could have destroyed the flying machine a long time ago, but for two reasons:

I felt an obligation to stay and keep you and those in my brother's party from harm. Also, with the specifications that Bartholomew and the Professor made, you would have just built another one. So, I waited until the time was ripe.

I have destroyed both the machine and the specifications of how to build it again.

Kang rushed out of the room, and Celwyn buried his face in his hands.

Captain Nemo continued reading.

To my brother, you should know that I enjoyed our reunion at times and found your supercilious attitude trying at others. However, I tolerated it to obtain my goals.

*Did you know that Miss McFein is not
only a vampire but also a witch? I doubt
it. You are so besotted with her that you
barely notice anything.*

*Perhaps we may meet again, hundreds
of years from now, when you have
forgiven me.*

Pelaez

"That is all," Captain Nemo said, folding the
paper as carefully as possible to keep from crushing
it. Unfathomable anger darkened his eyes. Then his
proud shoulders slumped as profound disappointment overlaid his indignation.

"Pelaez killed them all?" Bartholomew demanded
as he stalked to the window and back. "Why?"

The emptiness and betrayal Celwyn felt went
so deep he physically hurt. This time, the glasses by
the bar didn't shake or shatter—instead, they began
to melt, turning to liquid like his tears and falling
like rain.

Celwyn could not speak.

"Or … it was the witch, perhaps…" Captain Nemo
speculated.

Kang returned, and before he sat down, his face
told them what he'd confirmed; Pelaez had indeed
stolen the specs from his room. Celwyn remembered
his brother's overstuffed knapsack the morning he
left. More tears streamed down his face as an intense
sorrow enveloped him and wouldn't let go. After all

these years, Celwyn had found his brother and lost him again in the worst way.

Captain Nemo regarded the magician for a long moment, and with uncharacteristic pity, said, "I'm sorry, Jonas." He turned and instructed the remaining guard, "Valdez needs food. Have someone stay with him." The guard saluted and ushered Valdez out of the room.

Kang asked the magician, "Would Pelaez really kill them all?"

"Yes." Celwyn heard the certainty in his voice. "I have no doubt of it."

"Or, the wi ... Ginnie did it," Bartholomew suggested, as Nemo had.

The Professor said, "We just don't know."

Celwyn raised a tortured face to Nemo. "Take the Professor to Prague and his wife." He glanced at the big man who stood beside him. "Bartholomew and I will hunt Pelaez down."

"What is the point?" Nemo threw his glass across the room. "Revenge will do no good!"

"But—"

"Stop, Jonas." Kang patted his shoulder and pushed him down when the magician tried to get up. "Revenge is another place, another time." The automat made sure he had Nemo's attention and said, "Bartholomew and I will recreate the specs on the way to Prague, and we will build another flying machine. Near Prague, if that is acceptable? We can devote all our time to it."

Morose horns entered the room, exploding in anger and bleeding with the pain of treachery. Qing flew to the magician and nudged his chin. Celwyn's tears fell on his feathers as the ornate organ began to play, uniting with the music of the horns, soaring high and resounding sorrowfully above them.

"I will find Pelaez." With a growl, Celwyn stroked the mechanical bird's shiny feathers. His thoughts turned inward.

"No." Kang confronted him, his voice firm, but infinitely kind. "I need Bartholomew's help with the flying machine." With Celwyn sitting and the automat standing, they were on eye level as Kang challenged him. "You know we need you too."

Bartholomew said, "Come back to Prague, Jonas." The magician shook his head.

Bartholomew played the one card that broke through Celwyn's grief. "After Annabelle's wedding, we will talk."

Celwyn hesitated, picturing the disappointment on each of the faces inhabiting Tellyhouse.

"After we rebuild the flying machine, we will find Pelaez together," Kang promised.

The magician sat still and tried to think as logically as everyone else. He was surrounded by scientists and a military genius. Celwyn turned to Captain Nemo. "Sir, do you have an idea where the new compound will be located?"

Nemo took off his cap and shook his head. "At the moment, I am disheartened."

Celwyn said, "I am too ... however..."

From his favorite spot at the chess table, Jules Verne asked Celwyn, "What do you propose?"

The author had been so quiet the magician had forgotten about him. He hesitated a bit more before saying, "After reflection, I bow to the Professor and Bartholomew's good sense." Celwyn inhaled, his normal equanimity returning and the forlorn music fading. "Rebuilding the flying machine is more important than revenge."

Bartholomew rumbled, "Are you sure?"

"Yes." The magician thought about Annabelle and Patrick and the boys, Zander and Otto. Revenge was selfish. *And it will be private.* As a delectable distraction, he produced a tray of pastries, tea, and coffee on the table between them.

The Professor selected the fattest fairy cake with lavish frosting and bit into it. "It will take months to set up a new laboratory and a test field for flying. Of course, we will be there as it's built."

With a nod at the magician, Captain Nemo added, "We should build your kind of security into it, too."

Celwyn poured Earl Grey, and the aroma alone helped. He wiped the last of his tears away and glanced out the aquatic window. At the edge of a nearby kelp forest, a white silhouette hovered just far enough away that he couldn't identify it through the water. "I agree."

Nemo asked, "What will Pelaez do with the specs?"

"His purpose was to destroy the flying machine. By now, the specs no longer exist." Bartholomew slammed a fist into the arm of the sofa. "By god, we worked so hard on them."

"All the specs?" Verne had been playing with his fountain pen, not brave enough to take notes in front of Celwyn in his emotional condition. Considering recent events, he might find himself on top of the ship as she swam through the water.

Kang asked, "What if Pelaez didn't find the set of plans that we hid for Dr. Maeler?"

"I wager he did. We also don't know if Ginnie survived or if she was the one who killed them all." Celwyn cursed under his breath and strolled to the window. The conservative academic, Dr. Maeler, had been hired to build the next prototype of the flying machine. To make things interesting, he had brought along his flouncy, flashy, and bawdy paramour. Looking back on her behavior, Celwyn realized that Ginnie Ford was all of that purposely, and it may have been staged to divert them from the sabotage she planned. Celwyn stared. The white, shadowy image no longer floated near the ship. Only tendrils of black seaweed remained, undulating in the water like long ghostly arms as the ship drifted closer to the kelp.

"We will go back to our compound after all." Bartholomew did not appear happy about the prospect, and his frown deepened.

"It will be grim." The automat thought for a second and repeated his prediction.

Nemo rubbed his face hard. "You are all much more resilient than I from this tragedy." He joined them on the sofas. After a moment, he selected a pastry and bit into it like he would like to bite into Pelaez.

Kang said, "We're angry, and we won't give up."

The Captain dabbed his lips with a napkin. "There is no doubt we will rebuild. Tomorrow we will return to our compound, and I will bring more than a full complement of guards with us in case of an attack." He checked what he planned to say and then finished with, "Initially, we will head toward the mountains to the south, not the route we took getting here. The threat to us no longer exists." Nemo pulled down his cuffs and made sure they matched. "After that, we will journey to Prague."

"Thank God we aren't going back the same way." Verne shuddered.

Bartholomew echoed him with a shiver of his own. "Thank God."

Pictured across everyone's face was the memory of the ordeal they had just gone through in the nearby forest. It felt as fresh as if it had happened only minutes ago. The warlock, Duncan, would not soon be forgotten.

The automat half-smiled at the others. "How close can we get to our destination with the *Nautilus*?"

Bartholomew saw his expression. "Oh, no..."

The magician interrupted his morose thoughts to squint at them until he understood. *Poor Bartholomew.* At over seven feet tall, the muscular man from East Africa was as brave as he was tall ... but he feared many things, including every known superstition, and especially what the automat had just hinted at.

Captain Nemo nodded. "Yes, I can get us much closer by taking the ship through the underground rivers."

Verne asked, "Why didn't we go this route initially?"

"None of these rivers went far enough inland, and the ship was already at sea with the Mafioso's eyes upon the ports." The Professor told him, "As you remember, we took a calculated risk that Duncan would follow the other villains that Jonas and Pelaez led on a merry chase. It failed." They were all silent for a few minutes until Captain Nemo spoke again.

"For our return trip tomorrow, we will surface at a lake about ten miles from the old compound."

Bartholomew gulped and seemed to shrink into his clothes at the news, wishing to be anywhere but here to hear of a plan he considered extraordinarily dangerous.

"We will be fine, and I trust the crew of this ship." The magician did his best to assure him. "We won't be open to attack like the last time, and we can do this in one day." Celwyn's mood cleared, responding to action and planning.

"I like it." The automat turned to Bartholomew. "While we are underground, Jonas will do something to calm you like he did before. Will that suffice?"

"My claustrophobia is horrible. What he did before—" Bartholomew's voice sounded a bit more hopeful, "I didn't even notice."

Celwyn said, "You won't notice anything tomorrow either, my friend."

"All right, but I still don't like this, you know."

Of all people to respond, it was the most terrified participant from their ordeal. "It is better than chancing what happened on the way here by going the other route." Verne sounded like he had relived each detail vividly.

"Duncan is dead," the magician reminded them and wished he could kill the bastard again. Qing rubbed his beak on Celwyn's chin, his form of bird comfort.

Verne tugged on his little beard, and his voice trembled. "Who knows if another warlock might be lurking out there..."

"We don't. We also don't know our plans beyond tomorrow." Captain Nemo regarded them from under lowered brows. He twisted the brass buttons on his uniform jacket, the only indication of his personal turmoil, as if he twisted Pelaez's neck. "For now, we'll retrieve the specs if they still exist ... and perhaps some of the tools." His tone adopted a false hope that none of them felt. "It is possible we will recover someone alive."

"I don't wish to be indelicate, but what will we do about the dead we find?" Kang asked.

Captain Nemo stood.

"We will bury them there."

PART I

PART 1

Chapter 1

WITH THE EARLIEST HINT OF DAWN, when daylight was only a faint suggestion against the blanket of darkness, the *Nautilus* inched away from Trabzon, traveling east through the Black Sea and hugging the coast. By ten in the morning, they had reached the point where their route would change and made a wide arc about thirty feet below the surface. A series of gongs resounded in her belly as the submarine hovered, awaiting orders.

In the study, Celwyn and the others arranged their chairs in front of the aquatic window, watching the water change from blue to dark green against a strong current, and the ship slipped into the underground river below Ordu.

"Does this river have a name?" Celwyn asked Kang.

Glad for an excuse to discuss something he enjoyed, the Professor popped up and rummaged in the maps. He spread one across the chess table behind them and studied it long enough to develop a frown. "No, there's no identification here, but this is another underground runoff route for the melted snow from the Taurus Mountains. Like the one that we used on our way here." He turned to Bartholomew. "It will be deep."

The big man swallowed and slowly pried his lips open. "I understand." He loosened his tie and stared out the window.

Celwyn tried to help. "The Captain reports that we will only travel about two hours in this manner, depending on how much the ship must fight the outgoing current. Coming back, it will be much faster."

Bartholomew nodded, but a fine sheen of sweat broke out across his face as the earthen walls of the river drew closer, and darkness swallowed the ship. The sconces in the study came alive with a soft glow.

"Do you want Jonas to help you now or wait?" Kang asked.

For another moment, they gazed through the ship's exterior lights to where the water lightened, revealing tendrils of greenery that flattened as they cruised by. In the last few minutes, the passage had narrowed further. Bartholomew stretched his legs and knocked over one of the backpacks at their feet. "Not yet."

Verne asked, "What do you plan to do when we arrive? The Captain requested that I remain on the ship."

"He wants to ensure your safety," Kang told him, "in case there is trouble. You don't want to run into Pelaez, do you? I didn't think so." The automat pointed to a spot on the map. "The lake by Cerzin is remote and large. We will surface there without any problems, and with luck, we won't have to back out again when it is time to leave."

"What else are you going to do?" Verne asked, not to be deterred in his curiosity.

Celwyn shrugged. "Retrieve tools and bury the dead."

From the look on the author's face, Verne wished that he had not asked.

———————⏜———————

They elected to have a late breakfast in front of the aquatic window, eating silently while immersed in their thoughts instead of the small talk that usually accompanied a meal. Much of that talk centered on teasing Celwyn. Instead, the magician thought about their destination and relived the expected carnage the crewman had described to them last night.

He had just finished his third cup of tea when the submarine began to ascend, escorted by clouds of bubbles. Bartholomew's sigh could be heard all the way down the corridor.

"As the bard says, 'The game is afoot, gentlemen.'" Kang led the way out of the study. Once they arrived topside, they found a pair of Nemo's crewmen with spyglasses already scanning the forest to the south and west. Bartholomew and Celwyn began checking north and east.

"We are alone," Bartholomew reported and lowered his spyglass.

Celwyn finished a last survey and nodded to a waiting crewman who ducked back inside the ship to relay the information to the bridge. As another precaution, the magician blocked the area around the *Nautilus* so no one could see her.

A quarter of an hour later, three boats rowed away from the submarine. With a pistol resting on his knee, Captain Nemo sat by Kang in the lead boat, and Celwyn and Bartholomew were right behind them. As they drew closer to shore, the magician checked the area again, noting only a few feet of dirt separated the forest from the lake.

A fat trout rose into the air and pirouetted for the crew in the boats. When everyone turned to stare at it, Celwyn gestured, and a collection of carts filled the nearest clearing in the trees. By prior arrangement, Captain Nemo kept the crew offshore while the magician walked into the brush and scouted various hiding places until he found what he wanted.

Celwyn emerged from the trees, herding a collection of field mice in front of him. When he caused a tall waterspout to shoot upward in the lake, the crew turned toward it. A full complement of horses stomped and snorted in front of the carts by the time they turned back again.

Kang gave the big man a little push toward the first cart. "Don't ask."

"I do not want to know," Bartholomew announced with his chin up.

Chapter 2

I T ONLY TOOK A FEW HOURS TO COVER the ten miles through the rolling hills to the compound.

As they passed the outer perimeter fence, everyone stared at a single boot lying next to the fence post, a grim reminder that things here would not be the same as they had left them only days before. Everyone watched the cluster of buildings where they had lived and worked as it came into view.

On the far right, the hangar door stood open on the largest structure, something that would never have occurred when they were in residence. The shadows inside prevented seeing anything from this distance, but in front of the hangar, a hatless and shapeless body lay propped against the building, representing the caricature remains of a guard. Crows hopped over the body, tearing at the flesh.

Celwyn made a face and waved a hand. The birds scattered fast. "Captain, I suggest that the others wait in our transport for a few minutes, please."

Nemo wiggled a brow at him. "Because of...?"

"To give me a few minutes to find the bodies and bury them."

"That is considerate. My guards knew some of these men. However, I'll go with you and search for the specs. We do not have long here before we must return." Captain Nemo gave the order and climbed out of the cart.

Shoulder to shoulder, they headed up the walkway to the main building. The first thing the magician saw was the body of a guard dangling over the edge of the roof. At first, Celwyn thought the man had taken a shotgun blast in the face and then realized the crows had been at work again. With a gesture, the magician cleaned and dressed the corpse in a fine suit and put it in an open grave in the field. He elevated himself to the top of the roof to verify the two other guards. Soon, he added their rifles to a pile behind the cart and their bodies to the same grave.

"I suggest you dig a deeper hole." Kang arrived in front of the main house. He, too, did not mind the macabre; being alive for hundreds of years and seeing the worst of the world had inured him to it. "What killed them?"

"Their necks were snapped. It was done in a most violent manner."

When they entered the house, the magician caught a glimpse of himself in the mirror above the dining table, as handsome as usual with his dark hair and fine profile, but he also saw the worry in his eyes—*Damn Pelaez.*

Celwyn cursed and began the process with several more of the guards. They found Mrs. Sogun on the floor beside the stove and Fatima alongside her, still wearing a blood-splattered toque. Their necks had been slashed with a sharp blade. *Were these intended as more merciful killings?*

With his handkerchief covering his nose, Kang examined them briefly. "The stench is becoming unbearable." The automat pointed at the women. "Why a different way to kill them?"

"I do not know. I remember how Fatima was afraid of unnatural occurrences." His voice dropped. "It came true for her." As Celwyn finished readying their bodies for transport to the field, he remembered how Fatima had thought Pelaez resembled her son. *God damn him.* She would not have been afraid of him. "We're done here."

Captain Nemo waited by the front door with a thunderous expression. "The copy of the specs is gone."

"As we assumed." Kang flung open the door and stomped outside.

When they arrived in the courtyard, Bartholomew joined them, his eyes searching for the carnage while fearful of seeing any.

"No survivors." Kang took care as he told him about the way they died. "We do not know why there is a difference in the method."

"Perhaps it suggests two different killers?"

Celwyn heard that last idea but faced with the corpses, he didn't really care.

"All the bodies have been buried in the field." He pointed to an area beyond the transport carts.

The Captain asked, "Shall we check the hangar next?"

Bartholomew and Kang led the way as they approached the building where they had spent months constructing the product of their imagination and scientific talents. Celwyn stopped and took care of the body lying in front of the entrance.

With a deep sigh they all heard, Captain Nemo said, "That was Mr. Dobbs, supervisor of the guards. I will write a note to his widow."

"Is she nearby?" Bartholomew asked.

"Ankara. They have a large family." Nemo's mood darkened further. "They will be compensated for this."

Celwyn added Dobbs' body to those already in the field. With a groan, he realized where the rest of the guards would be.

"What is the matter?" Bartholomew asked. "You look angrier than the Captain now."

"Nothing pleasant, my friend." The magician clapped the big man on the shoulder and said to the others, "After we are done here, we will find the rest of the dead in the barracks. Any survivors would have approached us already."

By the time he finished speaking, they had reached the middle of the hangar and what awaited them.

"It is one thing to imagine the damage, but—" Kang stared at the shell of the flying machine.

It still smelled faintly of smoke. Celwyn assumed his brother had dissolved the fuel in the tanks to eliminate the possibility of an explosion. The bastard would want to watch the machine burn when he torched it.

Only a few streaks of yellow paint striped the tail section of the charred remains. The carcass reminded Celwyn of a large bird caught in a firestorm; he had no trouble picturing it on fire. The stench from the ruin almost covered the odor of decomposition. But not quite.

"There is another body here. I smell it." Celwyn expanded his search as Bartholomew opened cupboards and bins. Kang did the same. Their job was to find tools; his was much grimmer. Nemo heard them. His anger over Pelaez's crimes turned his complexion red.

"Pelaez," the Captain growled the word.

"There is decay here; I smell it also," Kang said.

Sometimes it surprised Celwyn when the automat displayed traits of a flesh and blood species. Kang had been made with leathery skin over a metal skeleton, long black hair, and elfin ears. Over the hundreds of years since, he had developed a great capacity and fondness for whiskey and cookies. When they had first met, Celwyn had listened to Xiau's explanation of his sentiments and his curiosity and love of life as they sailed west on the *Zelda*. The automat felt emotions such as hate and love. He also enjoyed teasing and worrying about his friend, Jonas Celwyn.

The magician gazed upward. A man lay face down in the rafters with an ax embedded in his back.

"Remind me of your helpers' names?" he asked.

"Martin and Kirk." Bartholomew followed Celwyn's gaze. With a sigh, he said, "That is Martin."

Celwyn dressed the body and sent it outside with the others. "Enough of this," he cursed. "I'd like to get the rest of this business over with. Perhaps you two could gather the tools you want while the Captain and I visit the guards' quarters."

With a nod, Bartholomew squatted beside an upended cabinet that used to house a collection of wrenches.

Captain Nemo sighed. "I'll search the house for the specs once more while you deal with what is in the barracks. It is possible Dr. Maeler moved the drawings if he felt threatened."

"He probably found a good reason to be," Bartholomew said as Celwyn and Nemo headed out the door.

More than twenty paces before the barracks, the magician detected cloying wisps of decay. When he stared into the interior of the structure, he saw only corpses. From the furniture to the lamps, everything inside seemed fuzzy, reminding him again of how the characteristics he'd received from Thales faded each day, including the optical ones. For several long minutes, he studied the way the men had died, mostly with surprise painted across their faces. He cleaned them up and sent them to the field.

As he stood in front of the building, something tickled the magician with the feathery touch of unease. He glanced at the hangar, only spotting Kang and Bartholomew as they dragged hunks of metal and other things toward the carts. They made quite a pair, the diminutive automat, and the seven-foot-tall African. He swiveled. A quick check through the walls of the main house revealed a contemplative Nemo staring at the bookshelves. Celwyn looked further, seeing nothing living in the bedrooms at the rear of the house.

What was bothering him?

It must be in the barracks. The magician removed all the windows from the building and sent a cleansing wind whistling through it from end to end. As he resolved to go inside, Captain Nemo slammed the door to the main house and tramped over to him.

"Something I should know?" Nemo growled the question, evidence he hadn't found the specs.

"The dead have been removed." Celwyn frowned. "We should check inside. A while back, Fatima told me there's a spring there."

"Very well."

They opened the door and walked in, stepping around a fallen bookcase and the broken dishes surrounding an overturned dining table. Bugs and maggots crawled over the rotting food and through the appalling stench. However, Celwyn preferred it over the sweet scent of decomposition. The magician stopped still, listening. The silence waited as well ... as if expecting them. A dark and shrill breeze raced through the house, like death riding bareback and shaking a bone over its head.

They remained by the front door. Nothing else breathed here. Yet Celwyn put an arm in front of Captain Nemo, holding him back. To the left, an open living room with sofas welcomed them, and a pinball machine and game tables occupied different corners. Stairs led to the bunks upstairs.

"That leads to the spring and storage room." Captain Nemo stared at a closed door across the room.

Celwyn moved forward, detouring around the upended furniture toward the door. Whatever they found wouldn't improve by waiting. He threw light inside and caused the door to swing open, revealing an enormous shadowy room.

To the right, bags of rice and other supplies filled shelves. Someone had placed a row of buckets in front of a knee-high stone wall that curved around the length of the room. The air felt heavy with dew. As they approached the parapet, the magician felt a certain reluctance. Perhaps it was fear. Captain Nemo stood quietly beside him, too grim to speak.

The magician somehow expected what happened next.

From the depths of the spring, something moved, rising to the top.

Pale, pink skin broke the surface, bobbing face up with the swell of the water.

Nemo's lips tightened, keeping his fear and disgust in check as they stared at a dead pig. It had been gutted snout to tail, and Kang's wooden replicas of the flying machine had been tucked inside its belly. The carcass floated there in a small fetid lake.

Without a word, Celwyn and Captain Nemo walked outside, welcoming the heat and normalcy of the midday sun. They met up with Bartholomew, who stood nearby talking with Kang about the merits of the tools they had salvaged from the hangar. When they saw the others' expressions, they stopped.

Celwyn rubbed his face, trying to wipe away the image of what he had seen; it took a most twisted mind to do something like that. "We need to get back to the ship. Do you agree, Sir?" He glanced at Captain Nemo and received a distracted nod in return.

Bartholomew didn't want to ask. "What happened? More bodies?"

"Only what we knew to expect. They're all properly buried in the field now." The magician pointed to the transport cart. "Do you have everything from here that you want?"

"Yes." Kang said, "We gathered a few things that will help when we rebuild. What is wrong?"

Celwyn waited, and Nemo took over. "We found something in the barracks." He urged them toward the carts where one crewman stowed the rest of the rifles, and another handed off cases marked *Vino*. "It was a gutted pig. Your carvings of flying machines were inside it." At their reactions, he added, "It was a real pig, not Pelaez's companion."

Bartholomew did better than the magician expected with the news. He blinked rapidly and licked his lips. "Oh, my."

"Oh, my, indeed," Celwyn repeated as the cold hand of premonition wiggled down his back. "Let's return to the ship."

"Before we do, I brought one of the *Nautilus* crew with us who serves as clergy." Nemo waved at a short crewman sitting in one of the carts. "He will say a few words over the grave for all the faiths represented here. If any of you would like to add your thoughts, it would be appreciated."

Chapter 3

WITH DELECTABLE SCENTS FILLING the air, they began a late luncheon of baked trout and freshwater mussels steamed in a basil garlic sauce, along with fresh bread. The submarine's crew had spent the last few hours successfully fishing the lake while Celwyn and the others dealt with what they found at the compound. As the *Nautilus* prepared once again to head to the coast, everyone breathed easier.

Without Pelaez, the five of them could squeeze into Captain Nemo's private dining room for meals. Qing had not been invited, so the magician provided the bird with a lively silver frog to chase across the study while they were gone.

The murmur of their luncheon conversation rose and fell like waves sloshing against the shore. As Celwyn ate, he couldn't help thinking about their disturbing find at the compound. In the end, he concluded that since he had no idea of the significance of the gutted pig, he simply would ignore it. With effort, he would also forget it.

The magician's concern grew about a situation across the table from him. After their return to the ship, Nemo announced that the circumference of the lake was not big enough for the submarine to turn around, compelling them to back out of the underground river and heightening the big man's anxiety. Bartholomew couldn't hide his nervousness, and his eyes quivered as much as his hands.

By design, the Captain had asked Bartholomew to sit beside Kang, facing away from the aquatic window. It did not work. The big man kept involuntarily glancing over his shoulder every other minute.

"Would it help if we closed the window?" Captain Nemo asked.

Bartholomew dropped his fork, and a crewman retrieved it while another replaced the fork. "No. Perhaps, instead, we could talk about our plans. The complexity of them should be distracting."

Kang continued to eat his trout, faces and all. The magician grimaced at that and tried not to look again. If he'd been Bartholomew, the crunching of fish faces would undoubtedly distract him.

"As you wish," Nemo said. "I've given our situation some thought. Like we discussed, it will take time to set up another compound, including a flying field and hangar." He regarded them. "I don't need to remind you of your social commitment in Prague."

"I am certainly aware." Celwyn could imagine what awaited them. "I will be blamed if we do not appear for the nuptials." He leaned back as a crewman served a compote of grapes and oranges immersed in cream and decorated with pistachios. "They will be anxious to see us."

"Sir, that reminds me," Kang said. "Before we travel too far, I'd like to send telegrams to Prague, letting them know we're on our way."

"But, what will you tell them? We do not know where we'll build the next compound." Bartholomew frowned, then he brightened. "Perhaps that is best, so they do not worry."

"Certainly, we will stop. What to say is always up to you." The Captain sampled an orange slice. "We will be near Zonguldak before sundown." The sugar bowl lay within his reach, and he stirred some into his compote. "I plan to take the western route around Gibraltar and eventually journey to the North Sea. We will surface as close as possible to Prague. Or, you may prefer to have your train meet us near Odessa again." He hesitated. "It all depends upon where we decide to build the new complex." Nemo took his time, eying each of them. "If possible, I want your suggestions for the new location before Tripoli, so I can telegraph to make the needed preparations."

Celwyn spoke as he thought. "If the new compound is to be located near Prague, some things become clear." Kang's head jerked up, sensing the magician was either up to something or holding something back. Jonas grinned at him.

"Perhaps we could use Nicobar Island, as before?" As Verne asked, his face lit up, probably at the prospect of a stop in Singapore.

Nemo shook his head. "I thought about it. But, no. The only flat land there for landing and taking off won't work according to our latest calculations. The island is too short. The other islands are even shorter."

"I see. So, our choices are open, then?" Celwyn asked, batting his eyes innocently.

The automat saw him and narrowed his eyes. "You're up to something, Jonas. You prevaricate worse than Bartholomew."

"I am?" The magician laughed.

Kang scowled at him.

Verne rubbed his hands together. "I hope the place we choose is full of new animals and interesting flora. The more exotic, the more fascinating."

Bartholomew regarded the magician from under lowered brows. "You are up to something ... like Xiau says."

At least they had successfully distracted the big man. Celwyn finished his fruit, and his spoon danced through the air to land inside the bowl. "All right. We talked about some of this before. I would like to be very involved in the building of the new compound to ensure our security and hopefully extend the life expectancies of our guards. Therefore, choosing a secret—and defensible—location is highly desirable."

"I agree, very much so," Captain Nemo said. "What do you have in mind?"

The magician blew on the spoon, and it spun in the air with a whirring sound. "A question first; do you expect to rebuild the prototype and then turn everything over to others? Or do you plan to do more improvements, or other models, after building a new prototype?"

Nemo folded his napkin and checked his pocket watch. "Let's adjourn to finish our discussion." He addressed Bartholomew, "We will be on the open sea within minutes."

The big man's sigh of relief followed them across the hall to the study.

With cigars, pipes, and a fresh pot of tea, they settled in front of the aquatic window. Qing streaked over to them and dropped his frog in the magician's lap. It was missing a leg. Celwyn made another frog, and both amphibians hopped away with the mechanical bird in pursuit.

As they watched the frogs' antics, a companionable silence filled the room. Captain Nemo smoked more than half of his cigar before answering Celwyn's question. "Men have passions, and they have dreams. Mine, Gentlemen, are in conflict." He did not glance at the others; his attention had turned inward.

After a moment, Kang surmised, "You want to be at sea, but you also dream of the flying machine."

"Yes." The Captain studied his smoke rings as they floated to the ceiling. "To answer your question, Jonas, I must tell you all of something I have told no one else." He turned to Verne, sitting beside him, and said, "Please, do not record this or speak of it." Nemo's gaze pinned the author to his chair.

Verne put down his pen and managed a nod. "Thank you." Nemo went on. "My initial thoughts centered on making a viable flying machine only. Then, as I remembered Jules's book, *From the Earth to the Moon*, I began to think differently, imagining the unknown as he did when he wrote it."

The author nodded. "The Captain provided inspiration for the story."

"Initially, yes. Anything technical in the book is from Jules's imagination. Since then," Nemo sighed, seeming frustrated with himself, "the idea of flying beyond the earth has become an all-encompassing desire in my heart. It will not go away."

"Indeed!" Celwyn exclaimed in satisfaction. He had experienced his own visions about the skies and beyond. The magician enjoyed this; Nemo intended to do something about his dreams.

Bartholomew clasped his hands together and stared out the aquatic window without seeing anything. "Most interesting. The idea does take your breath away." After a moment, he began fussing with his cuffs like they must be perfect, or he couldn't think. The big man had taken to wearing fancy vests and custom shirts after their shopping jaunts in Naples. Considering his height and breadth, they must have taken several fittings.

Captain Nemo regarded each of them in turn, unblinking and still deep in thought. "So, you see why answering your question is not simple, Jonas?"

"I do."

The automat steepled his fingers and, with the authority of high logic, said, "If I may, perhaps we can make a few decisions. No matter the eventual use of the machine or complexity of our efforts, we require several things to begin."

Celwyn asked, "A good quantity of tea?"

Kang laughed. "Probably, but I had something more concrete in mind."

"Secrecy, security, and more security," Bartholomew intoned.

The magician rubbed his chin thoughtfully. "Even if we eventually move the compound several times, I think Bartholomew's list is exactly right. We do not have to make too many decisions now."

Captain Nemo nodded. "That is sensible."

"I agree also," Kang said. "The location is open. In my opinion, the three of us can go wherever the Captain wishes. After the wedding, of course."

From deep within the ship, a series of gongs sounded, one right after the other. Nemo did not react. The automat shrugged.

Bartholomew held a match to a cigar and eventually got it going. "There is that. I hear young Zander is refusing to even wear underwear to the wedding at this point. It is no longer just a revolt against a necktie."

The magician smiled. "Not my responsibility."

"And I prefer it isn't mine either." Bartholomew puffed and inhaled sweet tobacco. "I also have yet to buy a new suit."

"Mine needs a few things. All right, out with it, Jonas." Kang stared at him.

"Well. There is a possible solution, my friends." Celwyn scooped up Qing and stroked his feathers.

"A very long time ago, when I was about fifteen, to the consternation of my keepers, I sailed a small boat out of a port near Middleborough by myself. Pelaez had left home long before. It was just me, my sense of adventure, and the North Sea." Kang snorted and rolled his eyes. The magician tossed another silver frog in his lap, and Qing went for it, making the automat jump. "Anyhow, a strong wind blew me north—or eastward—and I discovered an island. Much later, I found out it was reputed to be haunted." Celwyn raised his brows. "I came to agree that it was."

Bartholomew regarded him. He did not want to ask, but he licked his lips twice and did. "How did you decide that?"

"Once I made it ashore, the island appeared uninhabited, and I spied a series of buildings and a great house at the base of a hill." Celwyn shrugged. "It had apparently been a family estate in the previous century. Ouch." Qing had returned and rubbed the magician's ear with his beak.

Captain Nemo asked, "Would it be comfortable as our base?"

"It could be."

A tea service arrived, replacing the other one. The magician thanked the crewman and poured.

As he leaned over the map at the chess table, Kang asked, "Where is the island exactly? I am looking at the coast of southern Britain."

"About twenty miles north, or northeast, of Middleborough." Celwyn turned to Captain Nemo. "I explored several caves on the island. It was my first experience dealing with the perils of the tides that rise and fall in them."

"I'm sure you learned quickly." The automat grinned at him.

"Ha. In my young mind, the caves seemed enormous. Perhaps even big enough for what this ship would require."

"Were they on the windward side?" Kang asked.

The magician shrugged. "All I remember is that they lay near where I landed the boat."

"How would this ship get into a cave?" Bartholomew asked. "Could we use something like that?"

Captain Nemo replied with studied casualness, which the magician concluded was an effort to protect the big man from further upset, "Perhaps. What is the island called?"

"Findbar Island. Does it appear there?"

Kang waved a hand at them as his nose moved closer to the map.

"We'll have to check." Captain Nemo's eyes twinkled as he thought about the possibilities. He asked the magician, "Is the island big enough for a landing field?"

Celwyn said, "I think so. My memory is good, but it has been hundreds of years since then. Is it possible we can forgo the underground rivers on the way to Prague, which Bartholomew enjoys so much, and instead cruise by Findbar along the way?" He had a different approach to dealing with Bartholomew's phobias.

"Humorous, Jonas. Although, I like the idea of seeing Findbar," Bartholomew said.

The rest of them nodded, and Qing squawked his approval.

The Professor returned from a quick trip to the map room. With a smile, he said, "Let's take a closer look." He spread another map on top of the first. Within a minute, everyone stood over his shoulder with growing excitement. The automat regarded Celwyn. "Tell us what you do remember."

The magician lifted his hands. "It is hard to describe what I saw as a lad. I didn't have a great deal of experience in caution. Or knowing when to retreat if I encountered something dangerous."

Bartholomew laughed and took his seat on the couch again. "This is when Xiau says that you still don't."

Kang blinked his restraint while the magician tried not to laugh, and the big man chortled. "Humph." Celwyn wondered what color the automat would like his elfin ears to be.

"Please continue." Nemo nodded at Celwyn.

The magician cleared his throat and elevated his chin. "Now that I've entertained you, I will do so. I left my boat on the beach and wandered to the forested area behind the mansion. That was the center of the island, near the cliffs. It must have been high noon. The sun had dried my clothes, and yet, as I walked into the trees, I remember shivering."

Kang posed a question, "At fifteen, were you adept at magic? Did you know of other beings ... such as vampires and daemons?"

"Or witches?" the big man asked.

"Witches, yes. The others, no." Celwyn nodded, his memories coming back. "At that point in my education, I could control nature rather well—a sudden rainstorm, for instance."

"Oh, really?" Kang drawled. "Like the one you used on us this afternoon?"

The magician smiled at him. He enjoyed teasing the automat. "Of course. By that time, I could also change objects and manipulate music as I desired. On that day, I entered the grove of trees and heard the wind. There was also a somewhat forlorn Celtic horn—none of them of my making." He opened his eyes at them. "Which I found intriguing."

"I certainly would have. And then left as fast as possible," Bartholomew said.

Verne stabbed a finger on the map. "If this is the one that I think it is, the island was occupied by the Celts long before years of smugglers, and then Lord Spencer took possession of it." The little author shrugged. "This is one of the islands I've done some research on, but I didn't follow through with it."

"It might be interesting to know more," Nemo said.

"Agreed. Anyhow, the music from the horn sounded like an ancient dirge. It had grown much louder by the time I reached the higher ground." Celwyn could visualize the moment clearly. "The lichen grew wild, covering everything. The trees were tall and blocked most of the sun and shadowed the rocks. Moss covered everything."

"Go on," Kang said, his eyes bounced with excitement.

"The ground appeared soggy. In the middle of summer, mind you. As I stood there, more horns joined the first one ... everything seemed off ... it had all been painted in sadness so profound that it became palatable—so real I could have touched it."

"Something frightened you?" Verne guessed.

"Yes." Celwyn experienced a chill of remembrance and, with effort, controlled it. "I hadn't been away from the family castle but a few times before that and had little to compare the situation to." He stared at the ocean outside the aquatic window. "As I drew closer to the raised clearing, I could *see* under the ground. And the bodies laid out below."

"Marvelous." Verne's pen zinged across the page of his notebook.

Judging from his widened eyes and intake of breath, Bartholomew did not consider this exciting.

"A burial ground." Kang pursed his lips. "The Celts were known for that. What was the significance of the horns? If it had been you supplying them, I wouldn't ask."

Verne stopped writing to ask, "Then what happened?"

"A warning, perhaps? Right after the shock of it all, the ground by my foot moved. A skeleton's hand clawed at me." Celwyn shrugged again. "I flew upward, using magic. Then I fled back to the beach again." He hesitated, reluctant to further entertain the automat. His audience waited. "Oh, whatever—I went into the mansion."

"I knew it!" Kang shouted.

Celwyn plowed on. "That experience was even worse, so I departed in my little sailboat as fast as I could."

Bartholomew asked, as if he wished the magician wouldn't answer, "And then?"

"I brought forth a strong wind to fill my sail." The magician inhaled deeply. "It took more than that to get through the tide and rocks. A frightening experience, and one I can understand much better now."

"I agree." Nemo got his pipe going again. "You are afraid of very little, Jonas."

Kang leaned back, touched the tips of his toes together, and smiled. "Except losing at chess."

"A marvelous idea." Verne capped his pen and stood. "I need to push a knight around for a bit."

As the clock in the study chimed the midnight hour, the gongs in the ship's belly answered with twelve bells. Celwyn opened the door to his cabin and stifled a yawn. It had been a good day, and he needed to sleep.

He sat on his bunk and removed his boots, again remembering the summer he had found Findbar Island. Perhaps it was a good thing that he had so little innate fear at that age. Over the years, he had run into some truly frightening things and, to survive, had displayed a strong and swift reaction to them. A recent example was the trip into the catacombs a few months ago. It did not hurt to have friends; if it weren't for Nemo, they all would have died.

The magician removed his vest and wound his watch as he thought once more about the apparition he had seen on the *Nautilus* before they reached the catacombs. And then saw it again as they went underground.

In both instances, a thick, sinuous dragon-like creature covered in scales had appeared. In the first version, it had measured twice as long as a man as it twisted and turned, threading its way along the *Nautilus'* corridor in a heavy mist just under the ceiling. Yet, weeks later, in the catacombs, the creature could not have been more than a few feet long as it wiggled its way through the tree roots in front of him. Celwyn recalled it appeared real both times and how its eyes had met his own. After he described it to the automat, Kang suggested that it could be a wyvern. Through the centuries, there had been reports of these creatures all over the world, which made his opinion more likely.

After he finished winding his watch, the magician raised his head, and his breath caught; he wasn't surprised at what he saw.

The green eyes of the wyvern met his from only a few feet away.

Like a Ruben nude, it reclined across his trunk, belly up, while most of its body continued to the floor. Its silvery scales reflected the light and appeared inter-connected, lizard-like. It had no arms or legs, but a pair of nearly transparent wings lay flat on its back.

"Indeed," he murmured. As Celwyn spoke, the creature turned slightly, displaying its profile. Its mouth and nose resembled something he had seen in one of the pyramids in Egypt for Ramses II. The magician willed it to open its mouth.

The creature's jaw opened, exposing an excellent view of its pointed teeth. The magician had always had a way with animals, especially non-traditional ones. When it closed its jaws slowly, Celwyn realized he closed his own at the same speed. Did it mimic him?

What was this? He knew he had not made the wyvern. It wasn't magical. Its first appearance had been within hours after they visited the museum in Mondragone. Now that he had a close-up view of it, he realized that he had seen the same image in one of the museum paintings by Marino Negra. Celwyn tapped his fingers on his knees until he remembered the title of the painting. *La Obsesión del Dragón.*

He eyed his visitor and waited, watching it without fear. The thing did not strike him as malicious or evil. *But why was it here?* As he studied the creature, it rolled onto its side and rested its head on the trunk. Of all things, the magician did not want it and Qing to meet. Anything could happen.

"Why are you here?" Celwyn asked.

It blinked at him.

He had not expected an answer. This might all be his imagination out of control. He did think it was gorgeous, and its eyes were a brilliant green, very much like his own. *Coincidence?*

For the next hour, he worked with the wyvern, getting to know more about it, making silent suggestions, studying, and testing its responsiveness. It complied when he requested it to open its wings. Before the wyvern faded away, Celwyn fell asleep. His last thought an intention to name his new friend.

Chapter 4

Findbar Island

L ESS THAN THREE WEEKS LATER, with stops for sending and receiving telegrams, sampling wine in dockside cafes, hunting for delicious pastries, visiting every book proprietor in each city, and participating in enjoyable excursions across the seafloor to view ancient wrecks, the *Nautilus* entered the waters off the coast of Margate. The North Sea welcomed them with tall storm clouds and rough seas.

The submarine remained a few miles off the coast, cruising near the surface. Through spyglasses, they had excellent views of green cliffs decorated with herds of fat sheep, wind-weathered farmhouses, and majestic formations of limestone rocks. They continued east, submerging as they entered the shipping channels between Britain and Denmark. An hour more, and the *Nautilus* veered north slightly. According to Kang and the maps he enjoyed so much, they would hold that course for another hour or more. Findbar Island lay about twenty-two nautical miles to the east, between Middleborough and Scarborough.

At the appointed time, Celwyn and the others gathered in front of the aquatic window to wait for the ship to surface. Into the silence, the clock beside the bookshelves chimed the three o'clock hour. As seawater sloshed against the glass, the submarine ascended to reveal a foot of cloudy sky above the waves, a pleasant change from the endless blue-green water and interested fish. In the distance, something shadowy began to take shape on the horizon.

"Is that Findbar?" Verne asked.

"I hope so. I am very curious," Bartholomew said. "It would be nice to stay and explore this, but we agreed to be in Szczecin by tomorrow to meet the *Elizabeth*. We could always blame Jonas if we're late." He grinned.

"I'm sure they'll do so anyway. Did you hear everyone will be on the train to greet us?" Celwyn gazed down his nose at the automat. "We need to make our wagers on how much bigger the boys are."

"You probably asked Patrick already." Kang snorted and went back to scanning the waves.

Celwyn eyed him. "Would I do such a thing?"

"To win a bet, you would," Kang answered.

"Pfft."

"I've already asked Patrick how tall the boys have grown." Bartholomew waved a telegram at them and stuffed it back into his pocket. "I will be the judge for your wagers."

"Here you go, my friend." The magician refilled the big man's wine glass and sent him a cigar.

"Really?" The automat's mouth dropped open. "That is cheating!"

Verne patted the air. "Is it the Captain's plan to cruise by Findbar but not stop?"

"Yes," Bartholomew said. "His men will measure the island as we go by, using the speed and distance between different points, and some of the crew will be up top with spyglasses to see how much of the land is flat."

"And verify Findbar is really uninhabited." As Kang regarded the magician, his lips twitched in amusement. "We do not want to meet anything frightening now, do we, Jonas?"

Celwyn made a face at him. "I'll ignore that. By the way, we will not be able to see the great house from offshore. Especially with the trees in the way."

Verne said, "My research showed that the mansion on this island was most recently used as a sanitorium. For the criminally insane."

Bartholomew gaped at him.

"This was years ago," the author hastened to add.

The minutes ticked by slowly until they drew close enough to view more details, including how the cliffs overhung the shore like a wide-open mouth. "We're on the back side of the island now.

The beach where I went ashore is on the opposite side. The mansion is in the middle, along with the Celtic burial ground and the trees."

"Figuring this out will be an activity for the Captain and his men while we're getting fitted for wedding costumes." Bartholomew yawned and patted his stomach. "I hope I am not any fatter than the last time I wore formal wear."

"I usually travel with a suit, just in case." Verne smoothed the lapels of his jacket.

After a moment of silence, Kang pursed his lips and asked, "Do you think Captain Nemo would like to attend the wedding?"

"I broached the subject. He said he would consider it. Yet," Celwyn studied the others before adding, "it may be just as well if not. I hesitated to tell him about one of the guests."

"I can guess who." The automat nodded to himself. "Also, Nemo covets his privacy; this ship is a well-guarded secret. The clamor to know more about her would be tremendous if someone saw her." He stared at the island. "Our danger—and of someone discovering the flying machine—would increase tenfold."

Bartholomew asked, "Which guest?"

"Prague's premier witch may redeem her fee for protecting Tellyhouse by attending the wedding. Francesca remembers you very well," Celwyn told him with a chuckle. "And she could actually be there, from what Edward has reported."

"A witch!" Verne exclaimed. His eyes widened. "Oh, my dear. I remember the talk about her last year."

Kang said, "We shouldn't pressure Nemo to attend. Witches are a particularly sore subject for him because of Ginnie."

The magician remembered another witch, who was also a vampire and someone he missed very much. He hadn't seen Miss Tara McFein since their adventure in the catacombs.

The others nodded at what the Professor had said and thought about Ginnie Ford. She had been sent by the warlock Duncan to infiltrate their compound in Turkey. After a moment, Bartholomew said, "For now, Nemo plans to circle Findbar Island. Like Jonas said, there is only one beach that could be used by a regular boat. The sea in front of it is a mass of rocks."

"I can see the spray above them." Verne pointed outside the glass.

Minutes went by as the *Nautilus* increased speed and turned in a wide circle to the north before heading back toward the island. Captain Nemo entered the study with a pensive expression and refused a whiskey. He stood with them in front of the window as the ship finished turning west again, facing the island. She slipped below the waves under a mantle of bubbles.

"You will see a glorious sunset later on, gentlemen." Captain Nemo addressed them with an expectant gleam in his eye. He winked at Celwyn. "First, I have a treat in store for you." He turned to the Professor. "I found another map, and it revealed something most interesting about the island." His voice held more hope than it had over the last several weeks. A gong from the bowels of the ship sounded once, twice. "Excuse me." He clicked his heels together and headed back to the bridge.

"He's just as mysterious as you are, Jonas," Kang drawled.

"That is a compliment." Before they dipped below the surface, the last things Celwyn saw were the towering cliffs above the rocks and the explosions of spray from the crashing waves below them.

"The island is forbidding to all but the brave," Kang noted, as if privy to the magician's thoughts. "Or the young and foolhardy."

"The ship is slowing." Bartholomew leaned into the window and gazed downward. "I can see indications of sand far below us."

Qing waddled across the chess table to Verne's fountain pen. The author got there first and pocketed it. The bird clicked his tongue and flew to Celwyn for sympathy. The magician patted his back as the ship slowed further, the sea whirling like a miniature typhoon around her. She hovered, buffeting from side to side as if waiting for word to go forward.

In the next minute, the sea grew far worse. The water sloshed hard against the aquatic window as the *Nautilus* swayed and corrected, and the current bombarded her. The lights blinked once.

"What is going on?" Verne grasped the chair in front of him.

Before anyone could answer, the ship's engines revved, hurling her forward as if shot from a cannon.

The submarine surged ahead, slamming the automat back in his seat as she headed straight at the island. Bartholomew gulped and glanced around with panic filling his eyes. Celwyn grabbed his arms and held onto him. Verne squealed and hid under the table with Qing.

Kang jumped up again and fell against the aquatic window, his face alive and not at all afraid.

"What do you think is happening?" the automat asked them with a breathless smile.

Celwyn suspected him. "I wager you have an idea."

Kang's lips curled. Yes, he knew.

The magician released Bartholomew's arms but stood close enough to catch him if he collapsed. Sweat poured off the big man's face, and he pointed. "We are slowing somewhat. Look at that water!" The current swirled as if stirred by a whirling dervish, and the sea sloshed up the side of the ship, covering the window completely until receding again.

"And the rocks." Verne had crawled out again from under the table and pulled himself up by the window. "So many rocks ... they appear sharp," he murmured. "And so close!"

"Interesting." Celwyn noticed a change. "The water doesn't seem as crazy here."

Boulders wider than a carriage rose from the sea-floor, ascending and surrounding them like over-sized teeth. They seemed so close—Celwyn could have stretched an arm and touched them. Above the surface, the sun streaked the water while the currents agitated the sea gently in smaller swirls, like a chef stirring a giant bowl of cream.

The *Nautilus* continued forward at an even more cautious speed, and, of a sudden, the water darkened completely. The ship's internal lights brightened to counteract the darkness, and the submarine slowed again until it just perceptively floated forward. Outside the glass, less than ten feet from the side of the ship, a wall of rock climbed upward and then widened away again into the murkiness.

"That is very close." Bartholomew licked his lips.

Kang slapped him on the back. "Yes, it is. However, I think we're stopping soon." His prediction proved true as the *Nautilus* drifted forward and stopped. Try as he might, Celwyn could not see through the inky water at all.

"Note that above the surface, there are only shadows." Kang frowned at the window. "Like a cave."

Bartholomew leaned into the glass, trying to peer beyond the ship. "Yes ... in front of the ship, there is a bit of light ... but I still can't see anything."

Celwyn could detect more than they could and wondered if that was really a good thing. He bowed. "After you, gentlemen."

"I ... I think I'll stay here," Verne whispered, his face pale. "Some of the things I read about concerning this island..."

"Are you sure?" Kang asked him. "Jonas will protect us."

The author shook his head.

"As you wish."

When they reached the spiral stairs at the end of the corridor, Captain Nemo's man, Granger, met them.

"We're still securing the area. The Captain requests that you wait here, please."

Kang spoke before the magician could. "An excellent idea."

In his opinion, Celwyn could have handled any situation. But before he voiced it, the hatch opened, and another crewman motioned to them.

Bartholomew led the way. The magician brought up the rear, throwing illumination onto the platform as they crowded onto it. In every direction, darkness reigned. They could see glimpses of shiny black walls with dark, mysterious silhouettes fading into more shadows. When the running lights of the ship flickered, they revealed a large cave. The *Nautilus* rested in a pool of black water that smelled ancient.

The big man sucked in his breath, and the magician laid a hand on his shoulder to steady him.

A cloud of mold seemed to cover everything, along with a layer of brininess from the heavy air. The combination reminded the magician of a basement in Alexandria under a seaside bar that he'd once hidden in. Celwyn felt a distinct chill. He glanced at the pair of crewmen who stood on the bow with torches, splaying arcs of light up the shiny black walls.

Kang murmured so that the big man did not hear, "This cave appears to be a little longer than the *Nautilus* and maybe twice as wide. We can't turn around."

When Celwyn nodded, then lit up the entire cave, he almost immediately wished he had not; the big man sucked in his breath and backed up. The magician tightened his hold on his arm.

All along the walls of the grotto, intricate carvings as tall as a man stretched upward more than twenty feet above the water, bordering the walls surrounding the ship. Celwyn was not an expert, but wagered Kang would call them ancient deities. More of the carvings continued below the waterline. It must be high tide now; only the very top of the ragged entrance to the cave showed above the surface. As they studied the carvings, Captain Nemo climbed through the hatch and joined them on the platform.

"Thank you for the illumination, Jonas." Captain Nemo made a panoramic inspection and grunted approval. "This may work well for us."

Bartholomew breathed deeply and, after one last look, turned his back on the carvings.

Celwyn spied a set of limestone stairs in the far-left corner leading upward, disappearing into darkness. Before the stairs, a flat area of the stones had been arranged into a platform large enough to hold several men and supplies. Otherwise, nothing could be seen above the waterline except the carved walls.

As the crewmen rolled out the floating pier toward the stairs, Bartholomew pointed and asked, "What do those carvings mean?"

Ever the chicken, Kang raised his brows at Celwyn to deliver the news.

With a sigh, the magician said, "They appear to be devils. Celtic ones, to be exact."

There was little comment until Kang caught up to Nemo, navigating his way on the pier, and asked, "Sir, can you describe your method to enter this cave?"

"Certainly."

They discussed it until they reached the end of the pier. When the others caught up, Nemo led the way across limestone worn smooth from hundreds of years of use. The soft sound of the water lapping just below accompanied them in a regular rhythm, yet it didn't seem as comforting as it should have been.

As they went forward, Celwyn tried but could not see anything in the inky water, and without more light, it appeared opaque. He assumed that the tide freshened the pool on a regular basis ... yet, it would be nice to know what lay down there.

The path appeared to be about five feet wide and continued all around the grotto. It glistened with algae from the seawater continually seeping over the walkway ... reminding the magician of something ... perhaps the Nile flowing inside to lap at the walls at the bottom of a pyramid he had once visited in Darfur?

"I assume no one else could fit in here with us?" Celwyn asked.

"At low tide, perhaps, if the boat was small enough," Nemo said. "Never fear; my crew will be on guard. At high tide, the maelstrom of currents prevents boats, and nearly this ship, from entering."

"I certainly agree." Celwyn had just experienced how a ship as heavy and powerful as the *Nautilus* had a fight on her hands.

Nemo nodded. "I instructed my crew to employ speed through the turbulence. As you can see, we were successful." He gestured to the automat and added, "The Professor found this cave on the second map, along with a strong caution not to enter. I found another map with much more detail, which provided the sea route in here."

The magician asked, "How will we get out again? It is high tide now—do we use it to leave or spend the night here?"

"Good question."

Bartholomew did not find the Captain's answer comforting. Sweat shone across his brow. Nemo saw his distress and said more seriously, "We have about a half-hour before we must leave again, or we will stay here until tomorrow."

Bartholomew said, "I vote that we hurry. I do not want to stay here alone."

The automat gave him an encouraging glance. "We will be quick."

Once more, Captain Nemo led the way. Up the stairs they went with twin guards bringing up the rear. Bartholomew had his pistol ready, as did Nemo. Celwyn felt that pistols would not be effective against anything they found here. The cloying moistness that enveloped them increased.

To be sure, the magician checked behind them; a team of armed guards stood on both ships' platforms awaiting their return. Good. For some reason, Celwyn glanced upward. It took effort not to react and upset Bartholomew further. Instead, he touched Kang's sleeve and pointed with his eyes.

Center to the cave, directly over the ship, an eye in the shape of a large medallion was embedded in the rock ceiling above them. With a tug on the big man's arm, Kang herded everyone forward to where Captain Nemo waited at the top of the steps.

Celwyn and the automat may have hurried a bit more than usual as they passed through a creaking wooden door and into a corridor paneled in thick oak beams and cobwebs. The ceiling appeared just high enough and the walls wide enough for Bartholomew. Instead of stone, their steps echoed across a beautiful 17th-century parquet floor.

The guards held lanterns, and Celwyn broadcast a bright light in front of their procession. On the walls, unlit, baroque candleholders appeared at eye level between vintage paintings. The magician flicked a hand through the spider webs that tickled his face. He found it interesting that some of the paintings measured nearly as tall as the automat. A few were only a foot square.

Captain Nemo stopped dead still in front of a portrait. The others gathered around him as a shrill wind blew up the hallway, alerting the magician. With speed, Celwyn shielded them, including the guards at the rear. In an undertone, he told Nemo, "I have protection around us."

The magician sighed inwardly. Everyone expected danger now. Gone were the days of a boy exploring an island or a group of friends taking an innocent train ride across Bangladesh and drinking their weight in Irish whiskey. Yet, Celwyn admitted, it did make life interesting. Especially if they did not encounter someone such as his father. He shuddered and, with effort, stopped thinking about him.

Kang had drawn close to a painting. "This is by Culpepper. Do you think it is authentic?"

"Perhaps, but he only painted gentle countryside scenes." Bartholomew frowned in confusion as he studied it.

Captain Nemo did the same. "This is certainly not gentle." In the picture, a Victorian woman held a child's face under the pristine water of an idyllic lake. If that wasn't horrible enough, the painting next to it depicted a devil devouring a child in intricate detail and vivid color.

Really? Celwyn shook his head in wonder. Here was an example of something that would upset a patient from a sanitorium if they ever wandered down here. It upset him just standing here. The magician cleared his throat. "Perhaps we should move along? We only have minutes left."

Captain Nemo took a few steps forward. "Yes. Certainly."

The hallway ended. Nemo nudged the door in front of them open with his pistol while his guards trained rifles at it. In front of them, a pit of blackness receded into shadows and the faint whiff of burned wood. The stench increased as they stepped into the back end of an enormous fireplace. Celwyn threw more light ahead and kicked ashes over a skull next to Bartholomew's foot.

"We passed another door." Kang retreated a few feet and disappeared. Seconds later, he met them in front of the fireplace.

"Prop this door open," Captain Nemo ordered his crew.

Everyone else had continued forward across an expanse of deteriorating carpet into a grand ballroom with open mouths and words of amazement. Under a thick mantle of dust, tufted velvet furniture ringed the dancefloor, reminding the magician of things he'd last seen in the court of King Charles ll.

"We only have a few minutes," Captain Nemo reminded them.

Bartholomew examined the drapes and chandelier while the automat trotted down the neighboring hall and back.

To the right, glass walls separated the ballroom from an empty conservatory. On their left, beyond another arch, more doors led outside to dead and overgrown formal gardens. The garden statuary appeared to be seventeenth-century and predominantly religious depictions of mother and child.

Celwyn froze—he heard something... He listened, but it was not repeated. Instead, a deep chill rushed by him with cold fingers.

"You paled." Kang asked, "What is it?"

Celwyn did not want to say, and Bartholomew would not want to know, but he should.

"l thought l heard a woman crying."

Chapter 5

THEY RETURNED TO THE SHIP MUCH faster than when they left it. Kang scampered down the stairs with Bartholomew and Celwyn close behind. Captain Nemo followed his crew inside, and they closed the hatch.

As they marched down the corridor, Bartholomew exclaimed, "That mansion is very unsettling. Very."

"With all those unusual relics from the past ... it won't affect what we intend to do. But..." Celwyn bowed the big man ahead of him into the study.

"Make mine a double, please," Bartholomew requested as he collapsed beside the Professor on the sofa. Celwyn flicked a hand, and a collection of beverages floated around the room. With one glance at their faces, he resisted the urge to have the trays accompanied by ghostly butlers in full uniform and white gloves. Perhaps another time.

"I wonder about this island." Verne's ears almost wiggled as he regarded them from the chess table. "What did you see? You appear unsettled."

"The others will tell you. I must return to the bridge." Captain Nemo did not sit down. "Professor, to answer your earlier question, we will back out. It is a short distance. Then pivot the ship 90° and open the engines all the way. The ship will survive the currents, and we'll note if there is a better way for when we return." Nemo touched his cap. "Gentlemen." And hurried out again.

The automat gave Verne a capsuled report of what they had seen in the mansion. Without any sign of embarrassment or check for the magician's displeasure, the author scribbled notes. Celwyn frowned. Last year, Jules had nearly brought disaster to their doorstep because of his association with reporters.

With a squawk that Celwyn called his "let's play" signal, Qing flew onto the arm of the sofa and gawked at Bartholomew. The big man stared back. "After what we just saw, I think there are worse things than you out there, bird." Qing translated that as an invitation to walk up his leg. He eyed the big man's belt buckle.

"He isn't in the mood for you today." Celwyn scooped Qing up and opened his collar. The mechanical bird chirped in his ear and settled down. A moment later, the magician felt the vibration of the ship's engines under his feet. "We're on our way." He gestured out the aquatic window. Bubbles filled the glass until they couldn't see, probably just as well for the state of Bartholomew's nerves.

As minutes passed, the ship backed out of the cave, and the bubbles cleared to reveal rock walls once again. Everyone seemed to be holding their breath until they entered a wild and undulating swath of seawater. As Nemo had projected, the *Nautilus* began a 90° turn, rotating north while the devilish currents buffeted the huge ship.

The submarine ascended, hovering in place as a series of gongs resounded in her belly, and when they stopped, she slammed forward, cutting through the roiling currents. Her engines grew even louder and stronger than the time she sped away from Palermo, outrunning a homicidal warlock.

Seconds more and they broke free into calm water. To the cheers in the study, the *Nautilus* made a majestic turn, heading east toward Szczecin and Annabelle's wedding.

Chapter 6

UNDER THE SUBDUED LIGHTS OF the Captain's dining room, a pensive mood colored their dinner activities that evening. Candlelight flickered in the center of the table and reflected flames in the aquatic window. After Captain Nemo joined them, he apologized for his lateness and unfurled his napkin. Qing squawked a greeting to him.

The wine was sampled and poured; the toast was made first by Nemo, then by Bartholomew. Celwyn especially enjoyed this time of day. It was rare anything untold occurred while they dined.

After the platter of grilled octopus and shrimp had been sampled and the soup bowls filled, Nemo regarded them. "Quite an interesting afternoon."

Bartholomew nodded, but his eyes could not settle.

"Yes, in many ways, it was," Kang said. "What is your opinion, Jonas?"

Celwyn smiled around a spoonful of turtle soup. The Professor had such a playful mind, nearly as much as his own. He flipped the responsibility for what they saw back into the automat's lap. "You tell us."

The magician had not been the only one who recognized Kang's tactic. Captain Nemo's lips twitched as he said, "Other than the supernatural elements we encountered, there are several aspects to consider for our purposes. When we arrived, my crew roughly measured the land we could see. If there is enough flat land on the island, the island itself is more than long enough for the new landing field."

Kang beamed. "Excellent." He gave Bartholomew a thumb's up and turned back to the Captain. "Can we assume that after you deposit us in Szczecin, you plan to explore the island?"

Bartholomew blinked his nervousness.

Celwyn told him, "Please don't worry. If it is not safe, we will not use it."

"That is absolutely true." Nemo sampled his fish, grunted his approval, and ate another bite. "Have you had salmon before?" At the question, Kang and Verne nodded. "The island must meet several criteria, including security, size, and access. Not just a landing field."

The Professor tilted his head at him. "Sir, the only beach would not be usable for a supply boat. What do you have in mind?"

A school of thumb-size fish with yellow stripes darted by the aquatic window, terribly busy and seeming to have a purpose in their journey. "Jonas and I spoke of this on the way here." Nemo chewed. "If possible, I would like to keep the beach area inhospitable to passersby, and any enemies searching for the flying machine."

Bartholomew tapped the pristine tablecloth as he thought. "You expect to bring a supply boat into the cave?" He considered the situation. "It is obvious that other boats have docked there before, and that was the purpose of the cave."

"Also, the stairs leading out of the grotto are well-worn," Kang said.

"I don't know much about currents and tides, but I assume a combination of them would allow a regular boat to safely enter the cave?" Celwyn asked.

Captain Nemo said, "Exactly. The size of the boat would also be important."

Kang buttered a roll and double-checked that nothing else had been added to it before taking a bite. Celwyn smiled a playful smile at him. The automat made a face and said, "These details are all needed for the decision ... after you confirm the viability of the landing field?"

"Yes." Captain Nemo added, "There are many other factors we have to consider."

More than an hour later, the magician sent a post-prandial tray of cigars around the study, followed by tumblers of whiskey. While they got their cigars going, he produced a tray of something much better and poured some. After everyone had taken their first puffs, he asked a question.

"Sir, while we're in Prague, where do we send telegrams to you?"

"The Hague has a quaint bookshop called Middleboys along the waterfront. It has a telegraph desk." Captain Nemo puffed and blew smoke rings. "My crew will retrieve messages from there weekly unless you request them sooner."

Kang's brow went up. "A bookshop, eh?"

"I don't think this ship can hold any more books, Xiau," the magician drawled in his best imitation of the automat.

Bartholomew grinned. "How far is Szczecin from Findbar?"

"A bit less than twelve hours." Nemo nodded at them. "We'll travel all night and arrive in Szczecin before we're due."

"It is appreciated." The big man rubbed his belly, seeming more at ease.

"Not at all."

"That was a wonderful dinner. I had not sampled salmon before." Bartholomew smoked a moment and savored the contented atmosphere. "I found it very flavorful."

"Salmon caught near Dunkirk and Ostend have a completely different texture and taste than that from the Pacific Northwest." Kang pursed his lips. "It would be hard to choose a favorite."

"We may or may not be able to sample it on a regular basis, depending on where we rebuild. There is also a healthy salmon population in the upper reaches of the North Sea." Captain Nemo gestured outside the ship. "As promised, you'll be in Szczecin by noon tomorrow, gentlemen. Within a week, you'll hear from me as to whether Findbar Island will be our new home for the flying machine."

Chapter 7

BY MID-MORNING, THE REMAINING mist over the Baltic Sea had burned away, and the *Nautilus* hovered close to the coast while her crew, assisted by Bartholomew and Celwyn, unloaded luggage. When almost everything had been piled into the magically improvised carts, they knew it was time. Everyone faced the wind, quiet and hesitant to say goodbye.

"I feel hopeful, Sir. Much more so than after my brother's treachery." The magician shook the Captain's hand in farewell. The others did the same. Qing wiggled out of Celwyn's collar and squawked at Nemo. "He will miss you until we meet again," Celwyn told him.

"I'm sure." Nemo stared back, not blinking, imitating Qing as he patted the mechanical bird's back. "What else about the island should I know? Have you remembered anything more about the mansion?"

Celwyn shrugged. "As a lad, my memories are likely to be filled by how many paintings with nudes I could find or disgusting things involving insects. I didn't explore the ballroom or most of the house."

When Verne would have spoken, Bartholomew held up a hand.

Celwyn had gazed into the distance, seeming to squint into the past. "Like I said, I remember fighting the currents by the rocks. At the time, I thought it fun when I keeled over and back again a dozen times. Then I shot through it all to the beach. A wild ride, I can assure you."

Kang rejoined them and stood listening while the crew finished unloading their trunks and boxes.

The magician closed his eyes and opened them again. "No one had walked through the sand on that beach for a long time; it was so smooth, just faintly rippled by the wind. The beach seemed small, probably no longer than the *Nautilus*, and it ended against mounds of horse-sized rocks at each end. I made my way through the trees until I found evidence of a path. Eventually, I saw a dirt road ... and the bones of a cow."

As he talked, Kang lit his pipe and gazed out to sea. They had surfaced about five miles north of Szczecin. When they arrived, Celwyn had detected a farmhouse in the distance on the winding road paralleling the beach. He checked again; none of the locals appeared to be out on the water. Satisfied, the magician resumed his recollection of Findbar Island.

"Anyhow, I came upon the mansion. In front, an old sign read, 'Pembrook Asylum. Originally Spencer

House,' or something like that. The manor was huge. When I opened the main doors and called out, my voice echoed for a long time."

The clouds above them danced across the sky. The automat said, "Better finish up, Jonas; our train will be here soon."

"True. Above the mansion's foyer, I heard noises. They were not rats." The magician paused, not from a pleasant memory but from remembering his fright. "Still, I went upstairs. I'm sorry, I can't remember finding anything there. Just a feeling of unease I wouldn't give in to."

Bartholomew had started rearranging boxes in the cart and stopped. "You were brave even then, Jonas."

"No, just foolhardy." The magician handed over more boxes to the big man.

"Please continue." Kang glanced at his pocket watch. "We need to get going."

"The hallways upstairs went on forever, and I remember seeing barred windows inside the rooms as I went by." Celwyn stopped and frowned. "For some reason, I was drawn to the last few rooms." He made a face of distaste. "Because I smelled something metallic."

"Like blood?"

Celwyn shrugged. "It could have been, but I didn't find any. Just a feeling... It was like my nightmares..."

Kang asked, "What was it?"

"They are not something I wish to dwell upon for now."

Bartholomew straightened a stack of the boxes. "I still say you were brave even then, Jonas."

"No, my friend, just reckless."

─────⌣─────

The big man drove the second oversized cart behind the one with the automat and Celwyn. The magician jiggled the reins to put more urgency behind their 'horses.'

"What time do we expect them?" Kang asked as they neared the train yard, passing several carriages heading away from Szczecin on the coastal road.

"They plan to arrive before one o'clock, the last I heard." The magician kept an eye on the other carriages, checking for anyone interested in them. "Thankfully, it isn't raining." He squinted in the bright sunlight. "Your books would get wet."

"And your tea."

"Let's hope the train can still move again after we transfer all this," Celwyn told the automat. "The horses worked hard to pull this load uphill. You should be relieved they made it to the top."

The Professor laughed. "I wish I had more."

"Bartholomew set a better example. He mostly bought art supplies. Watercolors, I believe."

The carts rolled to a stop in front of the last set of tracks. Because most of the terminal activity seemed concerned with the other platforms, and no one showed any interest in their party. Even the yard dogs ignored them and went back to fighting over a piece of trash.

"We had a good trip, despite some of our adventures," Bartholomew said. "The Captain was sorry to see us go." He hopped off the platform to stride down the tracks and back again.

Kang glanced around. "After we leave, I assume no one will notice when the carts disappear."

"You assume correctly," Celwyn said. "The horses will scamper away too."

After a moment of silence in which everything in the world seemed to be suspended, their excitement and anticipation grew until the automat asked, "I wonder what the boys will do with their lives? They are growing up so swiftly."

"They are brave and intelligent. They would make excellent pilots, you know." Bartholomew wore a proud smile.

Kang reached and helped him back onto the platform. "They would."

"Ha," Celwyn said. "They are as bad as Xiau and probably can't keep secrets about the flying machine."

"It is true." Kang laughed. "Zander already told Elizabeth what I purchased for her birthday. But for something serious, he would hold our confidence if asked."

"Oh." Bartholomew's expression grew serious. "What did you buy? I have yet to think of something."

Kang blinked at him in surprise. "A new hat, of course."

"How husbandly of you." Celwyn shook his head. "I would strongly suggest that we don't mention the possibility of the boys becoming pilots to anyone at

Tellyhouse." The magician knew better. "I would be blamed for the idea."

The Professor smirked. "That is too bad."

"Pfft." The magician wondered if now was the best time to mention the wyvern. The three of them would not be alone again for days or weeks, and they needed to know about it. He doubted the creature remained on the *Nautilus* to bedevil Nemo's crew. The wyvern had a connection to him, and it would follow him off the ship.

He asked Kang and the big man, "Do you remember my description of the wyvern on the way here?"

The automat turned to face him and replied slowly, with a high degree of suspicion. "Yes."

"I assumed you were a bit overwrought because of the incident in the catacombs." Bartholomew regarded the magician. "Why do you ask?"

"Because I've seen it again, perhaps a half-dozen times in the last few weeks, usually just before I retire for the night."

Kang plopped onto his bag and stared. "Tell us more."

Celwyn complied with a moderate amount of details.

"Are you having fun at our expense?" Bartholomew asked, his voice filled with hope as much as skepticism.

"Not about this."

"I wonder why you see it. What causes it to appear?" Kang played with the buckle on his bag as he speculated. "It only appears before you sleep?"

The magician shrugged. "Not always. It can be any time."

As if to demonstrate, a cloud of green mist appeared at their feet. The magician said, "Show yourself."

This time, the creature could not have been more than a few feet long. As it wrapped itself around the magician's ankles, Bartholomew gasped. Celwyn put a restraining hand on the big man's arm. Kang's eyes widened, and he grabbed the big man's other arm as the wyvern solidified between them, blinking in the sunlight.

Bartholomew squeezed his eyes shut.

"It is harmless, and as far as I know, it does *not* come from my magic."

"Unbelievable," the automat said. The wyvern blinked at Kang and then Bartholomew, perhaps noting the friendliness in the air.

"It is fascinating," Celwyn agreed. As he spoke, Qing tried to get out of his collar. The magician pushed him back inside and buttoned every button.

Bartholomew said, "I will be all right."

"If you say so." Kang kept a grip on the big man's arm.

Celwyn told them, "I have been working with the wyvern. This is the first time he has obeyed me to appear."

"Unbelievable," Kang repeated as he studied the creature.

Bartholomew inhaled, held his breath, and opened his eyes. Sweat poured off his face. "You may release my arms. I will not faint." The wyvern had grown bigger and fatter until it resembled a chubby lamb. "Good grief. Where did it come from?"

"I don't really know." The magician used his most calming voice for both the big man and the wyvern.

When the creature rolled onto his side. Kang murmured, "Those are wings. In the 13th century, wyverns flew."

"Hold on." Bartholomew stepped across the platform, and he hung over the side. "We might want to leave discussing this for another time. See the puffs of smoke? There they are!"

Celwyn scanned the railroad tracks. "I will do my best not to think about my new friend while we're at Tellyhouse." As he spoke, the wyvern faded away, as if it had never been there.

Chapter 8

THE GROUND UNDER THEIR FEET vibrated. Soon, they heard the rhythmic huffing of a train engine and the screech of her brakes.

Kang leaned around the big man and squinted against the sun. Bartholomew's height had advantages. He yelled his excitement. "It's them!" The noise level escalated as her whistle blew and clouds of steam from the *Elizabeth* billowed high into the air. When Kang stood on his toes trying to see down the tracks, Celwyn resisted the urge to elevate him onto Bartholomew's shoulders.

The train rounded a bend and coasted to a stop. They could hear Zander whooping and shouting, and Otto appeared at the window waving at them. A few seconds more, the train shuddered a final time, and its doors opened.

Zander raced down the stairs with Otto close behind. Much more carefully, Patrick helped

Annabelle to the ground, and Ricardo followed, handing Mrs. Elizabeth Kang into her husband's arms.

Like they had never left, Zander sat on Bartholomew's shoulders, talking as fast as he could, while Otto grasped Celwyn's hand and stared unspoken words at him. The magician bent down to his level and gave him a big hug. "I am glad to be home, Otto. I have missed you, too."

Annabelle and Patrick approached hand in hand, relief painted across their faces. Annabelle appeared as pretty as ever with her blonde curls and aristocratic profile. She could also drink most men under the table, including Bartholomew. Beside her, Captain Patrick Swayne beamed with relief at their arrival. His nearly white hair contrasted with his deeply tanned skin, courtesy of his tour with the Queen's army in Punjab. Celwyn suspected the military man had trouble staying indoors after so many years in the Indian bush. Although the magician enjoyed such a warm welcome, he had a hunch they were experiencing the calm before the storm. He was correct.

"Uncle Celwyn," Annabelle got close enough to count his teeth, tilted her head back, and said sternly, "We are awfully glad you all survived. Patrick and I want to get married. We're not letting you out of our sight now." She smiled and hooked her arm through his. "We've waited long enough. Let's go home."

Patrick slapped him on the back and then shook his hand. "My sentiments exactly."

Elizabeth disengaged from Kang's embrace long enough to say, "I concur. But I also knew you would return." She regarded her husband with the kind of scrutiny he could not look away from. "We will hear about everything that happened on your trip before we arrive in Prague, and I mean *everything*." Her set smile brooked no quarter. The automat managed a nod and a glance at the magician for support. Celwyn blinked at him innocently, chuckled, and turned the other way.

Zander and Bartholomew headed toward the stairs to re-board the train, and the others followed. Celwyn bowed Otto ahead of him, noting the lad and Zander appeared almost the same height. Otto came from solid German stock and was developing the muscular physique of a young man. They had no idea where Zander's parents had come from, but the magician predicted he would become a tall and wiry man.

"I see both of them have filled out in the months we've been gone," Kang said.

The magician stopped next to him. "Patrick has been organizing calisthenics in between their studies."

Zander ran back to them. "Ricardo is making us lunch. It is going to be good!" He grabbed their hands and tugged them toward the train.

With a smile, Celwyn inhaled the satisfaction of being on the *Elizabeth* again. Jackson approached, and they shook hands. "It is good to see you again," the magician told the burly porter. "I trust you have enjoyed your stay in Prague so far?"

"Oh, yes, sir. It is a busy city." As Jackson spoke, the magician turned the man's mustache into something elaborate, with curls and character. After all, it was time to celebrate their return.

The Conductor nudged his assistants, the muscle-bound, red-headed twins Abe and Andy, forward. After more handshaking and congratulations on their return, he said, "Sirs, it is good to have you back."

"It is wonderful to be on board again." Celwyn saluted him. "We'll have to spend some time together when we get home to hear about what everyone has been doing." The magician added in a quieter voice, "I hope you've decided to stay with us."

The Conductor nodded. "I have, for as long as you will have me."

Nearly an hour later, with Bartholomew and Celwyn helping the porters bring their luggage aboard, the boys finished relating most of their adventures over the last several months. Ricardo hurried over, bringing the tantalizing aromas from the kitchen with him, and announced that lunch was ready.

"I'm hungry!" Zander shouted, and raced across the room to pull out Annabelle's chair.

As everyone got comfortable, Elizabeth asked, "Where is Mr. Verne?"

"We may see him at the wedding," Kang told her as he dug into his salad and savored it. "I say, Ricardo has only become more talented since we last saw him. This is superb." He asked Bartholomew, "What do you think?"

"Most excellent," Bartholomew agreed. "Aboard the ship, we ate a great deal of succulent fish and vegetables. I hope that is lamb I smell coming from the kitchen."

The magician sniffed and said, "Yes, it is lamb. With rosemary. Do you agree?" he asked the automat.

"I do. I also think there is ginger in the salad dressing, too."

"Notes of lemon, I wager." Celwyn tried not to give away the teasing by glancing at the women.

Annabelle had been squirming in her seat. She sputtered, "Uncle Celwyn!"

Bartholomew laughed; he never could prevaricate and remain serious. Kang elbowed him and giggled at Celwyn.

"The food is wonderful!" Annabelle exclaimed. "Now, please explain what happened and where you have really been for the last eight months!"

Patrick patted her arm. "Now, dear. The wedding is next week, and you shouldn't get so upset—"

The magician glanced at the boys as they eyed the platters of lamb and roasted potatoes Jackson had just set on the table. Boys had their priorities.

Certain aspects of their recent adventures should not be heard by the lads. While the magician thought about them, both benign and nightmare-inducing, the train hit a trestle, and everyone grabbed their water glasses.

"I've missed this train and all of you very much." Celwyn blocked what the boys could hear, and Jackson also, for good measure. Then he regarded Elizabeth, Annabelle, and Patrick. "I suppose now is as good of a time as any ... since it is still three hours to Prague."

Elizabeth's eyes flared in annoyance. "Yes, now is a wonderful time. I suspect our telegrams were just a part of the story, not the real story." Mrs. Xiau Kang remained a most beautiful woman with her fine profile, genuineness, and hair the color of a flame. Celwyn smiled to himself; Xiau got burned at times.

Kang wriggled in his seat. "We promised before this excursion that we would share everything with you. What was not discussed was that you would worry for weeks or months at a time when you heard of these things. We also didn't know how long it would be until we returned." He appealed to his wife. "You do understand?"

"Yes, I do." Elizabeth pecked him on the cheek. "Now, tell us."

"I understand, but I don't like it," Annabelle grumbled.

The automat turned to Celwyn for help, but the magician pretended to be enthralled with his roasted lamb. Kang snorted. "Fine, I will explain. As you all know, Jonas lay near death in December. What you were not aware of is that whatever was killing him could only be fixed by someone who could heal someone of Jonas's unique makeup. Captain Nemo found Thales, a healer of immortals, for us."

Ricardo pushed the dessert cart into the room and noticed Jackson, frozen in place with an out-stretched hand, ready to pick up the water pitcher. Celwyn took the block off Jackson. The porter shook himself and began removing empty plates. After

nieces; vampires were not something the women and Patrick were fond of whatsoever.

"What is it, dear?" Elizabeth poked him with her elbow. "Just before you prevaricate, your mouth twitches."

Annabelle blew smoke into the air and said, "Just tell us."

Both Bartholomew and the automat turned to the magician. "Jonas should do it."

Celwyn shrugged. "Thales's price, as it were, was that I convince my father to go to him."

Annabelle's mouth fell open. "You have a *father?*"

"Yes."

"I'm still wondering about your brother." Patrick stared at him. "His name is Pelaez? Where is he from?"

It was then that the magician realized the trip home to Prague would be a long one. Over the next hour, with a bit of help from Bartholomew and Kang, he related everything that had happened after his brother boarded the *Nautilus*. When he got to the point of telling them details about Pelaez, the magician's voice faltered.

"We'll finish the story of Pelaez another time," Kang said.

Not realizing the sensitive nature of the subject, Annabelle asked, "Could you talk about your father?"

Nor did she have a way of knowing that would be worse. The magician sighed. "His name is Wolfgang Augustus Griffin. I hadn't seen him in the last 300 years until we found him in the catacombs."

"This is going to be an interesting story, isn't it?" Elizabeth eyed Kang. "When Jonas tells the story, it is on a high level, and I get the distinct feeling much is left out."

"I wonder why," Annabelle drawled.

The automat hurried to say, "We never discovered Thales's underlying motive in requesting that we go to Jonas's father. But since he had saved Jonas, we felt an obligation to comply. Wolfgang is much more powerful than either of his sons. And deadly. Before we reached him, Pelaez reconciled with Jonas and went with us to Palermo to assist. They expected to find their father in the catacombs there."

Elizabeth regarded her husband with narrowed eyes. "There's nothing untoward about that, so why do you hesitate?"

"We do not wish to upset you," Bartholomew told them in his most diplomatic manner.

"Save it, my dear," Annabelle said. She and the big man were fast friends, and she didn't put up with much from him or the others.

Celwyn rubbed his face. "In Casablanca, we met a group of individuals sent by Thales to help us."

Patrick said, "Why, I wonder."

"To offer their assistance ... as directed by Thales." The magician inhaled deeply. "They were vampires."

Anabelle reared back with a hand to her mouth, horrified.

Celwyn hurried to say, "They were good vampires—"

"There's no such thing!"

"Hear us out—" Kang opened his hands, appealing to them. It took several minutes for him to explain. By the time he finished, including how the vampire

Valentine had taken care of Mrs. Karras and Crazy Mary and how smitten Celwyn was, Annabelle laughed along with Patrick. Elizabeth's mouth was open, and her eyes popped like she had been goosed with a hot poker.

"Who is Valentine?" Patrick asked.

Bartholomew said, "He is the head of the vampire family and the uncle of the vampires who helped us."

"What is her name?" Annabelle teased Celwyn.

The magician inhaled, burning his bridges in the face of the expected mockery. "Miss Tara McFein."

"How adorable." Annabelle smiled at him, enjoying his discomfort.

"And the other one lusted after Bartholomew," Kang giggled.

Patrick slapped the big man on the back. "That sounds interesting."

"I will tell you more later," Bartholomew confided in a low tone.

Elizabeth found her voice. "Finish the story, please."

"We continued to the catacombs." Celwyn produced another tray of tea and poured it. Sometimes even tea did not help, but it couldn't hurt. "With the vampires' help, we tricked my father. Things became quite exciting. Unbeknown to us, Captain Nemo had followed us in the *Nautilus* to an underground lake." The magician shrugged. "He rescued us."

"The submarine was there?" Patrick exclaimed. "You were very lucky."

Elizabeth said to Annabelle with palpable sarcasm, "And here we were patiently waiting for them and deciding on the wedding flowers."

Annabelle lit another cigarette and glared like an annoyed cat.

"Captain Nemo transported us out of the catacombs after one of Jonas's most complicated magic displays. One intended to distract Wolfgang and fulfill his obligation to Thales," Bartholomew said. "It was more fantastic than anything I had ever witnessed."

Kang said, "And a supremely risky answer to an extremely dangerous situation."

"I think of it as an enjoyable adventure." Celwyn tried to suppress a smile but couldn't.

"It was dangerous! When he found us, your father nearly strangled you to death!" Bartholomew's face broke out in a sweat.

"Oh, no!" Annabelle cried.

"Then we found ourselves in an enormous underground amphitheater and had to run for our lives." The big man started to shake, just remembering.

Elizabeth turned to her husband. "You shouldn't endanger everyone!"

"But—"

"Bartholomew showed his bravery through it all. He was not afraid until the ship had to back out again." Celwyn patted his friend's shoulder and gentled his voice. "All is well now." He told them with a proud smile, "I have an excellent recovery system, both mentally and physically."

"Oh, for God's sake," Annabelle sputtered.

Elizabeth stared at her husband, and not with affection. "I'm sure it is. Xiau's telegrams basically said nothing, so I knew it was extremely perilous."

"Now, dear—"

"Don't try it, *dear*." She kissed him.

"I wish I had been there," Patrick said. "After that, you consulted on the flying machine for Captain Nemo? That is what the telegram said..."

On the other track, feet away from their window, another passenger train passed them heading the other way, toward the coast. When the noise abated, Kang said, "Yes. While Jonas recovered, we had to be sure he did not attack his brother. Or the other way around. An interesting situation, I assure you. Pelaez has no problem assuming the appearance of anyone he chooses, which made things more difficult. His hearing is acute, meaning he heard everything on the ship. Bartholomew and I kept the peace as much as possible."

"Don't forget Pelaez's pig." Bartholomew wrinkled his nose.

When his audience demanded details, the automat supplied them.

"And now," the magician faced the Professor, "Considering what Pelaez did, don't you wish you'd allowed me to eliminate him, Xiau?"

"I doubt we would have made it out of the catacombs without him, Jonas." Bartholomew didn't seem happy either at the memory or saying something nice about Pelaez.

When Kang did not answer, the magician went on. "We left out a little something in the story." At

Celwyn's words, Bartholomew smiled broadly, probably reliving the gunplay. "During our stop in Naples, my brother was attacked. Due to Bartholomew's excellent marksmanship, we extracted Pelaez from a serious situation." The magician watched the big man a moment. "I think it is your turn to deliver the more exciting details, my friend."

Bartholomew told the automat, "We should have drawn straws to see who had to do this."

"I agree." Kang refilled his whiskey glass and sat down again. "Jonas would have had to deliver the news since he usually loses our wagers."

Annabelle growled, "What *is* it?"

Bartholomew looked at Celwyn, who grinned at him. Kang pretended interest in his refilled glass.

"The longer you wait, the worse it will sound," Patrick advised.

"Very well." Bartholomew said, "In Palermo, we … misplaced Pelaez and found him in the clutches of a powerful warlock. His name was Duncan, and he was beating the daylights out of him when we arrived. Like Jonas said, with a bit of gunfire and his magic, we escaped. I enjoyed it very much."

"*A warlock?* You didn't tell us!" Elizabeth accused her husband and moved away from him on the sofa.

Bartholomew added, "At the time, we didn't know what the consequences would be and didn't want to worry you; Duncan was in league with the Mafioso."

"No wonder you were worried about our reaction." Annabelle struggled to get free of Patrick's restraining arms to express her surprise.

The big man nodded at her. "They were working together to find the flying machine."

Patrick whistled. "I have heard of the Mafioso ... my God!"

Chapter 9

AT THE NEWS ABOUT THE MAFIOSO, Elizabeth made noises like she had just found a raccoon in her skirts. She pushed Kang's concerned hands away and exclaimed, "Warlock? Weren't vampires bad enough?" She turned back to her husband. "Good grief, Xiau!"

Celwyn patted the air. "Please." He appealed to them. "Sometimes the circumstances find us. Our enemies were after the flying machine this time. In the end, we were incredibly lucky, and we are here." He treated them to his most charming smile. "Captain Nemo saved our lives."

Annabelle sputtered, "But—"

"Er, Jonas. You left out the part about saving his." The big man inched away from where Annabelle sat, fearing another explosion.

Annabelle wailed, "I don't *understand*. Why would you endanger yourselves?"

Celwyn said, "Please." He sent a cloud of pastel-colored birds smaller than a thumb to hover over her. They trilled softly. The calming effect appeared soon, along with a sideways glance from Annabelle that told him he was not really fooling her. The magician continued, "Over a period of weeks, Xiau and Bartholomew built improvements into the flying machine and fine-tuned it."

"This part of the tale doesn't sound dangerous, but I'm sure it won't last." Elizabeth sent the automat an expressive glance.

Qing must have heard the magical birds. He poked his head out of Celwyn's collar and inched his way free. By the time he had reached Annabelle on the sofa, the small birds had been replaced by his favorite green snake that slithered across the floor toward the dining room table. The mechanical bird squeaked with joy and chased it.

"Wonderful, that damn bird is back." Annabelle lifted her feet out of the way.

"Allow me." Kang faced his wife. "You'll recall that at Odessa, Bartholomew flew above us in an early version of the flying machine. Jonas was so ill, we had to wait to work on it until later."

"I remember," Elizabeth said.

Qing sailed by them at eye-level with the snake dangling from his beak and onward to the windowsill.

Bartholomew ducked as the bird made another pass by. "Well ... that flight in Odessa was actually a bit of a risk because the machine was an experiment and not really finished. Please, do not worry; I won't do that again." He bestowed a sheepish grin on them.

"Anyhow, Captain Nemo shipped the flying machine to his compound near the Turkish mountains while we took Jonas to Thales and then on to the confrontation at the catacombs."

"You were all very busy," Elizabeth murmured. Kang patted her hand and kissed it.

"Yes, we were. After that experience with Jonas's father, we headed to Turkey. Once there, the *Nautilus* traveled through an underground river to the mountains, and then we journeyed to his compound to work on an improved version of the flying machine." Bartholomew could not help the tremor in his voice at the memory of their adventure, and his face shone with sweat.

Patrick eyed the adventurers with envy.

Annabelle shook her head. "There's something you're leaving out."

Celwyn said, "Please. We didn't want to upset you." He gestured for Bartholomew to continue.

The big man shuddered. "I hope to never travel in an underground river again, but the others enjoyed it immensely."

Kang elbowed him fondly. With a sigh, because he expected fresh reactions, the automat said, "Once we arrived at the compound, we knew the Mafioso and Duncan would be watching. You'll recall that they had tried to beat the location out of Pelaez." Kang shrugged. "When the flying machine became as complete as we could make it, Captain Nemo hired a scientist to carry on the next phase of development." He regarded the magician. "I think Jonas should tell you the rest of the story."

"Oh, really?" Celwyn glared at him. "All right. When it was time to journey home, my brother and I took care of the Mafioso while Captain Nemo and the others headed through the forests to the Black Sea, where the *Nautilus* waited. Along the way, something happened."

Bartholomew shuddered in his chair.

"Heavens—" Annabelle growled, "Give me another cigarette." Patrick complied. She lit it, inhaled, and said, "I know you are leaving out what really happened. We have at least an hour until Prague." She shook a finger at them. "It is time to come clean, you three."

"I agree," Elizabeth said.

Patrick shrugged and suggested, "It will be more peaceful if you do so."

The magician laughed grimly. "Your turn," he told the automat.

Kang finished the rest of the story, including the identity of the enormous raven, Nemo nearly dying, the demise of Duncan, the destruction of the flying machine, and the betrayal of them all by Pelaez. By the time he finished, Patrick had held Annabelle as she wept, and the others watched Kang trying to reason with Elizabeth.

"Dear, if you'd been there, things would have turned out much worse—"

"*Worse*? How can you say that?" Elizabeth cried, her color high.

Kang held her arms. "Because Duncan would have used you to make us comply with his demands and then killed you. There is no doubt."

Elizabeth checked on Celwyn and Bartholomew, and both nodded in agreement.

Bartholomew added, "That warlock would have killed everyone in a most horrible way. Without Jonas and Pelaez, we would be dead. As it is, he almost killed Nemo. Jonas saved him."

"Uncle Celwyn," Annabelle put her hand out and said in a much gentler voice, "are you all right about Pelaez?"

Elizabeth softened her voice too. "The betrayal was even worse because it sounds like you had lost him so many years ago and found him again."

"It is as you have said." The magician finished the last of his tea and nodded. "However, I look forward to better things, as I always have." He regarded Kang. "I'm going to finish the tale of our adventures because otherwise, Xiau will only fluff his chicken feathers and run."

"Really?" Kang snorted.

"Really."

Bartholomew laughed. "You already have, Xiau." He laughed some more.

"We're going to rebuild the flying machine." The magician told them, "After the wedding, probably in a week or so, the three of us will rejoin Captain Nemo. It is an obligation we can't ignore."

With curses and exclamations, the others reacted. Celwyn popped a peyote button into his mouth and chewed. He must remember to ask if more buttons had arrived from Santa Fe.

PART II

Miss Tara McFein

Chapter 10

London Docklands

*I*T IS NEVER THIS WINDY IN LATE *September,* Tara thought as she drew her coat closer.

The temperatures had dropped even lower by the time she arrived at the London docks. Still, she felt relief to finally disembark from the *Mayweather.* As a vampire, she did not feel the chill like the other passengers crossing the Channel, but she simply detested what the damn wind did to her hair and hats. On the journey here, she had lost a lovely box hat while leaning over the rail in Marseilles.

The dockside overflowed with travelers and families who shivered together and skirted mud puddles. While they waited, a few other nasty elements hovered about also, and by the time she descended the gangway and walked through the horde, she had counted eight daemons. Those creatures usually sussed out that she was both a witch and a vampire, and it gave them pause. The more intelligent of them also backed away.

She scanned the throng. A dozen welcoming signs emblazoned with arriving passenger names filled the waiting area, including one that brought a smile to her lips; a diminutive man wearing a dusty bowler hat held a sign under his chin that said, "My true love!" She wondered who would approach him. As she checked the crowd, there did not appear to be any of the Queen's secret police milling about. Tara knew most of them by sight, and out of habit, she always checked for them.

She ducked around the edges of the mob and stopped to take her bearings. The terminal lay to the right, where a massive amount of freight was unloaded. An almost welcome scent of horse manure from the carriage park floated across the gravel to her; she had been at sea more than three weeks while the *Mayweather* worked her way out of Lisbon, Porto, and Bilbao before sailing north. They had stopped at every port along the way, and the monotonous diet of sea air had become tedious long ago.

Someone laid a heavy hand on her shoulder. She lashed out with her umbrella, connecting hard, and whirled away. From the *whoomph* of air expelled from Thomas Hardy, along with a colorful curse, it had been a direct strike in his midsection.

"You scared me. I hope I didn't hurt you badly."

Hardy remained doubled over, which put him on Tara's level. When he held up a hand for her to wait while he dealt with the blow, she noticed that he had not changed much in the last several years. Still prominent was the high forehead of an intellectual, the delicate ears of a woman, and the sallow complexion of a writer. Today, he had tidied up and wore his best suit and a red carnation.

"Good grief, woman!"

Tara laughed. "I had no idea you would be here."

Hardy took her elbow, and they strolled toward the carriage park. Tara's porters dutifully followed with her luggage and trunks.

"Yet, I am. A big fat bird, who thinks he can write better than Shakespeare, told me you were arriving today, and," he handed her into a well-appointed carriage, "I thought you would enjoy a stroll in Kensington Gardens before a pleasant luncheon."

"Oh?" She arranged her skirts as he settled into the opposite seat. "Do you have my evening planned also?"

Hardy had the grace to blush. "Perhaps. Since you do not appreciate comical farces or Marlowe's plays, there is something you will enjoy." The loading of Tara's trunks began with thumps and the occasional jostling of the coach. "We are to have a meeting of the Wessex Club this evening. You are the invited guest."

"How delightful!" she exclaimed. Years ago, she had heard of the club and had always wished to know more. It sounded literary and most secretive ... yet, *why would they invite me,* she wondered?

The driver tied down the last of her trunks as Hardy lit his pipe and tossed the match out the open window. "Yes, mam. It will be an entertaining evening if I've recovered from your greeting."

Tara remembered the vague references in her missives from both Hardy and Oscar that mentioned their friendship with other men of letters. Reportedly, the informal group not only enjoyed an opportunity to drink great quantities of alcohol, orate on politics, and complain about the prices of cigars, they would finally talk about their writing. Her lips twitched; the Wessex club represented many of the great names in Victorian letters, and perhaps they thought of Tara as a novelty, like a singing parrot in a dress. Or ... there could be another reason for their invitation.

"Where are you staying?" Hardy asked as their coach rolled forward to join the queue leaving the port yard.

"Bailbrook House."

"I will call for you there at nine tonight. But first, an invigorating walk in the park awaits us!"

Chapter 11

For hours, Tara's anticipation had been growing for what would happen tonight. The air seemed heavy and the evening quiet, as if waiting to give forth her secrets. As their carriage pulled up in front of the Old Royal Naval College, Hardy finished a short history lesson, and they prepared to depart the coach.

"The Rolly here, as it is known, has been the home of many scholars and military men. Over the years, several architectural geniuses have influenced the structures." He joined her at the curb, and their steps echoed as they walked the darkened path between a modern building and one from the 15th century embellished with twin gables.

Further ahead, an acre of rose bushes spread out before them, along with more buildings closed for the night. The campus appeared deserted. On a Saturday evening, students would have social obligations, and even if still here, they would likely not be interested in drunken frivolity from the Wessex Club. When Hardy stopped in front of the roses, Tara read the posted card.

GRAHAM DARBY, ROSACEAE, GENUS.

This was a teaching garden. She inhaled the spicy perfume wafting around them. *How beautiful*, she thought, a night of flowers and literary intrigue.

"Do you see the tall tower over there?" Hardy waved his pipe, and the sparks flew everywhere. At her nod, he continued, "That is a campanile designed by Arbus. He is a founding member of the Wessex Club and a wonderful storyteller."

"It is most interesting." Tara studied the bell tower that rose nearly a hundred feet above them, with its open hexagonal arches climbing the walls of the circular structure. As they drew closer, she noted the intricately carved flowers and animals decorating the façade—England's version of hieroglyphics.

Hardy opened a side door and ushered her inside. "The Wessex Club welcomes you, M'lady." He bowed.

The steep, curving staircase that led to the tower was a reminder of how small a visitor in the fourteenth century would have been. Hardy was not a heavy man, yet he had to twist and contort himself as they went up the steps. Every few feet, they passed a window through which a few stars twinkled brightly in the beautiful night. Moonlight appeared to come and go as it painted the trees and other buildings, and from deep within the darkened building next door, a lone light shone.

Murmurs from above them grew louder as they ascended, and traces of sweet tobacco tickled her nose. For some reason, the aroma reminded her of Jonas; he would be curious about this group. The Professor and Bartholomew would want to experience even more of what the Wessex Club represented. Every day, she missed Jonas's knowing smile and so much more about him.

When Tara attained the landing, Oscar Wilde stood there, waiting to hand her into the room. The 'fat bird' that Hardy had referred to smiled widely. His outlandish tie hung loose, and he had spilled wine on his dress shirt, most likely during a fancy dinner party. Wilde kissed both of her hands.

His deep voice and height could be intimidating, but not to anyone who knew him. "Welcome, my dear. I pray Hardy did not bore you with stories of romance gone mad. It is his latest obsession." Wilde gestured to the others sitting around a brazier in front of an enormous brass bell that took up most of the room. All of them smoked, and a cloud hung above them like a noxious storm.

Oscar bowed. "I have the honor of the remaining introductions." As he presented the youngest member, Tara studied William Butler Yeats, taking time to interpret his thick Irish brogue and marveling at the brooding intenseness in his eyes. He should be walking down a peaceful country lane in muddy boots and singing odes to his ever-true love. Because of his long hair and unfashionable lack of whiskers, she assumed he had not been in London very long.

Wilde steered her forward. "This is Henry James."

"Good evening, dear." A spindly, elderly man hovered over her with the kind of probing scrutiny that strangers often gave the vampire when first introduced. His glasses magnified his dark eyes until it seemed like a near-sighted beetle was examining her.

"Pleased to meet you," Tara said. She knew little of James, except that he was an American and wrote plays.

Wilde introduced the final member, a tall man about town and one clearly appreciative of the female form by the way he regarded her. He stood and pushed an upholstered chair into the circle, urging Tara to sit. Hardy took the chair on her other side.

"Good evening, Miss McFein." The man's eyes tried to hold hers, and with a twist of her lips, she resisted.

Where Yeats had been countrified, George Bernard Shaw wore stylish breeches and a topcoat that complemented his muscular frame. He had parted his dark hair with precision and displayed a smile that could have charmed a nun. Of all the club members, Jonas would develop a certain level of jealousy about Shaw if he ever met him. Oscar would not cause the same concern; the fat bird had recently been censored by the church for what an unenlightened society deemed unseemly sexual activity. Judging from Oscar's level of jocularity, it had not broken his spirit.

"Please be seated." Shaw stayed close until she did so, and with a bow, Yeats delivered a glass of wine to her.

"I am honored, but do not fuss over me," she told them.

Oscar's deep laughter rattled the rafters. "None of us will listen to that request, fine lady."

"I agree," intoned Shaw. "We are honored that you accepted our invitation."

Tara lifted her glass. "I've been friends with Thomas and Oscar for so long they even know my preferences in wine." She sniffed the glass she held and decided it was a bit on the dry side but of good quality. "But this group ... is a surprise. Tell me about the Wessex Club, please."

Several of them spoke at once, but of course, Oscar won the privilege.

"Over the years, we had noticed that we have much in common, not just a love for the written word and passion for expressing it." He drained his glass, and Hardy refilled it. When Wilde stopped to drink, Yeats took over the narration, probably knowing it would be his only opportunity.

"We also have political opinions, some of which aren't popular with the Queen's government." His serious expression displayed the fervor and fire of a young radical. "Yet, above all, our writing is the most important thing we live for."

"Speak for yourself, Willy," Oscar intoned.

Shaw edged his chair closer to Tara. His breath reminded her of singed tobacco and traces of onions.

"I, for one, enjoy feminine wiles more than the quill pen."

"Ha!" Hardy laughed. "She has a wicked backhand you should be wary of."

With a smile, Tara turned to Yeats. "Please continue."

"To be sure, our club is fairly new, and it is basically an exchange of ideas and perhaps a few well-written letters of complaint to Parliament." Yeats rubbed his chin. "You were invited not only because you are acquainted with the fat bird here," he nodded at Wilde, "but because of your unique abilities."

That could include several things, she thought.

Through the open window, the hoot of an owl startled them, becoming louder until it flew inside, circled the room twice, and settled atop the T-frame holding the massive bell in place. Taking care not to step into the hole through which the thick bell ropes dangled dozens of feet to the ground, Tara approached close enough to confirm the owl was just that and nothing more.

When she was seated again, Yeats told her, "You've just demonstrated one of the reasons we sought your company."

"My caution?"

"Yes, and your ability to recognize unusual things."

The group exchanged a glance. Hardy said, "Your invitation also pertains to a project we would like you to attempt."

Oscar stared at her for a moment. "I haven't requested Valentine's permission regarding what we would ask of you." He topped off her goblet and passed the bottle to Yeats, who drained it. "I admit, your uncle terrifies me at times."

She controlled a laugh. "You did not ask because you knew that he would say no." Valentine and Wilde had only run into each other a few times, and she made it a point to sit between them to prevent a colorful incident.

Yeats cocked his head to the side, studying her, not offensively. "From what Oscar has said, probably so. None of the rest of us have met your uncle. However, I am familiar with most of the vampire families of Eire." His expression seemed to be a mixture of awe and fear. "I respect their wishes."

"Which leads us to our request," Hardy said. He eyed Wilde pointedly.

The fat bird patted his round belly. "My dinner seems so long ago. Did anyone bring any food?" When the others shook their heads, he complained, "Such an ill-prepared gathering by my fellow hosts." He swiveled and made direct eye contact with Tara. "So. Through a well-placed source, we understand that you perform clandestine services for the Crown. We want you to do the same for us."

"Oh, my goodness." The full impact of the request came not only as a surprise but also in the level of danger it represented. Valentine enforced the family rule to not become involved in social issues or cause notoriety. Her work as a royal spy sometimes blurred that line. "I don't know what to say." Spies in the last few centuries were employed because of their ability to blend into the royal courts in various countries. Tara had found the monarchs who patronized the dark arts also sought unusual entities as guests and confidants, such as herself. She regarded Oscar.

He did not appear embarrassed, nervous, or anything but focused. "Shaw here is exploring Marxism. Yeats isn't sure yet about anything except saying that all aristocrats should be—"

"And I agree with him," Hardy growled.

Henry James tapped his cane on the floor three times. "I would have to know more before diving into a political cesspool."

"What do you want, Oscar?" Tara asked.

"I want to know when they are going to arrest me again for kissing someone I am enamored with." The playwright snapped his red suspenders in anger. "We also want to know of political decisions that concern us."

"Well." Tara thought more. "We might be able to work on some of this. I can't tell you what I do for the Crown, though."

Wilde uttered a mild curse, low enough he had hoped she would not hear. He lifted his hands. "I do not understand. A long time ago, I consulted with Valentine, and he indicated you would probably help us. Do you have allegiance to the Queen? What is your motivation?"

Shaw stood and paced to the window and back. The owl watched him without blinking. "Have we put our foot in it? I did not know you worked for the Crown."

Hardy's drawl sounded as dry as the wine bottles at his feet. "Apparently, Oscar did."

"You should have told me," Shaw accused him.

She held up a hand. "Like I said, this may work out. Please listen."

With an abruptness bordering on rudeness, Shaw stopped in front of her and said gruffly, "Please excuse my outburst."

Tara laughed, and some of the tension in their faces relaxed. "I think you all are making this more complicated than it needs to be."

Oscar opened another bottle, passed it along, and opened another. "How?"

Tara watched the owl for a moment and said, "I cannot tell you precisely what I am doing for the Crown, but can say that it is on an international level. It has nothing to do with political issues or cultural ones here. In that respect, our purposes will not clash."

"This is wonderful news," Shaw said. "Yet, I suspect there is more?"

"Yes." She made sure they were all at least partially focusing on her. The wine was having an effect. "I cannot bring notoriety to my family, either as a witch or a vampire." When they appeared relieved, she added, "I do this work because of this country and the monarchy. I believe in both, but also believe things should change for the better because there is so much suffering."

"Child labor." Shaw's face was grim.

James intoned, "Smallpox and diseases."

"We understand. Correct?" The fat bird asked the others. They all nodded.

"Within those parameters—and without getting caught—I will see what I can learn for you," she said.

"Such as?" Shaw inquired.

"General things, the way the wind blows, as it were. We would talk again at that point." Tara finished her wine. Walking a fine line between dueling loyalties was not new to her. Part of what she did for the Crown involved planned subterfuge; this endeavor would add to her experience and help those involved, too.

Henry James had said little until now. "That is more than we could have hoped for."

"My pleasure."

"Your proposal is logical. I hope the effort is not difficult or dangerous," Oscar said.

Shaw managed to get his pipe going and puffed in quiet contemplation while Wilde again rubbed his stomach. Shaw laughed. "Next time, we must have pheasant and caviar for Oscar. He is ready to bite someone's boot."

Tara caught a few secretive glances and smiles between the friends. "You have another request?"

"Yes, young Willy here has a favor to ask."

Yeats shot Oscar a peeved look. "I do, but I am reluctant to impose." His brogue sounded so thick a fly could not have swum through it.

Tara extended a hand. "Please? I would like to know."

"No laughing from any of you." Yeats glared at the others. To Tara, he said, "I want to write a novel about a vampire. One like what Bram has done. Will you help me?"

"Of course. It would be my pleasure," she assured him. Bram Stoker's *Dracula* had a few inaccuracies, though it had merit as a drama and, in her opinion, a comedy.

⌣

Tara stood again, ready to depart. Then she pivoted. Her nose twitched as if she smelled a mouse, but detected no rodents. After another moment, she relaxed when Shaw took her arm and led her toward the stairs leading downward.

If she had searched much further into the far corner of the room before she departed and checked behind the stacks of crates, she would have seen a pair of small eyes, not unlike a rodent's, from a corpulent face that watched her exit. The man in the shadows finished a notation in a notebook and listened until he could hear no more from Miss McFein. Instead, Wilde's baritone filled the room as he sang. The club members joined in and uncorked more wine.

> *Mickey Maloney ducked his head*
> *when a bucket of whiskey flew at him*
> *It missed, and falling on the bed,*
> *the liquor scattered over Tim.*
> *Now the spirits new life gave the corpse,*
> *my joy!*
> *Tim jumped like a Trojan from the bed*
> *Cryin' will ye walup each girl and boy,*
> *t'underin' Jaysus, do ye think I'm dead?"*

"The hell with the Queen!" Yeats warbled.

The rest joined in, adding speculations about the Queen's amorous activities.

Wilde said, "Now, now, fellows. We are leaving out—" His voice lowered to a whisper.

Over their laughter, the bells in the neighboring clock tower rang the midnight hour.

What better time to leave? The corpulent man asked himself. He wiggled his stomach through the trapdoor in the floor and clambered down a ladder, more stairs, and out into the night.

Chapter 12

Prague

THINGS BECAME A MITE FROSTY aboard the *Elizabeth* for the remainder of the trip back to Prague. Kang explained and tried reasoning regarding the details of their latest adventure, as did Bartholomew, but the atmosphere still felt chilly. As they rounded Mount Kladno and started down the hill toward St. Vita's church, Mrs. Xiau Kang grudgingly addressed her husband.

"I understand most of this and why you must again help Captain Nemo. But how much of it is an obligation, and how much of it is scientific fervor?"

While Kang thought of how to squirm out of that question, Bartholomew said, "For me, it is half and half. Because ... when everything is over and done, I want to be here in Prague for the boys while they grow up ... and for all of you."

"The same," Kang managed.

Elizabeth tried not to smile and failed. "It is all right, Xiau. I understand."

"What about you, Uncle Celwyn?" Annabelle asked.

"My position is a bit different." He closed his eyes and opened them again. "You have probably noticed that I have a wide streak of wanderlust in my past and no discernable scientific talent."

"You don't say." Patrick laughed.

Annabelle slapped his hand. "I don't think it's funny if it is dangerous."

"Exactly my point to Jonas," Kang said with his brand of virtue, if not adorable hypocrisy. The magician knew his friend enjoyed their dangerous adventures as much as he but would not admit it, especially in front of Elizabeth and Annabelle.

"You fuss too much," Celwyn added leaves of lettuce to the automat's ears. "In any case, I am not concerned with science, but I am very concerned in keeping everyone here, and Captain Nemo and everyone aboard the *Nautilus,* safe." He stared at Kang's ears, adding cherry tomatoes for color. The automat's physiology prevented magic for structural changes, but cosmetic enhancements usually worked well. Elizabeth enjoyed them as much as Celwyn did, but in her present humor, they may not be as well received. "I can't tell a yaw from a propeller; however, I want to be present to be sure no one is hurt."

"By whom?" Elizabeth saw her husband's ears, and her mouth abruptly closed as she hid a smile.

"We hope there is no one else to fear but require Jonas's abilities to be sure," Bartholomew said.

The *Elizabeth* slowed to switch tracks and enter the Prague terminal. As the screech of her brakes increased, her whistle shrilled, and they bounced over a trestle.

Celwyn raised his voice. "At this very moment, Captain Nemo is scouting for a place to rebuild the flying machine, one that is as secure as it can be. It must also have flat land for a landing field and preferably be close to Prague. Above all, it must be secret. We estimate that Bartholomew and Xiau will be needed for several months before the project can be turned over to other scientists hired by Nemo."

Elizabeth addressed the magician. "A few months. I see. And you would be there to keep them safe?"

"Yes."

"We would visit here every month until it is done," Bartholomew said.

With a disapproving eye on her husband, Elizabeth sighed. "I'm glad one of you has some common sense."

"Jonas doesn't. He hasn't told you everything about the proposed site." The automat batted at his ears and edged his way behind Patrick.

"Oh? You have a proposed site?" Patrick asked.

All eyes turned to the magician. He made sure Qing was watching and produced another baby green snake, this time on the Professor's collar.

"Findbar Island. It is about twelve hours north-west of Szczecin."

"That doesn't sound bad at all." Annabelle raised her brows in confusion as Qing dove toward the automat.

"It is haunted."

Chapter 13

A S THEY ENTERED TELLYHOUSE, something furry and nearly as big as Otto bounded down the stairs and galloped to the boys.

Bartholomew stared with amazement. The automat grinned and stepped forward. In one leap, the animal knocked him down and stood on his chest while Kang rubbed his ears. While Otto and Zander tried to remove him, the magician peered over Bartholomew's shoulder at the tableau.

"A Russian wolfhound." Kang swiped at his face where the dog had licked him.

Bartholomew beamed. "A very big one, too." He tapped his chest, and the dog stood up, putting its paws on his shoulders. The big man scratched his back.

Zander panted, "His name is Beastie!"

Beastie left the big man to greet the others. Like a gentleman, he waited for Elizabeth to pat his head and tell him he was a good dog.

The magician eyed Beastie and told him silently, "*Sit.*"

Like a swarm of bees buzzed between his ears, the dog shook his head and sat. The magician decided the newest addition to Tellyhouse was a most welcome one.

After things settled down, Celwyn addressed the pianoforte in the parlor, letting the music ring, celebrating being alive and at home. As the atmosphere enveloped him in warm, comforting arms, he concluded that Tellyhouse was the closest he had ever come to a family, and perhaps it would always be so.

With only a short time until dinner, the aroma of garlic, rosemary, and several chickens baking filled the air. The magician decided Ricardo must be a genius indeed to produce something that smelled that wonderful after being home for only a few hours.

Celwyn had just started the "Mephisto Waltz" when Otto joined him, leaning over the pianoforte to watch his fingers dancing over the keys. His face displayed the kind of fascination that should be rewarded. The last time Celwyn had seen the lad, he had been too sick to play for the boy. Otto deserved as much as they could provide for him. Despite being mute, over the last year, he'd lost much of his shyness and become part of the family, no longer hesitating when something interested him.

The magician stood and ushered Otto onto the bench in front of the keys. After he brought a chair closer, Celwyn reseated himself and asked, "Are you ready to learn to play?" Otto's smile came quick, with the delicacy of a baby bird's first flight.

"You will have to find time to practice when you are not doing chores. Listen to what you hear as you play." The magician pointed to the keys. "Place your hands on the keyboard like this."

An hour later, tentative notes floated from beyond the conservatory and past the dining room to the parlor, where the magician relaxed under the picture window. He listened to Otto practice and glanced outside as he poured his third cup of tea. It would be a while until the boy could read the notes, but he would. Celwyn sent a simple piece of music to the pianoforte without Otto noticing. Perhaps the lad could prove the adage that if a person lacked one physical sense, the others became stronger.

Annabelle and Elizabeth stopped their embroidery to listen, even when the notes sounded a touch discordant, before going back to their needles. With a yawn, the magician gazed at the front yard and saw Patrick throw a baseball to Zander, who caught it and laughed. From his nearby chair, Kang read one of his new books and said without raising his eyes, "I need to go to the bookstore." He turned the page. "I want to purchase a few copies of *Alice in Wonderland* so the boys will read it, and we can discuss it during class."

"I doubt that is all you want to buy," Elizabeth replied without missing a stitch.

The automat turned a page. "You are correct. We can go tomorrow."

On the other side of the window, Zander tackled Patrick, and they rolled into the rose bushes. Annabelle eyed them and muttered something about Patrick's white shirt.

Celwyn remembered what he had been meaning to say. "Xiau, we should probably buy a second carriage exclusively to haul books in, don't you agree?"

Even without counting the automat's penchant for books, when they arrived at the train terminal, transportation home had been a bit crowded. Their footman Edward had picked them up, along with two carts for their luggage. Both boys rode in the cab up top with Edward. Mrs. Thomas, Tellyhouse's housekeeper, would not have approved if she had seen them; young men of breeding did not ride with footmen and whoop and holler as they drove down the street.

"Has Edward left for the train station?" Bartholomew asked while trying to see around the rose bushes to the end of the driveway. Edward had announced that Mrs. Thomas was due back from her trip to Vienna later that afternoon. It seemed she loved the Belvedere Museum and had taken a short holiday to visit it before everyone returned home, and her responsibilities increased. Celwyn knew that she would describe the household more colorfully.

Jackson arrived and deposited a tray of cheese and crackers in front of the sofas. He addressed the room, "Excuse me, Sirs and Madams. Yes, he has. Edward stated that they would probably return by dinnertime." Jackson could not help a knowing smile and a wink at them. "Mrs. Thomas is looking forward to your return."

As he left again, Celwyn asked, "I wonder what he meant?"

"I do not know but can guess," the big man said. "By the way, where is Beastie?"

"In the stables with the Conductor." Kang turned another page. "I understand the dog is supposed to have his initial obedience lessons." He raised a brow at Celwyn. "Have you had yours?"

"Ha!" The magician stood and called to Otto, "Same time tomorrow ... for your next lesson?" When the boy nodded, Zander, who had been waiting in the hallway for the last several minutes, waved at him. The magician said, "You may be excused."

More than an hour later, just as Jackson began setting the dining table, Edward arrived out front with Mrs. Thomas. While she climbed out of the carriage, Celwyn checked the parlor for any evidence of magic or other things she would disapprove of. Their housekeeper ruled Tellyhouse with a strong will, and no one—including Celwyn—dared to cross her. At over six feet tall and stronger than a coal miner, she did not put up with any shenanigans. Sully, the footman of Tellyhouse and her sometimes wooer, approached to take her bag. She allowed it and followed him up to the house.

Bartholomew, Kang, and Celwyn lined up in the front hallway, partially in respect and partially in the hope of climbing back into her good graces. They helped each other confirm their ties were knotted properly and prepared to greet her. Everyone else had elected to wait in the parlor. If Celwyn was dubious, he would have suspected they already knew her reaction would be noisy.

Sully held the front door open. Mrs. Thomas marched inside in her serviceable shoes, wearing a glower across her sweet face. When she saw the three of them, she stopped short, causing the flowers in her hat to bob.

"Well! About time you Sirs returned. I must get to work." She started by but swiveled to face them. "I am glad you survived, Mr. Celwyn, but it would be nice if you stopped scaring us like that." With her last few words, the housekeeper's voice wavered, and her eyes filled with tears. She pivoted and hurried down the hall.

After she disappeared into the kitchen, the Professor said, "You certainly inspire strong reactions, Jonas." He laughed as he and Bartholomew headed back to the parlor. "By the way, do you know where Qing is?"

From the kitchen came an outraged screech, not from Qing.

The magician ran down the hall as fast as he could.

The next morning, Zander sat beside Celwyn as they gathered at the breakfast table. Otto occupied the chair on his other side and smiled with Bartholomew, who had just told him a joke. After the others straggled in, Jackson poured coffee, and Abe deposited platters of steaming waffles on the table.

"Where is your brother, Abe?" Kang asked. "I haven't seen him since we arrived home."

Their redheaded porter, who also doubled as a helper to the Conductor when the *Elizabeth* traveled the rails, said, "He doesn't like being inside as much as I do."

"I can understand that." Celwyn poured syrup on his waffle. "Perhaps we will travel again soon, and everyone will be happy."

Annabelle shot him a flustered look. "The wedding is eight days from now. I assume you won't be going anywhere before then."

"No, ma'am. We do need to get Bartholomew's suit ordered today ... and a few other things."

Zander asked, "Are you going somewhere that Otto and I like to go?"

The automat sent him a sympathetic glance. "The bookstore and a few other errands, possibly, before your classes this afternoon."

Zander sighed.

"I must remain here," Annabelle said. "There are many things I still have to do concerning the reception."

"You recall Buckworth, the tailor that I need to visit?" Bartholomew told Kang. "I believe he is about three blocks south of your bookstore."

The Professor nodded and chewed. "I'll go with you to the tailors. I need a new cummerbund, according to Elizabeth, and both these rascals need final fittings."

Patrick regarded the lads. "You will be most handsome at the wedding."

"I guess," Zander said, and started kicking his chair.

"Could you reword that, please?" Kang requested.

Zander turned a little pink. "Thank you for the compliment."

"It is true. You will both be most dapper at the festivities." Celwyn chewed and realized he missed the breakfast fruits on the *Nautilus* and speculated whether Ricardo could find the same exotic things at the market. "Patrick will need your help that day, too."

Bartholomew asked Patrick, "Have you planned your honeymoon?"

"In September, we will go to London." Annabelle frowned and touched her hair. "Who knows what hats will be fashionable by then?"

At the news, Celwyn mentally sighed and caught the same corresponding reactions from Kang and Bartholomew. There was a chance they would still be with Captain Nemo, and someone should be here with Elizabeth and the boys. "We expect a telegram from Captain Nemo soon." The magician couldn't help but wonder how they were coming along on Findbar Island.

"If there are any messages, we generally see a messenger about four in the afternoon," Patrick told them.

The magician stared beyond the dining room and out the parlor window where the sun appeared strong, blanketing the yard and highlighting the red of the roses. It would be a pleasant day in town today. With luck, there would be a tiny breeze capable of stealing the automat's hat while he was trotting in and out of the bookstore.

Bartholomew emptied his juice glass and asked Annabelle, "Is your aunt still in Prague? Will she attend the wedding?"

"Yes. I see her every week. She will be there." She glanced at the magician with an impish smile. "My aunt will have dinner with us next Thursday and expects to be reunited with all of you."

Celwyn well remembered Mrs. Pearse ... and not fondly. But his thoughts remained on Nemo. He wondered what they had found on the island. Or who?

Chapter 14

Five days passed without a telegram from Nemo. The magician did receive a bedtime visit from the wyvern one night and took the opportunity for a spot of training. From this point forward, Wye would appear upon Celwyn's command. He hoped.

During those five days, the magician observed clear signs of impatience in the scientists. Bartholomew spent as much time as possible out in front, theoretically smoking but watching for a messenger. In contrast, Kang could not sit still at his desk in the parlor, and the wadded-up sheets of paper at his feet grew like a herd of misshapen rabbits.

For the magician, everything at Tellyhouse settled back into a pleasant routine of tea, music, and pastries. When Annabelle and Elizabeth's time became more and more consumed with the nuptials, he found himself drafted to oversee the transport of the wedding party and manage the boys' education until after the wedding.

Celwyn couldn't be sure if the idea originated from the magical scene of Prague Castle that he had created months ago, but Annabelle and Patrick's wedding would take place at St. George's chapel on the castle grounds. In the early morning, the carriage carrying the women would leave Tellyhouse and have their finishing touches done at one of the castle's apartments. Other well-appointed carriages would transport everyone else.

At high noon, three days before the wedding, Celwyn strolled along a shaded path of the castle's grounds that led to the abbey and the castle behind it. The abbey's ancient bells rang in overlapping, headache-inducing harmony. As he stepped around a gaggle of gardeners who occupied the paths and flowerbeds, he enjoyed the heavy air, fresh with turned earth.

Edward walked with him, regaling the magician with tales of his weekly visits to Francesca's coven. When Bartholomew joined them on their trip, Edward had taken over the task of paying the witch her fees. His visits had evolved to early morning arrivals, where the least amount of witches would be awake to pinch and grab at him. The downside of that approach meant he faced Francesca's aversion to rising before noon.

Celwyn stopped and smelled one of the yellow roses, enjoying the scent. "Has Francesca said she will actually attend tomorrow?" The witch's notoriety rivaled that of her coven.

"Did you invite her?"

Celwyn said, "Not exactly; it was her price for one of our requests for protection spells last October."

"Oh. I haven't heard." Edward scratched his head. "Would they allow her in the chapel?"

"We'll find out soon." The magician shrugged. "A question. Has anyone told you what happened on our recent journey?" They continued toward the end of the gardens, passing several devotees clutching prayer books, turned, and headed back toward the abbey.

"No, sir."

"I think you should hear about it. Not because of any danger, but because you would probably appreciate knowing what occurred."

"And be able to recognize anything out of place. I agree. But, won't you Sirs be here too?"

"At times." They found a bench, sat down, and the magician told him everything that had happened, from Captain Nemo and Thales to Pelaez, Duncan, and the Mafioso. When he reached the part about Findbar Island, they began walking again.

"One more thing."

"Sir?"

"Could you please call me Jonas?"

"Jonas," Edward repeated as if it were an obscure Chinese dialect, "what exactly was on that island?"

"Please still address me formally if Mrs. Thomas is nearby." After Edward winked like someone well aware of the housekeeper's rules about propriety, the magician continued, "I don't know exactly, but Captain Nemo is investigating the island now to verify if we can build our new compound there. It is one of the reasons I wanted to tell you of all of this and count on your discretion."

"Of course." Edward eyed him. "You are leaving again."

An astute man. "Yes, I'm afraid so. At the new compound, Bartholomew and the Professor will build another flying machine, and my role is to protect them, Captain Nemo, and the venture itself. I failed miserably the first time."

"If you don't mind me saying so, it sounds like you did a marvelous job of it but were betrayed."

"Perhaps."

"I couldn't believe Mr. Bartholomew was so far up in the air when I saw that machine," Edward marveled. "The sight was fantastic."

"It certainly was, and it is nothing I would do." Celwyn stopped thinking about the scientists and watched as a contingent of palace guards in red uniforms marched by.

"When do you leave?"

The wistfulness in Edward's voice again reminded Celwyn of his notion of bringing Edward along on their adventures. He speculated how difficult it would be to replace him at Tellyhouse and if Patrick and the other residents would still talk to him if he corrupted Edward into their activities. Bartholomew and the automat would love it.

"I hope it isn't before Miss Annabelle's wedding."

"Sorry." Celwyn had been distracted with thoughts of what awaited them on Findbar. "We leave after the wedding when Captain Nemo sends for us. Bartholomew and the Professor are anxious to proceed. You can see where your role has again become important to protect everyone in Tellyhouse."

"Yes ... more vampires?" Edward asked with a certain amount of trepidation as evidenced by the twitch in his jaw, but the resolve sounded just as strong.

"Yes, and no." The quartet of the palace guards marched by again, continuing down the path and turning toward the north side of the grounds. "There are some in Prague, but Mrs. Karras is no longer a threat. She has been dealt with. The two threats I know of are my brother and anyone who sympathizes with that warlock we killed."

"Who will your brother threaten?"

"The residents of Tellyhouse are not in danger this time." Celwyn had given this question much thought and could not see why Pelaez would bother. He either had kept on going, traveling far from them, or found something else to occupy himself now that he'd destroyed Nemo's dream. "There could be someone new."

Edward guessed. "Because it is you or the Professor and Bartholomew that they want."

"Exactly. Mostly the latter two," the magician said. "I would only be targeted for revenge ... or if I got in their way."

They started back toward the carriage. "I keep thinking about that big black ship under the water I saw you carried into—"

"The *Nautilus*. She is a submarine."

"If I may say so, that is a fantastic sight. Just fascinating." His eyes gleamed with the kind of fervor Bartholomew and Kang reserved for the flying machine. "Sea ships are incredible."

"The Vltava here isn't deep enough for her in spots, or Captain Nemo would have brought her upriver to deliver us here."

"Err ... that would have been a problem." Edward spent a moment visualizing the possibility before saying, "I will be on guard and hope all goes well with the new compound."

When they finished their promenade, they once again entered the parking area.

"Thank you." The magician climbed up to the cab of the carriage with Edward. "Where are we off to next?"

With the waning sun behind them, Edward drove up the circular drive of Tellyhouse just as Otto and Zander burst out of the front door, racing each other to reach the messenger who had followed their carriage through the gateposts. He parked his bicycle and handed Celwyn two letters. The first envelope had been sent from California and was addressed to the Professor. After the magician tipped the messenger, his attention centered on the second envelope. At last, they had an answer.

Otto held up his tablet.

The magician read it. "I am pleased to see you, too," he told him with a smile. "We will start our music lesson as soon as I've spoken to the others."

Zander jabbed Otto in the ribs, and they took off running down the driveway toward the gardens.

Celwyn thought it best they did so; he expected a heated discussion after he read the letter to the others. When he arrived in the parlor, he found everyone present except Annabelle. Patrick spied the blue-green envelope and Celwyn's expression and went to get her. Elizabeth put down her embroidery while the others turned to him with either curiosity or caution in their eyes.

The magician handed Kang the other envelope and produced a tea tray.

"Otto and Zander will probably be here any minute," Celwyn told them as he filled a cup. "Ah, there she is." As Annabelle joined them, she stared at the envelope in his hand like it might turn into a snake and hiss at her.

"It is from Captain Nemo." The magician read.

Dear friends,

> *Please forgive my tardiness in writing, but we have been extremely busy, and I finally have news.*

Findbar Island will suit us. There are several major projects we must complete here before we are ready for you. I anticipate further information soon.

Jules requests that I tell you he misses our bridge games. He also does not think he will be able to attend the wedding.

If Bartholomew or the Professor have any special tools they need for our endeavors, I will be picking up messages again soon. Jonas, I presume you will make anything you need.

Please give my best regards to Mrs. Kang, yourNiece and her betrothed, and everyone else at Tellyhouse.

Sincerely,
Captain Nemo

Kang jumped to his feet. "Yes!"

Bartholomew jumped up, too, striding to the windows and back. "This is wonderful news." The gleam of anticipation in his eyes could have lit up the chandelier of the Opera House.

The Professor grabbed his arm. "We need to get our list to the telegraph office before they close—" He ran out of the room with Bartholomew close behind. As they climbed the stairs toward their office, they bounced ideas back and forth like a tennis ball on fire.

"I will alert Edward to await the message—" Celwyn said and rose.

Patrick had been gazing out the front window. "No need. He is coming in the front door with the boys on his heels."

"Quickly," Annabelle said. "Before they arrive, tell us why this is good news."

"Because the island is about twelve hours from Szczecin, and we will be able to visit Tellyhouse fairly often."

Elizabeth rolled her eyes, not as well as Kang could, but she conveyed her sarcasm just as well. "*Such* good news..."

Chapter 15

"Two souls with but a single thought;
two hearts that beat as one."

Friedrich Halm

The Wedding

BY THE TIME CELWYN HAD HERDED
everyone at Tellyhouse across town to the
castle, he was seriously considering swimming out
to Findbar Island, with or without the *Nautilus*. It
would be less stressful. Annabelle, Elizabeth, and a
pair of maids departed at eight that morning, leaving
Celwyn to begin getting everyone ready and into the
carriages.

Several times, Annabelle had impressed him
with a warning; do not let the boys go outside

because they would either get dirty or be hard to find, and the magician agreed. Lately, he had spied them coming back to the house much more filthy than usual.

By eleven, Ricardo, Jackson, Conductor Smith, and Edward stood at attention in their finery, prepared to board the hired carriage. Even Andy wore a top hat and gloves, ready to drive them. After they climbed inside the coach, the magician felt that he had at least accomplished that. He went upstairs and continued searching for Zander. Minutes later, he cornered the scamp coming out of the classroom, straightened the boy's tie, and sent him to Patrick's room along with Otto. They were to either help or at least be where they could be found.

That left Kang and Bartholomew. They weren't in the automat's suite. When Celwyn arrived at Bartholomew's door, he found Kang with his hair askew and on his tiptoes, trying to tie the big man's tie. Celwyn fixed it. Without turning around, the Professor said, "Jonas is here."

"Correct. Are you ready? Everyone else is waiting. I'd wager you had your noses in the specs until ten minutes ago."

"No comment. Let's go."

⌒‿⌒

Under a cloudless blue sky, the carriage with Ricardo and the others led the way out of the driveway and down the street. The second carriage followed with Abe's twin, Andy, driving. After a few minutes, the

magician said, "I think the twins are racing." His prediction proved true when Abe took the next corner
nearly on two wheels with a whoop and a gesture.
Celwyn slowed the carriages and sent both drivers
strong suggestions to take their time.

When they arrived at the Castle, the boys followed Patrick and Celwyn down a fairytale path
to the apartments set aside for the groom. They
crowded inside. Patrick had chosen to wear his military uniform, complete with sash and medals. He
was most handsome as he sprawled on the suite's
loveseat with a lost look painted across his face.

The magician handed him a flask of whiskey and
distracted the boys with a slender yellow snake in
the tree outside the window. Qing's head popped
out of Celwyn's collar, and he made a metallic
clicking sound in his throat. "No." The magician
pushed him back inside his collar. "And don't chew."
Annabelle was not an admirer of the mechanical
bird, and Qing would have to behave, at least until
after the ceremony.

Patrick emptied the flask and handed it back.
"Where did the others go?"

On cue, the Professor and Bartholomew, both
appearing pleased with themselves, walked up the
path and joined them.

"We toured the chapel. It is beautiful." The big
man scanned the room. "How long until we begin?"

"Soon, I hope." Celwyn pulled out his dress pocket
watch, an exquisite E. Bourquin. "Zander, no, you
can't climb the tree."

Zander turned away from the window and opened his mouth. "How did you know—"

"I just know. Do you remember what you are supposed to do during the ceremony?"

"Yes." Zander nodded as Otto joined him at the window with a nod. "Otto does, too."

A few minutes later, an officiant escorted them to a side door of the chapel. As Patrick's best men, the Professor and Bartholomew wore solemn expressions befitting the occasion. The magician bet he could do something to make the big man laugh, but decided not to when he thought about Annabelle's reaction.

As the wedding party entered the ancient room while the pipe organ played a wedding dirge, the pews filled, and Patrick's nervousness grew. The magician added another full flask to the groom's pocket before heading across the grounds to the bridal suite. His last duty was to give the bride away, preferably without having to defend her against a vampire or anything else.

Above all, he was not to use magic. That was a request from both Elizabeth and Annabelle, stated as sternly as they could make it with the automat grinning in the background and Bartholomew trying to hide his amusement.

Chapter 16

I T WAS TIME.
As the magician started down the aisle, the music of the wedding procession swelled, growing in majesty as it filled the chapel until it met the ornate ceiling. The music couldn't hide a prickle of warning that sent an icy hand wiggling down Celwyn's back, not to signal danger, but of awareness. No matter. It would be best to hide whatever it meant from Annabelle.

She walked beside him, wearing a brilliant smile frozen in place, as she concentrated on not tripping on her dress. To Celwyn, the dress, with its long train, intricate beading, and lace, rivaled those at the royal weddings Celwyn had attended in the 1600s and 1700s. As Annabelle's escort, the magician knew he appeared quite handsome in his new suit that fit him perfectly for the occasion.

"I would kill a vampire with my bare hands for a cigarette," the exquisite bride whispered.

Celwyn resisted the urge to send her a silent word of encouragement since it would only annoy her. Instead, he patted her hand resting on his forearm.

The abbey held about a hundred people. As they passed rows of ancient pews, the magician broadened his scrutiny, scanning faces and noting most of them would not account for the sense of alarm he had experienced, even a gentle one that told him things were not as they seemed.

They had almost reached the altar, where Patrick, Kang, and Bartholomew awaited them, when the magician spotted Mrs. Pearse in the first row, dabbing her eyes. He did not recognize the other people on each side of her. When he checked on his right, Celwyn almost tripped.

Jules Verne, who he thought to be on the *Nautilus* and unable to attend, sat there. Next to him sat a darker-skinned man in a pristine white suit, thick mustache, and wearing a serious expression. The magician decided Captain Nemo needed coaching on the art of applying mustaches. He also noticed Nemo did his best to be inconspicuous by avoiding eye contact with others—a nice touch.

It took all Celwyn's concentration to listen to the cleric, who appeared as glorious in his flowery speech as his vestments, while he talked about the state of wedded bliss. Bartholomew and Patrick listened carefully to each word, as did Annabelle, while Kang made a point of catching the magician's eye with a raised brow and a nod toward the front row.

The magician winked at him. He did not consider it anything to worry about; none of the guests had seen Nemo before or expected him here.

The ceremony concluded, and the newly-weds walked hand-in-hand, back up the aisle to the accompanying well-wishes. Elizabeth and the others came next, with the boys bringing up the rear. The lads had done a marvelous job as ushers. Bartholomew saw Nemo and stared. Kang elbowed him forward again.

In the throng of people in the courtyard, Celwyn lost track of Kang. So had Elizabeth, who did not appear amused. With a snort of displeasure, she lifted her skirts and pivoted to rejoin the newlyweds.

Bartholomew grunted. "There he is—" They trotted down the rose-lined path away from the chapel. Near the carriage park, they found the automat amid the shrubbery off to the side, partially hidden by a flowering hibiscus.

When they arrived, they discovered Kang was not alone.

"Captain. Jules." Celwyn bowed. Bartholomew shook Nemo's hand. The magician said, "I'm so pleased you could attend, Sir."

"I am, also. A fine family you have." He glanced beyond the bushes toward the abbey. "I think Mrs. Kang recognized me; I'm not sure."

Kang pursed his lips and didn't quite suppress an impending-marital-discord expression, along with a furtive glance over his shoulder. "Let's deal with that later. Do you have news for us?"

From beside Nemo, Verne beamed at them. "A very nice service, very nice." He hesitated and then pursed his lips in a pout. "I wish we could stay for lunch."

"Jules was approached by a reporter he knows," Captain Nemo growled. "We must depart before he finds us."

The magician asked, "Are you going back to Szczecin and the ship?"

"Yes. Almost immediately. But if you could meet us at the telegraph office on Ovida Street after your luncheon, we will be able to confer."

"Hey!"

Celwyn turned. A young man in an ill-fitting suit, clutching a notebook, ran toward them.

"I did nothing!" Verne insisted. "He found me. I swear!"

"Captain, please take your leave. We will meet you there in a little more than an hour." Celwyn shook his hand. "I'll take care of this."

Nemo grabbed Verne's elbow, and they headed toward the carriage park. The magician allowed the reporter to approach. When the man rounded the curve in the path, a sleek panther sat in the flower bed, its eyes glowing in anticipation. The reporter stopped dead still and then backed up as the panther stood and swaggered toward him.

The reporter's retreat started slowly at first, but soon he sprinted. When he glanced back, the panther broke into a lope, gaining on him. The magician, Kang, and Bartholomew strolled up the path until they could no longer see the reporter. Celwyn dissolved the panther.

"You could have been more flamboyant, I suppose," the automat allowed.

Bartholomew made an observation with the mock seriousness of someone who had just enjoyed himself. "It is doubtful anyone will believe anything from that man. There are panthers residing in the castle's zoo near the north gate."

"I hear there have been a few escapes from there, too." Celwyn stepped onto higher ground to see if Nemo and Verne had reached their carriage. "I wonder what Captain Nemo wants to talk about."

"Us," Bartholomew guessed.

"I hope so." The automat rubbed his hands together and then stopped. "Oh, drat. We've been spotted." He waved a greeting, perhaps an olive branch, to his wife as they neared the abbey.

"There you are." Elizabeth met them. The automat hooked his arm in hers and pecked her cheek. "Come along." She led them to where the other guests had gathered.

The courtyard seemed much more crowded; the tables for the luncheon had been set up. More guests arrived by the minute, and the level of good cheer rose higher, stimulated by intoxicating beverages and the romanticism of the scene.

The bride and groom stood under an arch of white roses and stained glass, greeting the well-wishers, while the Professor squeezed Elizabeth's hand to reassure her he wouldn't disappear again. Zander and Otto flanked them, standing at attention and shaking hands like proper young men who had been coached for hours. Celwyn and Bartholomew joined them. Elizabeth whispered something in Kang's ear with a set smile, and the automat managed a nervous grin.

"I'm most curious about what Captain Nemo wants," Bartholomew confided in Celwyn in a whisper.

"I do not know, but hope it is something to do with the new compound." The magician murmured, "Have you figured out how we will get away to meet him after this luncheon?" Celwyn shook the hand of a man he did not know and said in an aside to the big man, "Smile like we're not talking about Nemo. Elizabeth has her eye on us."

"I would suggest it would be all right to take her with us, but that probably wouldn't go over well with the boys and the newlyweds." The big man smiled broadly at a couple standing in front of him.

"All right." Celwyn lowered his voice again. "I'll take care of it, but you'll need to help; Annabelle listens to you."

***

Edward drove them to the telegraph office. They had a pass from Annabelle that would last an hour only because Bartholomew talked her into it. From Patrick's torn expression, the magician deduced he wanted to go with them but knew better than to ask. Elizabeth had been invited to demonstrate newfound candidness in their planning; she also had a fairly open mind about their activities, no matter how she fussed at her husband. The invitation was well received but declined, along with her remark about someone needing to be gracious to their guests.

As they walked into the telegraph office, Celwyn spied Nemo and Verne standing off to the side, holding newspapers, seemingly engrossed in their reading. Edward stationed himself outside the door in case they had been followed.

"We meet again." The magician shook Nemo's hand. "No danger is present." He nodded at the room. "We may speak freely."

"We have only thirty minutes before we must return." Bartholomew also scanned the patrons in the office. "There are no reporters here."

Captain Nemo kept his voice down. "This should only take a few minutes. Over here." He led them to a pair of unoccupied wooden benches.

"Findbar Island is ready for you, gentlemen."

Kang and Bartholomew grinned broadly.

"The *Nautilus* is waiting in the waters off Szczecin." Nemo asked, "Are you prepared to join us?"

"Yes. This is even sooner than I'd hoped." Kang pulled at the knot of his tie. "I have given this some thought."

"I have, also." Bartholomew said, "We have most of the specs re-created, but in doing so, we have discovered that the design requires further refinements."

With a quick glance at the entrance, Verne asked with a certain amount of nervousness, "What happened to the reporter?"

The magician laughed at him. Verne gulped.

Kang said, "We will need the newest texts on lift. And any articles in periodicals to be found about it. Can we assume you have the tools we salvaged from the compound in Turkey?"

"Yes." Captain Nemo studied a pair of muscular men who entered the office and took seats near the pickup counter. "What else?"

They discussed the availability of types of fuel until the magician consulted his watch.

"We will pack for an extended stay." As Celwyn spoke, he entered the thoughts of the muscular men. It didn't take long before he backed out again and shook his head at the Captain, who nodded and took his gun hand out of his pocket. The magician went on, "Allowing for packing and other details at Tellyhouse, we could take the *Elizabeth* to Szczecin about three days from now if that would suffice? We must spend time with the newlyweds and the boys."

"And Elizabeth. Or she will insist on going with us," the automat said.

"They realize that the sooner we do this, the sooner we will be home for good." As he spoke, Bartholomew watched Edward walk by the window with his eye on the carriage park.

"As expected. We have some errands in the area and will wait off the coast until then." Captain Nemo stood. "We'll check for you at the headlands where we left you before."

"Mid-day, three days hence, Sir," Celwyn promised him.

Chapter 17

They returned to the wedding reception with a minute to spare and found Annabelle and Patrick dancing to the *Duke of Kent's Waltz*. Celwyn could think of worse waltzes, but not by much. As they danced, the newlyweds expressed their profound relief that the wedding had finally occurred.

The three friends joined the other guests near the bar. As they accepted glasses of champagne, Bartholomew elbowed the magician.

A few feet away, Zander walked up to Elizabeth, bowed, and took her hand to lead her to the dance floor just as Bartholomew had taught him. With utmost seriousness, Otto stood close by, studying Zander's performance. When Annabelle tapped him on the shoulder and invited him to dance, he checked with Bartholomew. The big man nodded at him. Otto offered her his arm and stepped onto the floor. His smile came, but he spent more time watching his feet than enjoying the dance.

Patrick sighed with happiness and joined Celwyn and Kang. They watched the boys as they moved across the dance floor.

"We seem to be short on younger female partners." Celwyn nodded at the crowd of well-wishers.

With a nervous glance, Patrick asked, "Planning to fix the situation?"

"But of course."

With her head held high and a corsage pinned to her dress, Mrs. Thomas floated by in the arms of Sully, who had shaved and wore his Sunday best. They made an interesting couple with the top of the footman's head coming up to her shoulder. A minute later, the upstairs maid, Flossy, and Ricardo went by, both wearing festive smiles. Ricardo proved he was as light on his feet as he was talented with a soup spoon. By searching, Celwyn eventually found the Conductor and Jackson toasting each other and laughing at Sully as he sailed by.

After Zander finished his waltz and returned Elizabeth to the Professor, he stopped short and studied at the edge of the crowd displaying even more interest than he displayed toward reptiles. A girl with chestnut curls and a pixie mouth stared back at him. With a glance of nervousness as much as interest, Zander searched for encouragement and saw Celwyn's nod. A moment later, the lad offered the girl his arm, and they walked onto the dance floor.

Otto spotted them, and his eyes widened behind his spectacles. Annabelle spied them too, and frowned as she tried to place the girl as a guest. Otto kept a fascinated eye on his brother as he wandered back to Annabelle and Patrick, who ruffled his hair and pulled him to his side. When the music ended, the magician added a brace of horns and a collection of violins heralding hundreds of white doves that had entered the castle grounds to circle the crowd.

"Oh!" Annabelle clapped her hands in delight, and Patrick embraced her. Celwyn's violins serenaded them to the consternation of the hired musical ensemble, who had lowered their instruments to their laps and tried to find the source of the music. Above the crowd, lights twinkled in the windows of the castle. A most pleasant fairy tale, the magician thought. Zander and Otto took turns pointing out faces peering down at them.

When the doves flew into the trees, the violins faded away. The other musicians hesitated a moment, then began to play once more. After the transition, the little girl with the chestnut curls could not be found—no matter how hard Zander searched. Luckily, he was easily distracted by another suggestion from the magician. Celwyn expected him to find romance without any help from anyone else.

The trickle of awareness that Celwyn had felt while walking Annabelle down the aisle had been derailed by the magician's discovery of Verne and Nemo. Now, it had returned, much stronger. Too late, he realized what it meant.

"Good afternoon, *darlings*," Francesca purred as she flowed through the crowd and approached them. In a slinky dress and fur wrap, her choice of attire would have been more appropriate for a theatre production of Cleopatra. Her jewelry rivaled the treasures in the castle behind her, and she held a long cigarette holder that trailed smoke in her wake. With a muffled squawk of delight, Qing's head pushed out of the magician's collar as if he could sense that everything shiny and wonderful he had ever dreamt about had come true. Celwyn patted his back and shoved him back inside his collar.

Elizabeth's grip on her husband's arm tightened as she stared at the witch.

"Aren't you going to introduce us, Jonas?" Francesca raised a painted brow.

Annabelle and Patrick had edged closer together. Thinking quickly, the magician forwarded Otto and Zander silent messages about snakes in the trees north of the courtyard. They faded out of the crowd and ran toward the trees.

Over the last half-hour, the crowd had grown, and to Celwyn's dismay, the reporter had returned and infiltrated the perimeter. *Wonderful.* The magician sent the man a compelling urge to visit the lavatory, then turned toward the witch.

"Yes, I will perform the introductions." By now, silence surrounded the wedding party in a tense cloud, despite the melodic waltz and dancers only feet away. Someone must have recognized Francesca. The whispering began, and dozens of faces stared and glanced away again.

The magician cleared his throat and used all the charm he could summon.

"Over the last year, we have been fortunate to have assistance from Francesca." He bowed to the witch. "She, and her coven, have provided the protection spells for Tellyhouse. They guaranteed yours and our staff's safety here in Prague."

Celwyn knew Francesca's ego very well.

Elizabeth appeared incapable of speech. Annabelle appeared ready to climb into Patrick's pocket.

"May I present Captain and Mrs. Patrick Swayne? This is Madam Francesca Commescu." The magician turned to their right and gestured. "This is Mrs. Elizabeth Kang. You've already met her husband, the Professor, and Bartholomew."

At this inopportune moment, Mrs. Thomas swanned by with Edward. She goggled. Edward recognized Francesca, flushed, and whirled her in the other direction.

"Why, thank you, Jonas. It is very nice to meet all of you. Finally." The witch nodded at Annabelle and the others, enjoying their restrained discomfort. That gave Celwyn enough time to realize that the situation had to be handled exactly right, or it could be explosive. Or worse. Kang must have thought the same from the desperate glance he sent the magician.

"Would you care to dance, Francesca?" Celwyn offered his hand.

"There is only one person, besides that prince over there, that I want to dance with." She turned a full-wattage smile on Bartholomew. Recognizing his role as a lusty sacrifice, the big man presented his arm, and away they went, his expression split between terror and bravery.

To Annabelle, he said, "I really didn't think she would actually attend, and right after that, I found myself too sick to do anything about it."

The excuse sounded weak as he said it. To help compensate for the situation, or distract from it, he produced a rainbow of hand-sized fairies just like the ones he'd made once before when he magically depicted their wedding, only now the wedding had finally occurred, and the sprites hovered above the newly married couple in clouds of tiny stars and glittering fairy dust.

"No one else can see," the magician assured them as Elizabeth managed a smile and relaxed her death grip on her husband's arm. Annabelle and Patrick held hands and enjoyed the moment as the fairies fluttered around them.

The magician bowed. "Am I forgiven yet?"

In answer, Annabelle kissed his cheek.

"Yes, but you have another problem." Patrick pointed.

Amid gasps and a few shrieks from the crowd, Zander and Otto approached, disheveled and muddy, each holding a writhing, yard-long spotted snake and wearing silly grins.

Chapter 18

B Y AGREEMENT, BARTHOLOMEW, THE magician, and Kang elected to wait until breakfast the next day to tell the others about the meeting with the Captain and Verne and what it meant.

"Thank you," Celwyn told Jackson as he refilled his water glass. As Mrs. Thomas pushed another cart into the dining room, he smelled bacon. Otto grinned at the magician.

The boy reminded the magician of himself at that age, interested in everything and unsure socially of what to do. The lad wiggled in his chair and listened to everyone; his shyness as strong as his curiosity. That reminded Celwyn of something he wanted to do; helping Otto to develop a skill he could be proud of was in order.

Before they left Prague, he would arrange for a piano teacher to visit Tellyhouse several times a week. He should be able to find a nice baby grand for the conservatory. Celwyn's original pianoforte had been relocated to the *Elizabeth,* and the new pianoforte sounded wonderful in the parlor, but a richer instrument, truer in tone, would be more appropriate for the boy to learn on. When everyone returned from Findbar Island, Bartholomew would have beautiful music echoing from the conservatory when he took up his painting again.

The lovebirds arrived last at the breakfast table, yawning and wearing secretive smiles. They took their places beside Bartholomew, exchanged a grin, and started to laugh.

"We finally did it! We got married!"

When he stopped laughing with them, the big man said, "It would have occurred sooner, but Xiau kept enticing us into perilous adventures." He pretended to fan himself with his napkin. "Oh my. We were *always* in danger."

Kang sputtered, "Me!"

The magician laughed. "I am just glad the era of enemies is behind us." Celwyn kept his face as neutral as he could when unbidden came a quote from Jules Renard: *"There are moments when everything goes well; don't be frightened; it won't last."*

"You think so, eh? Things will be fine." Kang spoke too slowly to convey confidence in the prediction. He looked at Bartholomew and then at the magician. "We are thankful we survived everything. Without our friendship, we may not have."

Zander stopped devouring pancakes long enough to ask, "What happened?"

Patrick hid a smile in Annabelle's shoulder and covered it with a peck on her cheek. Everyone turned to the magician.

"So much for handsome sacrificial lambs, eh?" Celwyn sighed. He regarded the boys. "All right. There are certain adventures that you're old enough to hear about and ones that you are not. I need both of you," he regarded them with the kind of sternness he rarely used. "I need you to discuss what you think you are ready to hear. Some of it is frightful. Some of it is not pleasant at all."

"How old are you now, Zander?" Elizabeth pointed a spoon at him. "Your real age, please."

Two years ago, when they'd found Zander orphaned and starving on the streets of Pushkari, he had told them he was eight. The next year Otto told them he was fifteen years old when they discovered him in dire straits and took him aboard *Elizabeth* as a porter. Celwyn suspected they were nearer the same age.

"Fourteen," Zander said.

Annabelle pinned him with a frown. "How old are you really, young man?"

Zander giggled and said, "Twelve."

Otto held up his tablet.

"And you are fourteen," Annabelle read. "It is nice that you are honest with us. I'll need to correct your information at Doctor Lloyd's office."

Elizabeth sighed. "All this time, I thought Zander was much younger." She eyed the boy. "But I didn't want to upset you by asking."

"But now that you're getting older," Celwyn got the boys' attention again, "and you know that you have a family who cares about you, no more fibbing. Understood?"

They both nodded.

Just as Mrs. Thomas pushed the coffee cart into the room, Qing escaped from Celwyn's collar and hopped onto the breakfast table between the milk pitcher and the plate of rashers. The magician thought fast. He blocked the table from her view and scooped the bird up and back into his collar, where he shook himself violently.

Zander jumped to his feet, searching the table. "What—"

"Nothing." Elizabeth tugged him back into his chair. She turned to Mrs. Thomas and said disarmingly. "I'll skip coffee this morning, thank you."

Annabelle said, "I require some, please."

Everyone regarded Mrs. Thomas with so much benign goodwill she couldn't help but be suspicious. She stared at the table for a long moment with her lips compressed and then began dispensing coffee without a word. No doubt, she held in an explosion. When they were all served, she asked, "Will you, Sirs and Madams, be at home today? I know Ricardo is planning a roast for dinner tonight."

"I have several errands." Celwyn raised a brow at Kang.

The automat said, "Bartholomew and I do also," and raised a significant brow at the big man. Bartholomew nodded understanding. The magician assumed it must have to do with the texts or tools for the flying machine.

Patrick took his wife's hand. "Annabelle and I wanted to take a stroll by the river."

"And we can feed the ducks!" Zander bounced in his chair.

That simple statement brought the magician's buoyant mood low, as he remembered when he fed the ducks with his brother in Palermo and how Pelaez had added singing piglets to the mud to tease Bartholomew. With effort, Celwyn shook off the memories.

"I plan to stay here and catch up on things," Elizabeth said as she gazed at her husband. "Because of my husband's habits while you are on your escapades, I need to reorganize the bookshelves upstairs. Again." She rolled her eyes. "When he returns home, Xiau's idea of an errand is buying more books."

"Should we purchase more bookshelves?" The automat reached over and kissed her hand.

With a final suspicious glare at the table, Mrs. Thomas pushed the cart out of the room, and Bartholomew and the Professor exchanged a rather conspiratorial glance.

"What are you two so pleased about, and why are you looking at Jonas like that?" Annabelle asked as she poured another glass of juice for Otto.

"Jonas has an announcement," Kang said.

Bartholomew confided, "He drew the short straw."

"It only proves I don't cheat on bets." The magician shrugged.

Bartholomew eyed the boys. "Aren't you two due at the stables right now for your chores?"

"Yes!" Zander jumped to his feet again. "Are we going to hear the announcement, too?" Otto gulped his juice and stood also.

"You will. Later today. Don't forget to think about what I asked you earlier," Celwyn reminded them.

"You may be excused," Patrick told them. "Please walk, not run, through the house."

After they left, the magician debated whether the parlor would be better for what he had to say. When she heard the news, Elizabeth might want something to throw or a large whiskey.

Through the windows, Celwyn saw the boys racing along the side of the house toward the stables. Otto was in the lead and laughing.

Patrick asked, "What is it, Jonas? You appear a bit nauseous. Didn't your breakfast agree with you?"

"It was wonderful as usual." He took a deep breath. "We have news that concerns other guests at the wedding yesterday."

"Was this before or after the three of you left to send a telegram?" Annabelle asked with suspicion tightening her voice.

"Before," the magician said. "I may seem a bit uncomfortable because this news borders on violating our pact to share everything with you."

Bartholomew took pity on him. "Captain Nemo and Jules Verne enjoyed your wedding very much."

"*They were there?*" Annabelle demanded. "So that is who you rushed off to meet?"

Patrick blinked at them. "But why didn't they say hello?"

"Because their ship, the *Nautilus,* is a secret, and so is Captain Nemo. He couldn't chance you reacting and drawing attention to him. Considering the festivities, you had more than enough to do yesterday." The magician waited for the ladies to rise before leading the way into the parlor. When they had settled, he continued. "Nemo has hinted off and on that there are a few governments hunting him. He took a big risk to attend the ceremony." Celwyn added, "I think Jules just likes weddings."

Annabelle asked, "Why did the Captain take a chance like that?"

"He wanted to meet you and the boys, but a meddlesome reporter tried to corner him before that could occur. Don't ask what Jonas did to him." Kang selected a book from the newest collection he'd procured. "I consider Nemo's visit a tribute to our friendship. He has heard many anecdotes and stories about all of you, and he also wanted to talk with us." He snuck a wary glance at Elizabeth, who did not see it, instead frowning at her embroidery. "Jonas will tell you about it."

Really? Instead of growling at the automat, a chicken appeared on top of Kang's head as Celwyn turned back to the others. The automat tried to swat it off, but it held on. "By prior arrangement, we met them at a telegraph office."

"I wondered about that," Annabelle frowned and received a confirming nod from Elizabeth, who snipped a thread and waited for them to finish.

"You are dragging this out," the Professor told Celwyn. "Tell them, please."

The magician added petite chickens on his ears. Artistry was important, after all.

"The purpose of our meeting was to hear an update." The magician edged his chair a bit away from where the women sat. "We have accepted Findbar Island as our new compound, and Nemo is ready for us. We leave in three days."

"*What?*" Annabelle and Elizabeth exclaimed at the same time. The magician decided he did not have to bear the rest of the conversation. He whispered, "Your turn," in the automat's ear and, as a moth, flew out the door and on outside.

The rest of the day became a whirlwind of activity. At a music store recommended by Mrs. Thomas and the maid next door, who had heard of it from the assistant pastor at her church, they found a baby grand piano Otto would love. It would be delivered the next day. The instrument's tone sounded beautiful, in Celwyn's opinion, and he enjoyed every minute in Marantha's Music Store as much as the automat did in his bookstore. Marantha's also recommended a piano teacher who would begin the lad's lessons the following Monday.

At the moment, they waited for Edward to pick them up after retrieving the love birds from their walk along the river. When their carriage arrived at the bookstore, Celwyn ended up carrying a hefty parcel for them because Bartholomew and Kang had bought so much.

After he shut the cab door, Edward leaned through the window and confided, "I wish I was going with you, Sirs."

"I do, also." Celwyn agreed. "I hope you will be with us on the train tomorrow, at least."

"I will be," Edward said. "Of course, I still have my duties here." He couldn't help a glance behind him. "We need to discuss the witches' spells before you leave."

Kang leaned out the window to ask, "Oh?"

"Yes, Sir. At the wedding, Francesca told me she was doubling our fees."

Celwyn growled, "That witch." He should have let Wye lick her ear.

All the way home, they debated if they still needed the protection spells. Bartholomew mentioned that he had done his duty for the foreseeable future after dancing with Francesca for hours.

Kang giggled. When he sobered, he asked, "Let us decide. Do we still need the spells?"

"I'm glad we're not talking in front of the others," the magician said. "For what I'm about to say."

Bartholomew grumbled, "I can guess, and I don't want to hear it."

"It must be said. Pelaez."

The automat glowered at him.

"Exactly," Celwyn sighed.

"But he would want to keep away from us after what he did, wouldn't he?" Bartholomew reasoned. "Nemo would kill him."

Kang lit his pipe. "Maybe. Maybe not."

Their carriage turned onto Berria Street in a leisurely manner, following a rambling coal cart. The magician suspected Edward of providing an opportunity for them to talk privately. Indeed, a very conscientious man, Edward Murphy.

"Who knows?" Celwyn said, "But to keep everything and everyone safe, I vote we retain the spells for the time being."

Bartholomew asked, "What would happen if Pelaez tried to get into Tellyhouse?"

"Initially, he would be rebuffed. Knowing him, he would keep at it until he was successful." As he thought about his brother, the magician frowned and packed tobacco in his pipe, concentrating on it instead of what Pelaez could do.

"But by then, the witches would know about it," the big man surmised. "What would they do?"

During the discussion, Kang had been silent and as pensive as a constipated chicken. With a snort, he said, "Your brother would probably go after them. There doesn't seem to be any hint of shyness about him."

Celwyn scratched Qing's back. "Again, another reason to have Edward and the witches on guard. I also told Edward about Pelaez and gave him something that might be handy."

"Such as?" the big man asked.

Celwyn smiled a smile of certainty. "If Pelaez threatens him, Edward will mention he knows about him and that I will retaliate. Probably by mentioning him to Thales. The idea that our father or Thales would visit him might make Pelaez stop."

The big man nodded. "That might help."

Celwyn asked, "And about keeping the spells?"

"I agree," both Bartholomew and Kang said at the same time.

"Ha! Harmony." The magician enjoyed it with satisfaction. It reminded him of music and numbers, which brought a bit of clarity. "Now, I know what we are."

Kang tilted his head at Celwyn. "What?"

"Listen to us: you are a tenor, Bartholomew a bass, and I'm a baritone. We are a perfect choice as opera singers." The magician raised his brows. "How can you deny it?"

Bartholomew chuckled. "And which opera do you have in mind?"

"*The Merry Wives of Windsor?*"

They spent the rest of the day sorting books and clothes for the trip, with the promise of a family discussion after dinner on their minds. As he packed his trunk, Celwyn again considered moving his bedroom upstairs. The enticing aromas from the kitchen always rose to the upper stories, never to the back of the house where he could enjoy them. He felt deprived.

After dinner, they gathered in the parlor and heard stories from the boys about the horses and detailed explanations of how compost benefited the garden. The automat agreed about the effects, quoting a few facts about the chemical compound of the compost and why it was good for the flowers. Zander insisted the horses made the compost.

Beside him, Elizabeth smiled and elbowed her husband. On his other side, Bartholomew snickered and enjoyed the high spirits of the room. Even Qing, who sat atop the armoire, seemed on his best behavior—he had left the crystal decanters alone all day. The bird might be worried he would be left behind with Mrs. Thomas when they departed for Findbar. As Celwyn thought about it, Qing blinked slowly at him. Pitifully. Celwyn thought, *really? Now who could read minds? Impossible.*

"We will have a complete science lesson tomorrow about fertilizing plants," Kang told the boys. He held Otto's tablet and read his message aloud. "Yes, we have to leave again, and we will come back to visit on a regular basis during that time."

Zander kicked the sofa and stared at his hands.

The magician hugged him. "This is something we need to do. When you are older, you will have to leave to go into the military or work. But," he smiled at the boys, "that makes coming home that much better."

"It is true," Bartholomew assured them.

"I completely agree; it happens enough that I appreciate the visits." Elizabeth raised a teasing brow at Kang.

Otto held up his tablet to the magician. Celwyn handed it back to him. "I will be careful."

Kang cleared his throat. "All right." Well aware that the others' eyes had watered and emotions ran high, he made sure he spoke to both boys. "This time, your Uncle Celwyn isn't sick, and we have a schedule to come back and forth every month until we're done."

"Done with what?" Zander asked.

"Good question. But first, do you remember when I asked you and Otto to decide what you felt ready to hear?" Celwyn, Annabelle, Patrick, and the others had already held their own discussion about what to tell the boys, finally coming to an agreement.

Otto nodded to Zander. "Yes, sir. We talked and decided we want to know some of the stuff, just the easiest parts." Zander glanced at Otto and received a confirming nod. "And if it has to do with tigers and monkeys and elephants, tell us now."

Annabelle laughed. "You're very logical, both of you." Over the top of their heads, she sent the magician a look that asked him to be careful.

"Do you remember the genie man and his friends from last year?" Celwyn asked Zander. "And the lady with bees in her ears?" Vampires had hounded them, eventually killing Telly, the lost girl they had rescued when they found Zander.

Zander made a face. "Mrs. Karras." To Otto, he said, "Bad lady. The genie man is bad too, but he is gone."

Celwyn told him, "Good news. They are all gone now." He made a mental note to thank Valentine again for ridding Prague of the predators.

From Otto's tablet, Kang read, "He asks, 'Why are you telling us this?'" The automat answered, "Because even though they are gone, you should continue to learn wrestling from Patrick and how to defend yourself."

"We will." Zander pretended to punch an imaginary opponent.

The magician asked, "Do you have friends in the neighborhood here?"

"Yes." Zander named two boys and a girl. "We get to play with them sometimes."

Annabelle had said as much during their earlier discussion. Celwyn made sure he had the boys' attention and said, "We are going to share a secret with you, but you won't be able to tell your friends ... or anyone outside this house. Do you understand?"

The boys exchanged a silent question, orphan to orphan. Zander said, "We agree. Can we tell Ricardo?"

"He already knows. So do Edward and the Conductor." Kang studied them, and with a furtive check of the doorway, said, "Mrs. Thomas does, also, to a point, and it upsets her. So, it is best not to talk to her about it." Everyone laughed somewhat nervously, either because they wanted to be on the good side of the housekeeper or because they did not want to have to explain something magical to her.

The magician said, "You asked when we're going to be finished with our traveling. Do you remember the wooden toys the Professor made for you and Telly on the journey here?"

"Yes." Zander turned to Otto and held his hands about eight inches apart. "They were this big."

"Bartholomew and the Professor are going to build a real one of those toys. Bigger than this room. It will fly in the air."

Otto jumped to his feet, and Zander raced to the window and back. "When can we see it?"

"Not for a few months," Bartholomew said.

As they sat again, Celwyn said, "Remember, tell no one of what the Professor and Bartholomew are doing. Do you understand?"

"Yes, sir."

"This is why we will be gone, and when we're done, we will come back here for good," the big man grinned at them.

"What do you know about magic?" the magician asked Otto. He'd told Annabelle and the others of the magical scene that Otto had witnessed and how he'd drawn closer to it instead of being afraid.

The boy cocked his head to the side, wrote on his tablet, and showed it to Celwyn.

The magician summarized, "You like it, and you saw a little of it on the train as we journeyed here. And you?" he asked Zander.

"I haven't seen anything except a picture in a book." He frowned and kicked the sofa. "It was of a lady in a painted box. They were sawing her in half!"

Elizabeth watched Otto and Zander with an encouraging demeanor while Annabelle asked, "Would you like to see some?" Both boys nodded and checked behind them.

"Where?" Zander demanded.

"Here." The magician opened a hand, and a collection of elephants, bears, and other animals no bigger than a child's teacup appeared on the table in front of them. As the elephant lifted his trunk and bellowed, one of the lions crouched and sprung across the table and into Bartholomew's lap. The largest monkey scampered onto the tray holding the tea service. It climbed up the handle of the teapot like it scrambled up a tree trunk and sat on top of the lid.

Otto backed up, but he didn't run. Elizabeth put an arm around him. Zander moved closer to the lion and slid onto his knees until he stared at it nose to nose. He offered the lion his finger. The lion licked it.

"So far, so good," Kang murmured.

Celwyn gestured at the table. "This is magic. It isn't an illusion, nor is it a trick. Yet, it isn't real." He did not add that it could be real—if he chose for it to be. The lads would not be ready for that for a while. Some of this still scared Bartholomew. The big man had controlled his superstitions when he deposited the lion on the table and smiled as best he could at the boys.

When Otto hesitated, Celwyn said, "It is permissible to get closer." The magician eliminated all of it except the lion and the monkey perched on the teapot. "They won't last much longer, in case Mrs. Thomas joins us."

Behind his spectacles, Otto blinked fast as he moved close enough to touch the back of the monkey. It squeaked, climbed onto his hand, and wrapped its arms around his wrist.

While the boys admired the animals, Celwyn said, "Please remember, magic is just like the flying machine; it is a secret."

"Yes, sir." Zander picked up the lion. It stood on his stomach and twitched its tail. "It is so soft."

Otto saw him and smiled. He watched as the monkey ran up his arm and onto the top of his head. The boy giggled.

"You can take them upstairs and play with them until they fade away."

Zander licked his lips. "Where did they come from?"

"I made them." When they gaped at him, Celwyn said, "I'm a magician."

Chapter 19

"WHEW!" BARTHOLOMEW exclaimed as the boys trudged up the stairs, whispering and laughing while cradling the animals.

Kang's reaction was a cross between sarcasm and boredom. "Those are better examples than the snakes they found yesterday."

"That was you?" Elizabeth demanded.

Celwyn nodded. He did not mention that the snakes *had* been real; it would only upset them. He could absorb the blame and even have room for more when he deserved it.

"I knew it!" Annabelle tried not to laugh and failed. "What are you going to tell them when they start asking more questions?"

"Jonas will think of something," Patrick said. "My vote is that they know enough not to be afraid if they see something by accident. However, perhaps it would be best not to describe all your escapades."

"Such as the warlocks, the catacombs, and the rest of the dangerous and disgusting situations." Elizabeth frowned. "The boys should be a little bit older for that."

"I agree." Annabelle nodded. "Otherwise, they'll want to participate."

As Celwyn listened to them, he appreciated the balance of feminine intuition, scientific logic, and the camaraderie the inhabitants of Tellyhouse shared. He doubted everyone had that.

"I feel like the harbinger of doom, but need to ask something." Bartholomew did not appear happy but asked anyway. "What do we do if Pelaez attacks? I know Jonas has a threat ready for Edward to use. But what if something happened before he uses it?"

"We need to discuss this more." Patrick rubbed his chin. "Also, what if Ginnie didn't die by his hand? You said you never saw her body when you returned there. She could be another powerful enemy against us," Patrick said. "Or just annoying."

Everything that they had found at the compound, from the murdered guards to Mrs. Sogun's look of surprise above her bloodied throat, and finally to Pelaez's betrayal, it all came back in full color, even the crows pecking at the eyes of the corpses. Celwyn cleared his throat. When a glass by the bar shattered, he stopped himself before his anger got worse.

"We don't know, do we?" Celwyn produced a fresh pot of tea. The broken glass dissolved just as Jackson arrived.

"Everything is fine," Bartholomew assured him. The porter kept his face blank, whirled, and retreated up the hallway.

The Professor retrieved a box from under the sofa and produced his woodworking tools and blocks of wood. He asked Patrick and Annabelle, "You remember the original toys I made for the children? The ones that Jonas mentioned to Zander?"

"Yes. Zander has them in his room." Annabelle turned to Elizabeth and said, "They are replicas of a flying machine with a little man inside. At the time, it was a secret between these three." She indicated the magician, the automat, and Bartholomew. "*Eventually*, they told Patrick and me."

Elizabeth eyed her husband. "Oh, I see. That was before you joined forces with Captain Nemo, I presume?"

Kang applied some muscle as he scraped the wood. "Yes, dear." Wood chips flew like a barn blown apart in a tornado.

"In the spirit of our promise to share everything with you, you should know that when we returned to the compound to see what Pelaez had done, we found the new ones Xiau had made floating inside a butchered pig."

Elizabeth reared back. "Why?"

"No idea. The Captain had none either." Kang blew sawdust in the air. "However, it was a real pig, not Pelaez's pet."

"We need to talk about defenses," Patrick said. "I like what we have so far, but there's more we can do for when you are gone."

Chapter 20

JUST AFTER DAWN TWO DAYS LATER, everyone once again boarded the *Elizabeth* for the trip to Szczecin.

Professor Xiau Kang and Elizabeth sat together in the dining car, wrapped in their romance and imminent separation. No matter how she worried, Elizabeth loved her husband dearly. Several times, Celwyn heard her lecturing him about being safe and not taking chances. Now Celwyn knew where Xiau got his fussy speeches from.

Patrick kept Celwyn company in one of the matching bar chairs while Bartholomew played checkers with Zander at the dining table. Otto had parked himself in front of the pianoforte and ignored everything else.

With her skirts swishing, Annabelle paced by the window and smoked like a stevedore. To anyone watching, she would appear to be the epitome of

Victorian femininity in a lovely lace dress, bustle, and curls, making the contrast more pronounced.

"I know why all of you are doing this." She nodded at the automat. "But I don't like you going away again." She pointed at the boys with her eyes. "They need you, too."

"I'll be able to send letters several times a week with the Captain's supply boat to Skegness. There's a telegraph office there, too. The boys will receive letters and questions to answer in class." The Professor pointed with his chin at the others. "Jonas and Bartholomew will also be writing to them."

Annabelle plopped onto the chair next to Patrick. "That will help. Tell me what you will actually do on this island."

"I wish to know, too." Elizabeth watched Zander jump his checkers across the board.

"Good game. We will play again, young man." Bartholomew tousled the boy's hair and joined the party in front of the windows just as the *Elizabeth* blew her whistle and bounded onto a new set of tracks. "I think I can see a sliver of the ocean in the distance, a bit north of Szczecin," the big man reported.

"Then we probably have another hour before arrival." Celwyn nodded at Bartholomew. "You two can answer these questions much better than I."

Bartholomew nodded at the Professor.

"As you know, Pelaez destroyed our prototype and the supporting papers that we call the specs," Kang said, growling a curse. "We have re-created most of the specs and found opportunities for improvements." He held up the wooden carving that depicted the body of the machine. "We will rebuild and refine the flying machine."

"It will be better than the first prototype," the big man said.

Elizabeth licked her lips. "Must you actually go up in the air with it?"

Behind them, Otto ran a scale up the pianoforte perfectly, from the lowest keys to the highest. Like a plane taking flight. Celwyn wondered if that was a coincidence. Some instances could be, and some things, the music directed.

Bartholomew and Kang exchanged a glance before the big man said, "Yes. But we are incredibly careful."

Celwyn saw the connection and reasoning in how the big man said that and how Zander and Otto would say it; both a type of double-talk that promised something they could not control. Hiding a grin, he chanced a glance at Elizabeth. She winked, proving she was not fooled, just waiting.

Meanwhile, Kang said, "We will learn how long it takes for the machine's wheels to leave the ground at the speeds we go. Also, we need to measure how long the field must be for the variances. The engine and weight of the prototype affect that. Sometimes we must change our assumptions."

"Several times, we have had to change the speed of takeoffs to get lift," Bartholomew informed them. "Even if my calculations are correct, it is not a guarantee of success."

"If you are not going fast enough..." Patrick's eyes widened as he reached the logical conclusion.

Annabelle pried her lips open enough to ask, "How fast do you have to go?"

"As fast as possible," Kang replied and started to carve the wheels, digging into the chunk of wood, not making eye contact with his wife. She inhaled her reaction but didn't speak.

Bartholomew said, "Nemo will give us men to assist and everything else we may need."

Minutes went by. Otto played a scale in staccato, imitating an ascending bird or a flying machine ... proving he was listening to them.

"Every month, we will come back to Tellyhouse to visit." The magician made a face. "I am going to miss Ricardo's cooking very much. The Captain does not believe beef or fowl belong at his table."

Proving logic to be a family trait, Elizabeth asked, "What is the total time you'll need on the island?"

Bartholomew and the automat exchanged glances before he said, "About three months if all goes well."

"What will you be doing?" Patrick asked the magician.

Kang had no trouble answering that. "Entertaining himself with magic at our expense."

"He wouldn't," Elizabeth countered with a half-smile.

The automat said, "He made it rain on us."

"Really?" Patrick asked with a broad grin.

"He will also be sure that no one disturbs us or hurts us." Bartholomew nodded at them and grinned. "And then entertain himself with magic at Xiau's expense. I'm usually spared."

Annabelle lit another cigarette and puffed. The smoke covered her hair like a gray wreath. "I expect you all to come home soon. The boys need science and mathematics lessons. Elizabeth helps with history and other things, but those two subjects belong to you."

Kang smirked. "You don't want Jonas to teach them numbers?"

Everyone laughed.

"We left some lessons for you that will get you through the next few weeks," Bartholomew said.

"And when we mail letters, we will send more lessons." The Professor shaved wood off the flying machine and admired the line of it.

"I think she means that she needs questions from the boys answered, also." Celwyn received a confirming nod from Annabelle.

"Yes, that is what I meant."

Bartholomew rubbed his chin. "A suggestion; you could concentrate on English and military history, which Patrick can easily handle, for the next few months. In addition to the regular numbers lessons, I will send them simple scientific experiments with household ingredients to round out their education until we finish the flying machine."

"An excellent solution," Kang said. "We would provide instructions on what the results would be. Hopefully." He caught a nod from the big man. To the others, the automat said, "During the experiments, I highly recommend continual supervision over their activities." A moment of silence passed while they all imagined what the boys could think of doing with fizzing and bubbling beakers.

"...Mrs. Thomas will not be amused." Patrick frowned, and a moderate amount of fear danced in his eyes. Several of the others nodded in agreement.

Annabelle reached into her pocket and, with a nod from Elizabeth, handed the magician, the big man, and the automat a tissue-wrapped package the size of her hand. As they opened them, Patrick said, "We had these made while you were gone and wanted you to have them."

Bartholomew was the first to react, and a big tear slid down his cheek. "I can't thank you enough."

The automat gazed at the photograph in his hand and hugged Elizabeth. "It is beautiful."

Like Bartholomew, Celwyn felt tears forming and blurring the image of the boys sitting in front of Elizabeth, Annabelle, and Patrick. In the picture, they hugged the boys, very much relaxed and contrary to common practice for portraits, their happiness evident.

"I'll keep this safe, no matter where we are. Thank you," Bartholomew said.

"You had better," Annabelle told him. "It takes weeks to have them made. And the boys were told they would keep you safe."

Otto and Zander had been in the classroom at the rear of the train car while they talked and returned with long faces.

"What is wrong?" Patrick asked.

Otto turned to Zander. The boy said, "Telly's toys are in there."

The magician put a hand on each of their shoulders. "The trip back home will be a good time for you and everyone else to go through her things, decide what you will give to the church, and what to keep at Tellyhouse."

Zander's bottom lip protruded. "It will be sad."

"But necessary," Bartholomew said.

Zander sighed his agreement.

The clock behind him chimed eleven.

"I think it is teatime." The magician beamed.

Kang rolled his eyes. "Of course you do."

Chapter 21

A FTER HUGS, HANDSHAKES, AND promises, they disembarked from the train.

As they traveled north from Szczecin, the anticipation of Findbar Island and the flying machine gradually replaced their regret over leaving the inhabitants of Tellyhouse once again. Bartholomew and Kang's spirits flew high as they drew closer to reuniting with Nemo and their dreams.

"How many books did you two bring?" Celwyn asked as he glanced at the overfilled cart following along behind their carriage. "There is probably a limit on how much weight the ship can hold." As he spoke, for the first time in hours, the sun emerged from behind a low bank of clouds and lit up the expanse of sea. The waves lapped the shore in a gentle rhythm, like a mother rocking a child.

"Humorous, Jonas." Kang studied the sandstone cliffs that rose before them and the Baltic Sea. "I say, are you sure Nemo is expecting us this early? It is not even one o'clock."

"He will be here." Celwyn shaded his eyes from the glare and scanned the water. In the far distance, a barge inched westward, its smokestacks belching puffs of black smoke.

Bartholomew licked his lips and eyed their driver through the cab window. "Are these real drivers?"

"Yes. I found them on the other train platform." Celwyn kept his voice low. "When Nemo arrives, they're going to suddenly need a refreshing nap while everything is transferred to the ship. I'll leave them enough coins to lessen their questions."

"Or heighten them," the automat guessed. He borrowed Bartholomew's binoculars and inspected the water.

As they pulled to a stop on the rough track under the cliffs, the big man turned to the others. "We might want a more circumspect method of transportation for our future visits between Tellyhouse and here."

"True." Celwyn caught the glint of another spyglass just above the surface about a mile out. The nearest commercial ships were at least ten miles further to sea. "The *Nautilus* is here." He used magic to signal back and put both the carriage driver and the other driver to sleep. "You are correct, my friend. We'll have to think of something."

"Welcome back," Captain Nemo said as they filed down the spiral stairs into the belly of the submarine. He shook their hands. "A pleasant journey?"

Bartholomew answered, "Yes. Except for having to say goodbye again."

"As you know, the wedding turned out very well." The magician led the way down the corridor. "On the trip here, Otto serenaded us on the pianoforte for several hours, and Zander has begun to favor pastels over charcoal in his drawings. We will miss them all."

The Captain followed them into the dining room. "We will make a stop at The Hague and one at Great Yarmouth for supplies we can't find at Skegness. By five tomorrow afternoon, we'll approach Findbar from the south. Expect the same optimal conditions as before to enter the grotto under the mansion." He bowed. "Please have a seat. Our luncheon is ready."

As they took their places, Qing inched his way out of Celwyn's collar and squawked his excitement. The aquatic window in Nemo's private dining room measured much smaller but no less interesting to the bird. Qing greeted a cloud of yellow-eyed sardines, who scattered in every direction.

The magician inhaled the moment with the kind of satisfaction that rivaled Qing's happiness and one that represented his own sentiments at being back on the *Nautilus*. Was this his real home? In some ways, he thought it so. Celwyn doubted he would ever lose his wanderlust. The *Nautilus* defined discovery and adventure. What had changed? He gazed at the answer sitting before him with the fondness that he still found amazing.

Bartholomew and Kang's enthusiasm lit up the room. The magician could almost see the sparks of electricity bouncing between them. With a glance at Nemo and a sigh of regret, he resisted the urge to make the sparks more visible; the Captain did not like 'the disorder' of magic. However, Nemo did appreciate his efforts for something exceptionally beautiful or necessary; for instance, to save their lives.

"It is good that we are together once more." Celwyn tasted his wine and aimed a pensive glance at Nemo. "We have discussed various things and made plans."

Kang agreed. "Yes, we had enough time for reflection and new perspectives. However, we did not completely decide what to do about Pelaez. Nor about the future of the flying machine ... since so much is unknown."

Captain Nemo watched a crewman serve the salad. "I have been busy readying the island. But agree, we do need to plan our time together." They toasted, and the clinking of crystal rang around the room. "In order to expedite preparing the island, I brought in all the men I have used before from this hemisphere. They have finished the field. Before meeting you in Prague, I deposited them again on the coast. Only my original crew remains here."

"I hate to bring up an unpleasant aspect, but can we count on their discretion about the island?" Bartholomew asked. "Considering what happened recently, I worry about being watched. And the Mafioso. They have their tentacles into many of the large cities here in the north as much as the ones in Italia."

"Yes, I trust my men implicitly." The Captain savored a bite, then added, "They have earned my faith in them over the years with even more ... shall we say, controversial tasks." He watched the cart with their entrée as it arrived. "I also pay them handsomely for their silence. But to answer your concern, I can't definitively say if we're being watched."

"Is the crew exactly the same as before?" the automat asked.

Nemo thought for a moment. "My normal crew plus two more. They are your new assistants."

Somber silence fell like a heavy blanket had been tossed across the room as everyone recalled the fate of the last two assistants.

A distraction was in order, and Kang supplied one. "When we are ready for another scientist and engineer to take over our work with the flying machine, I have someone to suggest."

"Who?" Bartholomew's eyes lit up with interest.

"Doctor Martha Rogers from Stanford. She is the inventor of the new type of fuel we plan to try."

Nemo chewed. "Tell us more?"

"Her doctorate is in chemistry, plus she has degrees in several types of mathematics. The last I heard, she was in Macao, hunting a particular lizard, just one of her hobbies. She is also cataloging butterflies, one of her other passions," Kang said.

"At least it isn't snakes." Verne made the comment as he dissected a piece of tomato.

Nemo said, "This sounds promising."

"She could be a wonderful addition to our team." Bartholomew suggested, "Perhaps you could inquire about her level of interest without letting on where we are and exactly what we're doing."

"It shall be done. She met Elizabeth years ago, and they exchange letters occasionally."

Nemo addressed Kang, "If you gain her interest and trust her discretion, I suggest we invite her to Findbar Island in a few months to talk with everyone."

"It will be done."

"By the way, who owns Findbar?" The magician had wondered if they might get legitimate visitors. "It would be a shame to continue full steam ahead with this operation and then have to move again."

The big man tapped his spoon on the tablecloth. "I was curious, too."

"I did not know and have asked Jules to research a few things." Nemo leaned back while his salad plate was removed and eyed the platters placed before them.

Everyone turned to Verne, who treated them to one of his Gaelic shrugs. "The city records in The Hague and Szczecin are limited. So, I resorted to interviewing a few people, err ... discreetly."

"*Reporters?*" The automat growled, and the bits of salad newly arrived in his metallic stomach probably whirled like a tiny hurricane.

Celwyn stared at Verne.

The author blinked fast and turned an interesting shade of pink. "Just ... just one. I used a different name."

"That might help," Bartholomew admitted.

"Just so." Verne nodded. "Well. The others I interviewed were from the historical society. And a few from the Szczecin hotel, The Essen. It is quite an interesting story.

"It will be ... if they gossip and a reporter shows up at Findbar." The magician stared with enough menace for Verne's knife to slip from his fingers and into his lap without him noticing it.

While they talked, Qing watched the water as the ship moved through a curtain of thick seaweed before breaking free. It headed west, across the sea, churning the water and leaving the fish behind. His metallic beak rapped on the glass, the sound quite unmusical.

"We're listening, Jules," Celwyn prompted.

Verne checked behind him and then the rest of the room. When nothing untoward happened, such as a tiger crouching at his feet, the author opened his ever-present notebook. "All right. Niall Island belonged to smugglers for hundreds of years until James IV chased the last of them out and claimed the island for Britain. It was renamed Findbar in..." He nibbled on a roll. "Let me see ... 1630? I'm not sure. After that, in about 1650, the mansion was built, and a family, the Spencers, lived there into the late 1600s when the Crown took it over."

The magician felt an unexpected shiver. "Why?"

When the author hesitated, Bartholomew licked his lips, suspecting he would not like the answer. "I only had a few days for this research." Verne finished his plate, patted his round belly, and seemed not to hear the question or think it did not require an answer.

Captain Nemo said, "I am expecting a pleasant evening of bridge, so please resume Jules. We'll get this over with."

"As you wish. Spencer Manor, as it was known, represented several things. Pirates and smuggling—which did not stop, as the Queen expected—with the death of the entire Spencer family. A host of ghost stories are connected to the mansion."

Bartholomew paled.

Celwyn thought the big man was going to faint. So did Captain Nemo. They both reached for him at the same time. Bartholomew swayed and squeezed his eyes shut. A low chant escaped his lips.

"Perhaps we should postpone—" the magician suggested.

"No!" Bartholomew shook himself. "We need to know."

"This will not be easy to hear. If you are sure?" Nemo gestured to Verne.

"Yes." Bartholomew picked up his wineglass and drained it.

Verne said, "I'll relate the most sensational and pertinent part first." He noted Nemo's approving nod. "Adolphe Spencer reportedly killed his own children by drowning them in the same cave where we surfaced. His wife's throat had been cut, and she

177

was supposedly beheaded, although that was not confirmed."

"I'm fine..." Bartholomew's white-knuckle grip on his dessert spoon bellied his words. "Please continue."

"Er, if you are sure." Verne flipped to a new page in his notebook. "The servants ran, and Spencer chased them through the woods like a hunter would wild game. The report said he was naked. It is unknown if there were survivors, but a few of the staff tried to swim out to sea and drowned."

"Good grief," Kang muttered a curse as Qing flew into the room again, and a crew member departed with a loaded tray. Celwyn opened his collar, and the bird snuggled in.

"To this day, there are stories about Adolphe Spencer," Verne reported. "These tales were allegedly found in the records of a sanatorium which operated at the mansion until about fifty years ago."

Celwyn observed, "That accounts for the fine but dusty furniture we saw."

"The criminal histories of the patients made them too dangerous for other institutions to house and guarantee they couldn't escape. Findbar Island, with its wild surf and treacherous rocks, prevented that." Verne gathered his papers together as a crewman began serving their dessert.

"An island with a haunted reputation would discourage visitors, also," Captain Nemo said.

"I wonder if the reputation was truthful or fabricated because of the smuggling." Kang studied his empty wineglass for a moment. "Smuggling on the southern coast of England during that time was so prevalent that more illicit spirits were reportedly smuggled into the country than what came through legally on London Docks."

"What drove the sanatorium away from the island?" Celwyn asked.

Verne checked with Captain Nemo, who nodded and said, "Jules, I can't think of anything you've discovered that should be withheld. We're all in this enterprise together."

"As you wish. By 1819, the sanitorium only had a skeletal staff and a dozen patients. One day, their supply boat arrived and discovered that they were all gone."

"Gone?" Bartholomew stopped eating.

"No bodies?" Kang asked.

"None. No sign of violence. They just ... disappeared, according to my research. There is a lack of information about this." Verne admired his cake and sampled a bite.

"Theories?" the magician asked.

"Too many to count," the Captain said. "Many of the sources Jules investigated did not agree with each other. But, to answer your question about who owns the island, who would want to?" Nemo hesitated. "Except perhaps for investment for a future mining operation or similar."

"Or something illegal, as the Professor suggested," Verne said and went back to his cake.

Kang said, "Could we assume that the island will suit our purposes for now, but we may relocate after the prototype is built?"

"Yes." Nemo said, "That seems reasonable at this point."

As they prepared to adjourn from the lunch table, the magician asked, "Has anything untoward occurred the last few weeks since you've been on the island?"

Captain Nemo raised a brow. "That is what I find most odd. Nothing has happened. Of course, everyone stays inside the ship at night, and we keep her sealed up tight after we go to bed."

Chapter 22

THE NEXT DAY, A LATE AFTERNOON storm hovered over the island as they approached, the rain light and the clouds low as they moved swiftly across the sky. The *Nautilus* once more slipped between the teeth-like rocks and exploding surf surrounding Findbar.

In the distance, the tower above the mansion peeked over the trees. Celwyn pictured a wild-eyed Adolphe Spencer running through the shrubbery and brandishing a long knife. For once, he appreciated the interruption to his thoughts when Kang rejoined them. "At least it only takes a few minutes to enter this cave versus forty miles up an underground river." He patted Bartholomew's shoulder.

"It is much better, I agree."

They had gathered in front of the aquatic window, able to see above the water level where it stopped about ten inches from the top of the glass.

Having a little surprise for Verne and Kang in mind, and not wishing to upset the big man, Celwyn sent Bartholomew an urge to visit the lavatory. The big man excused himself, and soon, the door to the water closet closed behind him.

The ship moved at a slow speed, and Verne happened to be staring out the window at the rock wall a few feet away as it smoothed out, becoming glassy. Celwyn caused the ship to stop, just for a second.

Verne shrieked. Kang turned and saw it, too. Before the automat could glare and ruin his entertainment, the magician said, "A wonderful likeness, is it not? A most handsome devil." Celwyn had imbedded his profile in the rockface, his eyes the same startling green.

"Jonas!" Kang exclaimed.

Celwyn laughed until he heard the door from the lavatory open. He released the ship and dissolved the image before Bartholomew rejoined them. Verne's eyes still bulged, and the automat looked like he'd swallowed a lemon. Like Qing, Celwyn sometimes had to make his own entertainment.

The big man led the way out of the study and up the stairs to the hatch. When Celwyn arrived topside, he found Bartholomew and Kang staring with a measure of approval at another addition to their new compound.

A forty-foot transport boat painted a dull and nondescript green had been tied up on the far side of the grotto. As a pair of crewmen unloaded boxes of produce, more of the crew added to the cases of water and wine already piled against the wall. A long time ago, *Golden Mädel* had been painted across her stern with an artistic hand, and a bust of an elderly woman adorned her prow. Celwyn wouldn't have given the boat a second glance, which was exactly what they needed to maintain their secrecy.

Captain Nemo hopped off the *Nautilus* and strode across the floating pier to the foot of the stone stairs. Kang caught up to him. "The new boat comes in at low tide?"

"Like clockwork." He pointed to stacks of crates. "Because the boat must be small, we need a daily run for fresh supplies for this many people."

"Where did you get her?" Bartholomew eyed the craft.

Nemo said, "From the harbor on the north shore of The Hague. We bring in water nearly every day from Skegness."

With a modicum of caution, Kang asked, "I hate to bring this up, considering what we found after the massacre at the first compound, but shouldn't there be a spring or a well here? Especially so, to support a number of patients and staff in a sanatorium?"

They began climbing the steps to the mansion. "We have checked extensively but have not found a water source," Captain Nemo answered. "Jules brought back several books he found in Szczecin. It is possible they contain a clue about water sources."

"It would be like a treasure hunt, only we seek water instead of gold." Bartholomew chanced a glance into the shadowy corners of the grotto.

Celwyn said, "I like that. Since you two will be extremely busy soon, I will do the searching myself ... unless Jules wants to come along." He held the door open that led into the hallway of the mansion. A damp moldiness greeted them, along with a chill despite the clear day outside.

Verne hesitated, probably remembering Celwyn's prank from a few minutes ago, and entered the corridor.

"It will be most helpful to find a spring," the Captain agreed.

"I would like to attempt something." Bartholomew had a speculative gleam in his eye. "It may be possible to build a water system to purify seawater."

"Charcoal filter?" Kang asked.

Bartholomew nodded.

The automat rubbed his hands together. "Nice idea."

"Excellent," Nemo agreed as they walked down the paneled hallway leading to the main part of the house. The same sense of unease and despair overlaid the dank smell of the cave, and it seemed so thick, he could touch it—at least, in Celwyn's imagination. The murders of the Spencers and the disappearance of the sanatorium patients could not be ignored.

"Sir, I believe you said that everyone continues to sleep on the ship?"

"Yes. I think it is best for now." Nemo regarded the magician. "As I mentioned, the extra workers have already departed, and the *Nautilus* can accommodate a normal crew, plus yourselves, easily."

They stepped out of the ballroom and onto a bricked courtyard that measured the length of the manor. The big man said, "It has been years since I slept under the stars. Perhaps if things remain quiet here, it would be possible to do so."

In front of them, a carpet of grass led to a low ridge before the first stand of trees, and further out, the North Sea glimmered in the near distance under the setting sun. Shelves of dark clouds promised them another storm.

"Look!" Bartholomew pointed.

Beyond the trees, the beginning of a landing field stretched southward as far as they could see. A row of flags fluttered on poles at least a mile away.

"Oh, excellent!" Kang trotted off the courtyard and onto the grass to see better. "It is flat. Captain, how long is it?"

The Captain said, "Approximately seven miles."

"More than enough." Bartholomew stretched to his full height and peered at the far end of the island. "We are fortunate to have Findbar. Most fortunate."

The magician had turned to study the turrets of the mansion tower. "I hope so." He did not want to spoil his friends' happiness as they basked in scientific bliss, but he called Nemo's attention to the uppermost tower window.

"Are any of your crew upstairs?" he asked in a low voice as Kang and Bartholomew jabbered and walked toward the landing field.

"No. What did you see?"

"Part of a person, watching us. We will want to keep an eye on those two," he indicated the scientists, "and have a few of your crew with them at all times ... if we aren't."

Nemo rubbed his face hard.

"I agree with the suggestion. I had so hoped our enemies would leave us alone here." He stopped short of cursing. "Why haven't we seen this until now? My crew has been everywhere here while they prepared the site."

The magician shook his head. "Unknown. It may not be an enemy."

"Was it a man or a woman?"

"I have no idea." Celwyn sighed. "Imagine the warrens' nest of secret rooms and passageways in a mansion of this size and age."

"Inspired by the need to hide from agents of the Crown ... or from other smugglers." He kicked a rock as far as he could. "I should have expected this. I'll tell the crew and issue a curfew on activities in the house and on the grounds." He shivered and drew his coat closer. "I say, it is almost dark. And getting cold. What are they doing?" He pointed at Kang and Bartholomew.

"Enjoying a discussion about wind gusts or similar?" Celwyn caused a small downpour to hover over the scientists as he bowed Captain Nemo ahead of him. "They'll be along shortly."

A festive atmosphere of camaraderie and scientific euphoria accompanied a dinner full of anticipation that night. Just before it began, a crewman arrived, saluted, and delivered a whispered message to Captain Nemo. After he left again, Nemo caught Celwyn's eye and shook his head, the message clear; nothing had been found in the mansion's tower.

Throughout the grilled Seabass and fresh peas, the magician listened to what Kang and Bartholomew planned first in rebuilding their creation. While they talked, the magician thought about the tower window. Had he seen a very unlovely woman or a man? It seemed like more of a *suggestion* of a person standing there. No matter. He felt certain he had seen something.

"Please pass the butter, Jonas," Bartholomew said. "And tell us what is worrying you."

As Celwyn handed the butter across the table, he tried to recall more of what he had seen in the tower.

"What is the matter?" Kang demanded. "Are you unwell?"

Bartholomew said, "You are pale, Jonas."

Knowing it would be best not to distract the scientists, Captain Nemo stepped in front of the inquisition. "Your new hangar is located beyond the courtyard and lawns. It has all the tools and everything you requested."

"Wonderful." Kang rubbed his hands together. "We will start at first light." He eyed the magician

187

with a modicum of suspicion. "I am assuming you aren't sick, considering what you did an hour ago."

"What did he—" Bartholomew started to ask.

"Nothing." Celwyn blinked innocently and hid his smile. "Xiau has an overactive imagination, is all." Yet, he felt pensive still. What had he really seen in the tower? Could it have been as simple as a play of light on the glass?

Kang gazed from Nemo to Bartholomew. Celwyn saw a nod between them he did not like; it usually spelled teasing. The automat asked, "Is it the wyvern?"

"No. Best we do not talk about it, eh?" the magician suggested.

Nemo raised his brows.

"Oh, hell." Celwyn gave the Captain an abbreviated summary of the wyvern, including how talking of it seemed to attract it. "I've blocked Jules from hearing this."

Nemo asked, "You are sure of ... it?"

"Yes. The creature appears when I think or talk about it—that was why I hesitated. Let us not push our luck and perhaps speak of something else."

Verne had been quiet while the others talked. With precision, he cut his pears and apples into small pieces. "I would like to explore the mansion tomorrow." He eyed the magician. "The Captain has been too busy to accompany me for more than a few minutes at a time."

"That situation will continue for a few more days, Jules." Nemo resumed eating his dessert. "And tomorrow, I must be at the hangar to ensure things go smoothly as work begins again."

"Tomorrow it is, Jules. And we'll find the island's water source," the magician told him.

Bartholomew eyed his dessert as if seeing it for the first time. He had other things on his mind. "This evening, I'll finish the lesson plans I promised Otto and Zander." He laughed. "That means you will be playing bridge, Jonas."

Verne licked his lips and announced, "I want the Captain for my partner."

Chapter 23

THE NEXT MORNING, THE SUPPLY boat chugged its way out of the cave just as everyone left the warmth of the *Nautilus* and climbed onto the platform over the murky water. Kang coughed and fanned the exhaust from its engine away.

The low tide exposed more of the slick walls and the unsettling sculptures depicted on them. From what Celwyn could tell, the images on this level of the grotto seemed much older than the rest and more primitive. Bartholomew pointedly ignored the figures and headed across the floating pier. Because of his size, the way the pier swayed, and the water sloshed, everyone else waited to cross until he made it safely ashore.

It took only a few minutes for them to pass through the Spencer mansion and outside to scientific Valhalla. Bartholomew led the way, with Kang trotting as fast as he could to keep up and talk at the same time about wind conditions. It seems he'd brought along a book on historical weather patterns. Nemo and Celwyn followed at a distance, with Verne nattering at them.

"For the last couple of weeks, I have been at a critical stage in my book." The author raised a fist in triumph. "It is finally done! And now, I am truly ready for a spot of fun."

The magician wondered what the dapper little man considered entertainment. He did not appear to drink to excess or visit dance halls or prostitution lairs. He did, however, enjoy the opera and, it soon became apparent, strange experiences.

Verne continued, "Like I mentioned last night, I am interested in supernatural occurrences. From a safe distance, of course."

"I'm sure Bartholomew's definition of enjoyment is not the same as yours. What if nothing like that exists here?" Celwyn asked as he stepped onto the mist-filled path that meandered through the shrubbery. Less than a mile away, fog shrouded the low hills before the cliffs and muted the rhythmic pounding of the waves.

"I think it does." Verne's eyes took on a faraway, glazed appearance as his imagination enhanced the scene, performing somersaults, calculating, and inventing as he thought. Perhaps his interest stemmed from his experience in building literary plots.

Across the landing field and for as far as they could see, fog hugged the ground in lumps and clumps like a flock of crouching fat sheep. A gust of wind blew several aside, revealing muddy earth and clusters of hearty weeds.

The magician smelled the dampness surrounding them, heavy with something metallic—like blood.

"I don't like fog." Verne sidled closer to Celwyn. The magician patted his shoulder to comfort him.

"There it is," Captain Nemo pointed. "Just beyond the trees."

Bartholomew and Kang had spotted the hangar and raced each other to it. The Captain and Celwyn broke into a trot, both aware almost anything could be waiting for them in the structure. They passed a pair of guards on patrol and arrived just as the scientists disappeared inside.

"How interesting. This used ... to be a big barn." Celwyn panted as they reached the front doors. The scientists stood in the entrance making excited noises and deciding what to do first.

Nemo straightened his jacket and said, "That is true." They waited for Verne to catch up and walked inside.

Over the next few minutes, Celwyn inspected the interior and decided the Captain had recovered from his disappointment in Turkey. Nemo expected success. No expense had been spared in the new set-up; from the wide worktables and elevated carts, to an extensive array of tools mounted on the walls, everything and more had been built into the workshop. Piles of wood had been stacked next to sawhorses, and cabinets of glass jars contained screws and things Celwyn didn't recognize.

Bartholomew scrutinized shelves of chunky metal pieces that the magician assumed made up the engines. A dozen round cylinders,. bigger around than Kang lay against one wall.

At the far end of the hangar, a large, coiled hose abutted a cistern nearly the size of a carriage. 'Water' had been painted on the outside in several languages. The magician instantly thought of Pelaez burning their original flying machine.

"We funnel rain into the cistern." The Captain gestured at a set of pipes running down from the ceiling. "If needed, we can eventually lay a pipeline from here to the main house."

"Ingenious. And there is more." Kang pointed. "Much of the ceiling rolls back like a window shade if we need more light." His voice rose in excitement. "Captain, this is fantastic! You have thought of everything!"

"There's even an icebox to keep food." Bartholomew crossed to the desk area on the west side of the building. "Here," the big man showed them a foot-square box with brass knobs and sliding tabs. "An arithmometer." He grinned. "It is obviously needed to help me with my calculations."

Verne stared open-mouthed at the rows of tools and measuring devices. "My, all sorts of things." He removed a long ruler off the wall and examined it.

"There was a hayloft there." Nemo indicated the overhang above them. "Although one end had collapsed, we were able to rebuild it." They moved to the north side of the shop to stand beside rows of cables bigger than vines from a jungle. "Observe how these descend from the center of the hangar to the outside doors. Do you see the pulleys?" he asked.

"Yes." The magician cranked the handle for one of the cables. It turned effortlessly and silently. "This is used for?"

"When the four pulleys are operated at the same time, the flying machine can be wheeled in and out of here easily instead of everyone having to push it. The process will take half the time." Nemo inhaled in satisfaction.

Verne marveled at the cables. "Very efficient. It would work like a giant puppet suspended on strings."

While they talked, Kang and Bartholomew donned their overalls and began unloading paperwork from their knapsacks.

The magician said, "That is a lot of paper."

The automat waved some at him and went back to what he was doing.

"They seem to have been successful in re-creating their specs." Verne sounded a bit wistful. "It is a testament to incredible memories."

"Ha! Xiau certainly has one. He still nags me about things that happened the first week I met him." Celwyn wished he would forget a few of the other things that had happened.

Without looking up from his paperwork, Kang said, "I heard that, and leave my ears alone." Bartholomew giggled and went back to the specs.

Nemo led them forward, and they wandered the length of the hangar, passing by two assistants awaiting orders with clipboards at the ready. The magician said hello and shook their hands.

Verne asked, "Sir, I understand you are spending the morning here?"

"Yes. Some of their enthusiasm and inventiveness may rub off on me." Nemo placed rolls of maps, a fancy compass, a divider, and a parallel ruler on the table and sat down to work on his charts.

Verne turned to the magician and blinked at him. "Jonas, I want to find ghosts."

Bartholomew dropped a chunk of wood he'd picked up and gasped. "*Why?*"

"Aren't you curious too?" Verne shrugged at the big man.

"No!"

Celwyn bowed. "But of course, Jules. After you."

Chapter 24

THE MAGICIAN FOLLOWED THE author across the courtyard, through the glass doors, and into the mansion.

"There's a sunroom and conservatory through here that the Captain had cleaned up." Verne led the way toward a side door. "I brought this," the author held up a package. "It is the information that I've discovered about the island and its history."

The first room they entered favored the morning sun. Bright light poured through glass panels, up the walls, and across the ceiling. Celwyn spotted some water damage in one corner, but overall, things seemed in good order. Although there were not any plants surrounding the reflecting pool, the overall effect appeared restful, especially if you happened to be a patient whose mental state required it.

The magician waved, adding a table, chairs, and tea service, and sat down. "Before we start exploring, let's take a peek at the research you have."

The author separated the information into three piles. "You know, I have come to like tea a bit more since our association began."

"How could you not love it? I quote, '*If you are cold, tea will warm you; if you are too heated, it will cool you; If you are depressed, it will cheer you; If you are excited, it will calm you.*' William Ewart Gladstone."

"If you say so." Verne sipped, added more sugar, and fussed with his papers. "To our business." He handed the magician a packet. "Those pertain to the period before the year 1680. The rest are from that point onward. I'll review them." He pointed to the third packet. "Celtic history from before 200 A.D."

A shadow passed overhead. Celwyn gazed through the glass overhead in time to glimpse a wing from a medium-sized bird. As he released the string holding the papers, he asked, "What birds inhabit this island?"

"Just auks and puffins, as far as I know." The author studied one of the handwritten sheets. "Do you want to know what we're searching for in these?"

The magician extracted a peyote button from his pocket and began chewing. "Please tell me."

"As you wish. This is a timeline of events."

1649   John Spencer marries Genevieve Octavia Davis, and renovation of the mansion begins.

1658 *Work concludes, and they move their household to Findbar Island.*

1662 *Their first child is born.*

1674 *They have four more children. The smuggling activity increases.*

1675 *Spencer completes fortifications around the mansion.*

1676 *A reported attack from smugglers is repelled, and their ship, The Rottingham, is found wrecked on the rocks.*

1679 *Criminal activity continues. The British fleet surrounds the island.*
   The smuggling activity stops.

1680 *The British fleet finds the corpse of a child floating against the rocks.*

"Years later, the fortifications were removed by the asylum. Probably to make the patients less anxious," the author said to himself.

Celwyn asked, "How did the child die?"

"Knife wound. It was a boy of twelve."

The magician had seen worse over the years, yet it was still hard to hear.

"Then what happened?"

Verne handed him another list. "This information is from newspaper reports. The initial reports were not accurate."

"Or the other way around." Celwyn speculated as he read and wondered about human cruelty and the definition of mental disorder. According to the report, all five children had been killed. The report stated that the household staff were also stabbed, except for Mrs. Teasdale, the housekeeper, and Jeffers, the butler. Their bodies were recovered on the lee side of the island, all drowned and bashed on the rocks below the cliffs. One of the nannies escaped.

On the north side of the island, in the woods where Celwyn had discovered the Celtic burial mound, the rest of the household staff had been discovered. Most of them had been stabbed, some bludgeoned. One of the Spencer children lay under the body of the cook. It appeared the woman had tried to shield her.

"Who investigated?" the magician asked.

"The British Royal Navy."

"Gruesome." Celwyn held up a sheet. "This says nothing about the fate of Mr. or Mrs. Spencer."

Verne waved his paper. "Mr. Spencer was found in the tower. Distraught and naked with a collection of weapons. He was reportedly covered in blood." The author unfolded a brittle, yellowed page.

"Wait. What about Mrs. Spencer?"

Verne shrugged. "Other than the initial reports of finding her dead in the grotto, nothing else. I'll read it to you."

"The suspect, Sir John Spencer, was incoherent and inconsolable. When questioned, he said, 'Kill all devils! Kill all devils!' He charged at the officers while holding a pistol. They opened fire. Subject is deceased."

"Hmm." The magician refilled his cup and immersed himself in the scene from long ago. It must have been a terrifying time, and it all occurred in the dead of night.

Verne licked his lips. "They did not find Mrs. Spencer's body. She was presumed lost off the rocks or the cliffs. Possibly, the other report of the beheading is true."

"I want to know what happened to Mrs. Spencer." The magician thought more. "What about the underground grotto?"

Verne shuffled papers until he found the right one. "The Spencer's boat, the *Octavia,* was still moored in the grotto. The British searched it thoroughly."

As a crewman passed through the room carrying a hamper, most likely filled with mid-morning coffee and cookies for the automat, the magician wondered what had caused John Spencer, by all accounts a sane man, to act so murderously. Little seemed to be known about his wife other than that she was fertile enough to produce a brood of children.

Verne pointed to the original packet of papers. "Those are copies of her letters to her father, friends, and others. Nothing unusual in them. There is no reason for what happened."

"Let's move along to the events after the Spencers."

They read for a minute before Verne said, "The first recorded date that patients were admitted to the Pembrook Asylum was in 1802."

They read in silence for several more minutes.

"Interesting." The magician asked, "Did any of the inmates in the sanatorium say they saw Mrs. Spencer's ghost?"

Verne shook his head. "Do you think she is a ghost ... here?" The author edged his chair closer to the magician.

"Perhaps."

Verne inhaled, trying to regain his nerve, and stuck his nose into one of the sanitorium transcripts to read a moment. "This is the most recent report about that. And yes, since the asylum opened, there were sightings. However, not of Mrs. Spencer. Most saw the ghosts of the dead children."

"Are you sure?" The magician didn't quite believe that. Although abhorrent, he had a feeling this was more complicated than dead children.

The Frenchman shrugged. "Each report states they saw the ghosts of the dead children."

Celwyn shuddered. He could not imagine how a patient in a sanatorium teetering on the brink of sanity would react to that. If an ordinary citizen found ghosts unsettling, the encounter would be a dozen times worse in their condition.

"Good grief!"

Verne said, "My sentiments, too."

The magician paced to the windows overlooking the courtyard. Past the shrubbery, a spotty lawn descended toward the trees, and before a crumbling rock wall, a sliver of seawater lay beyond the cliffs.

Celwyn did not want to know more about the apparitions the patients saw, but he realized for the safety of Nemo's enterprise, they should know. "Tell me about it, Jules."

Verne related when the children were reportedly seen. The dates ranged from the 1680s to just before the sanatorium ceased to exist. Some of the children had been spotted walking through the mansion or playing with toys on the stairs. Several times, they were seen pulling a wooden wagon across the ballroom floor. He continued, "Sometimes the children appeared lively and animated, but in other instances, they were dead and still as if posed in a painting. The reports vary on where this occurred, but most were reported to have occurred in one room."

The magician strolled back to the chairs and sighed. "Where do you think that room is located? There are four floors and a tower."

"I'm not sure I want to know." The author fell silent for a moment. "It is also unknown if that is where the children actually died. We would have to compare the text, notes, and drawings from the witnesses to each room. Not to mention the outbuildings. The Captain said his men found evidence the staff had been housed there."

The magician asked, "What evidence?"

"Beds, basins. Some toiletries and uniforms. We could explore the outbuildings before searching the house. It may be more productive."

"Your choice, Jules."

"I'd rather do the house first." Verne licked his lips and asked, "Have you ever seen a ghost?"

The magician laughed. "Several. Goffles the Clown in Marseilles was the most memorable."

"I heard stories of him. Why is he memorable?" the author asked.

"I made him." Celwyn saw the dawning of understanding on Verne's face. "To entertain someone with, of course." He laughed, and a thin copy of Goffles appeared behind Verne. "Haven't you ever wondered what made King Rudolph II so crazy? So nervous? I had to do something short of killing him because he had become dangerous to his troops and his kingdom... So, I gave him something to think about other than war."

"Oh, I see." Verne shot Celwyn an unsure glance and inhaled. "Be that as it may, shall we get started?" The magician dissolved Goffles before the author became more intimately acquainted with him. As they headed toward the staircase leading upstairs, Verne stopped still. "Did you hear that?"

The magician listened and shook his head, and they continued to the stairs.

"It sounded like someone laughing... it was not a pleasant laugh." As they climbed higher, Verne asked, "Were there other ... ghosts you made?"

"Ouch!" Celwyn patted Qing's head, pushed the mechanical bird back into his collar, and buttoned it. The magician could feel him chewing on his shirt as he answered, "Yes. Several. When I passed through Aspen in the United States years ago, I entertained some skiers coming down the mountain. Just a small show that came along with them." The magician stroked his mustache and relived the memory of the giant hairy man with wolf-like features that cursed in gutter Russian and chased a gang of bank robbers out of town and up the mountain. "A most memorable show."

Uncertainty filled Verne's eyes, mostly directed at the magician, as they reached the first landing, and Celwyn leaned over the unpolished rail. With its black-and-white checkered design, the floor below reminded him of a chessboard.

"Observe." Celwyn concentrated, and the floor filled with old-style chess pieces. He added a semiopaque image of a king in full regalia, life-size and without legs, sitting flush on one of the squares. His crown gleamed in the low light, as did the rings on his fingers. The magician stared, and more pawns and other pieces filled the spaces. The pawns had cherub-like faces, and the rooks resembled devious goblins with pointy chins, hooked noses, and jabbering voices. Celwyn stopped short of imposing Duncan's face on one of them.

With a squeak, Verne backed up until he stood on the magician's boot. He pointed a shaky finger at Celwyn's king as it glided smoothly across the checkered floor and stopped next to a bishop. The bishop's beard curled down the front of his robes like a hairy waterfall. As an artistic touch, Celwyn had given him tiny spectacles and a crooked staff that he clutched to his chest. The piece pivoted as if on a mechanical wheel to face the king, drawing another gasp from Verne when its eyes flickered.

"A wonderful game, is it not?" The magician wished these creations could fit inside the *Nautilus*. Such a beautiful scene. Above the chessboard, dust motes danced in the ribbons of sunlight falling from the windows.

Verne stuttered, "J-J-Jonas...You made those... Didn't you?"

Celwyn's smile froze.

"I made them ... but not the Queen."

As they watched, a diminutive figure in an ornate dress, also sitting flush on the chessboard, solidified beside the bishop. She wore the white gowns of an ancient monarch, including a crown and veil that did nothing to hide her heavy brows and cruel mouth. Before Celwyn could react, she brought up a broadsword from her side and whacked off the bishop's head. The magician backed his king away as the head rolled across the floor after him.

Verne fainted at Celwyn's feet.

"Ye Gods!" The magician threw Verne over his shoulder and elevated himself down the stairs, through the ballroom, and outside.

A moment later, Celwyn floated onto the lawn beyond the courtyard just as Kang, Bartholomew, and the Captain arrived.

"What happened?" the big man demanded.

"We had an incident." The magician laid Verne on the grass and scattered water from a nearby fountain over him.

"You're a little pale, Jonas," Kang bent over the author to verify that he breathed. "But you appear to be in better shape than Verne. What happened?"

Celwyn frowned and helped the author to his feet. A check on Bartholomew revealed a certain amount of apprehension in the big man, as evidenced by his nervous eyes and glances at the mansion. The magician would not lie to him. Something indeed had happened. Verne eyed the others with saucer-size eyes and clutched Bartholomew's arm. *For pity's sake.* "It is something that would upset most of you." The magician nodded at Bartholomew. "In case you encounter it, you should be prepared."

Nemo said, "I'm not going to like this, am I?"

Verne stammered, "I-I ... I wish I had never come to this island."

What the magician saw next was extraordinary. As Bartholomew extracted his arm from Verne's death grip, he patted the author's back and said, "You'll feel better after you think about it logically."

Celwyn and the Professor traded a glance with raised brows and withheld a reaction to what they had just heard; they had both used the same phrase to reassure the big man under trying circumstances. He must have listened to them.

The author regarded Bartholomew with a serious expression and sat down on the grass. Apparently, Bartholomew's advice was not helping. The magician stared at Verne until he rolled onto his side, and rhythmic snoring filled the air.

"I assume he didn't just fall asleep." Bartholomew watched Verne. "I prefer this method to feel better, even if you have to help it along, Jonas."

"I am at your service, any time."

"You seem more like yourself," Kang told the magician.

"I would prefer to receive this news with a whiskey and my lunch in my stomach," Bartholomew said.

Nemo said, "Agreed."

They started across the grass. Celwyn floated a prone Verne ahead of them as they reentered the mansion and headed for the *Nautilus,* a most beautiful ship at rest in her personal grotto and oblivious to the unusual goings-on above ground.

While they waited in front of the aquatic window for their luncheon, the magician told them what had happened. Verne woke up about halfway through his recitation and fainted again. Bartholomew took pity on him, scooped him up, and took the author to his cabin.

Celwyn waited until he returned. When the big man nodded, the magician continued, "I'm surprised he fainted again. I haven't gotten to the frightening part yet."

"Oh?" Nemo tossed off his drink, and Celwyn poured him another. Perhaps he loved a good story, too.

Qing's talons clicked like a miniature marching band as he paraded back and forth between the chess pieces under the sea window. The fish on the other side of the glass seemed enthralled with the aviary show, especially when Qing fluffed his feathers.

Bartholomew told them, "I will do my best. Go ahead."

Celwyn related it all in detail. When he got to the part where the Queen swung the broadsword, he made sure they heard exactly what happened. "She wore a veil, and her dress covered her completely. She did not walk across the tiles; she glided over them like a chess piece, imitating how I'd caused the pieces I'd made to move. She confronted the bishop and, without warning, brought up the sword."

"Did the sword appear, ah ... real?" the Captain asked.

The magician nodded. "Yes. As large as any other from medieval times. It had a gilded handle and measured perhaps five feet long, and was probably heavy as it could be. She used both hands like she knew what she was doing when she swung the weapon. The bishop's head went flying across the floor. The whole time, I could somewhat see through her—just like the life-size pieces I had made, but perhaps not quite as colorful." He frowned. "It was as if she imitated my craft."

Kang started to laugh, effectively breaking the tension. Bartholomew joined in until he roared, and tears streamed down his face. Even Nemo smiled. If this is what it took to keep Bartholomew calm in the face of unusual occurrences, the magician thought it well worth it.

"Someone, or something, stole your show." The automat whistled. "Does she want to play chess with you?"

The magician waited until the hilarity at his expense stopped. Captain Nemo continued to smile into his whiskey glass while Bartholomew provided his perspective.

"What I've decided is ... things happen. I'm ready to hear more, Jonas." He sounded serious. "Just don't leave me alone with them."

Celwyn understood; it only took himself being afraid to cure Bartholomew's fear. "There isn't too much more to tell. Jules fainted, and I panicked, and you know the rest."

Kang asked, "You saw nothing more?"

The magician shook his head.

Captain Nemo asked, "Who was the woman?"

"I think the original mistress of this house, Mrs. Spencer." The magician thought more and added, "At least, she greatly resembled the picture that Jules had shown me of her. Patrician nose, dark hair, and rather large ears. Not a handsome woman. When he is up to it, we will have to ask this of Jules, too."

"How do you know she was supposed to be a Queen?" Captain Nemo asked.

Celwyn thought for a moment. "She wore vestments appropriate to the 15th century. And a crown."

Kang grinned. "Lovely. A royal ghost." He nodded to himself. "Or, one pretending to be. It seems plausible the 'ghost' saw your magic and decided to participate." He slapped Celwyn's knee and chortled heartily. "You have a playmate."

"No, I don't."

Bartholomew blinked at them. "I'm not sure what it was, but I do hope we don't run into it again."

"There is the gong. It saves us from further speculation." Captain Nemo stood and shook his pant legs down. "Our luncheon awaits."

Chapter 25

A FTER THEY LEFT THE CAPTAIN'S dining table, Celwyn stopped two doors further along the corridor. He knocked on Verne's cabin, intending to check on him and make a request. He heard a weak response to come in.

Verne sat at his desk, fountain pen in hand, and wearing a blank stare. His tie had been discarded on the floor, and his lunch tray sat untouched on the table next to the bunk. The author's pipe lay scattered in pieces against the far wall where it presumably had been thrown. Celwyn seated himself on the bunk and reassembled the pipe before placing it next to Verne's hand. When he tapped the author on the shoulder, Verne turned to him with unfocused eyes.

"Jules, I know you can hear me." The magician gentled his voice. "And I know you are confused."

"Yes, I am."

Celwyn asked, "In the past, you have seen many strange and wonderful things, haven't you?"

"Yes."

"What was the most beautiful?"

A crease crossed the author's forehead, and his eyes cleared. "Why ... the Lalibela in Aethiopia, now Ethiopia. They are churches carved from solid rock with beautiful scrollwork and designs. Unbelievable."

"It sounds exquisite." The magician tried to remember exactly how he talked Bartholomew out of his greatest fears. "If that is the most beautiful, what was the most interesting?" He found Verne's pouch and packed his pipe for him. "The underground river that we took to the city of children?"

Jules shook his head. "No, no. That was engrossing, surely, but nothing to compare to the Neolithic stones of Easter Island. The obelisks are taller and heavier than I can describe. The Captain took me to see them."

"Put there by unknown forces?" Celwyn guessed.

"Yes. No one knows how, exactly."

"There are also the glowing tabernacles from Moses's time."

Verne stared. "I am beginning to understand your point."

"The world is full of unexplained occurrences and the unknown." The magician stared back with a degree of calmness he hoped the author would absorb. "I was frightened today, too."

"You recovered."

"Xiau would say it is because of my foolhardiness."

Verne's eyes took on an unfocused glaze again as he reflected. "I suppose."

"Or hundreds of years of seeing the unexplained makes me inured to it."

Verne's eyes strayed to his lunch tray.

"Would you eat if it was hot?"

The author nodded.

By the time the tray arrived at Verne's desk, Celwyn had warmed the food. The author spooned soup. "Thank you. This is very good." He sipped more soup and then asked, "Did you just stop by to make sure of my nerves?"

"Partly. I also wanted to borrow the rest of your research about the Spencers and the sanatorium."

Verne put his spoon back in the bowl and pointed to the cubbyhole above his trunk. "There's a book there too. You are welcome to them."

For the rest of the afternoon, the magician read about murders, madness, greed, cannibalism, and other delightful things on Findbar Island.

It seemed that officially John Spencer had made his money in banking. Unofficially, he smuggled rum from the Caribbean to supply the high-class tables and bars of Pall Mall. The operation was not controlled by a stranger; Spencer did everything himself. The irony of it all amazed Celwyn. For his service to the Queen and the banking industry, the unknowing monarchy fulfilled a personal request from her 'loyal' subject, John Spencer, and was awarded Findbar

Island. This included everything from the inhospitable coastline to its well-appointed underground cavern, also known as a smuggler's heaven.

Celwyn poured another cup of tea and glanced outside. As expected, the lower half of the view consisted of the grotto's murky water. The upper half revealed shadowy walls, the walkway, and the platform that led upward. No clues here as to the history he sought. To counter the gloom, Nemo's crew had strung a collection of lanterns across the pathways surrounding the water and up the stairs.

Walking heavily, more reminiscent of a stomp, Bartholomew entered the study and dropped onto the sofa, causing Qing to bounce off the cushion. He fluffed himself and abandoned them for the aquatic window.

"I need a break," the big man announced.

"From?"

Bartholomew made a face. "Thinking."

"Whiskey or wine?"

"Whichever goes well with a headache." The big man sighed.

Celwyn sent him a whiskey and waited.

Bartholomew sipped. "We have a problem with the fuel intake. Xiau wants to start over with it."

"And you?"

"I agree. But we can't figure out how to do it differently." Bartholomew tossed back the rest of his drink. "Xiau will be here in a minute. Perhaps we will do better without looking at it. A fresh view, so to speak."

"It will be dinnertime soon." The magician said, "Care to hear about the history of the island?"

"I do—" Bartholomew turned to the door as Kang and Captain Nemo came in and joined them on the sofas. The automat appeared frustrated and grumpy, as evidenced by his lowered brows, tie askew, and deep frown. Nemo seemed a bit more distracted than usual but still sighed with satisfaction at the end of a long day. If Celwyn didn't know any better, he'd assume the Captain enjoyed having guests on his ship, but he would probably prefer them with less magical tendencies and enemies.

He accepted a glass Celwyn floated to him and relaxed into the back of the sofa. "What is this?" He pointed to Verne's paper treasure trove on the table.

The author chose that moment to join them, his usual energy and affable mood restored. He trotted to the chess table and deposited his notebook and pens.

"Are you feeling better, Jules?" the Captain asked.

"Yes, I am. Jonas and I talked. It helped."

Bartholomew raised a brow of curiosity at the magician.

Celwyn shrugged. "Some things cannot be explained, but I might hunt down whatever it was that we saw this morning."

"What if it hunts you down?" Kang laughed.

"I am not afraid," Celwyn assured him.

Bartholomew raised his brow higher. "You appeared shaken this morning, Jonas."

"Perhaps."

"Even though I feel better," Verne said, "I do not wish to go into that room by the stairs again."

"Does that—" Kang pointed to the pile of research, "tell you who you saw this morning?"

"It might. There is quite a bit of information, and there are also a few photographs." Celwyn fanned them out so everyone could study them while he supplied details. "In the end, the report concluded that Mr. Spencer committed the murders, yet it was his wife who appears to be the lethal one."

"The authorities stated they found him covered in blood and brandishing weapons." Nemo cocked his head at the drawing of Spencer receiving his award from the Queen.

"It is possible he was defending himself," the author mused to himself as he filled his pen.

Kang said, "However, it was Mrs. Spencer who attacked someone this morning."

"That apparition resembled Mr. Jeffers, their butler." Celwyn shrugged. "The one the Crown says died by the cliffs."

"Perhaps he is the ghost in residence, not her." Bartholomew speculated.

Captain Nemo asked, "What happened to Mr. Spencer?"

"I read about him first." The magician shuffled through the papers to find the news stories. He passed them around. "The rumors in some news reports indicated Spencer was killed by the British Navy. Other reports said he journeyed to America and joined the Mormons."

Verne raised his brows. "What an odd thing to do."

"Or," the automat indicated the picture of her, "his wife killed him and buried him under the courtyard."

Although it sounded vaguely fantastic, the magician could not discount Kang's humor. "There is only one consistent aspect verified by the British Navy and the local churches and newspapers."

"The murders of the children," Captain Nemo guessed.

"Yes. And then, more than a hundred years later, the murders of the patients."

Kang made a face of annoyance. "But, by whom?"

"That is debatable." The magician consulted one of the articles. "This is a somewhat faded original from 1680." Celwyn wondered if Verne had obtained it by stealth or bribery.

"Listen." Verne stood up. "I hear the dinner gong."

"Shall we?" Captain Nemo tossed off the last of his drink and bowed them ahead of him toward the hallway. "I'm sure Jonas has more to tell us."

Chapter 26

AS A CREWMAN SERVED THE SOUP, the magician said, "If we go back to the island's history, during Spencer's residence here, it is an interesting fact that the British Navy only visited here on rare occasions."

"Because?"

"A lack of time, apparently. There were plenty of British wars waging around the globe. When the Navy did stop by Findbar, it was quite profitable; there are many reports of bribery by the pirates."

Into a lull in the conversation, Nemo tapped his spoon against his water glass, and the crystal rang. "We will continue this topic, but an announcement first. Under an anonymous name, I have optioned a fifteen-year lease for the island through my solicitor. It is a precaution in the event we decide to continue here for our other endeavors."

"Bravo!" Kang nearly upset his soup bowl in his excitement.

Celwyn joined in. "Wonderful news, certainly."

"Yes, most welcome news," Bartholomew said. "I imagine you'll have need of many solicitors to come, though." His voice radiated confidence. "For the patents and more discoveries. Meanwhile, we have enough room here to experiment and the privacy that we need." The big man grinned. "Who knows what we'll think of."

The automat pursed his lips. "I'm not sure at which point we'll need a larger compound, though. I am not keen on sleeping in that mansion."

They thought about the possibilities until Nemo said, "Please continue, Jonas. I want to hear more."

The magician picked through the paperwork to find answers. "As you wish. The Queen deeded John Barton Spencer the island on June 13th in the year 1649. There is strong evidence that he ran a successful smuggling operation of his own from out of this cavern—until he ran afoul of a rival smuggler, a one Dostal 'Red' Parker. The children could have been killed as part of Parker's plan to drive Spencer out."

As he cut into his fish, Kang spoke slowly. "You do realize that if any feminine presence, such as Elizabeth or Annabelle, sat at this table, our dinner conversation would be quite different."

Bartholomew's thoughts diverged in a dissimilar direction. "I wonder what reaction Annabelle would have to a ghost?"

"Unknown. Elizabeth would handle it well ... as long as I wasn't in any danger." The automat chewed. "She is usually fearless, which is good, considering some of the things we encounter."

"If either of you were in danger, she would ask me to make it stop." Celwyn smiled at them dotingly. "I think by now she would extend the request to all those present."

"It is appreciated." The Captain said, "Continue, please."

"Certainly. The ghostly bishop beheaded this morning could have been one of several of the local personages of the time: Boynton, Hopps, Jeffers, and possibly Wengman. I do not have pictures or good descriptions of them. In some of the accounts, Hopps was one of the King's men. Others list him as Parker's man, who infiltrated Spencer's smuggling operation." With a moue of distaste, Celwyn extracted a set of smaller sheets, yellowed with age. "From Mrs. Spencer's diary, it appears he was also her paramour."

"Or Jeffers, the butler." Verne bit his lip. "It could be someone else altogether."

"That makes things rather tawdry," Bartholomew said.

The magician agreed. "There's more. From what I can tell from these drawings depicting the bishop, the man we saw this morning looked very much like Sir Spencer himself, not Jeffers."

"This is all quite interesting ... and confusing." The Captain shook his head and buttered another roll.

Verne asked, "What did they smuggle besides rum?"

"Spices and exotic animals, such as parrots and snakes. And apparently, the means for a spot of fresh cannibalism for a particular client in Lyon."

At that last detail, Bartholomew appeared ready to lose his dinner.

Nemo rubbed his chin. "Wouldn't the motive for the murders be important for the patients and the Spencers? Was it about the business of smuggling or about problems within the Spencer's marriage?"

"Or was it about pure madness trumping everything else?" the Professor asked. A tapping on the window caused them to turn around; a large spiney fish brushed against the glass and then moved on, wriggling its way into darker water. "Who was it that reported Mr. Spencer went crazy and killed them all?"

"Most reports do not state where they found the information." The magician shrugged. "It probably came from the Crown or the Queen's Navy."

———

After they settled at the bridge table later that evening, Verne couldn't help but shudder. "Can you imagine your reaction if you were confined in the sanitarium here and the ghost of Mrs. Spencer approached you?"

"Perhaps the ghost kept the patients company or gave them someone to talk with." The automat appeared serious, but Celwyn suspected him.

Bartholomew whispered, "I believe in ghosts, but I've never encountered one."

"I certainly have," Verne said. His hand shook, causing him to drop his pen. Celwyn retrieved it for him.

The Captain told them, "It does make our stay here rather interesting, I admit. But I hope it doesn't distract from our work."

"Malignant ghosts were not one of the dangers I planned for." The magician thought about how to anticipate something like this. "It would be nice to know more."

Kang asked, "Such as discovering if the entity is a serious threat?"

"I vote it is." Bartholomew didn't hesitate.

"I went back to the ballroom this afternoon." Celwyn noticed everyone, but Nemo seemed surprised. "The bishop and his head were gone. Other than some mouse droppings under the stairs, I saw nothing untoward."

Verne licked his lips. "Did you go upstairs?"

"No. I want to finish reading the rest of the research you collected first." Celwyn pushed the scorepad across the table to the automat.

"Really?"

"You always say I'm not good with numbers." The magician smiled at him, and the pencil sat up. It had Kang's face. When it wiggled its brows, the automat flattened it with his hand.

"Would you tell us about the asylum, please?" Bartholomew shuffled the cards. Tonight, the magician partnered with Kang and the big man with Captain Nemo. Verne seemed content, scribbling in his notebook at the chess table.

"Of course. The patients were both men and women, young and old. As we were told by that witness, the male patients resided on the third floor, and the women on the floor below them." The magician noticed low whiskey levels in a few glasses and corrected the situation. "Most of the patients had been committed by the Crown to the sanitorium for heinous criminal acts."

Bartholomew winced and went back to sorting his cards. "Can you imagine being innocent and then sent here?"

"Your bid, Jonas." The automat concentrated on his cards as if it would be unlucky to do anything else.

Celwyn had been thinking about Bartholomew's question, not the bid. "Pass." He went back to pondering the situation on Findbar Island and thinking he did not feel fear for their safety. Yet, he was awfully glad they slept in a long metal tube that locked from the inside.

"Jonas—"

"Yes?"

With a raised eyebrow, Kang scrutinized him. "We have the bid. Pay attention."

Later that night, the magician finished studying the rest of the information that Verne had collected. It would be nice to answer more questions about the history of Findbar. Visiting a library, newspaper office, and museum on the mainland were in order.

London

DAYS AFTER THE MEETING WITH Oscar and the Wessex Club, the weather turned colder, bringing the scent of fall into the shadows and swirling under the eaves and alleyways of the Lambeth District.

One could call the neighborhood bohemian. Tara thought it was more than that. As she walked, she covered her nose and decided the streets just stank. Mostly with unwashed bodies made worse by the proliferation of seedy pubs washing out stale ale, vomit, and whatever else had landed on their filthy floors.

It neared mid-morning, and Tara expected to find her quarry soon. This was the very spot at which she had lost him last week. She considered the traitor a man of habit, and after stalking his every move for days, she knew he would appear here again.

For the better part of three years, Myles Gibson had been a double agent in London. The American President had sent him, along with his own brand of goodwill, as a diplomat of sorts to Britain. Once established in London's social and covert circles, Gibson had carried out clandestine duties as directed by the Colonies. With his cherubic face, delicate dusting of freckles, and wispy hair, he could appear rather innocent, which probably helped with his secret work.

Twenty minutes later, Tara wiggled into a more comfortable position under the eaves of St. Bernadette's church. Judging from the parishioners who shivered in the pews below, the place had no heat. It did have an impressive display of lit candles, and a thick stream of smoke from them funneled past her into the cracks in the ceiling. A rather fat mouse ran over her boot, causing her to smile. It reminded her of other mice—that were not mice—from their adventure in the catacombs. She missed Jonas and the others. The witch in her came alive, and she stared at the rodent until it emitted a squeak of alarm and ran back across the beam.

Over the last hour, not more than a dozen people had entered the sanctuary, and few spoke. The door leading to the street creaked open again, letting in the jingling bells of the horses, the rumble of carriage wheels on the cobblestones, newsboys yelling, smoky air, and William Butler Yeats.

Well, she thought. This was not expected. Only days ago, she had seen the man swilling wine with Oscar Wilde and the rest of the Wessex Club. Now, he hesitated before darting into the pews furthest from the altar. Tara watched him open a hymnal and pretend to read it.

Who is he meeting here?

The obvious answer did not seem possible until the door opened again to silhouette a pudgy man with a cherub-like face and freckles. *Ah, her traitor.* She always liked being right.

With care and again grateful she wore riding breeches, Tara scooted across the beams until she could lie flat a mere dozen feet above Yeats. Gibson took off his hat and sat down.

"Good evening, sir," Yeats said. As he spoke, a blast of cold air flowed over them as a woman cradling a baby entered the sanctuary.

Gibson watched as she walked by them up the aisle. "Did you bring it?" His voice sounded surprisingly deep for a small man.

Yeats pulled a flask from his coat and drank half of it down. He wiped the back of his hand across his lips, and his hand appeared steady. "Yes."

"So, give it to me."

As polite as ever, Yeats replied, "No, laddie." He uncapped his flask again. "Not until I see your money."

From the front of the sanctuary, murmurs from a pair of worshipers and the priest floated to them. Tara's hearing was excellent. It seemed the couple knew each other well; the woman wanted to marry, and the man did not. The priest standing between them appeared flustered as he patted each of them on the shoulder and reminded them to keep their voices low and faith high.

"It isn't my money. It is the Crown's." Gibson dropped an envelope in Yeats's lap. "I am not your laddie. Now, hand it over, fella." The American sounded mildly irritated but nothing more.

"As you wish." Yeats stood and flung a smaller envelope at his feet. "I have no idea what you'll do with this; it is not my concern." He made a point of not looking back as he strode down the aisle. Before the outside door closed behind him, a man in a beaver coat and large hat walked in.

Tara's perspective from directly above them kept her from recognizing him at first. But when she did, she tightened her grip on the beam and blinked rapidly. All speculation about Yeats stopped.

This man *should not be here.* Tara did not breathe in case he heard her.

The conversation a dozen feet below did not take long, and Tara heard enough to make her doubt everything she thought she knew.

This is not good. Not at all.

Chapter 28

I T TOOK OVER A WEEK FOR MISS TARA McFein to set a trap for the corpulent man she saw at the church with Gibson. She knew what to expect from the man, and as a typical American, he thought himself much smarter than anyone else. The man in the beaver coat, however, could be a much worse opponent; she must be careful and cleverer than him. If not, he would kill her.

To confirm the man's treachery, she needed proof, and while obtaining it, Tara would do her best to neutralize him and expose what he had done. All the while, she had trouble reconciling his actions to what she thought she knew of him. If there was an innocent reason for his actions, the trap she laid would confirm that. Or he would be proven to be an enemy of the Crown.

On a rather grey day, without rain or much sun, Tara climbed aboard a cab and directed it eastward.

She had enlisted the help of one of the street women who sold flowers on Grandview Street and her child. With a bag of candy for the urchin and a large coin for her mother, the girl Lolly would accompany Tara to the Royal Zoo. For her own disguise, Tara had chosen a much too-large moth-eaten coat, missing a few buttons and any sort of charm. Its color resembled dull bark, which would help her blend in even better with the crowds. Along with displaying stooped shoulders, a dejected air, and a dirty blonde wig, her quarry would dismiss her. She did not anticipate chasing the man through the nearby woods; all she needed to do was confirm he had taken the bait.

It had been agreed Lolly would call her Auntie, and Lolly's mother would be waiting for them at the zoo's exit. If this went well, Tara would use the pair of them again.

One of their predecessors from previous capers, a skinny young man with a bad complexion, would deliver the bait today. It hadn't cost Tara a great deal for his help, but she had included a ticket that entitled him to many free Sunday meals … for the near future.

"Come along, Lolly." Tara led her charge up the path between the other patrons of the zoo until they stood beside the bear enclosure, a popular feature here. It attracted enough people to gawk at the baby bears that Tara could observe and not be observed. As they took up a position where she could watch the path on each side of them, the sun deserted the city, and a light mist floated down. Lolly didn't mind at all. She chewed her candy and pointed at the bears.

The man in the beaver coat arrived early. As Tara finished straightening the child's hat, she saw him at no more than ten paces to her left. Tara pointed out the smallest baby bear as it waddled to the right, and they sidled that way to keep track of it. Tara knelt beside Lolly, putting the child between her and the man while she monitored him and the path. *Where was pimply Peter?*

The minutes went by slower than a pool of drying blood, and while she waited, Tara cursed Peter in Gaelic and French. Just as she tried to remember a particular word in Spanish, he trotted up the path, saw the man in the beaver coat, and approached, standing beside him to view the bears in their little hats and colorful tutus. The crowd laughed at their antics.

Peter passed an envelope to the man in the coat and received a smaller packet of money in return. That had been a bonus for Peter, keeping the bribe for his trouble.

"Now," Tara whispered. Lolly dropped her bag of candy just as the man in the coat walked by them. As they'd rehearsed, she began to wail, providing a wonderful deterrent to keep the man from lingering. Tara scrambled, head down, to pick up the treats. "Louder, please." Lolly yelled with more vigor, and the traitor walked faster as Tara noted the man's expensive shoes and recognized his cologne. *What a bastard*, she thought as he moved swiftly out of sight and down the path.

Lolly was proud of her performance, especially when Tara presented her with sticks of cotton candy on their way out, one for her and one for her mother. Would her mother be as sanguine if she knew a witch and vampire had just spent a pleasant outing with her daughter? Tara shrugged. Her thoughts remained on the man in the coat.

If he indeed was a traitor, she would soon know. And if he again met the American spy at the same church to sell his new secret, so much the better.

Chapter 29

Findbar Island

CELWYN HAD JUST SAMPLED HIS second cup of morning tea when a sleepy Bartholomew wandered into the study.

"How is work in the hangar coming along?" Celwyn asked as he poured Bartholomew's coffee, added two sugars, and sent it across the room to him.

"Thank you." The big man raised his massive shoulders and let them drop. "It goes well in some respects. You are aware that we made the decision to take our time, making improvements as we go, not just duplicating the model that Pelaez burned?" Bartholomew sipped coffee. "We're also recording everything we do each day."

"Those are logical decisions, certainly."

Bartholomew sampled his coffee again. "So far, we've improved the gauges. We have the frame complete. The new machine is longer than the first two versions and nearly two feet wider."

"Does that mean you'll need a longer field for takeoffs or landings?"

Bartholomew said, "Unknown yet. We must run tests. It will actually be more of an adjustment to the engine's power, in my opinion."

The magician finished his cup, eyed the teapot, and asked, "Do you know if there is a ferry, or boat service, from Scarborough to Great Yarmouth or Grimsby and other nearby cities? I also want to go to The Hague."

Bartholomew rubbed his chin. "Skegness is where Nemo gets our supplies from. However, I do not know anything about ferries."

The Captain arrived in time to hear the last of what was said. "Good morning. What about The Hague?"

"Is there ferry service between there and the rest of the coast? I need to pop over to the area for a day."

Nemo said, "Yes. It leaves about noon, but if you plan to return on our supply boat, you'll need to spend the night in Grimsby as our crew does. The supply boat can only return to its berth before noon because of the tides."

"That is fine." Celwyn stretched and sat once more. "I want to do more research about this island at either the city library or other sources."

"The *Newton News* originates in Durham. But there could be a smaller gazette or older local paper."

"What are you hoping to find?" Bartholomew asked.

"I am not sure yet."

The Captain gestured at the wall clock. "The supply boat will leave in about an hour."

Celwyn bowed.

"I better pack a bag, then."

⁓

Three days later, just after noon, the magician returned to the grotto. For the entire trip back from Grimsby, he had hunkered down in the cabin of the supply boat. It had been so blasted cold and gusty. As he unfolded his legs and climbed out, Celwyn asked the crewman on duty where he could find Nemo and the others.

"The hangar, sir."

"Thank you." The magician headed up the stone steps, carrying his cache of information. He had read it all and thought Kang and the others needed to hear what he had found as soon as possible, even though he knew it would not comfort them.

Celwyn walked the length of the ballroom, admittedly quicker than normal, and purposely did not glance toward the staircase or the checkered floor in the room behind it. He did not want to know. Not at all. The magician didn't mind encountering a normal enemy, but what lay in wait here ... he preferred to avoid.

A light rain accompanied him across the courtyard, over the grass, and into the hangar. Even before he strolled through the rolling doors, he could hear someone sawing wood and Kang calling out a series of numbers.

They had made progress. The frame of the new machine appeared so complete that Celwyn spotted where the engine would go and the pilot would sit. In front of it, Bartholomew fiddled with various coils of wire. At a table off to the side, Celwyn found Nemo behind a pile of maps with several bottles of ink and a notebook. A loaded revolver functioned as a paperweight.

"Welcome back, Jonas." Nemo regarded him. "Successful trip?"

Celwyn pulled out a chair and joined him. "Yes. I found what I was searching for and more. What are you doing, Sir?"

The Captain finished measuring a point on a map. "You can imagine that much of our underwater travels are through territory no one else has seen and recorded. Where the underground rivers run are not catalogued at all."

"Many people would not want to experience that unless necessary," Bartholomew contributed as he and Kang sat down.

Kang patted his arm and said, "Please continue."

Captain Nemo complied. "For the future travels of *Nautilus*, it is desirable to record depths and describe canyons, shelves, and other aspects of the seafloor."

"Such as steam vents or whirlpools, perhaps?" The magician had seen scores of those from the windows of the submarine.

"Or a proliferation of whales or unusual fauna," Bartholomew said. "I enjoy our ventures through the oceans thoroughly. But not when there is land above us."

Kang patted his shoulder, and Nemo nodded his understanding as he filled his pen and shook off the excess. "There are also underwater rivers within the sea. They run along swift currents on thousand-mile paths that have existed for thousands of years. We know enough to avoid them if we can."

"I wish we had time to see them all." The automat's eyes took on a faraway glaze as if his imagination spun as fast as he could think.

Once again, Celwyn enjoyed the contrast between Kang and Bartholomew. One of them would be quite happy to stay on solid land and pursue his interests safely away from anything not easily explained. The other was as adventurous as Elizabeth allowed him to be, preferably while blaming the magician for anything outlandish or dangerous.

"Noting the specific locations of the wreckage of ships is part of it, too." Nemo capped his pen and folded his hands. "Please tell us about your research."

"Certainly." The magician produced a coffee and tea service and poured. "Cookies?" he asked Kang.

"But of course."

With a grin he didn't conceal, the magician added a plate of oatmeal and walnut cookies. The first one Kang reached for disappeared before he could grab it. "Really?" He glared at Celwyn and changed the subject. "Is that the river under Fetheye?" As the automat eyed the map Nemo had been working on, the cookie reappeared in his hand.

"Yes. You'll recall the depths we measured."

While they talked, the magician arranged the various treasures he had found at the Great Yarmouth Museum and copies of the *Petherlee Mail* in front of them. He began his report. "These are the actual newspaper articles and published journals from 1660 to 1838." He passed them out. "I reproduced them from the originals. Please note that I can decipher most of the vintage script ... if you are not able to do so."

"What do they say?" Bartholomew held a page up to the light, his expression confirming it was a foreign language.

"At the time, the Crown investigated the events here, but not with enthusiasm. This one is from June 1733 when the report of multiple deaths on Findbar was recorded."

"And the asylum?" Bartholomew asked.

"Years later, in 1824, there were stories concerning a young woman, Mattie, who had rowed for hours from Findbar across the North Sea to Lowestoft. She was reportedly hysterical when found."

Captain Nemo asked, "Was she the only survivor?"

"That they found, and who spoke to the Crown, yes," Celwyn said. "Here is her account."

June 13, year 1824   0900 hours
Superintendent William David Warren presiding.

Witness: Mattie Hayes
Transcription location: Lowestoft, County Suffolk

Crown: State your full name.

Mattie: Matilda May Hayes.

Crown: State your connection to Findbar Island.

Mattie: I was employed there to help with the patients.

Crown: Referring to the events of the evening of June 1, 1824. When did you know something was wrong that night?

Mattie: I heard screamin'. It woke me up.

Crown: What time was it?

Mattie: 'ow would I know?

Crown: What happened?

Mattie: More screamin'. Like they couldn't get 'nough air to scream 'nough. (*Witness cries.*)

Crown: Who was screaming?

(*No answer.*)

Crown: Who was screaming?

Mattie: The patients. (*Witness whispers.*) The moonlight over the water looked so bright. Like daytime.

Crown: Explain. What did you do?

Mattie: I put on my clothes and went to the window. Between me an' the stables there were people walking toward the forest.

Crown: Walking?

Mattie: Yes. The patients were walking. Slow. In a row.

Crown: Who was screaming?

Mattie: The patients. (*Witness whispers.*) They was cryin' too.

Crown: Why?

Mattie: B'cause every time one of them stopped, they dinnit get up again. And there was blood. None of them had been out of bed for a long time. It was hard for them to walk all that way.

Crown: How do you know that?

Mattie: B'cause when I fed them, they had chains on their arms. Chains on their legs. Keeping them from escaping. That night when they walked ... I could hear the chains clinking together and dragging across the bricks in the courtyard. 'Till they got to the trees.

Crown: Please tell us what happened next.

Mattie: (*Witness whimpers.*)

Crown: Please tell us what happened next.

Mattie: Screaming. One at a time... (*Witness covers her face.*) No one came back. (*Witness mumbles.*)

Crown: Louder, please.

Mattie: After that, I waited a long time. I could hear noises downstairs in the house. Thump-like noises. M' friend Lucy came in my room. She had blood on her arms and face. I asked her what happened. (*Witness becomes agitated.*) She wouldn't talk and ran out again. I followed. She ran up the back stairs.

Crown: To the men's floor?

Mattie: Yes. Third floor.

Crown: What did you find?

Crown: I repeat, what did you find?

Mattie: Lucy ran fast. The main door was open. Silent. Everything so silent. It shouldn't be that ... quiet. The patients always yell ... or fight. Then (*witness stops talking and shakes her head*).

Crown: Tell us.

Mattie: Lucy screamed so loud. Louder and ... waited. A long time.

Crown: You opened the door?

(*Witness will not talk. Nurse is sitting with her. Calming her.*)

(*Interview resumed twenty minutes later.*)

Mattie: When I opened the door, Lucy 'as there. She was crawling in her blood. She was my friend! (*Subject cries.*) She lay down ... in the blood. Quiet-like.

Crown: Why?

Mattie: Are you daft? They were all dead, of course.

Crown: The male patients?

Mattie: All of them. I got around the blood and went back downstairs to the family quarters.

Crown: Why didn't you go to the women's floor?

Mattie: (*Witness screams obscenity.*) Are you mad? I told you because they were all marched into the trees.

Crown: Who marched them? One of the nurses?

Mattie: I'm tired.

Crown: Who marched them to the trees?

Mattie: Not saying what I saw.

Crown: What happened when you went downstairs?

(No answer.)

Crown: What did you do next?

Mattie: I ... I heard things.

Crown: Where were the noises coming from?

Mattie: *(Witness whispers)* ... the family quarters.

Crown: But they were not used. The staff slept elsewhere.

Mattie: There were noises.

Crown: Tell us.

Mattie: *(Subject begins to sing a nursery rhyme and sways from side to side.)*

Crown: What did you hear?

Mattie: I lit a candle ... and stayed to the side of the stairs. The house was very dark.

Crown: Continue.

Mattie: Bumps. Then nothing. I went on. But I didn't smell anything until I got to the old wing.

Crown: Why did you go there if no one slept there?

Mattie: I had to.

Crown: Answer the question.

(Subject continues to sing.)

Crown: Please go on.

Mattie: I opened the door. *(Witness hesitates for several seconds.)* In each room, I saw a child. They were wearing old-fashioned clothes.

Crown: Did they speak?

Mattie: (*Screams obscenity.*) You are so 'ffing stupid! No. They were dead. A long time ago. Every one of them. Understand? There were no children on the island, just patients. Now, do you understand? They were dead. All of them. The dead Spencer children.

Crown: Why are you smiling?

Mattie: They were so sweet ... (*Witness laughs and hugs herself.*)

Crown: Nurse, please check the subject. Make sure she is coherent.

Mattie: Get away from me! I am not crazy. I know what I saw.

Crown: Which is?

Mattie: (*Witness whispers.*) Ghosts. I ran away. All the way to the cave and the rowboat.

Crown: Was anyone there?

Mattie: (*Laughs and curses.*) Just more dead people, all bleeding. The cook, Mrs. Healy. She looked funny. I pushed the boat out.

Crown: And then?

Mattie: I rowed and rowed ... toward where the sun rose in the sky. It was just getting light.

Crown: They found you ten miles from Grimsby. Unconscious.

Mattie: Iffin' you say so.

Crown: That is all that you remember?

Mattie: There's one thing you didn't ask.

Crown: Such as?

Mattie: Don't you want t' know who killed them all? *(Witness giggles, and then becomes hysterical. She does not appear to be able to stop ... Nurse shakes her until she quiets.)*

Crown: I am asking now. Who killed them?

Mattie: Come closer, and I will tell you.

Crown: Who?

Mattie: *(Witness whispers.)* Mrs. Spencer and her long sword.

Crown: Miss Hayes, she has been dead for more than a hundred years.

Mattie: *(Witness laughs.)* I never said she was alive. But she killed them.

June 13, year 1824   End of session: 22:30 hours

"She paints a powerful picture without trying to." Bartholomew gazed at the pile of propellers beyond Nemo's shoulder without seeing them. "Can you imagine the horror of what happened that night?"

Kang inhaled. "She had a clear memory. And, if true, this raises more questions. If we separate the deaths into two separate timeframes, it is easier to understand what happened to the Spencers and what happened to the inmates and staff of the asylum."

"Well ..." Bartholomew shot a nervous glance out the hangar door. "I heard that the large building next to the courtyard was used as the dorm for the sanitarium's orderlies. It sounds like we don't know if they were all killed."

Kang hesitated. "True. Where did Mattie and the rest of the house staff sleep?"

Celwyn shuffled papers until he found a map of the house. "In the old servants' quarters behind the kitchen. Which does not appear to match her testimony. Since you are about to ask," he shuffled through a different file, "there is confirmation here that in the 1600s, the Spencer children slept in the bedrooms on the first floor, just as the girl says in the transcript."

"So, the information Mr. Verne found was only partially correct." Kang tapped a finger on the table. "Spencer did not kill them, according to this report."

"It changes things, does it not?" Captain Nemo leaned back and closed his eyes. "Is the rest of the girl's story verified?"

Celwyn said, "Yes, now it is because of the broader amount of information. Including the six female inmates found murdered in the trees. There were three more bodies near there, just as the girl described."

"All by knife wounds?" Kang asked.

"Yes."

The big man appeared to be doing fairly well with the grisly subject matter, and his voice sounded steady as he asked, "What happened to the rest of the staff?"

"The girl Lucy was found on the third floor, just as Mattie described. From the condition of the dead male patients, it appeared they fought back and that an axe or sword was used on them." Celwyn checked the papers. "The cook and her helper were discovered, just as Miss Hayes reported."

Captain Nemo asked, "How many doctors and nurses were there?"

"Two each, plus orderlies. The two girls were helpers for the nurses. All except Mattie were found next to a remaining boat in the grotto. Knife wounds again. According to this article, the boat wasn't even untied before they died."

Kang studied him, finally asking, "What haven't you told us?"

Celwyn frowned. "Something that is hard to explain. Luckily, I have pictures." He dug into the pile and handed two drawings to them. "The first drawing is supposed to be of Mr. Spencer."

Bartholomew finished his perusal and pushed them across the table to Captain Nemo. "Doesn't this remind you a little bit of Jonas?"

After peering at the picture, Captain Nemo hesitated. "Possibly. The doublet would be appropriate for the late 1600s."

Kang held up the second drawing to the light. "This is much more recent. Early 1800s."

"Hold them together," Celwyn suggested.

Bartholomew's brows drew together as he studied the picture and handed it to Kang.

After Captain Nemo studied it, he said, "They do seem alike."

"The 1800s one is labeled as a doctor, Doctor Samuel, from the sanatorium." Kang continued scrutinizing the picture until he stopped and turned his attention to the magician.

"It isn't me; I assure you." After everyone waited for him to go on, thereby providing the drama the moment deserved, Celwyn said, "But it closely matches the chess piece dressed in bishop's vestments who lost his head the other day. I forgot to mention that during the attack, the piece had a different face than when I made it initially."

"Heavens!" Bartholomew exclaimed.

"There is more." Celwyn placed a third picture in front of them. "This picture is of the man that we saw dressed as the bishop; it is of John Spencer."

Kang whistled.

Bartholomew lined up all three pictures. He licked his lips but did not say anything more. From across the table, Nemo raised a brow, first at the automat, then the magician.

Celwyn said, "By all accounts, Mrs. Spencer keeps finding him and chopping off his head."

Verne shuddered. "Well, let us hope she doesn't take a dislike to the rest of us." Before he spoke, the author had been so quiet only Qing knew he sat there.

"Agreed. We will be vigilant." Nemo stared at Celwyn for a few seconds. "We haven't had a moment to discuss the newest oddity that has occurred, the wyvern. Do you consider it a danger to our enterprise?"

"Not really." The magician shrugged. "I do not know much about it other than talking about the creature sometimes brings it forth. I do not know why it is attracted to me."

"Just as well." Nemo chewed on his lip for a moment. "We shouldn't have to worry about it with all the activity here, not to mention the apparition you saw."

"True."

"We have seen the wyvern... once." Bartholomew's intake of breath indicated he remembered it well.

"Twice." Kang pointed. "It is as much of a showman as Jonas is."

Only feet away, the wyvern had arrived and swerved in and out of the windowless cabin of the flying machine. Celwyn thought its scales seemed more pronounced than usual and loved how its eyes shone a brilliant emerald green in the low light. Nemo stared at the creature, not moving.

"What does it want?" Bartholomew whispered.

"Unknown," Celwyn answered. "But it seems to enjoy the flying machine immensely." The wyvern twisted in the air above the craft and dove back inside.

"What will it do?" Nemo asked.

The magician shrugged again. "Sometimes, it listens to me." He turned toward it and said, "Come here."

The wyvern made another circuit through the cabin window, its tail slapping the side of the craft as it passed through, then floated down the side of the machine to the floor. It undulated back and forth in front of the engine parts, flipped on its side, and turned to the magician.

For minutes, they returned the regard until it faded away as if it had never been with them at all.

Chapter 30

Six weeks later
The platform of the train depot, Szczecin

JUST BEFORE THEY BOARDED THE *Elizabeth* for their return to Prague, Professor Kang murmured in an undertone, "Since we have done nothing dangerous or untoward and have shared everything with the others, we should have a pleasant journey back to Tellyhouse." He darted a hopeful glance at his wife and Annabelle conversing a few feet away in front of the train. Behind them, the loading of their luggage onto the train continued.

Celwyn nodded. He well-remembered the interrogation and chilly atmosphere after their disclosures about the dangers they had encountered. Instead, today, a most festive atmosphere accompanied them on this return trip as a breeze blew the spicy scent of oranges through the train's window. He handed off his bag to a new porter.

"We haven't been introduced. I am Jonas Celwyn."

The man bowed and said, "John Fellman, sir." The porter met his gaze head-on without any nervousness. Associating with the strange elements they encountered might put the man's equanimity to the test. Even more to his credit, the magician did not often perceive such honesty as what he saw in Fellman. He also appeared calm. The magician had a hunch no one had told him to expect unusual activities. In fact, he would have placed a wager on it.

As they moved into the main part of the dining room, Celwyn noted the man's military bearing and pronounced limp, probably from the war in Burma. Fellman sported little hair above his ears but owned a full, luxurious beard well-suited to a Bedouin tribal leader if he should ever visit them. Fellman stood at not more than five feet, which put him a bit shorter than Zander, and Otto, who continued to grow by the day. On this visit, Celwyn had won the bet on how much taller the boys had grown in the months they had been on Findbar Island.

While he produced his tea, Annabelle brought a cardboard box to the dining table and began handing out their mail that had accumulated at Tellyhouse. The *Elizabeth* gained speed, leaving the city behind in a cloud of steam. "We even have today's mail. It is a good thing Edward noticed the delivery before we left."

"Where is Edward?" Kang asked.

Patrick said, "He is in the kitchen helping Ricardo. They tend to get along very well."

The *Elizabeth* lurched around a bend, and they began their journey south. Annabelle handed the Professor a bundle of letters and a heavier package.

"I'm surprised there aren't more books being delivered, too." Elizabeth bestowed a fond glance on her husband.

Kang assumed a moue of virtue. "If there had been, they would be for the boys' classroom, of course." He scanned his first letter. "Bertham says the new dean of Egyptian studies is corrupt."

"Or, just not agreeing with him," Elizabeth said. "I remember Professor Bertham's opinions caused a certain level of controversy."

"Here you are, Uncle Celwyn." Annabelle handed him a small box wrapped in wax paper and tied with string. "The label is obviously written in a feminine hand. Perhaps it is from your friend, Miss McFein?" Annabelle's expression showed she teased him and didn't quite approve.

The magician heard her question and hesitated as he examined the package. He had only received one letter from Tara ... and none recently.

Everyone jumped when a shrill whistle pierced the air and faded again as another train continued down the track. Celwyn turned the box over. "Indeed." A most feminine hand had addressed the box to him. "It is." A thread of trepidation wiggled its way down his back. He used magic to undo the string around the box.

While Otto played scales on the pianoforte, Zander sat cross-legged on the floor in front of him and watched everyone. He sat up like a startled gopher. "Where did the string go?"

Celwyn pulled it out of his cup and blew it into a ball that rolled toward him. "Otto, that sounds wonderful. I can tell you've been practicing." The boy's smile acknowledged the compliment.

As the magician unwrapped the box, he did not say anything but felt a second wave of unease as he relived Tara's voice, her eyes, her touch. But something else came with it, riding on a miasma of dread.

Kang moved to sit beside him, perhaps sensing something amiss.

The box had a simple clasp. At about six inches square, it contained a small book covered in fine leather and etched in gold tooling. Celwyn remembered Tara's words, "A book is an intimate caress between those who share it." He missed her even more, knowing she had given this to him. As soon as he thought of touching it, his unease grew stronger.

Qing chose that moment to leave the window-sill and fly to him, settling on his shoulder. While the bird rubbed his ear with his beak and made guttural bird noises, the magician stroked his feathers and regarded the book, more than ever hesitant to touch it.

Bartholomew leaned over his shoulder. "Are you afraid there is a spell on it?"

Very astute observation, Celwyn thought. "Yes." Yet it should not, considering the book came from Tara. "If there is a spell, it is from another witch." He used magic to lift the book cover and held his breath as he read the inscription. The magician sat still for a long moment before reciting Tara's message aloud to the others. Before he began, he made sure the boys could not hear.

Dear Jonas,

> *I am writing to you in the hope you can call upon*

> *me. It seems I am suspected of treason and sit in the Tower of London at the moment.*

> *An acquaintance was kind enough to visit me here and send you this book. Please enjoy the poems and think of me.*

I am thinking of you,
Tara

When he finished, he said, "There are several things of note here. Before we discuss this further, would someone tell Conductor Smith I will be exiting the train at the next town, please?" He noted their expressions and added, "I'll take the local from there to Calais and cross the Channel."

"This is so sudden." As Elizabeth spoke, Annabelle's eyes filled with worry, and Patrick patted her hand.

Bartholomew strode to the kitchen door and disappeared. When he returned, he said, "We reach Schwedt in five minutes. You'd better talk fast."

"Thank you, an excellent suggestion." Celwyn considered the possible dangers and frowned at the box. "There are traces of another witch's hands on this book. Not Tara's." He turned to Kang. "I will be careful when I arrive in London, never fear." He held up a hand at Xiau's expression. "Like you said, I am only fearless for myself. For Tara, I will be much more prudent."

"Good." Elizabeth eyed him. "Have you ever been to the Tower of London?"

"Years ago."

"I see. Are you going to enter the country as someone else? This may be a trap, and they may be searching for you." She raised a brow at him.

Annabelle said, "I am so happy you asked that."

"I am also," Patrick agreed.

Celwyn shrugged. "It certainly is a worthy idea; in fact, a very good one." Qing flew across the room and landed in front of the magician again. His squawk sounded louder than usual. Celwyn patted his back. "He knows I am leaving. You will take him with you to Findbar when you return there?" he asked Bartholomew.

"Of course." The big man shot a glance at Annabelle. "He isn't exactly a popular guest at Tellyhouse."

Kang had been silent ever since Celwyn opened the box. He stared at the book inside it. "Are you taking that with you?"

"Yes." Celwyn used magic to re-wrap the box. "And I will send telegrams to Tellyhouse and Nemo as things develop." He stood. "Nemo may end up meeting me in Calais on his way to Findbar when I return."

Bartholomew's attention stayed on the box. "You are very optimistic, Jonas."

"I need to get ready." The magician patted him on the shoulder. "Conveniently, my bags are still packed."

As he started toward the compartment door, Kang confronted him, hands on his hips. "Should Bartholomew and I go with you?"

Elizabeth's breath caught, but she did not say anything.

Bartholomew rumbled, "We are both ready to assist, as usual."

"You just want a chance to shoot some villains again, my friend," Celwyn teased the big man. "Thank you, but please continue your visit. I will let you know how things turn out."

"We'll advise Captain Nemo of where you've gone." Bartholomew sighed. "And perhaps we will have the new prototype completed by the time you return."

"The entire idea is upsetting, and I do not like it." The Professor tramped to the windows and back. "But I know you must go."

⌒‿⌒

Less than three days later, Celwyn crossed the Channel on a quaint vessel dubbed the *Eloise Marie*. She seemed a buoyant and happy craft, both in stability and choice of paint color. To ensure his trip would be memorable, she had been filled to the gills with scores of lively children and their parents on holiday.

Once inside his cabin, he realized he had not had time since his hurried departure off the *Elizabeth* to really study the book—*if* it came from Tara in the first place.

The magician detected notes of her perfume, and the wording in the letter came from her. Yet, something unsettling covered the message, like the faint odor of cream left in the sun too long. There was more. His sense of danger had been triggered when he discovered a malicious coyness overlying the book, which was very much unlike Tara. If anything, the condition of the book reminded him of Ginnie, the voluptuous witch who had toyed with them at the compound in Turkey. With a private shrug, Celwyn could admit he preferred that Ginnie had been the one to kill everyone there, not Pelaez. A tiny part of him still loved his brother.

The magician had purposely avoided thinking about the massacre in Turkey, and he was not ready to now. Yet, like a snake slithering through grass, an unwanted question came to him; what if both were responsible? He tried to remember every word or glance exchanged between his brother and Ginnie.

Celwyn growled under his breath and went back to contemplating the book he had placed on the petite table. Other than the bunk, it was the only furniture in the cabin. Whoever had decorated the cubicle had a fear of gentle colors. The

Eloise's cheerful purple wallpaper tried to distract him. Keeping to the theme, the ship itself could be seen from miles away with its peacock-blue smoke-stacks and gaily painted hull that reminded him of an English garden.

Although nearly fall, the *Eloise* chugged along, with the hordes of cheerful weekenders crowding her decks and braving the rain. Considering the thinness of the ship's walls, it surprised him that he could concentrate at all.

The magician sipped tea while the boat wiggled its way up each swell and down again. Although light filtering through the cabin's porthole dimmed as darker clouds moved overhead, Celwyn was not concerned. Since they had been underway for over an hour, with only thirty-odd miles between Calais and the London docks, they'd arrive before dusk.

Under the decreasing light, the box and book lay in shadow, a condition he had not seen them in before. Confirming Celwyn's suspicions, several fin-gerprints blackened the leather box, and even more covered the book. In his estimation, either a large-handed woman, which Tara was not, or a man had handled the items.

"Well, well," he muttered as he used magic to move the book closer and open it. *La Sagesse des Mots* was published by the Holistic Press of Amsterdam in 1845. Without touching it, he turned the fron-tispiece page and raised a brow. The picture of the poet Robert Mensonges seemed somewhat familiar, as if he had met the man, although he could not recall doing so.

At times like this, he missed the wisdom of the well-read: Kang, Elizabeth, or Bartholomew would know more about the poet, being much more literary-minded than he. Annabelle had never thought about poetry, instead developing excellent poker skills and an acumen for haberdashery shopping. According to Patrick, if a book was not a war story, it was not worth reading, which left out poetry.

Over the next twenty minutes, the magician read Mensonges's prose leading up to page seventeen and the poem Tara had mentioned. Outside his cabin, the rain changed from a whisper to a tantrum, beating a steady staccato on the tin roof of the *Eloise*. Through the lowering clouds, the cliffs of Dover became visible.

As the seas roughened and the rain worsened, he brought forth a quartet of horns playing *Die Walkure*, Wagner's march to victory for the Valkyries. He did so to keep his mood as buoyant as he hoped the boat would be. When he turned the next page and read the poem in front of him, it seemed important, but he did not know why. Yet.

Espérer

In love, there is danger, there is pain.
The ancients conquered their surprise at
finding another person they care about
more than life itself.
Beware! How treacherous the waters
they must be?

Interesting. Celwyn discovered a few of the telltale fingerprints on the poem, but he only found Tara's on the word "love." A variety of prints had appeared on the pages leading up to the text that Tara had wanted him to read.

The magician blinked in pleased surprise. Tara returned his affections! He certainly hoped he could rescue her from the danger she was in and tell her he felt the same.

He waved a hand, inviting a light breeze to flip through the rest of the pages. No other fingerprints appeared. In contrast, Tara's note had so many he could hardly read her message now. Most telling seemed to be the faint odor of cloves from some of the fingerprints. Impossible! He dismissed the thought. The individual that cloves reminded him of was long dead under the Arctic Sea.

'The game is afoot,' as the learned bard says. The magician readied his disguise. With luck, the *Eloise* would bump into the dock soon. Already he could spy tall ships at anchor and overloaded barges moving upriver.

Celwyn thought about what all this could mean as he used magic to pack the book and its paper into a hole in the cabin wall and shove the bunk in front of it. The owner of the malignant fingerprints would find that tracking Jonas Celwyn had just become a regularly scheduled activity as the ship traveled the route back and forth across the Channel.

Chapter 31

THE BLACKWALL REACH DOCKS HAD a certain charm if one enjoyed the smell of rotting fish and the varieties of strong perfumes favored by the painted ladies decorating the pier. Further to the south, dockhands unloaded containers from an army of freighters of the West India Lines.

"My goodness, aren't you a tall, dark one?" One of the women, with a man-sized physique, straightened from her languid drape over the rail next to the water. "And handsome, too."

"He is as old as he looks, Maude," a rotund blonde told her. "That white hair just makes him d'tinguished." She laughed and sidled up to the magician. "We could have some fun, t'ou."

Celwyn managed a smile and peered through the drizzle to verify that the porter he had hired to transport his trunk kept up. Satisfied, he regarded the shorter prostitute. In her thoughts, he heard a worry about a boy named Jack and how he wanted new shoes. "Madam, I have no need of your services, but you'll find that when they open tomorrow, Gadsby's on Wharton Street will have a pair of shoes waiting for your son, Jack. What is his last name?"

"D ... Draper..." Her open mouth exposed many missing teeth.

"Thank you," Celwyn said and stepped around her, reminding himself to leave a few other things for her by way of his hotel concierge. As he continued toward the street, he heard man-sized Maude say, "For a darkie, he sure is a nice one."

Celwyn controlled the urge to educate her further, instead scanning the crowd for signs of witches or anyone else who seemed to be scrutinizing the arriving passengers too closely. When he attained the other side of the street, he accosted the first hire cab he saw and climbed in. "You may drop me in Norwich at the *Gazette* office. After that, please take my trunk to Claridge's Hotel."

Chapter 32

THROUGHOUT THE REST OF THE DAY, the magician sat in the basement of various newspaper offices, reading about the rumors, history, and facts of the Tower. His assault must wait until dark. He especially enjoyed the older accounts of the ravens of the Tower, knowing much more about them than the tabloids did. Architectural maps, the weather forecast, and other periodicals completed his reading.

When he finished his research, he traveled to his hotel to send a series of telegrams. The missives all read alike: *"Arrived safely in London."*

By now, Bartholomew or Kang, or both, would have told Nemo where he had gone and why. After he sent the telegrams, he arranged with the concierge to deliver a collection of coats, books, and shoes for Maude's son.

The sun had finished its descent by the time Celwyn walked the last few blocks to the docks in front of the Tower.

The area around the Traitor's Gate had a forlorn and forbidding atmosphere which was not improved by the spiked gate itself installed long ago as a deterrent to those who tried to escape. It was a pleasant evening and moderately crowded; one moment, onlookers would have seen a tall, well-dressed black man strolling near the water. In the next second, they saw no one as Celwyn slipped behind the block wall and, as a sleek pipefish, swam through the moat.

He traveled as fast as he could past trash and other unspeakable debris, including a derelict rowboat listing to one side. Every inch of the water was littered with indescribable filth. The magician began to regret this method of entry. If Xiau were here, he would be most vocal, and sarcastic, about what Celwyn must have been thinking.

The magician avoided most of the disgusting debris until he reached the front of Develin Tower, where he continued forward to slip between the grates and into the second moat. There, he saw what he had been expecting and hoping for—an opening under the wall.

As he swam against the outgoing water, he fought the urge to gag and kept going. The architectural drawings had been correct; an overflow of the moat's uppermost basin eventually emptied here, only steps from the White Tower building.

By the time Celwyn reached the other side and shook off the water, he'd changed into a fly and congratulated himself on his sense of caution. Yes, he could have flown in without all this bother, but he needed an alternate escape route for Tara if need be. Even if he preferred not to think about it, he had to consider that she might be hurt, and being out in the open, he'd have a harder time protecting her. Another reason for caution? If he used magic to escape, their enemy would know he had arrived in town and be forewarned for future confrontations. Celwyn loved surprises.

His precautions paid off. The magician found confirmation of his vigilance as he lost count of the armed guards who patrolled—not just in pairs, but in quartets—in every direction. Either someone important was being held here, or this was a preparation for his arrival. As he flew by the guards, upon nearly all of them, he discovered a wisp of the telltale danger he had detected in the book and box. If the magician had simply come over the rag-stone walls, whoever was behind this would know he had accepted their invitation. Dozens more guards occupied the two-story keep where they stood elbow to elbow with field glasses trained on the grounds below. *Was Tara the reason for the extreme security?* Or, perhaps, she was not the only unwilling guest in the Tower.

Answers to why she was here could only come from Tara. He must find her.

Still, as a most handsome fly, Celwyn stayed about a dozen feet above the ground around the Tower perimeter. He flew too high for the guards to detect him in the gathering gloom and kept close to the walls, avoiding the vents and windows. As he went, the magician's mood grew darker. The danger he sensed seemed much stronger here. *Was a wizard, or a witch, behind this?*

He passed by a window from which harpsichord music rang, and his heart caught as if gripped by an iron fist that wouldn't let go.

Then he heard nothing.

If Tara was held here just as a formality or if she was revered in good standing, they would have placed her in the more opulent third-floor apartments where unlucky kings had stayed on occasion. King Edward I lived here for a time. However, if the Crown considered Miss Tara McFein dangerous, she would be kept in the basement dungeons. Instead, she had been imprisoned in between these extremes.

It neared the dinner hour, and the sun had taken a bow, leaving ribbons of gold, red, and deep blue across the horizon. In an evening pregnant with intrigue, the smell of wood-burning fires rode the breeze down the Thames.

As he passed over a group of guards, he heard the rumble of their laughter, then their words. It seemed unkind fates awaited several of the prisoners. Also, it surprised him that the Cardinal of Exeter had fallen out of favor and languished here. The guards did not think the Cardinal would leave here alive.

Celwyn circled until he once again hovered by the window where the harpsichord music had come from. It came again, ringing with beautiful intent. As the notes began to sound familiar, his breath caught. Someone played the music he had written for Tara, the same music he performed for her the last night they were together. Could it be anyone but her at the harpsichord? Only the occupants of the *Nautilus* had heard it.

He rested on a chipped brick just underneath the window and the source of the music. From within the room, he detected two heartbeats and something odd he couldn't name—perhaps a ticking sound. Sometimes subtlety is called for; he sent the next line of the music inside to answer and harmonize with the harpsichord.

With caution, he lifted his wings and rose to hover in front of the window.

His heart raced.

On the far side of a room, past the velvet furniture, antiques, and woven rugs, Tara sat behind a concert-sized harpsichord. Dried blood streaked her face from her hairline to her chin. Fresh tears fell from those remarkable eyes. Hearing his music, she stood and yelled, "Run!"

But Celwyn had already flown toward her, transforming back to himself. A small mechanical man with too long hair and elfin ears arose behind her. He held a knife to her throat. Talos, the automat—Kang's brother—faced him, his artificial face a picture of triumph.

As the magician lifted a hand to send Talos flying, something fast and shiny came at him from the side. He ducked and dived under the harpsichord, hearing the clatter of a knife against the wood. In the next second, he yanked Talos off his feet and under the harpsichord. Celwyn pivoted, flipping Talos in front of him as once again someone attacked, this time hitting Talos, the clang of metal-on-metal echoing across the room.

Celwyn remembered how strong Talos could be and wasted no time using the automat as a shield as he pushed back hard, driving whoever assaulted them backward. Then it suddenly stopped, the silence ominous.

Tara—

"Jonas..." She did not sound frightened, but she put all the warning she could into her voice.

Lying on his side and cringing from the stench of cloves, the magician tightened his hold on the automat as he peered around Talos's leathery cheek. But the only thing he saw was a well-made boot a few feet away. That was enough.

Celwyn inhaled, and violins entered the room, exploding with the same five notes as his magic intensified, becoming extreme and strong. The magician exhaled, blowing out the candles in the room. As he incapacitated Talos, Celwyn dressed him in the same handsome green jacket that he wore, silenced him, and pushed him out from under the instrument again. As soon as Talos cleared the bottom of the harpsichord, something lifted him high in the air. Tara screamed and fell to the floor on the other side of the instrument. Without speaking, Celwyn pulled her close, reassuring her in a silent whisper. A faint smile creased her lips.

The violins grew louder as the magician rolled toward the wall. He stood in time to see the back of a stranger as he pinned Talos, who he thought was the magician, to a wall with the point of his sword. In the semi-darkness, Talos struggled in his grip, unable to tell him he was not the magician.

Celwyn did not try anything fancy, not with Tara in danger. He miniaturized them both, and, hand in hand, they fled through a mouse hole in the wall behind the harpsichord, moving around several rooms and following the scent of the city that had seeped into the building. He blew open another hole, letting in the sounds of the night. As they ran through it, he tucked Tara under his chin. She clung to his neck as he lifted his wings, the black wings of a raven. Irrationally, he realized he really had come to like ravens, despite that damned Duncan.

He circled the Tower once, hovering in front of the window long enough to see the profiles of the two attackers. Talos stood in front of the window arguing with a large man who had turned to walk away. Celwyn could not see his face. No matter. There would be a time and a place, the magician promised himself.

Minutes later, he landed behind a sizeable tomb in the Nunhead cemetery, that of Sir Charles Frende, who had led the Queen's armies to victory in Spain.

When they were themselves again, the first thing Celwyn did was take Tara's face in his hands. He wiped the blood away as he embraced her, and she shivered in his arms. He asked, "Are you cold?" He did not think vampires could be.

She clung to him and shook her head. The magician kissed the top of her forehead and drew her nearer, inhaling her closeness. She felt so precious to him. Over the next few minutes, he repaired the tears to her dress and did his best with her disheveled hair. It would be best if she did not encounter a mirror for a while.

Tara glanced beyond the army of tombs to the gaslights that twinkled outside the cemetery. "We're about three miles from the Tower."

Above the tombstones, the moon glowed like a milky yellow orb through the shroud of smoke over the city. It painted the cemetery with enough light that Celwyn could verify they were alone. For minutes, he held her close as they stood in a cocoon of silence and intimacy. A distant siren echoed across rooftops along with the clomping of hooves and creaking of coach wheels on the cobblestones of Consort Road, reminding him they were not truly alone.

"May I suggest we enjoy some refreshment while we discuss what has happened?" He bowed her forward, and with her hand on his arm, they walked between the rows of graves toward the street. As they went along, Tara still shivered. Celwyn thought it best not to have her relive what had happened just yet, no matter how curious he felt. However, he could distract and reassure her. "I have a story to tell you that will explain some of this unpleasantness. I do not know what all is behind it, though."

She squeezed his hand, and they stepped off the curb, around aromatic slush, and across Brayards Road.

"About two years ago, I happened to be in San Francisco when a priest asked if I would board a ship, the *Zelda,* sailing the next day. That man was the smaller of our two attackers just now, and he wasn't a priest. His name is Talos, and he wanted me to subdue his brother Professor Xiau Kang, another automat who you know."

The magician stopped, sniffed the air, and scanned the street. Satisfied that he could not detect any warlocks or similar creatures. Tara did the same, her nose being more acute. After her nod, he continued. "Eventually, I discovered it was Talos who was filled with evil intent, not Xiau. When the ship encountered a severe storm, the gales blew her into the ice fields of the Artic, and the situation escalated."

Celwyn checked Tara's eyes. They showed interest in his tale, not anxiety. He congratulated himself—perhaps his story succeeded in distracting her from her fear.

"To summarize, I used magic to subdue and kill Talos. Then I trapped the hundreds of automats that he had brought with him."

A frown creased her smooth skin. "How did you trap them?"

"After a well-placed explosion, their ship became encased in ice, turning it into a frozen tomb." The magician developed his own frown. "You probably wonder why Talos is alive now. Each of the automats has a metal disk about the size of your hand that powers them. It is embedded in their chest. I tossed Talos's into the ocean, along with his body." He cursed under his breath. "Apparently, someone found him."

"It is probably Captain Dearing, the pirate king whom you almost met just now." When Celwyn raised a brow, she added, "If Dearing was in that area, I imagine he salvaged Talos."

Or... perhaps the pirate had been Talos's client all along. As Celwyn considered that unpleasant connection, they walked briskly past a pile of rags and a beggar who suddenly found his cup filled with silver. Before they reached the pub on the corner, they had to sidestep a group of men in front. Celwyn stared them down, and they backed up.

"To continue, you probably wonder what Talos wanted of Xiau and me. Back in San Francisco, Talos had said he wanted to take his brother to Junstan Island in the South China Sea. Even at that point, his intentions could have been centered on the confounded flying machine, but I doubt it."

Across the street, two coaches raced by, the drivers whipping their horses until they foamed at the mouth, their eyes wild. Celwyn growled under his breath, sending the whips flying into the night. The drivers followed the whips into the air with surprised shrieks that echoed as they disappeared.

With a nod of approval, she asked, "I'm assuming there is a great deal of money involved if that venture is successful?"

"Yes."

"Then that would account for Dearing's interest. He is fond of money and intricate plots."

"And Talos is fond of lying." Celwyn turned to the pub in front of them. The Mallard had the enigmatic and mysterious facade of all 17th-century London pubs: a tiny sign swinging above heavy oak doors and windows too small and dark to see through. The smell of stale hops oozed through the wood.

As they stepped inside, an urgent thought belatedly occurred to the magician. "We have to warn Xiau and the others." He escorted Tara around several groups of inebriated customers to a table. "One moment, please." He reversed his path and strode to the bar. A whiskey should steady Tara's nerves. He tapped his fingers on the bar while he waited to be noticed.

The publican fit perfectly with the snug's atmosphere. Along with a bulbous drinker's nose that took up most of his face, he had borrowed St. Nick's red cheeks. Most observers would also notice the man's large working hands capable of throwing out the most obnoxious drinker.

"Good evening. What will it be?"

"Two whiskies, please. May I ask where the nearest telegraph office is located?" Celwyn placed coins on the countertop.

Although he hadn't any hair to scratch, the publican scratched as he thought. "There are several over in the Farringdon district." He regarded Celwyn with the kind of polite speculation he probably reserved for strangers. "You would know that is about a fifteen-minute walk to the north."

Celwyn suspected that the man tested him and did not do a good job of it. "Farringdon is much further away, sir." The magician smiled at him.

"So it is, so it is." The publican slid the drinks across the bar top. "I do believe there is a telegraph desk at Elmer and Sons Greengrocer's. A block down the street." He thumbed the air to his right.

Celwyn nodded. "When do they close?"

"Lemme see." The publican consulted his pocket watch. "Another hour, maybe less."

Which meant any minute. "Thank you." The magician thought a bit about the man's attempt at misdirection. It could have been out of habit ... or something else.

After Celwyn set the drinks on their table, he told Tara, "We must send a telegram as soon as possible. Drink up, please."

"I should send one to Miss Redifer's hotel also," Tara said as she sipped.

"You made a face of distaste. The whiskey—"

"No, it is fine. I just do not want the rest of it." She allowed Celwyn to help her back into her cloak.

He asked, "Have you told Valentine of possible danger?"

Months ago, her uncle, and head of their vampire family, had participated in the foray into the catacombs of Capuchin in pursuit of the magician's father. His other niece, Miss Redifer, had accompanied them. It had been a memorable adventure.

They stepped outside into the evening air, still fragrant with sweet horse manure and burning coal, and the sounds of frivolity in Piccadilly Square. Shaking her head, she said, "Because that was how those men forced me to send for you. They already hold Valentine hostage."

"Damn."

She started trembling again. "Would you care to hear all about it now?"

Celwyn did not want to upset her further. "I must, so I can help resolve this. Will they harm Valentine because you have escaped?"

She snuggled closer into the shelter of his arm. "I do not think so. From what I can tell, they will not harm him until they have you. He will be destroyed afterward." In a voice he hadn't heard yet, she added, "I hope he tears them up."

Her last remark caused him to smile. So soft, feminine, and deadly. His perfect woman.

Chapter 33

A S THEY WALKED, OTHER EVENING strollers kept them company. Some with children, others in pairs and enjoying a night on the town. The man in a handsome topcoat in front of them smoked a pipe so fragrant Celwyn had to resist asking him where he purchased his tobacco.

Tara began her tale slowly, with her voice unsteady, but by the time they reached the barrels of flowers and bins of cabbage in front of Elmer's, she had calmed down and spoke with her usual confidence.

"After I left you in Florence, I traveled here without incident. For the next several months, I spent my time answering the Queen's questions and whims. Some of what I told her, I invented since I did not know the answers. She is an inquisitive and justifiably suspicious woman."

With really bad teeth, if Celwyn remembered correctly. He steered Tara away from the other patrons until they stood alone in an aisle beside an oversize basket of apples. "I have heard that about her."

"Just so," she said as she selected an apple and inspected it. "The day before this unpleasantness, I had been given my next assignment: spy on the King of Prussia and report on his navy and their intentions. The day before I was to leave, the Royal guards arrested me. Two days later, they came back to the Tower to bring formal charges of treason."

"Allow me to guess. The charges came from information supplied by Talos or Captain Dearing?"

"Yes, it could be either. There was something odd, too."

Celwyn had almost reached the end of his patience with the situation, too irritated to control his voice. "Such as?"

She inhaled and snuck a nervous glance at him. "I also had another assignment not connected to the Crown. So far, I hadn't done much with it, but," she stared at him, "it is possible I was followed and reported because of it."

"Can you explain?"

"It will take a while." She vouchsafed him a small smile. "And best done in quiet circumstances after we've settled for the night." The smile won. "I hope you enjoy Victorian poetry."

"I appreciate it even more now." Celwyn thought about the book she had sent him, no longer as irritated, just enjoying her as a woman of mystery.

"In the Tower, I was told to call the smaller man with the tiny ears Mr. Brown. The other man never introduced himself, but I heard Talos calling him 'Captain.' I'd seen a picture of Dearing before."

Celwyn took the apple from her fingers and brought her hand to his mouth for a kiss. "We're about to have company. Please continue."

As promised, an austere man in a rather worn coat sidled closer to them. Celwyn sent him a silent message; a reduced price on potatoes could be found inside the grocers. Not a second passed before the man about-faced and entered the establishment. The magician changed the sign over the potato bin in the store and added coins to the man's pocket.

"And our attacker in the Tower?"

"Captain Dearing was rather proud of himself, not caring if I knew who he really was." She touched the bruise on her forehead. "That was my first clue that they intended to kill us and not leave witnesses."

The magician did not want to tell her he thought the same. "I didn't see his face as we escaped. But that name is somewhat familiar."

She nodded. "He is extraordinarily strong and fast, and his knife work is legendary."

"That accounts for how he attacked me. If I had been more prudent, I would have made a more circumspect entrance." Though, at that moment, all he could think about was the danger to Tara. "I should have eliminated them."

"Then we wouldn't know where they took Valentine."

"True."

"You got us safely out of there." She leaned her head against his chest.

Celwyn did not voice his growing conclusion that between his fascination with Tara and friendship with Xiau and Bartholomew, his natural aggression seemed to be abating. *Good grief.* He hated it when the automat was right.

"Still, it could have been a more elegant exit and perhaps something other than a retreat." The magician berated himself silently. "Please describe Dearing. I saw him in profile only."

"About your age and height, quite hirsute. Fancies himself an aristocrat, judging from his affected mannerisms." Tara regarded him for a moment. "Thales's 'gifts' to you are wearing off, aren't they?"

"Yes." Celwyn shrugged. "I still have the strength but can't predict anything about to happen. At least I retain some of the enhanced eyesight." He ushered her inside the establishment, beyond baskets of cabbages and an impressive number of pickle barrels, to the telegraph desk in the far corner. On a stool, a clerk slept against the wall with a visor pulled low over his eyes.

The magician dragged the pad of telegrams closer and began writing. Tara read as he wrote.

Xiau and Bartholomew,

> *I have rescued my book lover. Your brother has been retrieved from the Arctic Ocean, alive and well. He looks*

exactly as before. He is after you. Take extreme precautions.

Your brother is partnered with Captain Dearing, a dangerous pirate king. Do not draw attention to Tellyhouse. You are safer where your new tools are kept. Go there as soon as you can.

Request the crew travel in disguise and take varied and circumspect routes when they retrieve supplies for where you'll be.

It is up to you and Bartholomew for how much to tell Tellyhouse. But you must warn them.

More tomorrow.
Your friend and tea lover.

"That is very 'circumspect,' and I admire your craftiness. Who is Mrs. Spencer? Should I be jealous?"

"A nasty ghost on Findbar Island."

"Oh."

"Let's get you settled in a comfortable room for the night." Celwyn straightened the collar of her cloak. "When we emerge outside, you'll find you have developed red hair and a much larger nose."

She laughed. "And my face?"

Celwyn tried to contain his laughter. "Much rounder with an adorable birthmark on your chin."

"Oh..." She glanced down. "My hips are suddenly much larger, also."

"I enjoy a voluptuous woman." He winked at her.

Tara bestowed on him her version of Kang's eye roll as she held his arm and stepped outside. When they reached the cobblestones, she gasped.

"My, you have aged."

The magician agreed. He had adopted the disguise he had last used in Turkey; that of a doddering elderly academic. "I perfected a shuffle, also." He moved to the left, turned, and shuffled back again. "As you can see. Come along, dearie."

Chapter 34

THEY FOUND A FINE HOTEL OFF Fenwick Road. The façade had been painted a pale blue with black shutters and trim. The style appeared Georgian to Celwyn's untrained eye. A succession of well-to-do patrons came and went as they stood there. When the carriage that brought them rolled away again, Celwyn added a few pieces of luggage at their feet. "It wouldn't do to arrive without bags and draw attention to ourselves."

They checked in as Professor Tinkerton and his niece. As a porter led the way upstairs, they passed upholstered chairs, overstuffed dowagers, well-fed bankers, and potted ferns waving graceful tendrils at them. Celwyn inquired about the Chrysanthemum Hotel's dining room.

"It will be available for another two hours, sir." The porter bowed them into their suite and asked if he should send someone up to help his niece unpack.

"No, thank you." Celwyn tipped the porter and closed the door after him. He turned to Tara. "Are you hungry?"

"Ravenous. They only fed me occasionally."

The magician approached where she stood in front of the windows. He closed the drapes. "We don't know who may be watching." As he pulled back her hood, he admired his work. "Your hair looks marvelous. I should kiss you to make sure this is really you."

"Yes, you should."

After their embrace, he excused himself, promising to return. He took a circuitous route to the kitchen, wrapped in invisibility. Once there, he selected a portion of raw steak for her. Just a tidbit to stave off her hunger for now.

Later, over new potatoes in parsley and cream and more rare steaks, they enjoyed a bottle of wine and the intimacy of being together. It was not until his potatoes were nearly gone that he asked her a more serious question. "Are you recovered enough to tell me more of your ordeal?"

She sucked on a morsel of her beef and discreetly put the remainder on her plate. "By tomorrow, I should be much better. This," she indicated the meal, "helps greatly."

"Having the dining room to ourselves is also useful for keeping our business confidential." Celwyn checked the waiters by the kitchen door, who stacked dishes and talked in murmurs. "By the way, Nemo's crew picks up their telegrams on Tuesdays. After they read what I sent, they will probably go back for more messages every day until they have been brought up to date on our situation. The same applies for Tellyhouse."

"I want to hear about Findbar Island, but first, let's get my report out of the way." She sipped wine and finished with a deep breath. "Like I said, on my second day in the Tower, the Queen's men arrived to read the charges against me. At the time, I felt thankful for one thing; if they intended to hang me, they would have left me in the basement in chains. The apartments at the top floor are quite comfortable."

"At least, there is that."

Tara sighed. "It did not remain so."

The magician felt his anger at Kang's brother growing as she continued. "First, that odious man, Talos, just walked in, and the guard left again, locking the door. Talos questioned me for a long time. Everything he did displayed his arrogance."

"When I knew him, that was my impression, also."

"He reeked of cloves." She made a face. "I'd like to know more about him." She hesitated as a waiter arrived to serve cake decorated with berries and to refill their coffee cups. When he left again, she said, "This is good. I wondered if I would have coffee again." She smiled. "With the breadth of my new hips, perhaps I shouldn't consider any cake, even if I wanted it."

"Do you realize that you are the first vampire I have ever dined with?"

"You should make a habit out of it."

She was also so unlike every vampire he had known. She had kindness and gentleness, too. Celwyn liked the way her eyes twinkled at him and her sense of humor. "I could do without myself—"

"No, no. Enjoy your dessert." She waved a graceful hand. "Over the last few days, Talos became frustrated at the lack of substance in my answers. At first, I thought he'd been sent by the Queen when he had not. It didn't take long for his questions to veer toward you and the Professor. Not subjects of espionage. He did not mention Captain Nemo or Bartholomew." She thought for a minute. "He never met them, did he?"

"We disposed of Talos about two months before I met Bartholomew and long before encountering Captain Nemo in Singapore."

He recalled what had occurred on Ijis Island in the Bering Sea about ten years ago. Or was it further south? "Wasn't this pirate the one who terrorized the China Sea?"

"Correct." Tara frowned, and her anger at the situation returned, lighting the fire in her eyes. "Dearing has a wide net of interests and vast wealth."

"He is human, not an automat," Celwyn stated with certainty.

"Yes." She seemed to retreat into herself, reliving her ordeal. Celwyn held her hand, realizing how small it seemed in his own. "When Talos kept asking about you and received nothing, he became angry. At that point, Dearing arrived." Her gaze dropped to her lap. "His approach was much different."

Celwyn's anger caused their water glasses to shake and slosh onto the table. "He hit you."

"Yes, but I have been hit before." Her chin came up. "Then, he suddenly stopped and smiled. A ghastly sight, I can assure you."

Celwyn put both hands over hers. "Perhaps we should stop and talk of this later."

She shook her head. "Through it all, it seemed like he was an actor on stage, and the performance was just for me." Her voice wobbled. "Then he slowly produced a lock of Valentine's hair. He showed me my uncle's ring—the one you saw. He made it clear Valentine would die in a short while if I did not write the message asking you to come." A tear escaped from those fine eyes.

He frowned. "I wonder how he knew of our association."

In answer, she raised her brows.

"Knowing I can take care of myself, you agreed to do as they asked and hoped that I would find Valentine? I understand." Celwyn wanted to assure her of his earnestness. With a fingertip, he raised her chin until she looked at him again. "I understand your allegiance to your family and would have been offended if you didn't turn to them, and me, in times of danger."

The waiters hovered by the kitchen door, polishing silverware, trying not to stare, and most likely waiting for them to leave so they could close for the evening. Tara noticed them. "Two more things; tonight, Dearing hit me until I played the harpsichord, saying they knew you liked music. They were ready for you. I so hoped that the song you wrote would warn you somehow."

The magician finished his wine. "If I'd been thinking normally, it would have. The second thing?"

"A few days ago, they blindfolded me, and then a woman came into the room with Talos. I could hear the taffeta of her skirts rustling as she walked and smelled her perfume. It sounded like she fussed with the book and the box on the table Talos had brought with him. She was a witch."

Celwyn pulled back her chair as he thought about who the woman could be who'd been in the room. Who did Talos know?

After they went upstairs, they sat on the suite's settee, immersed in their thoughts and each other. Celwyn found the settee damned uncomfortable but did not mind Tara's closeness. Just as he began describing Nemo's compound in Turkey and his brother's antics, she developed a most delicate snore and fell asleep in his arms.

Before the sun had warmed the sky on the morrow, Celwyn had composed another telegram to Xiau and Bartholomew. As Tara came into the living area of the suite, she patted a yawn and adjusted the bodice of a lovely lace dress.

"You make a fine dressmaker, Jonas. And the shoes fit very well. Could you let out the dress a bit up here?"

He did so. "Now?"

"Much better, thank you. I can breathe."

"Coffee or tea?" He stood until she sat across from him and smoothed her skirts.

"I will have what you have. Thank you." She held up a piece of the hotel's stationery.

"A draft of the next telegram to Xiau that we'll send right after breakfast. Your thoughts would be appreciated."

"All right." She read it with a frown.

Xiau & Bartholomew:

>*Do not come here. There is another development.*

>*I will stay in London until I free our friend with the gorgeous silver hair. My book lover is safe.*

>*Please ask the Captain to watch Qing for me for a bit longer. You might want to donate some cufflinks to his entertainment.*

>*Again, do not come to London. It is too dangerous.*

Sincerely,
Earl Grey

"What do you think?" he asked.

Tara stared at the telegram. "I admire your adorable sign-off and foresight. But perhaps you should go there to protect them while I find Valentine?"

"Yes, and no." Celwyn sipped his tea and thought a moment. "If you were a dastardly villain, would you be watching the docks to see if I'm leaving the scene? Or assume I am on my way to Prague? I wager they will eventually know about Tellyhouse, and I plan to write to them about that in more detail. Xiau and Bartholomew will warn them, too. If I do not, I will never hear the end of it."

Tara could not help a grin as he poured more tea. She added a lump of sugar to her cup but no milk.

The magician continued, "Or would the villains split their forces in two in order to have some of them watch the docks while the others journey to Prague to watch over Tellyhouse?"

Tara tapped her lips with a thoughtful finger, and Celwyn could not stop admiring her lips as she did so. "It would depend on the villains. I do not know either one of them."

"I will tell you more of Talos in a moment, but first, I'd like to make a supposition."

"Go on."

"Let us assume that Talos believes I will go to Xiau. That is what he wants, so he will convince himself of it." The magician's expression displayed a high level of certainty and amusement. "That leaves us with an excellent opportunity to rescue Valentine."

"Ah." She sat back in her chair. "Most interesting. And they may assume I am too frightened to do something about their treatment." She touched the bruise on her cheekbone.

"I can fix—"

"No, it is a reminder to be more cautious next time."

"As you wish," he said. Tara reminded him of himself sometimes, which was another thing he admired about her.

"You could kiss it; that would make it better."

Celwyn did as requested and moved to kiss her lips.

She caressed his temple and sighed. "As you expected, I agree that we find Valentine first and then take a circumspect way out of London."

The magician cocked his head to the side. "As much as I enjoy your company, I will not put you in danger. Our little party in the catacombs was forced upon me."

"I remember. Yet could I really stay here if I was suspected of treason? I must clear my name as part of this."

Drat. Her logic reminded him of the automat. Celwyn poured a third cup of tea. "It isn't a quandary, per se. We do have choices. Last night you enjoyed your raw steak but little else and still seem a bit wan." He studied her. "Perhaps I could take a walk to the butcher shop and find something for you while you think about where and how we'll find Valentine?"

"That would be lovely, but before you go, remember I promised to tell you of my other activities."

She did so, and by the time she finished, the magician had laughed several times, then developed a frown he divided between Wilde and the rest of them, but he made no comment.

Chapter 35

THE MEMBERS OF THAT DAMN WESSEX Club did not realize the peril they had put her in. With Tara's account of the dangers ringing in his head, Celwyn hurried out of the hotel. If he told her what he intended to do, she might be too proud to allow him to fight her personal battle. Luckily, he could do so without drawing attention.

He would stop at the butcher shop, as he planned, but first, Buckingham. He ducked into the first alley he crossed and emerged again as a petite but swift wren flying above the trees.

The castle lay about five miles due east, and Celwyn flew to it without mishap. He knew exactly which office in the north wing he wanted to visit. What he did not know was whether Pompero still occupied the office or someone else had become the Queen's hatchet man and Tara's employer.

As a much smaller fly, he hid in the oversized feathers of an elderly woman's hat as she entered the castle, passing by the liveried guards and their severe cases of seriousness. He noted that the usual line of visitors to meet the Queen, or visitors who hoped they would see her, seemed abnormally long today. Luckily, he was not one of them. He rode with the dowager as far as the north stairs before soaring upward and down a long hall. This particular corridor had a long history of intrigue, and many of Pompero's protégés and disciples had offices here. As he went along, he passed the door marked Sir Jones, the anonymous mastermind of the Scarlet Pimpernel, and that of James Wilkinson, a most scandalous individual.

The magician's luck held as he neared the end of the hallway. Pompero's name remained on the door in gold script. No title. A title would only encourage questions the clandestine mastermind would prefer not to answer. Celwyn flew under the door and onto a plush rug that smelled faintly of horse dung. He studied the room, seeing that it appeared like it did a dozen years ago, with the same desk between wide casement windows, surrounded by walls of books and extensive maps. Xiau would love it here.

Aldonis Pompero had not aged much, except his hang-dog mustache sagged a bit more, and grey predominated in the ring of hair around his delicate red ears. They stuck out from his melon head like handles on a jug. At the moment, the spymaster held a rather soggy cigar between his teeth and puffed while he read a report.

Just as Celwyn got comfortable behind the books on the man's desk, something slammed into him, knocking him to the floor. The magician shook his head to clear it and retreated.

"Damned flies," Pompero growled as he tried to swat the magician again with a handful of papers. As he flew under the desk, the magician sent Pompero a silent suggestion to ring for more tea. Celwyn assumed he would have accomplished his mission by the time the tea service arrived.

Pompero pulled on the silk rope beside him and plopped back into his chair. "Damn flies." When he picked up the paper he had been reading, Celwyn forwarded him another suggestion, an explicit one saying that Talos was lying and that Miss McFein was innocent of the charges. Any warrants for her arrest must be squashed before Pompero had his lunch. Celwyn checked for resistance to the idea but only heard suspicions about Talos and questions about another report Pompero had asked for that made no sense.

The magician sent him another thought; Talos kept company with an enemy of the Crown, a certain Captain Emilio Dearing.

Pompero must have already had doubts about Dearing, for he muttered, "Damn pirate," under his breath as the porter walked in with the tea tray, and Celwyn flew out the door.

Mission accomplished. Off to the butcher shop!

A little after ten that morning, Celwyn and Tara descended to the first floor of their hotel. As they passed the front desk, a shrill double ring filled the air, and the clerk lifted a black bulbous handle out of a matching box and brought it to his mouth.

Celwyn stared as the man spoke into it. "That is one of those new 'talking boxes.' I hear local businesses use them." He studied the cloth cord affixed to the side of the contraption and the wires running up the wall.

"Have you seen them before?"

"Not right in front of me, no. I doubt there will be one on Findbar very soon. I hear there must be wires between anyone who wants to talk on it. Only the rich, or businesses such as this hotel, have them so far."

They walked out the main entrance and hailed a cab. Minutes later, the pair again availed themselves of the telegraph desk in Elmer's Greengrocers to send Nemo, Bartholomew, and Xiau's messages. Celwyn stifled a gallows grin, imagining the automat's tantrum when he realized his murderous brother had returned to plague him. His smile disappeared with a correction; to plague *them*.

Earlier that morning, after returning to the hotel along with the package of blood for Tara, he had spent most of breakfast describing the events that occurred after the *Zelda* arrived in Singapore and how he, Xiau, and Elizabeth had met Annabelle. Shortly after that, Patrick and Bartholomew entered their world. The story continued to his near-death before meeting Thales. He skipped the rest of the events in Turkey because they had almost finished breakfast, and it would upset his digestion to discuss his brother.

⌣——⌣——⌣

With the new telegrams sent and once again ensconced on the velvet seats in a cozy brougham, they bumped across Penhall and Henrietta streets. During their visit to Elmer's, they had appeared as bustling, plump housewives intent on selecting vegetables. Now, the magician studied Tara beside him, thinking her profile was still beautiful, even with the enhancements he had made to her nose and matching white hair. Their driver might doubt his own sanity when they emerged at their destination, appearing so different from when they boarded.

"I have given Valentine's predicament some thought." Tara tried not to smile. "And I hope you are listening to me, not just staring at me."

Celwyn laughed. "How did you know I was staring?"

"I can feel it," she said. "It is like tiny ants crawling across me." She squeezed his hand. "Of course, in a good way."

"Oh, I see." He resisted the urge to use magic, seeing how serious she had become. But he could not help adding soft music from a pair of guitars to the cab. Their melody glided back and forth like lovers silently conversing.

"Why did you ask the driver to stop on this street?" Celwyn asked.

They passed the Devil and Cow pub, then Chancery Books. The shops here had a feel of something distinctly mysterious about them, such as Everyday Alchemy and Astrology, with its blackened windows. Some storefronts appeared perfectly normal, like Mother's Flowers, decorated in gaily painted shutters and sparkling windows. Or Edwardian Tailors. Then they would spy a grumpy warlock exiting a smoke shop, followed by a pair of giggling daemons intent on no good. It was quite a show. Their carriage pulled to a stop in front of Jermyn Street Perfumeries.

Tara said, "I need to pick up some toiletries since my bags and clothes are either in the Tower or Buckingham or donated to a brothel by now. I will also inquire about the last time some of the owners saw Valentine shopping there. He haunts the vendors here when he can." She frowned. "I do not know for certain that he was in London when they kidnapped him. His predicament may have begun in France or even further away."

"I understand."

"Please revert me to my normal appearance as we enter the shop. Otherwise, the owner will not recognize me and tell us what we need to know."

"As you wish." Celwyn held the door open for her.

Nearly an hour later, Tara had made several purchases, including her unique perfume the magician enjoyed so much. When she held the bottle under his nose, it smelled nice but not wonderful. That confirmed his hunch that the concoction must be mixed with her skin to become exotically beautiful.

As they chatted with the proprietor while leaning over a glass counter, the magician made a face. Mr. Cockerham's breath emitted a sour, garlicky essence that did not go well with the intoxicating scents in his shop. He also eyed Celwyn with a modicum of jealousy. Tara batted her eyes at the proprietor with a coquettish smile.

"What else can I get you today, Miss McFein?" Cockerham tied a string around several boxes and tried to look down her cleavage.

Tara pretended interest in the display case between them and, as if it did not matter, asked, "Has my uncle been in lately?"

Cockerham snorted. "He has. It seems Valentine has acquired a new lady friend who favors anything with musk in it." The perfumer wrinkled his nose. "He also has a much shorter temper than he used to." The man yanked down his collar and said, "See what he did?"

Tara leaned over the case, as did Celwyn. "I do not see anything."

The shopkeeper pulled his collar back in place and growled, "It's been two weeks, so I suppose it doesn't show as much, but you could clearly see his finger-prints on my throat. Unacceptable!"

Celwyn sent Tara a silent question to ask the man. She complied. "What was he angry about that day?"

Cockerham fussed with his receipts. "Something to do with missing his cufflinks and a witch." He raised nervous eyes. "No offense."

"No problem."

"I really do not know more. He was furious with me because I was out of violet musk. Then he insisted I check in the back and demanded I find him some."

Tara asked, "Did you?"

Taking his time, Cockerham fitted a cigarette in a holder, lit it, and blew a ring toward the ceiling. The magician itched his nose and resisted the urge to turn the ring into something memorable, perhaps a caricature of Valentine's face.

"Of course. I sent him to Miss Rowley's shop down the next block. That absolute hive of high prices and gossip." He smiled broadly. "I hope Valentine bit her."

They thanked Cockerham as he approached his next customer, an aged daemon with a lace-trimmed eyepatch and a tiny poodle on a sequined leash. Her fur wrap blinked at Celwyn, and with a start, he realized the fox was very much alive. The magician kept an eye on it all the way out of the shop.

After he stowed their packages in the first carriage they saw, Celwyn held up a hand to get the driver's attention. In a heavily accented voice, he asked the driver to meet them on the next block and strolled away with Tara's arm hooked through his. For the next shop, the magician had decided they should be a young married couple from Bangladesh in ornate costumes, memorable as being nothing like the couple who had arrived on Jermyn Street earlier. He had a hunch that the enemy they were dealing with would be crafty, and he would take no chances.

As they stepped inside Mrs. Rowley's establishment, Celwyn noted the two shops could not have been more different.

While Cockerham's store had appeared unconventional, perhaps eclectic, the Fleur Rouge favored opulence and the latest fashions in bows, flowery potions, ribbons, and lotions. The proprietress resembled a near-sighted giraffe with short curly hair and a long thick neck above a beanpole frame. She wore a pink, flowered dress and matching pink spectacles. Celwyn could easily imagine her in a zoo as an oversized flamingo. When she saw them, she fluttered a handkerchief in their direction and lurched forward.

"How do you do? What may I find for you?" Her wide smile revealed excellent porcelain bridge work. It took a moment, then the magician remembered what Mrs. Rowley reminded him of—the Cheshire Cat in Xiau's new book, *Alice in Wonderland.*

Celwyn glanced at the tins of bath salts and assorted perfumes. Yes, the shop had high-priced items. Behind the racks of intimate wear, lay tables of stockings and gloves. Near the sales desk, rows of bottled spices and mysterious liquids had been artfully displayed on satin pillows.

In the far corner, a silk drape led to a back room.

With a deceptive smile, Tara conferred with the woman about her wares and then began inspecting the labels on the various scent pots by the light of a nearby bay window. "You have a marvelous selection, Mrs. Rowley. I am hunting for violet musk. Do you have any?" She uncorked a jar of cinnamon and inhaled deeply. "I am so hoping you do. My mother desires some."

As Tara spoke, Celwyn watched Mrs. Rowley, noting that upon hearing Tara's request, suspicion flooded the giraffe woman's eyes. He felt certain she was not a vampire or witch or daemon. But he would wager she could be bought for nefarious purposes and had been.

"Perhaps I do. Follow me, please." Mrs. Rowley led Tara toward the rear of the shop, stopping to say, "Your gentleman friend may remain out here."

The hell I can, Celwyn thought. As they passed through the drape, he sped up until he entered right behind them. In the dim light, the storage room appeared larger than the main shop. He inspected a stack of boxes, and when he pivoted, he heard a commotion only inches away. Tara had slammed the woman to the floor, and a baton fell out of Mrs. Rowley's hand.

"She was about to cosh you with that." Tara shook the giraffe woman like a dog shakes a rat.

Celwyn bowed. "I love a woman of action!"

With a busy smile, Tara blew him a kiss and continued to shake Mrs. Rowley until her wig fell off.

"I've had a very bad time lately and won't put up with lies." Tara flipped the woman over and kneeled on her. Celwyn made himself comfortable against the door to watch. "What happened when Mr. Soriano came here?"

Mrs. Rowley's eyes grew wide, and Tara slapped her. "Tell me."

"I... I... He will come back—"

"Who?"

She blinked fast, like hummingbirds perched on her lids. "Mr. Brown. He gave me something for Mr. Soriano."

In his own voice, and not disguising his anger, Celwyn asked, "A little man with tiny ears?"

Mrs. Rowley's eyes took on a new level of fear. "Who... who are you?"

The magician dropped beside her, and his expression held the kind of menace the woman should respect. "Just tell us." Celwyn thought about making Tara into a crouching tiger to make his point but decided against it. They were in disguise for a purpose, and there was no advantage in anyone knowing that he was a magician. Yet.

Tara raised her hand to slap the woman again.

"All right! Mr. Soriano was here on the twelfth. In the afternoon."

Celwyn asked her, "Have you seen Mr. Soriano or Mr. Brown since?" When she didn't ask who Mr. Brown was, he added in a gentler, confidential voice, "If you happen to know where either Mr. Soriano or Mr. Brown are staying or have anything to tell us, not only will we let you live, but I will pay you."

The woman's eyes shifted to the left, and she swallowed.

"Don't lie to us," Tara warned her.

Mrs. Rowley appeared more afraid of Mr. Brown than she was of them. Celwyn could not help himself. He sent one of Qing's favorite green snakes wiggling up the woman's neck. As it approached her mouth, she shrieked.

"Yes?"

"He..." The snake slithered off and dissolved when it reached the shadows. "He... he said the wine at the Trafalger Hotel had improved. That is all I know! That is where the delivery of his musk was supposed to go."

The magician helped Tara to her feet and spun Mrs. Rowley onto her stomach. A second more, and she was trussed like a boney Christmas goose. He put a gold coin between her rouged lips. "Your payment, Madam."

As Tara and Celwyn left the shop, she turned the "Open" sign to "Closed," and Celwyn locked the door behind them. "I left the lights on, so when her bonds fade away, she'll be able to see."

"Very considerate of you, Jonas."

He bowed her ahead toward their carriage. "Remind me not to annoy you, my darling."

She chuckled and climbed inside.

"Could we make a stop at Falstaff's on Orange Street, please?"

The magician opened the glass and instructed their driver.

"Done."

"Thank you." She pursed her lips and nodded to herself, deciding something. "We have an arrangement of convenience at Falstaff's that allows us to send and receive internal family messages. Many of the vampire families use the service."

"I see. And you wish to request help in finding your uncle?" He guessed. They bounced along, passing a few shoppers with umbrellas over their heads and others making do without in the heavy mist. As they turned a corner, they rolled by a disabled coach with a detached wheel propped against the curb. A feedbag hung around the horse's neck, and the driver was nowhere in sight.

"Yes. It wouldn't hurt to have help finding Valentine and with anything we may face while doing so. I am going to send for Mercury." She watched the magician's brow rise as he hid an obvious comment that came to mind. With a slender finger on his lips, she said, "Mercury is a vampire in our employ who is extraordinarily fleet of foot, which is what we use him for. He has a speech impediment that hinders him for some of our activities. Our family is fond of him." She smiled like someone who enjoys teasing. "Once he finds out Valentine is around, he follows him everywhere like a puppy." The smile vanished. "And he will be upset to learn he is missing."

Their coach swerved to a stop, and they alit from the cab. Cardboard signs decorating the shop next door announced the availability of live mice and leeches. Celwyn grunted and switched to studying the front of Falstaff's, noting that the windows seemed clear one moment and blacked out the next. "May I accompany you?"

"But, of course." She hugged his elbow to her. "They also have a wonderful selection of tobaccos. Please revert me back to my normal appearance again as we enter."

───────

Twenty minutes later, they exited the shop. Celwyn held her arm and checked up and down the street with care; he didn't wonder if they'd see an enemy;

it was a matter of when he spotted one. "Shall we continue on to Valentine's hotel to search for him?"

"Yes. We must return here later to meet Mercury." Tara also glanced up the avenue and then turned to scan the streets to the south.

"Our coach awaits us." Celwyn escorted her to it, and they climbed in. The ride was short.

The Trafalgar Hotel took up the entire block of Waterstone Street. With its high hedges shaped like bears and lions, it reminded the magician of a pretentious manor in the Surrey countryside. As they approached the uniformed doorman, Celwyn noted the hotel's variety of clients. Everyone from businessmen in top hats to an elderly duchess waving a spindly walking stick decorated with flowers. How did he know she was a duchess? By the gaggle of hotel employees calling her name and trying to bow at the same time. They were not alone; dozens of sycophants and outriders passed through its doors behind them.

"Have you ever stayed here?" he asked Tara.

She shook her head. "Not since a horrible incident a few years ago involving a rabbit."

"Oh?" He raised a brow. "Tell me more."

Tara steered him forward. "Not now. It will only distract you."

As they entered the hotel's dining room, an appetizing aroma of roasted pork and fresh bread filled the air above a variety of patrons enjoying their luncheon. Many appeared conservative, dressed as if they could attend a funeral without a costume change as soon as their repast finished. With décor

that leaned toward the old Georgian pastels of flowered dells, the Trafalgar was a favorite alternative to
the more modern Madison House nearby.

"I count a half-dozen daemons so far." Tara
nudged him in the side. "Although we're disguised
again, that may not be enough if someone unfriendly
gets too close."

The magician agreed as he scanned the tables. "I
believe I know that wizard with the long mustaches
... over there by windows." He pointed with his chin.

"Yes, that is Rosario. Nice man. A bit stuffy,
but nice."

"Anyone else I should be aware of? I prefer a quiet
luncheon."

She cuddled up to him. "I would also. Do you see
the table in the far corner with three women?"

"With the outlandish hats?" Celwyn squinted
across the cavernous dining room and said,
"Annabelle and Elizabeth have kept me aware of fashions in women's hats with much more enthusiasm
than I ever thought possible. Yes, I see the scarlet
feathered creation and one with a birdcage, and the
one that I don't know is what the blonde woman
next to her is wearing."

"Correct," Tara said. "Those are three witches I'm
familiar with."

"Are they dangerous?"

"Perhaps. They are from Martha Raines's coven
here in London. They can see through disguises. It
would be best if you blocked me and if we sat on the
other side of the room."

"My pleasure."

When the maître d' had settled them near the windows and far from the witches, Celwyn stopped him. "How long have you been at this establishment?"

His smile lifted his oiled mustaches upward. The man responded, "Over ten years, sir. How may I help you?"

With a nod from Tara, Celwyn asked, "Do you recall the last time Mr. Valentine Soriano graced your dining room? A tall man with memorable silver hair."

As he asked the question, Celwyn entered the man's mind and found a touch of fear and a clear memory of Valentine sipping wine at the table where the elderly wizard now sat.

"No, sir. I am not familiar with that gentleman." He stared directly into the magician's eyes.

He lies very well, Celwyn thought.

"Thank you."

With a bow, the maître d' bid them an enjoyable meal and left. Their waiter arrived. After he had retreated again, the magician told Tara, "The maître d' lied to us. He saw Valentine recently. My judgment of him is that a bribe won't elicit the information we want. Violence or trickery is the answer."

"Both, most likely. Does our waiter know anything? I see they have fresh asparagus." She sighed. "I used to like it quite a bit."

"I don't know yet. Our waiter's thoughts center on the scullery maid in the kitchen that he suspects is forsaking him for one of the sous chefs."

Chapter 36

W ITH QUIET COMPANIONABILITY
and more than two hours until their appointment with Mercury, they spent a pleasant interlude
under a rather warm sun in Regents Park enjoying
a parade of toy boats. The miniature flotilla spread
out in every direction in the idyllic pond.

They tried not to hold hands since Celwyn had
adopted a new disguise: a shrill-voiced matron
wearing the latest fashions in bustles. To anyone
watching, Tara would appear to be her daughter
with a fondness for flounces and bows.

Earlier, they had stopped at a music store on the
Strand and then a pair of art galleries before once
again hailing a coach. The magician never would
have guessed Tara's preference in art and felt pleased
and surprised by her appreciation of Hiroshige ll. He
had never seen the artist's work before, and it took a
while before he could look away from it.

At the appointed hour, they arrived at Falstaff's. The main attraction for the magician here was the anticipation of the sweet smell of the tobaccos. It neared four in the afternoon, and they would soon have to leave for their surveillance of the hotel's maître d'. As their driver opened the coach door and handed Tara to the sidewalk, Celwyn glanced behind her. An albino dressed in a blue suit waited at the shop door. His cap perched on his head like a chicken on a nest. Blonde curls drooped over pixie blue eyes that regarded them openly. He stood exactly as tall as Tara.

Celwyn and Tara approached him, and the magician saw something that always made him doubt the existence of God. After Mercury bowed and stood again, the light caught his face full on. His deformity began above his cheek, bisecting his face in a terrible line to his chin.

Tara greeted him in her normal voice, and he lit up with pleased recognition.

"I ... h... have ... missed you, Miss McFein." He paused as he studied her. "If ... I hadn't heard ... y... your voice ... your hair and nose ... are—"

"Different, yes." She smiled at him. "I am in temporary disguise." She indicated the magician. "This is Mr. Celwyn. He is helping us."

"Pleased to meet you," the magician bowed. "Shall we go inside?"

Mercury eyed the matronly clothes Celwyn wore and widened his eyes at the magician's deep voice, which did not match his costume. The magician grinned at him.

Celwyn did not fancy standing outside need-lessly in case any of the automats associated with Talos happened to stroll by. He could not shake the feeling of being watched, especially over the last few days. It came and went, but occurred enough to be worrisome. If Bartholomew were here, he would know. The big man had a sixth sense of when he was being spied upon and would usually do some-thing about it.

The bell over the shop door jingled discordantly as they entered and passed tables of books and pipes on their way toward the office at the back of the store. Tara knocked on the wooden door and, after checking inside, motioned them into the sparsely furnished room. Celwyn stood as they took seats at a table barely big enough for a chess set and two glasses.

"It has been a long time," Tara told Mercury fondly.

"Heavens! Anything for you and M-Mr. Valentine. Please tell me what is wrong."

It only took a few minutes for Tara to tell him that they suspected Valentine had been captured and that they would need his help soon, perhaps as early as tomorrow.

"I am here to serve you." Mercury kissed her hand. The albino's expression turned dark. "Your uncle... I... I would do anything for him."

Tara and Mercury reminisced, and the magi-cian supplied a bottle of wine to help them. When it appeared next to his hand, Mercury stared into Celwyn's eyes and slowly blinked a measure of trust and acceptance. Would he have done so if Tara had not been sitting there? The magician wouldn't wager either way.

Celwyn said, "Tonight, we plan to follow someone who can provide the information we need. The man is probably in league with our enemies. In fact," he checked his pocket watch, "we must depart now."

"Can you meet us tomorrow?" Tara asked. "We will know more then."

The magician assured Mercury, "We will need your services, especially when we hunt down the villains who took Valentine."

"I c... can help now." The albino lifted his hands in confusion. "I do not understand."

"Do not worry." Tara hugged him. "We think whoever is behind this has dozens, if not hundreds, of men. We plan to rescue Valentine and then form a plan of attack to eliminate them." She described the automats. "They are mechanical men and extraordinarily strong. Beware of them." She smiled. "I've told Mr. Celwyn how fleet of foot you are. We will need your help when we know more."

The albino nodded his acceptance of the compliment. "I ... shall meet you tomorrow?"

Celwyn pulled out Tara's chair and helped her to her feet. "Yes. Please meet us here at noon."

Chapter 37

A S THEY APPROACHED THE FRONT desk of the Trafalgar, Celwyn said, "Our maître d' will leave for the day soon. I am quite curious where he will go."

After the magician asked for Valentine's room number, he examined the telephone contraption installed at the end of the concierge's desk. The ringer box appeared to be about eight inches square and quite heavy.

Tara asked the clerk, "By chance, is a Miss Simone Redifer registered here?"

"Yes, she arrived a few days ago." The smartly dressed young man sporting a yellow four-in-hand consulted the ledger. "She is in room 312."

The magician leaned closer to the telephone and murmured with envy, "We need one of these at Tellyhouse." Tara laughed and tugged on his arm.

As they approached the grand staircase, Celwyn lowered his voice. "Let's visit your uncle's room first, before Miss Redifer's, and then follow the maître d' as he exits. If need be, I'll plant some urgency in his thoughts to visit Talos."

"It is interesting that he knows Talos."

Celwyn growled, "Yes, it appears he is afraid of him."

Tara fell quiet as they ascended the wide, curved staircase to the second floor. Below them, a sea of feathered hats and homburgs went by, along with the occasional turban. "It is rather helpful to know that Miss Redifer is here."

"I had a letter from her a few weeks ago saying she would be in London before long." She sent him a frown. "What is puzzling is that she isn't fond of this hotel."

They reached the landing and turned right. "Possibly she and Valentine had a job to do, making the proximity of this hotel convenient?"

Tara nodded. "Perhaps." She still frowned.

"What else bothers you about this?"

"Both Valentine and Simone knew I was due to leave London for Paris and that I was incommunicado at the castle. I don't know what they were doing after they arrived." She shuddered delicately. "After my arrest, I certainly didn't know."

Celwyn squeezed her hand, and they started counting the room numbers as they neared Valentine's suite. "Can we assume from your uncle's messages that he was in London about a week before your arrest?"

Tara stopped before room 223. "Probably more. My captors had me write to you the second day after my arrest."

"I see." Celwyn unlocked the door, and they stepped inside.

If nothing else, Valentine had excellent taste. The room must be one of the hotel's finest. It sported pale silk draperies, a light blue settee, and fine Baroque pieces, including a handsome desk he would not mind having. The magician saw no evidence of violence, but a few things seemed curious: it smelled empty, there was no luggage in sight, and the bed had not been used.

The magician picked up a piece of paper off the desk, read it, and passed it to Tara.

Seeds
Indigo
Violet musk
Oyster shells
Rose petals
Snips of fragrant grass
Frog ears

"Items for a spell, perhaps? Valentine wouldn't need them ... interesting ... what he wanted at Mrs. Rowley's shop is listed here. Third on the list." He pointed to a paper-wrapped package with her shop's name. "If we can't find him otherwise, we can trace his attempts to find the other things on this list."

Tara bobbed her head in agreement. As they searched the room, she grew quiet.

"You're worried."

"Yes. We have just enough time to investigate Simone's room before we must leave."

⌣

Twenty minutes later, disappointment dogged their steps down to the first floor. They had found nothing in Miss Redifer's room except a vase of wilted roses by the settee. They walked in silence to the back of the hotel.

In keeping with the sophistication of the establishment, the Trafalgar's rear alley appeared free of debris, rats, and flies. Neither did it have packing crates to hide behind. The magician and Tara had to remain on the sidewalk fifty feet away.

"It is two minutes to the top of the hour." Celwyn frowned at his pocket watch.

"There is another way he may go," Tara pointed. "See the other end of the alley? That is Grosvenor Street."

Celwyn stepped into a new position behind a manicured hedge. "When he emerges, if he heads that way, I'll leave you to follow him and wait for you in the trees along his route."

"If he comes this way, we will both follow him." Tara nodded, keeping an eye on the exit of the hotel.

"Our task would be easier if we flew."

Tara eyed him fondly. "I would prefer not to, my dear. Only in emergencies." She scanned the street. "This would be much simpler after dark."

"It won't be for another two hours." The magician's attention centered on the door as several women in cleaning uniforms came out and down the short flight of stairs. A pair of men in dirty overalls appeared next. A minute more and the maître d' darted out, wrapped in a heavy coat and fedora against the cold, heading directly toward them.

"He's coming this way." They faced the street as if searching for a taxi. When the man exited the alley, he nearly walked into them before heading north at a rapid pace. He turned down Basil Street as a bright red omnibus approached.

They moved briskly, keeping a comfortable distance behind their quarry and dodging other pedestrians as they went by a quaint sweets shop that reminded Celwyn of Xiau. His worry escalated. *God damn Talos—what if he had found him?*

Celwyn hustled Tara into the bushes, and they emerged again dressed as dockworkers in none-too-clean clothes. Their caps were pulled low over dirty faces, and they carried carpet bags. In seconds they had caught up to the omnibus and climbed inside just as the driver clicked his tongue at the horses, and it rolled forward again.

Without any hesitation, they settled next to two women in the corner furthest away from the maître d'. As the bus crossed William Street, one of the women stared at Tara and said, "Good afternoon."

Celwyn piped up in a rough Cockney accent, "M'friend is hard of hearing, ma'am. Also, he's most shy." The magician did not add that she also had a sultry and feminine contralto that would confuse the woman to no end.

The woman's hat bobbed as she nodded her sympathy and understanding. Only a few feet away, the maître d' listened to them and then resumed watching the streets. On the next block, the women descended to the curb and bustled off toward Harold and Son's Cabinetry on the corner. That left their target alone with them in the omnibus.

They bumped along for a few more blocks, picking up a pair of ne'r do wells in grubby suits and an elderly man with the gentle mannerisms of a cleric. Celwyn wrinkled his nose at the pair of men, detecting a faint aroma, just a trace of something unpleasant, suspect, and familiar. *Perhaps these two should also be followed,* he told Tara.

Minutes later, it became necessary to do so. At the end of the street, the bus made a complete circle in front of one of the derelict buildings common to the older docks. It was an enormous warehouse that partially extended over the Thames, a common practice for receiving freight. Although massive, it appeared abandoned, with long expanses of wooden plasterboard missing.

The dapper form of the maître d' alighted from the bus and set off south on Paul Street. Much more slowly, the grubby men followed, with Celwyn and Tara a bit further behind. Celwyn shielded them from view as he took her hand and increased their speed. They passed the men without any reaction. He suppressed an urge to whisper something as they went by.

When the maître d' reached a set of stairs leading below the building, he disappeared down them into the windowless wing of the building. Although the former Balfour Fish Company appeared deserted, the dirt path leading to the stairs showed evidence of many visitors.

Celwyn stared through the walls and into the interior as far as he could, seeing nothing but crates and boxes.

Should we allow these two men access? The grubby men had drawn closer to the building.

Tara rolled her eyes at his teasing. "I think not."

"All right, then." Celwyn bowed Tara ahead and closed and locked the door behind them. They stood in a small vestibule about the size of a card table. When the men began pounding on the door, a much larger man approached from the hallway behind them. He stood beside the magician without seeing him and blinked a pair of eyes that bulged in a doughy white face with a fish-like quality.

"Go away—" the man yelled and shook a pistol at the door.

He cannot see us, the magician reminded Tara as they pressed themselves against the wall.

"Let us in, Smithy—" One of them smacked the door.

Smithy stuffed his pistol in his pants and tried the handle. The magician made sure it did not open. Smithy bellowed, "Back up! I'm going to blast it open."

The magician added more protection to the door and escorted Tara out of the vestibule and down a long corridor door, where the shadows mixed with the faint smell of rotting sardines. As they went along, Celwyn changed their appearance back again. Whatever lurked in this building would be more respectful of a magician and vampire than two scruffy dockworkers.

As they walked, the smell of cloves became stronger, competing with the other disgusting odors and sending a thrill of apprehension up Celwyn's spine. The scent of revenge was sweet!

Talos has been here, he told Tara silently. *Instead of waiting until tomorrow, we may be able to rescue Valentine now.* Her brows went up beautifully, but she said nothing. He added, *when we reach the end of this hallway, let me go in first, please.*

Celwyn slowed their pace, still hearing the faint sounds of Smithy's frustration from behind them. The blast from a boat horn came so loud that the vessel must be only feet away from them on the water.

They reached the end of the corridor. From an open door, the murmur of indistinct voices filtered out. Then silence. The magician doubted that whatever they found here would only have Smithy guarding it. As he took another step forward, sounds of combat reached them, and the body of the maître d' slowly rolled into the hallway. A large knife had been buried in his chest.

So much for that. Celwyn stared through the wall and gaped. What a surprise... But it made sense, too. He sent a message to Tara beside him. With the same surprise lighting her eyes, she acknowledged him. The magician handed her the pistol from the maître d's coat. The man would not need it anymore.

Before Celwyn reached the doorway, he fluttered the wings of a small fly. As he entered an enormous storage room, he ascended to the rafters above a mass of bright lights and impenetrable darkness. The storage chamber stretched for a hundred feet or more into shadows that swallowed the crates, boxes, and trash splayed across the floor. Directly below him, a long string of lanterns lit up every detail of a much smaller area, including a bound and restrained Valentine in an iron cage. In front of the cage, a quartet of automats, so like but unlike Kang, played Mahjong.

The magician cursed under his breath. There was no sign of Talos or Captain Dearing. Yet, Talos had been here. The place reeked of cloves.

Celwyn's attention moved to the other occupant of the room, and his buoyant anticipation for a spot of violence and revenge spiraled downward as the memory of his brother's painful betrayal returned.

Voluptuous, in a tattered way, still bawdy and devious, Ginnie Ford reclined on a divan on the other side of the cage. Celwyn well-remembered the witch. With a whiskey bottle to her lips, and a cigarette holder dangling from her other hand, she gazed through the smoke with a wide yawn. A fleeting question crossed the magician's mind; *how did she escape Pelaez?*

Just as Celwyn decided her fluffy blonde hair could have used a few hairpins, Ginnie sat up, dropping the bottle and her cigarette. She had gained some pounds since he had last seen her, and it aged her. Oddly, in this light, or perhaps it was the circumstances, she reminded him of someone. She had not done so before.

He regarded the situation in front of him. *It would have to be handled carefully,* the magician concluded, *and, of course, artfully.* He had to protect Tara as much as Valentine, which gave him pause.

The automats continued their game without talking or noticing anything amiss. A collection of nasty-looking guns, machetes, and knives littered the tabletop where they played. In the cage behind them, through the dried blood on his face, Valentine opened his eyes, and his nostrils flared. *He probably smells me,* the magician thought. *Good. He will be ready when things become livelier in a moment.* However, the witch would soon detect him also, and the magician had no idea how powerful an enemy she would be.

How to get Valentine out? The magician did not think quietly unlocking the cage would work if the vampire couldn't move without help. Celwyn would have to blow the cage open. A fascinating situation. He usually flung vampires into cages, not help them escape.

"Gaspardy? Where are you?" Ginnie called as she rolled off the sofa and onto her feet. She scratched under her arm as if no one else were present.

Slow, measured steps approached, and another automat strolled out of the shadows toward her. He not only wore much finer vestments than the other automats but also seemed a bit different—something about him put him on a higher level than the others. He wore the same glittering eyes and disdain as Talos as he regarded the occupants of the room. Celwyn could almost touch the man's arrogance.

"Again, it is Gaspard, Madam. Not 'Gaspardy.' What do you want?"

"Why did you kill that waiter just now?" Ginnie used her little girl voice that the magician found so annoying. "Poor, handsome thing. He just asked to talk to Talos."

Gaspard cocked his head to the side and regarded her like a lower species of rat. "He said some old woman inquired after our guest." Gaspard gestured at Valentine. "It would only be a matter of time until he was questioned again."

"Why do you think that?"

He swiveled. "Where is your 'Smithy?'" Gaspard asked with plenty of scorn.

Nice. The villains did not seem to be united. Also, the fact that Gaspard wondered about Smithy meant the time had come to act. Fish Eyes could join them at any moment. The magician sent a silent message to Tara, where she waited in the hallway.

As himself once again, Celwyn brought his hands together and floated to the floor.

Like giant ships colliding, metal clanged and echoed many times over as he caused the automats to slam together in a tight embrace over the table. Then he added a powerful magnet over them all, guaranteeing the metal discs in their chests welded together. A second, even larger magnet completely disabled them. Celwyn congratulated himself. He had recalled Kang's lecture on the composition of automats. Later, of course, he would remind Xiau he had used it.

The magician turned in time to see Tara rushing into the room. Ginnie had already tried to flee at the sight of the magician, and Tara took aim on the run and shot her in the rear.

At the same time, Celwyn blew open Valentine's prison and turned toward another automat who materialized out of the shadows. The new villain backed away from the magnetized bundle of automats. Tara emptied her pistol into his chest, the bullets ricocheting as he backed away.

"He's yours," Tara called as she passed behind Celwyn. When she turned toward the cage, a half dozen automats emerged from the darkness and swarmed over her. Gaspard had backed away and now joined the attack. The magician pivoted, scraping off a pair of them as Tara squirmed away so fast he couldn't see her. She produced a cord from her pocket. Like a thin snake, its iridescence flickered under the lights as she whirled it above her head and around them. She tightened the cord until they couldn't move. "My witchcraft may be limited ... but I am ... highly ... annoyed right now," she panted, wiping away a ribbon of blood from her cheek.

She had that under control. Celwyn turned to the automats who'd been playing Mahjong and dissolved the pile of them, leaving behind their metal disks that rattled to a stop on the concrete floor. He would have preferred to destroy them to the accompaniment of a full orchestra, but things appeared a bit rushed right now.

Tara nodded at him and rushed into the cage, where Valentine struggled to get to his feet and failed.

"Deciding?" Celwyn purred at the remaining automat and took a step toward him. "I suggest you go. Tell Talos I said 'hello.'"

The automat's eyes flashed as he faded into the shadows, and they heard him run. Then a door opened.

"God, I hate the smell of cloves," Celwyn said as he entered the cage and knelt before Valentine.

Pain contorted the vampire's face as he tried to smile through it. "As do I."

Celwyn regarded him. Using magic, he carefully removed the mountains of chains around the vampire. At the same time, the magician kept an eye on Ginnie on the other side of the cage. She had wrapped her dress around her rear end and retreated until she crouched behind the divan. He didn't see any fresh bleeding, and a bullet lay on the floor.

"I wouldn't try anything," Celwyn warned her as he helped Valentine to stand. The magician asked the vampire, "I have never tried to heal someone like yourself, but would you allow me to try? I can at least stop the pain."

"Please. I am very weak. They did not feed me."

He meant blood. Celwyn considered the options. They could not use Ginnie; there was no telling what was in her blood.

"Smithy, the guard, perhaps?" he suggested.

Valentine made a face of distaste.

"It would obviously do no good to use mine," Tara said as she studied Valentine.

Over the top of her head, the magician saw something that did not surprise him, but it certainly made the situation more interesting.

A full-size version of the wyvern wiggled its way across the mound of automats Tara had subdued, stopping to open its eyes and bare its teeth at them. His tail slapped Gaspard in the face with a satisfying sound. Wye turned on his side, and Celwyn could swear that he grinned at him.

From beside him, Tara let out a muffled shriek and grabbed his arm.

Valentine exclaimed, "What—"

"A wyvern. I will explain later." Celwyn and the others stood between Wye and the witch. For some reason he could not name, the magician did not want Ginnie to know of the creature. He told it, "Please go, and nice to see you too."

As they watched, the wyvern shimmered and faded away.

Celwyn assured them, "I will explain soon."

"I'm not sure it will be necessary, considering your normal activities." Valentine tried to nod, stopped, and grabbed his ribs. "A long time ago, I saw something like that. It ate a dozen villagers in Truro."

Tara managed, "I still want to know."

"First, let's see what we can do here."

Celwyn did his best to help Valentine's pain. He did not try anything elaborate, just repairing bones and muscles where they had cut or pummeled him. He asked Tara, "Please press on the area around his liver and abdomen. Your uncle will tell us where it hurts much more than it should."

Just as he finished with Valentine, the magician heard a noise and whirled.

"Stop that—" he yelled.

Ginnie had her wand out and scrabbled further behind the settee to point it at them. Celwyn elevated the witch to the ceiling, and with a flick of his finger, the wand went flying into the darkness beyond them. "Irritate me again, and I'll drop you."

He turned back to watch as Tara tested parts of Valentine's torso until he winced. Over the next several minutes, the magician continued to do what he could. "I've counted more than two dozen blows and deep cuts." As he left each area behind, Celwyn deposited something to help with the pain. Valentine sighed and would have fallen if Tara had not caught him.

He glared at Ginnie. "That witch has appeared to me in several enticing forms over the last few weeks. I had been buying her presents."

"I didn't know spells worked on vampires." Celwyn opened his eyes in surprise. Valentine started to growl a response and winced.

"Hence your hunt for exotic herbs and violet musk," Tara surmised.

"Yes. A request from the witch." Valentine patted his side. "This is much better, Mr. Celwyn; thank you. I will not forget your help."

As he spoke, a bullet zipped by Celwyn's nose and hit the iron bars of the cage.

Smithy stormed through the door and turned his gun toward Tara. Celwyn flipped a hand, sending him flying hard against the wall, and he slid to the floor.

"Aha! I believe your dinner has arrived, Mr. Soriano," the magician announced with a bow.

Chapter 38

A FTER VALENTINE HAD DRUNK HIS fill, he glanced at Tara, who wrinkled her nose. She threw back her hood and straightened her hair. "It has been quite a day." She regarded her uncle. "How are you?"

"Angry and tired. Let us depart." Valentine did not make it more than a few steps out of the cage before sitting heavily on one of the chairs the automats had used. "Give me a moment." He kicked the nearest automat.

As they watched Valentine catch up on his breathing, Celwyn asked, "Would you object if I fixed the cut on your cheek?"

Tara nodded. "I'd forgotten about it. Yes, please."

When he had done so, Celwyn rolled Smithy over with his boot. "Is he dead?"

Valentine shook his head. "No. He will recover after a while."

"Let us take the same route out." Tara took Valentine's arm. "Talos could be here any moment once that other automat reaches him."

Celwyn brought Ginnie down to her sofa. As she watched him, her eyes alternated between a furious glare and soft seduction. The magician laughed, which made her angrier. He used the same type of bindings that he had used for Duncan. They would tighten the more she tried to get away and last for a few hours until Celwyn and his party had traveled far into the bowels of the city.

"Now, Jonas honey, you don't want—"

He added a gag to Ginnie's expressive face between her over-rouged lips and took Valentine's other elbow to guide him forward.

⁓

Dusk bled amber and pink under banks of sooty clouds covering the city. As they walked, the Thames winked at them from a few blocks away, glinting like a silver serpent under the setting sun.

On Celwyn's left, Valentine moved carefully and used an ornate walking stick the magician had made especially for his height. It supported him well. Before they left the warehouse, Celwyn had also repaired his clothing and provided a mirror while the vampire tidied his hair, now a rich ebony courtesy of the magician. His profile looked much different also, his nose smaller and eyebrows heavier and lower.

Valentine had insisted that they walk for a short time to see if any automats haunted the area. Tara tried to argue him out of it, and they settled for using the magician's assistance to help him.

For their disguises, Tara and Celwyn resembled young men of the priesthood. Tara had raised her brows when the magician had requested her not to roll her hips as she walked. Celwyn propelled Valentine forward while Tara remained alert on Celwyn's other side. Minutes later, the three of them neared the fringes of a bawdy area, and the raucous voices from the gaming halls rose higher. They strolled on.

The evening enveloped them as the streetlamps came alive and the night complete. Judging from their speech and strange footwear, many tourists from America and Spain populated the streets. Celwyn considered himself up to date on fashions, and a row of buttons on the side of a boot just seemed odd.

They sidestepped a dapper, skeletal man speeding down the middle of the sidewalk like he owned it. Tara's fingers tightened on Celwyn's arm. "Daemon," she muttered under her breath.

Valentine stopped and glared.

Even in his depleted condition, the vampire emitted danger. The daemon paused, threw his hands in the air, and ran into the street. While the tourists were distracted, a calèche drawn by a pair of black Arabians appeared at the curb.

"You can't last much longer, Mr. Soriano," Celwyn told him. "We have been checking to see if we were followed." The magician touched both of their elbows. "We weren't." He helped Valentine into the seat next to Tara. "How much further?" he asked the vampire.

"Perhaps a mile." They'd talked about how Valentine had been attacked in his hotel. "I agree that it would be best if we did not go back to our hotel rooms. I know of a discreet and safe place for us to stay." Even under questioning by his niece, he would not disclose details other than to say they would be welcome and safe.

"It is not too much further. Keep north on this street."

Celwyn nodded and steered the horses in that direction.

"Rest, Uncle," Tara told him.

"I will. Take a right at the end of the next block onto New Cavendish. From there, it is close by." Valentine waved a hand toward the avenue. "I wouldn't have made it this far without your assistance, Mr. Celwyn."

As he drove, Celwyn had been trying but could not answer a question, so he asked, "You are welcome. How did they find you?" He studied the streets, seeing nothing amiss but knowing that as they neared their sanctuary, anonymity became even more important. Not a thing stood out as the avenues became more prosperous, as did the carriages.

"How?" Valentine snarled. "That damn Rowley woman from the perfume shop. She sent a message saying my order had arrived and that she would have it delivered."

They reached New Cavendish and turned, leaving much of the traffic behind in favor of well-manicured shrubbery and a profusion of flowers in front of majestic estates. The architecture appeared mostly Georgian, with red or blue painted doors behind short sidewalks. Regency-style windows overlooked the road.

"We should disembark here. It is only another few houses, and we do not need to be remembered by the neighbors as having a coach that seemed to disappear," Valentine told them.

"Good idea," Tara agreed.

The magician helped her to the ground, along with Valentine. "Please, continue." They attained the sidewalk and started forward again.

The vampire shrugged. "Initially, it was just one delivery man who came into my suite, but he left the door open, and three more entered, one of whom bludgeoned me on the head before I could tear them up."

Tara said, "That accounts for the pristine condition of your room when we searched it."

"They probably lowered you out the window to the alley to take you away," Celwyn surmised.

Valentine indicated the front of his coat. "That would account for the condition I found myself in when I woke up." As he spoke, they stopped in front of a freshly painted manor with boxes of bright geraniums on each side of a wide door. A dozen carriages, some with royal crests, were parked along the street, and their footmen had gathered on the corner to smoke. "I say—" Valentine led the way up the walk and asked Tara, "Did you talk with Simone?"

Celwyn saw Tara's moue of sadness and spoke up. "We checked in her room but did not find her."

Valentine had been about to knock, and his hand froze in the air. "They have her."

"Most likely. That was the assumption when we found you, but not her," Celwyn said.

"Let us hope not." Tara blinked away tears. "Who lives here?"

Valentine studied the bricks under their feet for a moment before he said, "A widow. Mrs. Polly Hatcher." He glared. "God dammit. We need to compare notes on what we know."

Celwyn said, "I agree. Can we talk in there?"

"Yes." Valentine thumped his chest. "Please, change my appearance back so the butler will know me."

The magician did so, adding a large hat to cover his silver mane, then reverted Tara and himself.

Valentine knocked. "The only thing to worry about here is the food. Polly's chef is a fiend, but my niece and I will not have to endure it. I hear he over-salts everything."

"I'm famished, Uncle."

Valentine patted her arm and knocked again. "Never fear. Polly has a variety of visitors and keeps a splendid assortment of our nourishment and wine on the premises."

Although the outside of the manor epitomized conservative England, as they crossed the threshold, they stepped into what Celwyn compared to an opulent hotel he had once seen in Carson City, Nevada. From the braces of Enfield and Colt rifles mounted across the walls to a pair of shiny spittoons in the corner and the bearskin underfoot, the wild American West surrounded them. The magician wondered what Qing would think of the five-foot-tall wooden Indian holding a tray in front of the door to the parlor. He would probably sit on the tray and squawk, proud of something new.

The butler finished hanging up their coats.

"Thank you, Gerald. Is Miss Polly home?" Valentine inquired.

"Yes, sir. This way, please."

The magician noted that Gerald did not bat an eye at a collection of interesting late-evening visitors. He led the way up the hall, past a settee made of what appeared to be buffalo horns and decorated with velvet pillows. Gerald looked the proper butler in his black museum-worthy funereal coattails and white gloves. Across the hall, Celwyn spied a luxurious sitting room. From within it, a grandfather clock intoned eight bells.

Tara's brow furrowed with worry as she regarded Valentine. "My uncle needs to rest."

"Please, in here." Gerald bowed them into the sitting room, where Celwyn imagined he could still hear the echo of the clock's bells.

The room contained matching red velvet sofas and a smattering of antique desks next to exquisite stained-glass lamps. Mr. Tiffany's artisans seemed to favor dragonflies this season. Through tall windows, the streetlamps outside glowed under an increasing halo of fog. As they sat down, Valentine sighed. The extent of the ordeal he had endured was painted across his face.

"Once we are alone, I will help you again with your injuries." Celwyn eyed him. "For broken ribs and the like, I am quite adept." He covered the vampire with something for his pain. "However, for anything more serious, it would be prudent to have a doctor familiar with you to direct my efforts."

The vampire heaved another heavy sigh. "Thank you. If things worsen, I will visit my doctor, but I would prefer to avoid the trip if possible."

Tara said, "I will be the judge of that, Uncle. Who is Polly?" She tucked a rug around her uncle's shoulders, despite his protests. "Yes, I know you aren't cold, but it can't hurt."

While she fussed over Valentine, Celwyn admired the grand piano taking up the rest of the room. A cathedral-like ceiling ended three stories above them in panels of beveled glass. *The reverberation must be marvelous*, he concluded with a strong pang of lust. Without getting up, the magician played a single key of A, letting it ring and enjoying the beautiful tone as the sound echoed upward.

Valentine had said they would be welcome here. Celwyn hoped it would be long enough for an extended session in this room.

"Let's discuss our situation," Valentine said.

Staccato steps clicked their way up the hall, announcing the arrival of their hostess. A woman of average size and enormous bosoms teetered on high heels in front of them. She swept her hands from side to side with excitement that appeared at odds with the seriousness of her formal gown. "Valentine!" She rushed to him and kissed both cheeks. "What happened? You look deathly!"

The vampire held her hands as she sat beside him. "My dear, it has been too long. Allow me to intro—"

"Not now. What happened to you?" she demanded.

"Perhaps I can assist," Celwyn said. "This is Miss Tara McFein, Mr. Soriano's niece. I am Jonas Celwyn," he bowed, "Lately of Prague. We helped Mr. Soriano escape from an attack and beg your indulgence. We seek shelter, Madam."

Polly reared back, causing her long strings of pearls to dance. "Is that true?" Her American accent contained a good measure of Alabama drawl.

Valentine shrugged.

Tara said, "My uncle is rather stubborn, Mrs. Hatcher."

"Call me Polly, both of you. Y'all have my thanks for helping him." She crossed to a corner and pulled on the rope. When a maid appeared, she requested, "Please have three rooms prepared upstairs. And send in tea service." She regarded Valentine. "And a bottle of the Bordeaux."

When she returned to the sofa, Valentine brought her hand to his lips. "Thank you, for your shelter, Polly. It is mid-evening, and I note your finery." He eyed her. "You are entertaining, and we have interrupted."

"Well, yes, but—"

Valentine said, "Please return to your guests. We'll retire upstairs after we've had our refreshments and see you in the morning."

Tara nodded at her uncle. "I can assure you he will rest."

"Thank you, dear." Polly stood and pecked Valentine's cheek. "All right. I do have the Earl of Welbeck and the Count of Milan in the ballroom spoiling for a fight over a woman young enough to be their daughter." She trotted out on her high heels as fast as she came in.

By silent agreement, they waited to talk until the tea service arrived, along with an impressive array of sandwiches and sweets. After the maid poured the tea, Valentine requested that she ask the butler to return.

Minutes later, he did so. Gerald excused the maid.

The vampire asked, "Could you bring a good portion of the type of refreshment that my niece and I prefer, please?"

"But, of course."

When he had left again, Celwyn said, "Let's talk quickly." He popped a fairy cake into his mouth and chewed. "I can summarize our situation succinctly; however, what to do about it may take lengthy discussion." The cake tasted exceptionally good. Xiau would eat a fistful of them. Bartholomew would have sampled a few, too.

Tara pointed her chin at him. "Please do so."

"I suspect that when we dissect this conundrum, it will look even worse," Valentine grumbled.

Celwyn held up three fingers. "The story consists of three parts. First, your niece was detained by the Crown and falsely charged with crimes. She was imprisoned in the Tower and forced to send for me."

"Were you injured?" Valentine demanded of Tara.

"Very few injuries. Mostly, I was angry and feared for you and Jonas."

"Who imprisoned you?"

Celwyn detected steps approaching. With their excellent hearing, the vampires had already heard them. Gerald entered with a maid in tow, and they placed a tray with silver goblets and two tall, covered pitchers on the table next to the fairy cakes.

After the maid had executed a nervous curtsey and ran out of the room, Gerald said, "Fresh chilled rabbit's blood. Will that do, sir?"

"Yes. It is appreciated."

"Please ring for me if there is anything else." He marched out again.

As Tara reached for one of the carafes, Celwyn said, "To go on, the villains were not from your past. Though they were partially from mine. I knew Talos from before." He selected another fairy cake and thought about Kang's fondness for sweets again as he took a bite. He missed his friends and Qing. He grinned; the bird had probably been more destructive than usual while the magician was gone. "Talos is Professor Kang's brother. He is also an automat. A few years ago, I destroyed him when he attacked us. Or at least I thought I had done so." The magician summarized what happened on the voyage of the *Zelda* and the trip to Prague that followed.

"So," Tara held a finger to her lips as she thought. "How did Talos come to be in London?"

"As a guess, it is because of the other villain who probably retrieved Talos's body and power source from where we threw it into the Artic Sea. Pirates do a bit of salvage work while searching for wrecks and treasure."

"Then they both came here," Tara deduced.

Valentine said, "I don't understand. Why?"

Celwyn noticed the vampire had lost some of his haggard appearance since he rested and had drunk more of his special form of nourishment. The magician topped off their goblets and did his best to ignore the metallic smell of the blood.

"To use your niece to get to me. She identified the second villain as Captain Emilio Dearing. I have never met him and only saw his boots during our escape from the Tower."

"He is the most famous and successful pirate on the Asian seas." Tara walked to the windows to study the street outside. After a moment, she shrugged and returned to sit beside her uncle. "His base is the Sulu Islands in the Philippines. It is quite odd; London is a long way from Asia. Whatever this is, it must be important to him."

"I agree," Celwyn growled. "Tara tells me that a majority of the people on those islands are slaves and prisoners Dearing captured to work on his estates."

"I hear that many are Christians. Some are sold back to their families, and a few of the women sold to the Arab sultans." She shuddered.

"What do they want with us?" Valentine asked.

"Ah." Celwyn held up another finger and regarded the vampire. "This is part two. The operation to capture you was designed to ensure Tara's cooperation."

Tara sighed. "It worked."

"Part three is what Talos and Dearing wanted from all this," Celwyn said. "If they had captured me, I would have become bait to entice Professor Kang to come here. Instead," a satisfied smile crossed his face, "I have warned him, Bartholomew, and Nemo to stay away."

"What do they expect from the Professor?" Tara asked.

Celwyn rubbed his chin and thought. "This is even more vague. When we were on the *Zelda*, Talos desperately wanted to subdue his brother and take him to Junstan Island in the South China Sea. He had hundreds of automats supporting him on a ship shadowing us, and they appeared most warlike."

Valentine finished his goblet and dabbed his lips delicately with a napkin.

"There is good news. Our situation has nothing to do with the confounded flying machine that everyone else wants."

"Yes, that is good news, and?" Tara raised a beautiful brow at him.

"Keep in mind I am not a scientist," Celwyn said. "In fact, at times, I bend scientific principles."

Tara saw the look in his eye and smiled at him. "No demonstration needed. The maid is already on edge."

Celwyn shrugged. "Well. In my opinion, they want Professor Kang because he has developed a powerful weapon known as atomic energy. The theory behind it is old. Per Xiau, in the 5th century, Leucippus and Democritus brought up the possibilities. The science can be used to help or destroy mankind." He waited for them to think about the risks. When Valentine nodded at him to go on, he added, "I will leave it up to you as to what Talos and Dearing would do with it."

Now that they had a moment to breathe and think, Celwyn's thoughts narrowed to an unsettling question. "Why was Ginnie, the witch, associating with the automats? She was after the flying machine the last time I saw her."

"They could have separate motives and do not share information with each other," Tara observed. "Yet, that reasoning confirms she only wants the flying machine."

Valentine had been lost in thought; now, he raised his eyes to Celwyn. "Why?"

From beside him, Tara murmured, "I don't like my answer."

"Let us hear it, please. I'm tiring," Valentine said.

Celwyn agreed. With his face lined with exhaustion, the vampire appeared much closer to his real age. Only his eyes seemed alive, blazing with anger.

Tara regarded the magician. "You said Ginnie was a disciple of that warlock. Her world isn't with pirates normally."

Celwyn said, "I agree."

"Someone new has gained her allegiance. Someone she either admires or who is paying her handsomely."

"Oh, hell—" Celwyn slammed a fist on the table, and the fairy cakes jumped. *Pelaez?*

Tara murmured, "Think about it. Why is she interested? She could still be after the flying machine for whoever she works for. Or she wants what Dearing wants. Why not both?"

Like a lion, the older vampire growled in his throat, and if the nervous little maid had been in the room, she would have climbed the drapes. Valentine's brows lowered, and his expression darkened further. "I never saw her until the week before last, and none of the other scoundrels spoke to her besides Gaspard."

Celwyn cursed, and the glasses on the tray trembled.

"What do you think?" Valentine asked them.

The magician rubbed his face hard. "I don't know. It depends on what they want from the Professor."

Tara touched his hand. "It could also be about you."

Chapter 39

THE NEXT MORNING, THEY MET IN Valentine's suite, a refined room of silks and polished wood with a view of an ornamental garden, a sleepy pond, and a gazebo. A vase of proud irises graced the table in front of the windows. By the time Celwyn arrived, Valentine had ordered their tea.

As he sat at the table between the vampire and Tara, Celwyn asked him, "Are you feeling better?"

"Yes, except for my side, where they continually battered me in an effort to bring me to consciousness."

"May I?" Celwyn asked, and with Valentine's nod, he reached to touch the vampire's ribs, doing his best with them. "Is that better?"

Valentine checked his side. "Much, thank you. What did you do?"

"Knit a rib together that I missed before. It would have healed on its own; I just hurried things along and eliminated the discomfort."

When Tara handed him a full cup of tea, the magician thanked her silently and intimately. After she smiled at him, she grew serious. "Without being rude, this is probably our best chance for a private conversation."

"Observant as usual." Valentine sat back, winced, and asked, "Are there ideas for our next move?"

Last night Celwyn had fallen asleep pondering this without any satisfaction. "Would you agree that we first need to discover Dearing's lair and find Talos?"

They approved. "And Miss Redifer, if they have her," Tara added.

"Could I assume that you have spells to track subjects of interest?" the magician asked her.

She again nodded, this time with a gleam of revenge in her fine eyes. "I'll need to visit the Tower and obtain something from one or both of my attackers."

"I will go with you," Celwyn said. Turning to Valentine, he continued, "We promised Polly that you would rest and recover."

"I suppose."

"There is another reason. I also need to change both of our appearances." He demonstrated this by changing Tara into a much taller, pale, bookish woman with large spectacles. For himself, he became a shorter male version of Tara.

The vampire studied the details of Tara's costume. As he looked at the face he did not recognize sitting beside him, he said, "I see."

Celwyn asked, "Do you mind having blonde hair this time, my dear?"

She laughed. "Your choice. We should depart." Tara stood. "There is no time to waste."

"Sir, if you need more than the common toiletries while staying here, please do not purchase them. Make do with what is here so they do not trace us. I will supply garments and other necessities with my magic. We do not want someone like Mrs. Rowley finding us."

"She is responsible for them capturing my niece. Both of them," the vampire growled. "I will take care of Mrs. Rowley when this is over."

Celwyn got to his feet and shook his pant legs down. "It is settled, then? We will revisit the Tower and find what we need to track Talos and Dearing."

"You need rest, Uncle," she told him.

Celwyn helped her into a shawl. "We will return here before we approach Talos. And we will wait until you have rested completely so you may accompany us."

"Of course." Valentine gazed out the window with a dangerous glint in his eye.

At the door, Tara turned and told her uncle, "I have enlisted Mercury to help us."

"He irritates me." The vampire complained with mild annoyance.

Tara laughed again, much to Celwyn's enjoyment. "Only because he worships you."

Valentine told Celwyn, "Every time I turn around, that albino is staring at me." He shrugged. "But he can be useful. Swift and fearless. He also drinks mouse blood, the Philistine."

"He is fast." Tara said, "We plan to meet him at Falstaff's at noon. We'll perform our errand first."

As they approached the Tower in bright daylight, Celwyn noticed the fortress showed its age. It was built in the 11th century and has endured many wars since then. Pot marks from rifle shots and cannon balls decorated most of the building. Celwyn could easily picture invaders, from Gauls to the Vikings, clambering out of boats, warbling war cries, and scaling the walls.

As part of the curious visitors, they strolled up the street next to the Tower's moat. Like the other night, it smelled of stale water, a dash of mold, and something decomposing. Celwyn hoped it was just an unlucky rat.

"I wonder how deep the moat is," Tara mused. "It couldn't be more than ten feet wide."

The magician knew exactly. "It is eight putrid feet deep." A film of something unpleasant covered the surface, like stagnant, sour milk. "Never fear. Today we will walk over the bridge, not swim."

Wiggling her eyebrows, Tara said, "I was rather hoping for a bit of excitement today."

"I have another idea." Celwyn laughed and steered her toward the back of a stall selling wax figures of the Queen dressed in her widow's weeds. She had been mourning Prince Albert's death for more than seven years and did not appear to be done yet. When Celwyn emerged again, he flew as a beautiful raven with a small Tara on his back and her arms around his neck. The magician had decided that another raven would not be noticed with the other resident ravens inhabiting the Tower. He did his best to ignore the reminder of how ravens had played a part in their adventure in Turkey.

He flew high, circling the Tower and peering through windows. On his third pass by, when he felt certain neither Talos nor Dearing lurked nearby, Celwyn landed on the sill of the same window he had entered to rescue Tara.

Someone had tidied the room since that night. The pillows on the two settees had been arranged just so, and on the desk, an assortment of pens had been lined up beside the ink wells, along with fresh stationery. Celwyn stifled the urge to write Talos a nasty note in case he came back.

All the sheet music had been removed from the stand next to the harpsichord, yet a small man sat there without touching the instrument. He wore a black suit and appeared to be a cleric of sorts, judging from his collar and melancholy expression. The magician checked the rest of the room, seeing nothing sinister.

The clock on the wall struck the midmorning hour, causing the cleric to jump.

What is he doing here? Celwyn wondered silently.

I do not know, Tara answered.

They watched him another moment, wishing he would leave. Behind them, calls from a busker by the docks filtered upward through the window. One of the real ravens cawed from nearby, and two more answered. Not being the superstitious sort but still practical, Celwyn could not discount other abnormal forces at work here.

They couldn't wait all day. He glanced at the harpsichord, and it began to play. Just one string, then another. By the time the cleric had widened his eyes and jumped to his feet, the five notes Celwyn played to reinforce his magic echoed lightly across the room like clouds blown across high mountains. When the instrument began to glow iridescently, the cleric edged back. As he ran for the door, he checked the painted ceiling for the source of the unnatural— and what he probably considered devilish—activity. By the time the door closed behind him, Celwyn and Tara stood side-by-side as themselves next to the harpsichord.

"I'll stay out of your way while you search for what you need," Celwyn told her.

Tara pecked his cheek and began to tour the room. "It's too bad they emptied the ashtrays," she remarked and inspected the desks. Minutes passed, with Celwyn keeping an eye on the door leading in and out of the room. He had locked it but still worried to a degree.

As the minutes ticked by, Celwyn hid his disappointment and watched Tara's frustration grow along with her string of adorable blasphemy. He admired her grasp of colorful and descriptive curses in several languages. She had found nothing. Willing to do his share, the magician checked behind and under the settee cushions. He elevated himself to the top of the chandelier so he could inspect the upper bookshelves. He sat there for minutes, checking the room, his legs and boots dangling between the crystals. Still, not a thing.

"We need to find something," Tara grumbled.

"Tell me about our villains. What did they touch or read?" He landed flat-footed beside her.

Tara stared at him. "Well ... Dearing seemed fascinated with the financial sections of the newspapers. He read every word."

"Did he smoke?"

"Terribly. A pipe that he tapped out—-that window!" She pointed to a smallish square window across the room.

By the time she reached the window, the magician had changed back to a raven. He wasted no time flying out and down to the garden below.

Thankfully, it hasn't rained, he thought.

Sure enough, he found several piles of embers under a rose bush directly underneath the window. The cinders that had landed on top of the bushes had presumably blown away. Not knowing what a witch needed for a tracking spell, Celwyn carefully transferred the freshest ashes into a pouch and flew back again.

As himself once more, he spread his treasure across a piece of stationary on the desk. "Will this do?"

It took several minutes for Tara to study his find. She sniffed it. She poked some of it with a finger, then a pencil. Celwyn produced two small drawstring bags and a spoon. Without looking up, she thanked him and sorted through the remnants. She leaned close to each pile and nodded before scooping several bags full.

"We have what we need and can go."

As she spoke, someone tried the door leading to the hallway. Celwyn took her hand, and they walked to the side of the doors. Someone shook the handle.

"When it opens," he told her silently, "we will be invisible and depart."

———

Celwyn and Tara discovered the only hire coach remaining in front of the Tower. As soon as they climbed inside, they knew why. The magician corrected the smell and cleaned the windows as the carriage rolled across the street, heading for Falstaff's.

"Will Mercury be on time for our meeting?" Celwyn asked.

"Oh, yes. The only time he was not prompt, Valentine became highly annoyed. Our friend in blue will wait in the back office if he gets there before us. Never fear; we will be there by noon."

Minutes later, they pulled to a stop a few storefronts south of Falstaff's. Some inner sense tickled the magician with cold fingers, and he changed their disguises again. Tara emerged from the coach as a much older and muscular woman resembling Mrs. Thomas, the housekeeper of Tellyhouse. When Celwyn attained the sidewalk reeking of tobacco, he could have been the diminutive footman of Tellyhouse with his curly whiskers and paunch.

"My, you are adorable," Tara wiggled her nose. "What kind of tobacco is that?"

Celwyn finished paying the driver, took her elbow, and approached the entrance. "I don't know, but it should be distracting enough for anyone we encounter."

An automat approached from the north. Celwyn turned Tara away as the mechanical man walked rapidly down the sidewalk. The magician watched until the automat disappeared into the crowd on the next block.

"Was that a—"

"Yes. This isn't an ideal situation. Let's go inside and get this over with."

The bell on the door tinkled behind them as, once again, they circled tables of books, pipes, tobacco, and a rotund proprietor who resembled Mr. Toad from *Alice in Wonderland*. Celwyn's dread rose as he regarded the shopkeeper. He had stopped stacking books to stare at them in a stupefied manner as if he didn't know where he was. The magician's unease grew stronger.

When they reached the door to the back office, Celwyn held a hand in front of Tara. "Please, allow me to go in first." He could still see-through walls somewhat, thanks to Thales, but not clearly. No one breathed in the room, and he heard nothing.

As the magician pushed the door open, he threw light inside. It would have been better if he had not. Knowing Tara would have seen worse many times before, he told her over his shoulder, "Mercury is dead. It is messy. I'll leave it up to you whether to come in."

"I'll stay here." Tara's voice sounded low and angry. "How did he die?"

"There must have been several of them," Celwyn said. "They tore him apart and used blades. It was a vicious fight." He felt his rage grow, but with effort, he kept his voice steady. "If you could instead check for more automats, that would be helpful." He watched her from the doorway; pain and sadness twisted her face.

She whispered, "Mercury wouldn't have gone quietly." A tear slid out of her eye, and she wiped it away. She scanned the rest of the store and then out the windows for the automats.

"It is possible more of them will arrive if the one we just saw reports that he saw us." Celwyn finished backing out, closing the door. "Even if we are in disguise. I do not trust them. Please excuse me while I check the proprietor. He should have heard this attack."

The magician moved behind the shopkeeper as he finished straightening several fallen books and entered his mind. Up front, Celwyn found a high level of wild, unfocused fear. When the proprietor's memory grew clearer, the scene became a band of automats entering the store, backing him into a corner and hitting him on the head, and then nothing. The fright remained with the man, and utmost in his thoughts, he feared that they would return.

Celwyn wiped away the proprietor's memory of himself and Tara in case torture was a part of the automats' game. The magician made a silent suggestion to the man to close the shop for the rest of the day and to bring an armed assistant with him on the morrow and for the next few days. For his part, Celwyn sent Mercury's remains to the alley in the back and covered them with a clean blanket.

After he cleaned the gruesome room, the magician returned to Tara, took her elbow, and they headed toward the door. "The owner is innocent. The automats knocked him out before the attack."

"Why did they kill Mercury? He was gentle and sweet."

"I know. I am so sorry."

Tara said, "It isn't easy to kill a vampire."

Celwyn stopped in front of the door leading to the street. He checked outside, seeing nothing unusual. "They must have followed him here. It would be prudent to leave. Now."

When the shop door opened, he flew through it as a handsome fly with a much smaller and exquisite fly on his back.

Chapter 40

B Y THE TIME THEY RETURNED TO
Polly's mansion, Celwyn had developed a
strong craving for his tea. Like Xiau said, it made
him grumpy when he did not have it by this time of
the day. During the ride back, he also had come to
terms with Mercury's death, along with a silent vow
to avenge him. Celwyn had not known him well, but
no one should die in such a manner.

As Gerald opened the door, Celwyn greeted him,
"Good afternoon." They stepped inside. "Where
would we find Mr. Soriano at the moment?"

Gerald closed the door and turned to face them,
a curious expression seeping into his neutral and
well-trained face. Something between amusement
and nervousness warred there. Considering her wide
variety of guests, the butler must have seen quite a
bit while working for Polly, and Celwyn wondered
what had unnerved him.

"Mr. Soriano is in the garden; I will escort you there."

As Celwyn ushered Tara forward, he asked Gerald, "Would you request some Earl Grey, please?"

"I believe Mr. Soriano is expecting you and has already sent for some."

They passed a vacant drawing room, then an overstuffed parlor. In the library, a pair of stern spinsters sat there as primly as if they were in church with their hands folded. During the ride back from Falstaff's and the murder, Tara had clutched his arm and wept. Only now, when they reached the fashionable French doors leading outside, did she release his arm. By the time they finished trailing the butler down the path between the forsythias and roses, they heard Valentine's voice and then Polly's.

They rounded a wall of tall shrubbery and stopped short. In the gazebo, a very naked Valentine and Polly held forth in a sweeping, dramatic fashion.

"Shakespeare's *Winter's Tale*," Tara murmured with a hand over her face to keep from laughing. "Your mouth is open, Jonas."

Valentine bowed and raised his eyes upward.

> "'I shall report,
> For most it caught me, the celestial habits,
> Methinks I so should term them, and the reverence
> Of the grave wearers. O, the sacrifice!
> How ceremonious, solemn, and unearthly
> It was i' the offering!'"

Gerald's façade of imperturbability had begun to crack. A fine sheen of perspiration appeared above his upper lip—for a British butler, the epitome of breaking strict training.

Meanwhile, his mistress, Polly, carried on.

CLEOMENES (Polly)
    "'But of all, the burst
    And the ear-deafening voice o' the oracle,
    Kin to Jove's thunder, so surprised my sense.
    That I was nothing.'"

DION (Valentine)
    "'If the event o' the journey
    Prove as successful to the queen, —O be't so!—
    As it hath been to us rare, pleasant, speedy,
    The time is worth the use on't.'"

CLEOMENES
    "Great Apollo
    Turn all to the best! These proclamations,
    So forcing faults upon Hermione,
    I little like.'"

DION
    "'The violent carriage of it
    Will clear or end the business: when the oracle,
    Thus by Apollo's great divine seal'd up,
    Shall the contents discover, something rare
    Even then will rush to knowledge. Go: fresh horses!
    And gracious be the issue!'"

Gerald coughed and announced much louder than necessary, "Miss McFein and Mr. Celwyn, Madam." He bowed, nearly knocking over the maid delivering the tea.

Since Valentine and Polly showed no signs of interrupting their performance, Celwyn steered Tara to a chair in the shade. As the maid poured, she stared at the gazebo, as horrified as if she'd found a salivating werewolf sitting on the kitchen table. Tea sloshed everywhere. Without touching the maid, Celwyn steadied her hand until she finished; there was never a reason to waste tea. By the time he took his first sip, the odd pair of actors had finished, bowed to each other, and donned robes.

"Thank God," Tara murmured. Her expression had turned serious, once more remembering Mercury's demise, "I knew of this hobby of my uncle's but had never seen a performance."

Celwyn drained his cup and poured more. "It is something I will not soon forget." He could not help but wish Bartholomew and Xiau were here for their reactions. He wanted to laugh when he thought about Nemo's reaction. More somberly, he admitted it was not the only reason he wished for their presence. He sighed; protecting them was more important than their companionship.

The magician observed Valentine as he made his way out of the gazebo and over to them. He did not seem as lively as during their adventure in the catacombs, but nearly so. Vampires had an excellent recovery system.

Polly's cheeks flushed with excitement, and her blonde curls shimmered under the midday sun as she approached their table. Like a plump fairy, she displayed no signs of embarrassment at all. Instead of sitting down, she paced to the nearby roses.

"I've decided," she whirled and announced, "*Richard II* is next. Do you agree, my lord?"

Valentine executed an elaborate bow and said, "But, of course."

"Excellent. I love Shakespeare to no end, but I must change for a luncheon appointment. Oh drat! Some members of the mayor's committee are waiting." She regarded Tara with a stern eye. "Whatever you and Mr. Celwyn must do, please watch Valentine. He isn't as recovered as he pretends to be." She started up the walkway toward the house, calling over her shoulder, "Yes, I know y'all won't be here for dinner."

Valentine leaned back and turned away from the sun, putting the hood of his robe up. "What kind of tea is that?"

"Earl Grey, of course."

The vampire made a face. Celwyn added a bottle of red wine and a pair of glasses in case Tara had been too polite to refuse the tea.

"Ah," Valentine uncorked the bottle and poured. "Thank you. Do you like Shakespeare?"

Celwyn's lips twitched, and he hesitated. "Yes ... I had never seen it performed this way before."

Tara touched his hand. "You can't hurt Uncle's feelings." Then her eyes misted, and she turned away.

"Something has happened, judging from my niece's expression."

Tara told him about Mercury's murder at Falstaff's. When Valentine stopped snarling, and his expression cleared, he said, "We'll avenge ourselves against these vermin. Mercury served my family for many years. This is an affront that cannot be ignored!"

He started to get up, and his niece pulled on his sleeve until he subsided.

"Were you successful at the Tower?" Valentine patted her hand.

Celwyn laid the bags of ashes on the table. As Valentine peered inside the pouches, he cursed in a language the magician did not recognize.

"To a point. I would like to have a plan in mind and know more about Captain Dearing before we attack," Celwyn said. "Violence is a bonus when we find the villains. Especially after our discovery at Falstaff's."

Valentine nodded. "I enjoy it at times, also. If they have Miss Redifer, her rescue will come first."

"Agreed." Celwyn nodded.

"I might know of someone who can tell us about Captain Dearing," the older vampire said as he smoothed his luxuriant mustache. "He is a nasty individual and can usually be found in a pub over by the Parliament buildings."

Tara asked, "Do I know him?"

If Celwyn had not been watching Valentine closely, he wouldn't have seen his eyes shift slightly and close. The magician congratulated himself on discovering more about Valentine, such as when he intended to prevaricate.

"No, you do not."

It would be best to change the subject, Celwyn decided. "Excellent. A field trip is in order." He finished his tea, stood, and pulled out Tara's chair. "After we freshen up, we will meet you in the front parlor."

"Perhaps I should go alone," Valentine suggested.

"No." Tara's glare at her uncle allowed no room for negotiation.

Chapter 41

"I COMMEND YOU ON YOUR CAUTION," Celwyn told Valentine as they changed broughams for the third time since leaving Polly's mansion. For his own version of caution, the magician had altered his and Tara's appearance to those of two well-to-do and fashionable women, with Tara resembling a much younger version of Polly and Celwyn, a close, obese relative of Marie Antoinette. Cake! More cake! Valentine remained as himself so that his acquaintance would recognize him, but the magician had added a high collar on his cloak and an oversized hat to hide his telltale silver locks.

As the carriage pulled to a stop in front of a respectable pub, Tara asked, "Who are we to see?"

Valentine handed her out of the carriage and, in measured tones, replied, "Sir John Cecil Winterset."

"The vampire hunter?" Tara gasped and froze.

Celwyn finished settling the fare with the driver, stepped back, and touched her elbow to show his support.

She demanded of her uncle, "Are you insane?"

"Let's not attract attention," Valentine said as he took her other elbow and approached the entrance of the Feathered Goose. "I have an agreement with Winterset. He leaves our family alone if I remove the destructive vampires he has trouble eliminating. He knows that this only applies to the ones *I* consider evil." He held the door open for them. "I also told him I would rip his eyes out if anything happened to you."

Celwyn suppressed a chuckle and walked through the door behind them.

Low murmurs filtered through a thick cloud of at least a dozen types of pipe smoke. The snug appeared appropriately secretive and gloomy, with cubbyholes for privacy that framed a room filled with resident drinkers. The magician spied a table in the corner occupied by a quartet of what appeared to be inebriated schoolmarms. As he watched, one of them threw her hat in the air and caught it again. Her companions whistled or tried to.

"This way." Valentine steered them toward the back, with Celwyn following in a somewhat comehither wiggle because of the womanly shoes he wore. One of the patrons grabbed at his rear. The magician glued the man's hand to his lap and smiled at him.

Valentine stopped at the last cubbyhole at a table just big enough for four. The vampire and Tara sat across from the man sitting there, leaving the magician the remaining chair. Two people of great girth did not belong in such a tight space.

At least the closeness had an advantage. As Valentine made the introductions, Celwyn entered Winterset's mind and wandered around. Their quarry had little regard for Valentine but a healthy opinion of his usefulness. As the man's thoughts darted in different directions, the magician found a few surprises. Winterset liked Marlowe's plays over those of John Webster. He also hoped to leave the pub soon to see his mistress.

Celwyn frowned. Winterset's thoughts bounced again in a more serious direction. Apparently, the fat man had a list of Irish vampires he wanted eliminated. Then Winterset turned to Tara. He expressed a modicum of curiosity, but not extremely so. He did think her hat a bit too much for the London fashions. Celwyn had noticed that hat styles seemed to be less flamboyant lately. He grinned, anticipating Annabelle's general outrage about any changes in haberdashery.

"Good afternoon," Valentine grumbled at Winterset with little graciousness. Celwyn suspected that was part of the dance between the two of them.

"Are you going to introduce me?"

"No need. These are my confederates. They wish to remain anonymous until they are sure of you." The vampire shot him a neutral glance. "Why are you here? Have I interrupted a *tête-à-tête* with someone?"

"No. Not right now. I was hoping to meet you here," Winterset gushed with the expansiveness of a horse trader. "I always expect to profit from our association." He signaled the barmaid. "What will you have to drink?"

After their pints arrived, Valentine trained a stare on the other man. "I understand that you have traveled extensively in the East. To Singapore, Beijing, and Hong Kong."

"Yes. And points beyond that." The fat man waved a hand that seemed small for a man of his size.

Valentine took his time sipping, and the magician suspected the intent was to increase Winterset's nervousness. Finally, the vampire gazed at the man from under lowered brows and said, "What do you know about Captain Emilio Dearing?"

"Ha!" The fat man slapped the table with delight. "I believe my price just went up. I happen to know a great deal about him. Not many people do."

"Excuse me." Tara batted her eyes at him. "May I ask why?"

Winterset smoothed his mustache flat and continued to grin. "As I stated, I have traveled extensively for years."

In a stilted upper-class voice, Celwyn asked, "From your expression, there is more, isn't there?"

"Excuse me, Madam." The fat man sneered at the magician. "How are you acquainted with Mr. Soriano?"

"We advise him when he is doing your bidding; to hunt vampires," Tara made a point of not looking directly at the man, probably to keep him relaxed.

"Oh. Well." Winterset rested his chin on his other chins. "That is appreciated."

Valentine eyed him. "And our question?"

"A simple answer. At one point, I was one of Dearing's hostages." Winterset enjoyed their expressions of surprise. "Over a period of months, I learned many things. Not to be immodest," he patted his chest, "but there are very few people alive who have survived Dearing's imprisonment and know as much as I do."

Celwyn simpered, "What do you want, sir?" After he asked, the magician sent Valentine a silent message saying he would help extract the information if the vampire preferred him to.

Valentine made eye contact, and it was not pleasant, but Celwyn understood that he accepted the offer.

Oblivious to their exchange, Winterset said, "I want the Muldane clan of vampires in Eire eliminated."

Tara sputtered, "I know Erin Muldane. She is a gentle, kind soul."

"She is a vampire who is close to Alex Muldane, who you will admit is murderous and unpredictable," Winterset spat.

"She is not like him!" Tara cried and knocked over her glass. "Neither are her brothers and sisters and the rest—"

"Hush, woman—" Winterset hissed at her.

Celwyn started a hand for his throat and stopped. Breaking their disguise was one thing; showing Winterset his true nature was another.

Valentine had no such restraint, and because he knew Winterset, the vampire had an advantage.

"Let's discuss a few samples of what you know and then come to an agreement on the *price*," the vampire suggested to the fat man.

Tara was ready to climb over the table and discuss things with teeth and nails. She settled for glaring holes through Winterset's corpulent face. To appease her, the magician covered the man in red spots and removed the hair from his head.

"Well, sir?" Valentine's lips twitched.

"Why is that barkeep laughing at me?" Winterset demanded.

"I'm sure I do not know," Valentine waved a hand at him. "Go on."

Winterset stared at the bartender again before saying, "It was the summer of 1859, just a few years ago. Dearing sank the ship that I sailed on, the *HSS Dolman*. She had been on her way to Hong Kong." He hesitated. "I was carrying the Queen's business for a trade proposal to a local dignitary there."

"Politics." Valentine dismissed it. "Then what happened?"

"I found myself on Dearing's main ship, enjoying the extravagant comforts he afforded himself. I was a prize, you see, and perhaps more educated than some of his hostages. Someone he could socialize with." He finished his pint and signaled for another. "We waited while he tried to ransom me. It took nearly six months for my family to pay him off." Winterset watched the barkeep drawing ale. "Dearing left me near Sardinia. Months later, I returned to London. After that, the Church asked for my help ridding the world of bloodsucking killers." Not only did he not apologize for the insult, but treated them to a nasty smile. "And here I am."

Tara appeared ready to do something about Winterset; the red spots were not enough. Celwyn silently implored her, "*Please wait. Think of this as a step to recovering Miss Redifer.*" She inhaled several times and subsided.

Valentine leaned back and patted a yawn. "We need to know Dearing's habits and everything about his fears."

"He is extremely good with knives." Winterset shrugged. "Fast and accurate."

"We know that and what his pipe smoke smells like," Celwyn retorted in a high, fussy voice. He told Valentine, "This man is useless."

"If you've met him, why do you need me?" Winterset reddened.

"He has something we want." Valentine slowly scratched inch-long nails across the table. "Again, tell us what he fears."

Nails or not, Winterset clearly enjoyed Valentine's irritation. He laughed, and his belly shook. When he sobered, he became helpful. "Very well. Like many sailors, he can't swim. But unlike them, he is convinced he will never drown. Let's discuss my payment."

"Why does he think this?" the vampire demanded.

From his expression, the fat man considered saying nothing, but finally did. "It is something to do with how Dearing thinks of himself—without limits and invincible ... if you will. Much of my knowledge comes from our dinner conversations together."

He consulted a gold watch ringed with twin-kling diamonds and stuffed it back into his pocket. "Sometimes Dearing elaborated on his thoughts, then other times he suspected me of gathering intelligence for the Crown." The vampire hunter sat up with his eyes filled with suspicion. "I say, how did you know I would know so much about Dearing?"

The vampire purred, "I'll tell you after we conclude our business."

Winterset hesitated, deciding if it would benefit him. "That remains to be negotiated. Anyhow, there is little else that I know of that he is afraid of."

Celwyn suspected Winterset of hiding his cards, and when he entered his mind, he found confirmation. A few more tidbits lay there for the taking. Once Celwyn silently passed most of them along to Valentine, and then Tara, the older vampire asked innocently, "Tell me, why is Dearing in London?"

Winterset squirmed like his drawers suddenly felt too tight. "I'm sure I do not know."

The magician tightened them further.

Valentine leaned over the table close enough to breathe on him. "Yes, you do." His voice held a threat no one could miss.

"There are witnesses here." Winterset's chins quivered.

"Yes, there are. All I want is information," Valentine whispered, which served to frighten the fat man more. "And I will continue to help eliminate the bad elements within the vampire communities." He gently patted Winterset's cheek. "We need more information about the pirate. Why is he here?"

Winterset exhaled loudly. "All I know is that he is in league with someone who has promised him a weapon. It is used to conquer kingdoms and rule the seas. I didn't believe it when I heard it, and I don't believe it now." The fat man drank off his pint and wiped his face. "That is all I know!"

Taking his unspoken cue, Celwyn stood and urged Tara to her feet. One of the drawbacks to this disguise was that he could not touch her. "We will be out in front while you conclude your business."

Tara was ready to help her uncle negotiate, perhaps by standing on Winterset's balloon-shaped stomach. The magician drew her to the side to whisper, "Valentine won't give him much. He will only eliminate those he feels should be. Have faith in him."

When Winterset turned the other way, she kissed his cheek. "I hope you are right."

Chapter 42

Twenty minutes later, Winterset observed Valentine as he crossed through the main room of the pub. A few of the drinkers glanced at him, and some of the women stared with interest. *Little do they know of his true and disgusting nature,* the fat man thought.

"Left me with the bloody bill." Winterset sniffed and flung coins on the table. As he wiggled himself into a position to stand, another pint appeared in front of him, and a man slid into the opposite side of the booth.

"Good evening."

Fascinated, Winterset hesitated and turned back. He watched the stranger sip ale, well aware the man returned the scrutiny. He knew this man, and why was he here? Like a surgeon dissecting freckles off a face, the man's eyes crawled over Winterset in the dim light. The vampire hunter had never met his new guest but, long ago, had seen a picture of him in newspapers. He knew of him.

"Excellent." The man licked foam from his lips. "I must try this house more often." The stranger enjoyed Winterset's stunned silence for a moment, and asked, "You wish to know why I am here?"

"Yes." Winterset gulped ale as he thought of the man's reputation and the possibilities behind this encounter. If rumors were true, it was dangerous just to associate with him. *Could this be an assassination or an arrest?*

The stranger scanned the room behind them, face by face, and when satisfied, said, "I have something to sell ... or perhaps trade. It would definitely be of interest to you."

Winterset stalled, taking time to finish his pint. He had heard of the trickery of this man and that he had no scruples while also doing things that could be termed illegal. *Yet, how intriguing?* It was not often Winterset met someone more scandalous than himself.

"Perhaps ... we can talk."

The stranger laughed. "How would you like to hold the fate of Miss Tara McFein in your hands?" He enjoyed Winterset's slow smile of understanding. "You could ask anything of Mr. Valentine Soriano that you wished. *Anything.*"

⌣

The magician felt it was high time for lunch when Valentine joined them in the hire carriage. The odors from the pub's kitchen had not set well with Celwyn's stomach.

As Valentine climbed inside, the magician announced, "I'll leave it up to you as to where we will luncheon. All I ask is that it does not include boiled cabbage and that the tea is hot."

A discussion ensued until the vampire opened the glass between them and told their driver, "Turow's Garden, please."

As the carriage set off down the street, the magician addressed Valentine, "I am going to disguise you. What do you prefer?"

Valentine hesitated, and Tara advised, "Tell him, or he'll get fanciful."

"If you must, make me a handsome Shakespearean actor. Or perhaps Oscar Wilde."

Tara gasped and shook her head. "Don't. Someone else, please."

A moment later, Celwyn said, "Done."

Valentine admired his new black locks, patrician nose, and velvet jacket in the reflection of the coach window.

Celwyn wondered if he seemed as vain as Valentine. When the vampire stopped staring at himself, the magician said, "We need to plan. Winterset had a variety of information that he did not tell us about. Did you know that Dearing led the siege on Tripoli a few years ago? Winterset not only knew of it but also participated in one of Dearing's bloody raids in Cyprus. He is as much a villain as the damn pirate is." The magician eyed Valentine. "You might want to use that tidbit during your next negotiation with him. The Queen wouldn't like that if she learns of it."

After Valentine nodded his agreement, Tara asked, "Does Winterset get paid for the killings, or does he just hate vampires?"

Valentine shrugged. "A bit of both, but to his credit, he does understand the difference between good and bad vampires to a point, until his prejudice overwhelms him."

"You do not trust him," Tara surmised.

Valentine said, "That is correct."

Conversation halted while a clarion siren went by with a wagon full of bobbies hanging off the side rails. Right behind it clattered a horse-drawn water cannon and more bobbies running by on foot.

"I wonder what is burning?" Tara asked as she tried to see down the street.

"Unknown. I do smell the fire. It is at least several blocks away." Valentine addressed Celwyn. "I have a hunch you explored much more of Winterset's mind."

"Thoroughly. Such a disgusting man."

As their waiter set a carafe of wine upon the table, Celwyn glanced at the Turow's dining room, enjoying the calm pastel colors and lace-covered windows so reminiscent of the cafes in Prague. The room could not have held more than a dozen tables, and at every one of them, the patrons enjoyed something French and decadent. Through the open doorway, he caught glimpses of customers arriving and waiting on the sidewalk. It seemed a fine day, which helped lessen Celwyn's guilt for leaving them outside while he ate.

After they ordered, Celwyn occupied himself, sorting through the telegrams they had retrieved on the way here. One from Patrick and Annabelle and one from Xiau and Bartholomew. The third originated with Captain Nemo, and the magician opened it first. Nemo's message was short and to the point:

> *Do you need my help?*
> *Are they after the flying machine?*

Celwyn composed answers in his mind for another stop later at the telegraph desk. No, he did not want Nemo, Bartholomew, and Kang in danger. And no, Talos was not after the flying machine. At least, not for now. But, if he found out about it, things would suddenly become more interesting for everyone.

The magician ripped open the message from Annabelle and Patrick:

> *Uncle Celwyn, you are always getting in trouble, but we understand. We will be on guard. Otto's piano lessons are progressing very well. If you can find Mozart's Die Zauberflöte music in London, he will be pleased. He knows it will be a while until he can play it, but he wants to learn it for you. Elizabeth says for you to be careful and keep the Professor out of London.*

> *Zander wants another dog as big as Beastie. Your problem.*

The waiter had left by the time Celwyn spoke again. "Things are normal in Prague. Nemo has offered his help. It will be refused at this point since Bartholomew and Kang would come to town along with it."

He ripped open the last missive with a feeling that Xiau would not be as easily put off:

Jonas,

> *I do not know what you are leaving out or how dangerous the situation is. Talos cannot be trusted. Bartholomew and I are ready to cross the Channel and help if you give the word.*

> *If you don't, we will wait for a short time and then come over to help anyhow. You usually display no sense of caution for yourself.*

Xiau

The magician held the telegram up. "As expected, nothing that can't wait until we have finished our luncheon." He downplayed the automat's intention since it was his problem to deal with, not Valentine and Tara's.

"Is the Professor coming to town?" the vampire asked.

Tara's brows went up with curiosity.

Celwyn watched a waiter deliver plates at a neighboring table. "I certainly hope not. I say... the lamb looks marvelous."

The vampire regarded his niece. "Once we follow your spell to Talos and Dearing's lair, what are our plans? Freeing Miss Redifer is important."

Tara said, "We will have to see what we find."

"Are you armed now?" Celwyn asked.

Her smile was just from her to him. "But of course."

———⌣———

An hour later, Valentine climbed into a hire cab, and the magician helped Tara inside after him. After the coach had bumped its way back into traffic, their conversation resumed.

"It is good that you are armed. We need to guarantee Dearing does not come after the Professor and everyone else." Celwyn sighed all the way to his boots. He had to tell them.

"What is it?" Tara prompted him. When he still hesitated, she added, "It can't be that terrible."

"It could." The magician said, "I wanted to deal with this myself, but I fear I've run out of time. We must hurry—between Nemo, Kang, and Bartholomew, they will probably arrive here soon to 'help' us. It could turn into a circus. An extremely dangerous one."

Valentine's answering glare could have lit a small fire in the carriage.

Their coach lurched to a stop. Many Londoners crowded the sidewalk, some holding newspapers and others reading cardboard advertisements in the windows of a small theatre. A boy on a bicycle whizzed by as even more people surged into the street, enjoying the evening.

When they alighted from the coach, a woman in the crowd caught sight of Valentine and exclaimed, "It's Richard Hume!"

Chapter 43

HOURS BEFORE, THE SUN HAD TAKEN her final bow of the day as Celwyn, and the vampires, walked away from Polly's and flagged down a carriage to take them to the Tower. While the magician kept an eye to the rear to verify they were not followed, Valentine kept a running description of his favorite play at Vienna's Grand Theatre. It involved woodland nymphs and a shoeless prince. Tara half-smiled, but it was clear to Celwyn that her mind was on their mission and Mercury's death.

They passed a young couple so entwined in themselves and their romance that they did not notice a daemon stealing the woman's watch. Celwyn waved a hand, and the daemon fell on his knees, extending the purloined watch toward his victim. Tara enjoyed the scene with grim satisfaction.

Minutes more, and Valentine handed Tara to the ground as Celwyn paid their driver.

The night seemed still as they watched their carriage roll away toward Buckingham. Celwyn took Tara's elbow, and they continued the rest of the way down Canon Street. When they passed under a burned-out streetlamp, the magician changed all of them into another, reluctantly agreed-upon, mode of transportation; it saved time if they did not have to depend on carriages and the discretion of drivers.

As a most handsome raven, he flew upward with a small Valentine and Tara on his back. When they arrived at the top of the Tower, the chamber was unoccupied. He and Valentine waited while Tara prowled the room, finally settling at one of the desks with a fat pouch filled with odd things. She poked a finger at a scrap of tree bark, a pinch of cinnamon, and string.

Minutes went by as she manipulated the objects, murmuring and directing them again. In the silence, the magician could hear the older vampire breathing.

Finally, Tara stood. "This will have to do. Let's adjourn to the street."

A few minutes later, the raven hovered above the entrance, waiting for a pair of guards arguing about a woman to pass by. Tara tapped the raven's neck and silently directed him toward the south. The city lights twinkled, and the evening air grew colder as Celwyn flew higher above the roofline. Headlines barked by newspaper boys floated up to them, along with distant cathedral bells. Far below, a short train chugged by, heading north. Wisps of steam from her engine blew upward and bathed the magician's face, the scent reminding him of their adventures on the *Elizabeth*.

Gradually, the city smells of horse manure and coal fires became overlaid with the salt and brine of the sea. As they neared the docks, the outline of tall white canvases above the barkentines and schooners glowed from within the darkness. He flew lower, in a wide arc around the ships.

Oh my. In Tara's thoughts, she began to curse again, loudly.

Where to land? Ah. The roof of one of the bawdy houses seemed flat, with plenty of dark shadows, and appeared unpopulated. By the time he had floated downward and changed their appearance back, their toes touched the roof. High time to rest.

Valentine patted his coat and checked elsewhere to see if anything had changed from their flight. He growled, "Why did we land? I see no one nearby."

"Your niece will tell us."

With a deep frown that made Celwyn glad it was not directed at him, she said, "We may as well leave. The spell stopped when we arrived at the docks. It can't cross the water."

"Damnation!"

Behind them lay the expanse of the Thames that opened into the North Sea.

Celwyn's reaction was the same as her uncle's, but to calm Tara down, he asked, "We assume they boarded a boat? That couldn't have been foreseen."

"Most likely. It must be a boat that hasn't returned, or I would see secondary evidence of it with the spell."

"Can you change the spell to bring the boat back?" Valentine asked.

She raised her eyes to them again. "I wish I could, but I'm not that powerful. My specialty is wind, and even with that, I have limitations."

The magician patted her arm and resisted the urge to comfort her.

"Don't let my niece tell you differently. She is a powerful witch."

"If you say so, Uncle. But you only see that power in times of extreme danger." Tara sighed. "If we cannot find our enemies another way, perhaps we can enlist the services of a stronger witch," she suggested.

Celwyn said, "There may be a less elaborate way."

"Such as?"

The more he thought about it, the more Celwyn enjoyed a measure of malicious satisfaction. "Everyone should have a fondness for tea, such as Captain Dearing and I do."

Late that evening, they dined on Polly's terrace by the gazebo. Celwyn was the only one wearing a coat and noticed that Fall had arrived with cold arms.

Valentine said, "Polly sends her regards. She had a prior engagement."

"Her hospitality is appreciated," the magician told him as he cut into a portion of baked chicken and savored it.

Tara glanced wistfully at his entrée before saying, "We can assume that Talos and Dearing are searching for us right now. Shouldn't we take the offensive and go after them?"

Celwyn loved a strong woman! The magician could have hugged her, but not in front of Gerald, who oversaw the table from a discreet distance away from the gazebo.

Valentine's face hardened. "They will pay soon enough. Mr. Celwyn, I could put out a call and gather a few of our family and others to help us. They will be most concerned if Miss Redifer has been abducted."

Celwyn rubbed his chin. "We just don't know, do we? It is also possible we don't have time for a rescue."

"That is true," Tara murmured.

They sat in silence for several minutes, each thinking and devising plans.

The magician finally put down his fork and sat back. "When I explored Winterset's mind, the only hint I found that might lead us to Dearing seems thin and a bit nebulous. Yet, it is all I can offer."

"You hinted earlier about a 'fondness for tea,'" Tara said. "For myself, I can't suggest anything except that blasted spell."

"Nothing from here," Valentine poured out the last of the wine. Celwyn refilled the bottle. Gerald saw it and pretended he didn't. Valentine continued, "I suspect that they have her." His face darkened. "Tell us of whatever you have, sir."

"Well. You must promise not to find this too amusing." The magician hesitated and when Valentine showed signs of impatience by again dragging his long nails across the tablecloth, said, "It seems that Captain Dearing, the supreme leader of the pirates, has a great fondness for teas, especially for the same Earl Grey that the Queen favors, as do I."

Tara burst out laughing as Celwyn soldiered on. "All we have to do is find the finest tea purveyor in London and wait for our enemy to place an order."

Chapter 44

Findbar Island

NEAR SUNDOWN, BONE-TIRED BUT proud of their work, Professor Xiau Kang and Bartholomew left the hangar. Any time Celwyn was not with them, Kang made a habit of scanning the grass leading to the thick grove of trees between the buildings and the cliffs. Satisfied, he switched his survey to the courtyard and then the mansion. He spied nothing unusual and noted that Nemo's guards appeared alert as they walked the perimeter in pairs.

Bartholomew asked, "Do we want to discuss the weight ratio tonight or sleep on it until tomorrow? I am sure of my calculations." He held the door to the ballroom open, and they crossed through to the conservatory. They did not dawdle, even though they verified the guards stood at both the north and south walls, rifles over their shoulders. Over the last few weeks, they had gotten used to the heightened security with the magician gone.

"Your choice. It will give me a respite from my worry about Jonas," Kang said.

"As do I. I hope he is—"

Jules Verne opened the door from the hallway that led to the grotto. He stopped still when he saw them. A practiced—and suspect—smile lit up his face.

"Good afternoon," the author said.

"To you also," Bartholomew replied, indicating he saw the subterfuge.

Kang noticed the author carried a single fountain pen and his ever-present notebook.

"I was hoping to catch you here," he said.

Kang raised a brow. "You wanted to see the flying machine?"

"Err ... no. If Jonas were here, I'd ask him." Verne's eyes shifted, and his words came faster. "I wish to visit the tower above us and for you to go with me."

Bartholomew blinked in disbelief and gestured at the guards. "Any of these men would go with you."

"I know." Verne sucked on his lips and said, "They have once before, but not all the way to the tower."

Kang regarded him. "And?"

"It didn't turn out well." The Frenchman shrugged, which spoke words. "Nothing happened. I think the ghosts are hesitant. Perhaps the rifles are a deterrent." Verne sighed.

Kang could not believe it. "Because a guard has a gun?"

"Excuse me, but as far as I know, ghosts do not feel gunshots—they are already dead." Bartholomew did not sound sure.

Verne said, "Perhaps, but I am hoping that bringing someone else will help." He scurried under the grand staircase leading upward and checked the floor above. He returned to them. "I am hoping to meet a specter, not that horrid woman from when Jonas and I came here months ago. Possibly we could encounter one of the ghosts from the sanitorium who can tell us what happened to the Spencers or the mental patients."

Bartholomew eyed him. "You aren't afraid?"

"Yes." Verne pulled on his lip. "I am. But, with you accompanying me, I feel safe. At least, I think I do."

Kang pointed to the notebook under his arm. "You expect to use information from this for a book?"

"Yes," Verne nodded. "I do. Not right away, but I'd like to have notes about it before we leave the island." His eyes took on a faraway mien. "It would be simply perfect to be in a snowbound cabin and write a ghost story."

Kang thought the man daft and tried not to laugh. At least Verne was not writing about things he shouldn't like he usually tried to do. Bartholomew's expression displayed his horrified reaction that anyone would want to see something like that.

"All right," Kang told Verne. "Lead the way."

Verne's resolve faltered along with his steps as they climbed the stairs above the black-and-white checkered floor—the scene of Mrs. Spencer's beheading of the bishop. Bartholomew urged Verne forward with a suggestion to not look at the room below.

The Professor did glance at it, seeing nothing untoward except a few dust motes in the corner. Nemo's crew probably avoided the place. He sighed. They had only returned to Findbar days ago after a visit to Prague, and like Bartholomew, Kang had hoped they could immerse themselves in science again. Not intrigue. Yet ... he checked on his big friend, glad Bartholomew could not read his thoughts; the automat could admit he liked intrigue better than science at times but, above all, would not tell the foolhardy magician so.

Bartholomew stood with his hands on his hips, gazing down a long, narrow corridor of closed doors to a small window at the far end. "This was the floor where the female residents were kept. Remember that girl's account from the information Jonas dug up? Lucy? Mattie?"

"Yes," Kang answered. "She said it happened here."

"Do you think it is true?" Verne asked as he hurried to keep up and joined them in studying the hallway.

After a moment, Bartholomew said, "I do."

Kang clapped him on the back. "Let's get this over with."

They returned to the stairwell and climbed to the third floor, continuing single file to the tower stairs in the north corner. Their steps echoed hollowly across the empty floors. By the time they ascended to the top of the stairs, Bartholomew had to stoop, and the stone ceiling grazed the top of Kang's head. The automat rubbed a thumb over the stone wall, noting the granite had been worn smooth over the years. He thought that odd since most of the inhabitants and patients had lived on the lower floors.

Behind him, Verne grunted as he followed Kang up the last of the steps. Bartholomew stopped before a rough-hewn wooden door and called down, "Are you ready?"

"I think so," Verne squeaked.

The door did not stick or creak; it swung open at Bartholomew's touch as if well-used.

Without a word, the big man ducked under the lintel with Kang and Verne close behind.

The automat blinked in surprise. He had not expected so much light, but the waning sun spilled through a half dozen tall windows that framed the circular room. Two of them were missing glass, and wood had been nailed over the lower half of another.

Kang estimated the diameter of the tower at fifteen feet and noted the ceiling graduated to a center point, a score of feet above them. In the east corner, he discovered a wooden wagon loaded with misshapen dolls and toys. Beside it lay a pile of vintage clothes with square brass buttons popular in the late seventeenth century.

As Verne approached a paneled trunk in front of the opposite wall, Bartholomew crossed to the windows with their excellent view of the cliffs and the sea. Kang assumed the tower had been used to spy on smugglers' ships.

Bartholomew's voice rose in excitement, "I can see our flying field and hangar from here. There is the—"

"Stop!" Kang shouted at Verne. The author had been about to lift the lid on the trunk. "Let's examine it first."

Verne backed up. "As you wish."

Bartholomew joined the automat in his examination. Noting the rusted steel clasps, Kang touched the broken studs and deteriorating strips of teak across the top. Some side panels appeared cracked, and more rust encrusted the metal bands holding the trunk together.

"Do you smell that?" Kang wiggled his nose. "I can't place what it is."

"Mold?" the big man guessed. "Dank, yet somewhat spicy."

Verne said, "It smells like old, wet food."

"Possibly," Kang said. "But there is something else." After another moment, he shrugged and said, "Let's look inside."

Bartholomew took one end and Kang the other, and they lifted the lid.

Verne inched closer. "It is empty!" he exclaimed.

Kang agreed. Not a shoe, hair comb, or mouse dropping in it.

"How interesting," Bartholomew said. "You'd think there would be something inside to justify keeping the trunk up here."

Kang squatted and searched for any stickers or indication of ownership. The style matched the 1680s period, but he felt certain it did not belong to the Spencers, although it seemed serviceable, not expensive, like someone of Adolphe Spencer's standing would own.

Just as Bartholomew had done, Verne crossed to the windows and came back to them. "You do believe that Jonas and I saw a ghost downstairs? And that she cut off a man's head?"

The big man straightened and swiveled to face him. He measured his words. "I believe you saw something most frightening."

The automat happened to check over Verne's shoulder. Kang could not speak. Thick mist rose from inside the trunk, solidifying into the shape of a man as it arose from within it. The man's mouth yawned open in a rictus grimace.

"I—I—" Kang grabbed Verne and pulled him so forcefully away they both fell backward and rolled to the far wall. The author scrambled up, unsettled and about to say so when he saw something worse.

By now, details of the apparition, such as the bishop's vestments and long beard, could be discerned. A silver cross hung from his neck and reflected the light. Although smaller than Bartholomew, the ghost regarded him with a vicious look. When Bartholomew turned and saw it, he froze.

The automat tugged on the author's arm, and they scrambled toward the big man. Kang started to speak and instead shrieked.

Behind Bartholomew, a rather plain woman matching the description Celwyn had given of Mrs. Spencer hovered only feet away outside the window. She had to be 500 feet off the ground. Kang could see through her and had no trouble reading the madness in her eyes and the gleam of sunlight on the broadsword in her hand.

She raised it high and smashed the window, the glass exploding everywhere.

In a blur, Bartholomew moved quickly, with Verne and Kang right behind him. They raced down the flights of stairs and across the drawing room, not stopping until they pounded down the floating pier and tumbled into the belly of the *Nautilus*.

Alarmed crewmen and some guards followed them down the spiral stairs. Kang paced and watched Bartholomew and Verne catch up on their breathing. When they seemed better, he told the crewman, "Please ask the Captain to meet us in the study." As they started down the corridor, he turned to another guard who tried to hide his nervous eyes by looking the other way. "Please round up the rest of the guards on the first floor of the mansion. Captain Nemo will let you know more shortly." Kang nodded Bartholomew and Verne into the study.

As Bartholomew poured a line of whiskies, the Captain ran into the room. The automat didn't know he could run so fast.

"What is it?"

Bartholomew did not appear happy, but at least he was not as petrified as Kang expected. The big man blurted, "We asked one of your men to gather the guards together until you hear what happened. I would worry about leaving them in the mansion right now."

Qing had flown off his perch by the aquatic window and landed on the bar to peck at the decanters, going from one to another like a percussionist tapping a row of crystal bells. Nemo cleared his throat, and he stopped.

"Go on," he said.

Kang grabbed a whiskey and tossed it off. "We went up to the tower with Mr. Verne." He held out his glass to Bartholomew, who refilled it.

"I wanted to f-find a ghost," Verne told Nemo. "These gentlemen were kind enough t-to accompany me." Verne appeared almost as nervous as he did when Jonas was angry with him. Nemo was not likely to use magic to scare him.

Nemo inhaled and took off his cap, crushing it in his fist. "I take it you found one?"

"Yes." Bartholomew herded everyone toward the sofas. "Mrs. Spencer again with her broadsword. Please make your guards safe, Sir."

"Excuse me a moment." Nemo marched out much slower than he ran in. By the time he returned, they were comfortable on the sofas and passing the whiskey bottle between them while pretending they were not frightened. Bartholomew's hand shook as he tried to sip his drink.

"We have your glass here, sir," Kang said.

Captain Nemo sat heavily next to him. "My men know nothing except seeing the three of you race by. I've asked them all to come aboard the ship for the night. Now—" He drained his whiskey in a single gulp and slammed the glass on the table. "Exactly what happened?"

Bartholomew told the story, his voice steady until he got to the part where they saw Mrs. Spencer hovering like a malignant fairy outside the window. He gulped, and Kang took over the narration.

When Xiau had finished, Nemo turned to Verne. "*Why* were you up there?"

Verne squirmed like he had worms in his drawers. "It is as Bartholomew says, I only wanted to see a ghost, perhaps speak to one. But not—" he trembled, "Not see that crazy woman again."

Nemo swallowed a remark and checked the wall clock behind them. "It is nearly the dinner hour. From your expressions, I do not need to ask you not to go up to the tower again or go anywhere in the mansion unless at least two of the guards are with you."

Kang said, "Agreed. If Jonas were with us, he might want to investigate further, but I doubt it. His last experience with Mrs. Spencer impressed him."

With a shudder that shook the sofa, Bartholomew said, "She certainly impressed me."

As they left the study for the Captain's private dining room, Granger, who appeared to rank high in Nemo's crew, approached the Captain and handed him a telegram. "From the telegraph office in Middlesbrough." He passed a second one to Bartholomew.

The automat's curiosity about the messages grew as they took their seats and unfurled napkins. Verne blinked his interest at Captain Nemo, probably assuming he would be most likely to share information. He was correct.

Nemo finished reading his and said, "Jonas says he would really appreciate it if I locked the ship up and didn't let you out." He eyed Verne. "After this afternoon's escapade, it isn't a bad idea."

Bartholomew had opened his envelope after Nemo opened his. He told Kang, "This is addressed to both of us from Jonas."

The big man read theirs aloud as a crewman began ladling the soup.

Dear Xiau and Bartholomew:

> *We rescued Valentine without casualties. We are trying to locate Miss Redifer. Talos' automats have killed one of our confederates, making this situation more dangerous and Valentine angrier.*

> *Talos seems to be after what he wanted before, not what is where you are.*

> *Do not come to London.*
> *I repeat, do NOT come to London.*
> *Please relate this news to the Captain.*

Jonas

"Humph," Kang grumbled.

Bartholomew glanced at Kang and said, "This Talos. He appeared before I met all of you."

The Professor had been lost in his thoughts about his brother, most of them unpleasant. Nemo saw him and said, "I believe Jules and I would also like to know what this means."

Kang inhaled deeply and dropped his spoon back into his soup. "You can't imagine how disheartening this is. Thank God Elizabeth doesn't know, or she'd hide me on top of the Matterhorn."

Bartholomew raised a brow. "That bad?"

"Yes. From what Jonas said, Talos must be after my work on atomic power, not the flying machine. So far." Kang studied them each in turn. "In a way, this is good news. Talos doesn't know where I am. That is why he tried to trap Jonas."

As Nemo finished his soup, he said, "I agree."

"We should wonder how he found out about the affection between Jonas and Miss McFein." Bartholomew mused.

Kang agreed. *Who had connected them?*

Verne announced, with a dash of daring, the kind he usually used when nothing else would work, "I would like to know more about this atomic power."

Bartholomew chuckled, amused at Verne's attempt to find out something that did not concern him. "No. You'd only get yourself in trouble for talking about it. And Jonas would be highly annoyed."

"If you brought Talos to our door, it would annoy me," Nemo warned him.

The author managed a contrite nod.

"My brother wants the information to sell it to unfriendly tyrants or use it himself." The automat regarded Verne and Nemo. "The knowledge could destroy much of the world."

"At least he doesn't know where we are." The big man nibbled a bite of poached halibut. He nodded with pleasure and ate more.

Captain Nemo said, "Jonas told me about Talos' demise on the *Zelda*. So, this turn of events is an unpleasant surprise."

Kang took pity on Verne; politeness dictated they could not entirely exclude him from the conversation. At least when Jonas was not around to block what he heard. The automat gave Verne a shortened version of Talos and the events on the *Zelda* and then pointed to his chest. "My brother's power source must have been retrieved." He turned to Nemo. "Sir, do you know of this Emilio Dearing that Jonas mentioned?"

The Captain had been enjoying the halibut, and when Kang asked the question, his expression turned as sour as if he had eaten rotten fruit. A vein throbbed near his brow.

"Yes." He clipped it.

The automat asked, "Could he have been in the South Arctic Sea?"

"Certainly." Nemo sat back. "Like you, I am about to lose my appetite."

Ever the diplomat, the big man suggested, "Let's table the discussion until later, before our bridge game."

Nemo nodded his thanks and buttered a roll.

After their cigars, and a discussion about the fuel intake for the prototype had been resolved, they enjoyed post-prandial brandies. Nemo dealt the cards. He sighed and said, "Captain Emilio Dearing is the son of Sir Robert Dearing and the daughter of the King of Spain. It was inconvenient for the boy to be raised at either court because of the political atmosphere at the time."

When they had picked up their cards, he went on, "I knew little of him until about ten years ago, when I began to hear of his nefarious activities."

Verne sorted his cards and asked, "Pirate activities?"

"Worse." Nemo made a face at his hand and stared at Bartholomew, who would open the bidding. "Dearing trades in slaves and also sells notable passengers from plundered ships."

Bartholomew looked up to find the others waiting for him. "Three hearts. What happens if their families do not pay?"

"Four clubs," Verne announced.

Nemo sent Verne an exasperated glance. "They are sold to one of the Arab sheiks or become slaves on Dearing's plantations near Manila."

"Sir," Kang asked, "May I inquire as to what happened when you encountered Dearing?" The automat assumed that they had met, to account for Nemo's animosity.

"Pass." Nemo put his cards down. "The most recent instance occurred when I took the *Nautilus* to the Azores, where Dearing and his fleet of ships were supposed to be." He studied his cards again as if wishing for a miracle or magic.

Qing jumped onto the table with them and strutted around, peeking at each of their hands. When he reached the author, he pecked Verne's cards and squawked at him.

"Perhaps he thinks you shouldn't have bid so many clubs," Nemo suggested.

"That bird reminds me of how much I miss Jonas." Bartholomew sighed.

"He misses Jonas, also," Kang agreed. "He has been more destructive than usual. I pass, by the way."

With a darkening expression, Nemo rubbed his chin. "We chased Dearing's crew into the jungle. In the ensuing battle, our rifles were evenly matched, but we didn't count on the bastard's tiger traps."

Verne piped up, "Those are deep pits in the ground, with leaves over them?"

"Usually," Nemo answered. "Only Dearing used them as a defense. He put sharpened stakes in them. I lost nearly a dozen men that day and, in the end, did little but interrupt his operation." The Captain growled, "Later, I heard that Dearing did something much worse than I'd initially heard." Nemo took the first trick. "As soon as we left the area, he executed nearly all the people from the villages, insisting they'd betrayed him to us."

"Oh, no!" Bartholomew exclaimed.

Through hundreds of years, Kang had become inured to abominations, but he still believed good triumphed. Eventually. "And then?"

"I sank several of his ships on the way out of the islands, but not his favorite, the *Primero*. She and Dearing sailed away while my men finished fighting his pirates in the jungle."

"You would welcome another battle with this man," Verne observed.

"I'll get him," Nemo said. "What was the bid?"

Verne grinned sheepishly.

"From all accounts, it appears we're going to London." Bartholomew checked the scorepad. "You and Mr. Verne still need to take a dozen tricks." He bestowed a confident smile on top of Verne's head.

Kang asked, "You have a plan, sir?"

"Yes. Tomorrow, we leave for England, despite the request from Jonas." A gleam of revenge lit up his eyes. "I know enough about Dearing and his habits from the many close calls we've had. We will find the *Primero*, and Dearing will be on her when I sink her."

PART IV
The Game

Chapter 45

London

T HE MORNING BELLS OF ST. PAUL'S
Cathedral rang, echoing across the city's rooftops.
Celwyn heard a knock just after he finished
knotting his tie. With one last admiring glance in
the mirror, he crossed to the door and opened it.

Valentine walked in without an invitation. "Don't
look so disappointed that it isn't my niece."

From what Celwyn could tell, the vampire had
completely recovered from his recent ordeal. His
color seemed good, and his movements smooth and
sure. The magician speculated how he would disguise him today; he had been running out of new
ideas. Although appearing healthier, this morning,
the older vampire wore a worried expression, not
the angry one that the magician had come to expect.

Valentine possessed a goodly amount of confidence. *What would worry him?*

"To what do I owe this visit?"

Valentine glanced at the closed door and lowered his voice. "We have a mutual problem. Mostly, it is mine, but I could use your expertise."

"Do tell."

The vampire could not relax enough to sit. He strode to the windows and back twice before he ended up at the door again. "Let's depart ... before Tara realizes we have left. I'll tell you about it on the way."

"Certainly." The magician put on his jacket and followed a frowning Valentine out the door. Like boys sneaking away to make mischief, they checked both directions in the hall and made for the back stairs.

Ten minutes later, and moving fast, they accosted a hansom cab on Jane Street. Valentine relayed an address in Hampstead to the driver as he nodded and shut the door. The magician deduced the cab's last fare had thoroughly enjoyed his tobacco, one a bit too sweet for Celwyn's taste. The carriage dipped and righted itself again as the heavy-set driver climbed aboard, and they rolled forward. Celwyn handed the vampire a cigar and lit one for himself.

"Not my brand of cigar," Valentine commented, lit it, and waved a hand through a thick cloud of smoke.

"Nor mine, but it isn't of importance now. Hearing what you have to say is." Celwyn had not been able to control his imagination over what could cause Valentine to worry about Tara.

At least, they would not be recognized at their destination. With a tall hat covering oily black hair, steely eyes squinting over fluffy muttonchops, and an elaborate mustache, Valentine made an excellent policeman. To make things more interesting and throw off any unfriendly observers, Celwyn had made himself a pair of handcuffs and adopted the drooping shoulders and downtrodden mien of a criminal who had been caught.

"You are probably wondering why our driver seemed to know the address I gave him."

"He even winked at you." Celwyn nodded. "Is it normal for bobbies to use coaches for transporting prisoners? And I do wonder, yes."

He tapped his uniform jacket. "He probably assumes bribery is involved." Valentine puffed on his pipe. "Before I forget, I've been meaning to ask how you came to acquire a wyvern?"

The magician explained, ending with, "...there is no evidence of why it likes me ... or what it wants."

"I have heard of another instance like this. The creature became increasingly possessive of its owner."

Celwyn asked, "And then?"

"I am not sure." He smiled. "Maybe it ate him."

The magician did not have a response to that.

They drew to a stop in front of a stately home with well-manicured hedges and sparkling windows. At each window, the curtains had been tightly closed. The magician wondered who lived here.

"Let's make a quick detour to that wine merchant at the end of the block, and I will emerge dressed differently, as will you."

"Excellent." Valentine paid their driver, and they hurried away.

"I love a good mystery, but perhaps you should explain what we are about to do. Start with why Tara isn't with us." Celwyn held the entrance door open with his now unshackled hands.

"Because this is about her. You know of her side activities, other than assignments for the Queen."

"The Wessex Club," the magician guessed. When the wine clerk went into the back room, Celwyn took the opportunity to change their appearance again.

Minutes later, a somewhat subdued Celwyn walked the short distance back up Jasmin Lane as he listened to Valentine.

"Winterset left a message at the pub where we usually exchange missives. It was most disturbing." They side-stepped a man in an expensive coat coming down the steps of the manor. Above the door, the numerals 431 in brass had been recently polished and shone in the weak sunlight. As the gentleman passed them, he deliberately did not speak or look at them. Celwyn noted nervousness in his eyes, not rudeness.

"I think that is a Parliament man, the Honorable Angus Truedove." Valentine pointed at him with his chin.

Celwyn had begun to be wary of their adventure. "Again, why are we here?"

"We are here for Winterset."

The magician guessed, "And you want me to enter his mind to find out who is threatening Tara and allowing Winterset to use that threat?"

Valentine started up the steps. "That is correct. Before I break his neck." At the magician's raised brow, he added, "I couldn't stomach his blood."

"Very well." Celwyn followed him, taking the steps two at a time as his character would; they were both now young men out to sample the carnal pleasures of the city.

"You would also like me to step aside while you eliminate Winterset or possibly change our appearance so that you will not be suspected."

Valentine pulled on the bell. "Yes. Being recognized would also impede our search for my other niece. It also depends on what you find. Winterset's note demanded my complete allegiance; he expected me to kill any vampire he named upon demand." Even in the low light of the porch, the vampire's expression would have frightened anyone. "He said our prior agreement was void. I was to do what he said, or with his evidence, my niece would die at the end of a rope."

"He is a very stupid man," Celwyn commented. All they had to do was eliminate whoever gave Winterset the club to hold over Tara. Then Winterset, too, for good measure.

"I agree."

The door was answered by a woman dressed like a puritanical governess, an expensive one. Her smile dropped a bit; she would have seen two gangly university men on the stoop.

Celwyn grinned at her as daftly as he could and said, "We want a girl. One for each of us!" The magician made the timbre of his voice a touch high, like an immature lad, not quite a man. As an additional misdirection, he also sounded as American as possible and flipped a gold coin in the air to be sure they would be welcomed. It did not take long.

"Oh, I see." The woman looked down an aristocratic nose at them with a patronizing smile. "This way, please."

On the second floor, they were shown to adjacent rooms and told to wait for their 'girls.' Celwyn became a tiny fly again and flew out the door after the woman. He waited until she started down the stairs, then began slipping under each door along the corridor, staying only long enough to see if Winterset occupied the room before flying to the next one. It was not until he reached the third floor that he found the fat man at the end of the hallway.

Celwyn landed on the nightstand next to where Winterset lay on the bed. The bleary-eyed prostitute had already dressed and leaned over the fat man to light his cigar, a most vulgar scene in Celwyn's opinion. He did not plan to stay longer than necessary and entered Winterset's thoughts.

The fat man had a most disorganized mind under normal conditions and now only wanted to continue with his carnal desires. Celwyn planted an image of Tara, with her fangs out, in his thoughts. Winterset jerked upright and checked the room for what he had just seen. He shuddered and lay back again. As he relaxed, he focused on his happy thoughts of newfound greed and power, thoughts decidedly not carnal. His ideas became more elaborate, including a detailed fantasy of standing on Valentine's chest and stomping his face. Above all, Winterset felt certain he would soon have complete control over Valentine and be rewarded by the Crown for killing dozens, if not hundreds, of vampires, no matter how good or bad. Celwyn waited.

Winterset's smug smile grew wider as he thought of Valentine begging for mercy at the end of a sword, which displayed his lack of vampiric knowledge. It took a bit longer until Celwyn discovered what he had been waiting for, a description of the danger to Tara. The magician did not linger. He sent the prostitute an urgent need to visit the lavatory and an image of the fat man developing a series of blistering sores. She would stay away from Winterset's room for a while.

All the while lying quite nicely, saying that she would soon return, she rushed out the door. Celwyn flew after her as fast as he could. He detoured down the stairs to Valentine's room. Before he reached the door, another much older prostitute exited the room, more than irritated, and slammed the door behind her. She cursed Valentine for wasting her time if all he wanted was to be left alone. The magician flew under the door and became himself again.

In a low voice, he told the vampire, "I found Winterset. It is worse than you thought. He wants to use you to destroy all vampires. He has already sent a message to the Queen to have Tara arrested again, saying he has proof of her treason. Tara's activities for the Wessex Club were mentioned."

Valentine stood to his full regal height, and the lethal fire in his eyes scorched the room. He started for the door.

Celwyn blocked him. "Wait a moment. You should know that it was the spymaster Pompero who betrayed her. He supervised her work and had been selling the information she and others gathered. The bastard probably knew it was a matter of time until she exposed him."

"I'll take care of him next," Valentine growled. "Get out of my way."

Celwyn told him where Winterset was located and stepped aside. "You are still in disguise. I'll create a diversion for you and then take care of Pompero myself." He grabbed the vampire's arm. "Time is not on our side. Please hurry."

Valentine nodded as he opened the door.

"Use the side door when you depart." Celwyn pointed below them. "We'll meet again at the wine shop on the corner."

———

Appearing as a successful businessman in a well-fitting suit and homburg, the magician waited in front of Treadway and Sons Wine Merchants. In the distance, a siren from the fire brigade echoed, then a second one. From the direction of 431 Jasmin Street, a tall man in an expensive topcoat hurried by, swiveling to aim a nervous eye at the rear. Seconds more and a pair of ladies in garish cosmetics and their hair in disarray trotted by. They also checked over their shoulders.

Celwyn stepped onto the cobblestones and looked down the street.

Smoke billowed above the gables and out the windows of the house. *Where was Valentine?* Celwyn began to worry. If the magician stayed this far away for too long, the vampire's disguise would start to fade. Celwyn did not want to consider what would happen if Valentine failed or was caught in his elimination of Winterset.

Just as the magician debated if he should send Valentine a message or go back there, the vampire appeared in a blur at his side, a reminder of how fast they could run. He had lost his hat, or it had already dissolved. Except for a torn sleeve, he looked presentable as himself. The magician handed him a large floppy hat to cover his locks.

"Shall we depart?" Valentine asked. "Yes, I was successful. The fire is a distraction."

"You should go back to Polly's and entertain Tara before she begins to suspect we're helping her, even if she doesn't know why."

The vampire stared at him until he understood. "Do you require my help with Pompero?"

"I know Pompero. The bastard." The magician stalked away from him, saying, "This time of the day, he will be at his desk in Buckingham Castle eating scones with too much cream." Celwyn thought about the danger the man had brought to Tara. "I will do this alone."

Chapter 46

FOR THEIR OUTING LATER THAT DAY, Valentine elected to disguise himself as a distinguished butler in search of tea for his master. Tara became a rather wan housemaid with a limp and mop of disheveled brown hair. With luxuriant whiskers and a courtly manner, the magician dressed as a footman greatly resembled Edward in that role at Tellyhouse. Celwyn held the elbow of the housemaid properly as they marched along behind the butler.

Business in the Pall Mall district seemed brisk even at the end of the workday. Prosperous men in Chesterfields met on street corners, orating and gesturing with their long-stemmed pipes to make a point. Behind them, their clerks and assistants stood at attention, holding umbrellas and armloads of documents and displaying more self-importance than their employers. Dancing around them, newsboys hawked their wares, and uniformed messengers waited by their bicycles, smoking French cigarettes.

Rolling fog from the river approached as if liquid, pouring across the avenue to swirl above the streetlamps. Dusk seemed sinister, thickening and bringing the kind of dampness that went through thin coats to the bones underneath. Mysteries and watchers stood on every corner, behind each brolly. For Celwyn, it was high time to get on with this adventure.

Tara took his arm, and with Valentine on her other side, they crossed the street and approached the tea shop.

"The shop closes soon, and we may have to visit here several times before we find them," she commented as they stepped around a prune seller. The boy could not have been over ten years old. Celwyn added a coat to the boy's skeletal frame and coins in his pockets.

"That is true. But we may have some luck, too," Valentine said.

As Celwyn closed the door of Floyd's Teas behind them, he scanned the room, feeling his hopes drain to his boots. Over the years, he had occasionally visited here and considered it the premiere teashop in all of London. At the collection of petite tables in front of them, half were occupied by women sipping tea and nibbling cakes. At the counter, a pair of men in flamboyant theatre attire argued with the proprietor about an ornate tin in front of them.

Valentine steered their party to a table near the windows where they could observe whoever walked by, and more importantly, who entered the shop.

It had been decided the magician would explore the shopkeeper's thoughts as soon as possible, and preferably before any pirates or automats arrived. After his initial disappointment over the patrons in the shop, Celwyn did not have any great expectations, but he still tried. The shopkeeper stood only a few feet away, trying to keep his voice low as he continued the argument with the thespians.

Within seconds, the magician sat up straight and uttered a mild and amazed curse under his breath.

"Yes?" Tara tried to control her optimism.

Celwyn eyed Valentine. "Your suggestion to look at him," he aimed a thumb at the proprietor, "has borne fruit." He teased Tara, "You must be my good luck charm."

As she touched his hand and pretended not to hear him, Valentine's smile should have caused anyone looking to pause. "Do tell."

"One moment, please." Celwyn waited until their order had been taken, and the server left before nodding at the shopkeeper.

"He is directly acquainted with Captain Dearing." The magician stared at the proprietor, a slight, sandy-haired man with baby-pink ears and a wide forehead. "He calls Dearing by his first name and expects one of his men here tomorrow when they open. The pirates bring him a quantity of a sought-after product; Chinese mountain lavender tea sells for a high price in London. In return, Dearing arranged to purchase his usual quantity of Royal Earl Grey."

Tara waited while their cups were filled and served before saying, "We could approach the owner and ask for a substantial amount of the lavender tea, causing a second request to Dearing. Or, they might find it more convenient for one of Dearing's messengers to deliver the tea to us."

Celwyn admired how she thought. Valentine did, also.

"A most worthy suggestion. I agree that we order the tea, as my niece has said, and verify how the proprietor would fill our large order." He nodded at Celwyn. "Wouldn't it be fortuitous if we could follow the messenger who takes our request to Dearing?"

The magician enjoyed his own smile. "Yes, it would."

Mr. Horatio Floyd turned out to be a gregarious businessman and most efficient at supplying tea. After his surprise at Celwyn's affinity for a large quantity of lavender tea, he assured them he would have their order within a few days.

⁂

Valentine held the door open, and Celwyn sighed as he left the wonderful scents from the tea shop behind. As they stood at the curb waiting for a hire coach, the magician said, "It is getting late, and I need to pick up and send some telegrams. Would you mind continuing to Polly's? Or do you prefer to accompany me?"

Valentine and Tara exchanged a look before her uncle said, "I think we should all go. I want to send a few, too."

With a nod of agreement, the magician stepped into the street and waved down one of the newer large curricles pulled by a quartet of lively Arabians with tall purple feathers. In contrast, the driver wore a dirty coat and a sour expression. They climbed into the coach, and Celwyn gave the driver instructions to take them to Elmer's Greengrocers. During the ride, Celwyn asked the vampires what plan they had for watching over the tea proprietor.

Valentine lit his pipe and puffed peevishly, producing small clouds of pungent smoke. "Our priority is to locate Miss Redifer. The more I think about it, there won't be time to enlist others from my family on the Continent to help us."

"I agree," Tara murmured as she gazed out the coach window. "Floyd's Tea is in between Stratton and Fraser Streets. Starting early tomorrow, we need to cover the tea shop night and day and have transportation ready."

"As much as I enjoyed our nighttime flight over the city," Valentine told Celwyn with a seriousness that bordered on laughter, "I do not wish to do so again ... unless it is unavoidable."

"I understand."

A rain shower began as their coach turned onto Caxton Street, the drops bouncing off the backs of the horses and cobblestones. Already, a herd of umbrellas moved silently across the sidewalks, their owners anxious to get home to sit in front of a fire.

The remnants of dusk had nearly disappeared, and the gas lamps hanging over the streets came alive.

"It is a problem," the magician thought aloud as their carriage slowed for a turn. "We must all three be available to follow the man Dearing sends. Do you agree?"

Tara pursed her lips, and Celwyn found the gesture fascinating.

"Yes, all three of us." She frowned. "We'll need to be inconspicuous, too."

Their coach came to a quivering stop opposite barrels of apples and bins of cabbages. When his companions would have gathered their things to alight from the carriage, Celwyn stopped them. "One moment, please—just in case someone is watching. Allow me to scout the area." He rapped on the glass and asked their driver to wait a few moments.

When Celwyn left the cab, he again wore the stoop and shuffle of the elderly academic Dr. Tinkerton. Although a favorite disguise, he used it sparingly.

He meandered around the fruit bins and breathed a bit of relief that he detected no one out of place among the onions and no smell of cloves. "God damn Talos," he muttered under his breath. The magician sidestepped a matron who dug into the tomatoes as if she were hunting for gold nuggets. When he reached the glass door leading into the establishment, he stopped short.

"Oh, *hell*—"

Professor Xiau Kang held the door open for him and bowed with a sarcastic flourish. Bartholomew came out the door eating an apple and trotted down the steps. "Nice whiskers, Jonas."

"Your mouth is open," Kang observed.

Celwyn growled, "Of course it is! What the devil are you *doing* here?"

"We're here to help," Bartholomew announced with one of his biggest smiles. "All we had to do was find the shop that sent your telegrams."

"Good grief!" The magician rubbed his face hard. "Come with me," he pointed to the hire coach at the curb. "We can talk freely inside." He stomped to the cab and held the door open for them.

As Kang scrambled up, he said, "Good evening, Miss McFein, and Mr. Soriano. I'd hoped we would see you again." He handed Tara a telegram. "I took the liberty of bringing your waiting message." He laughed at the magician's snort from behind him.

"Thank you." Her answer came slowly and from far away as she stared at the envelope.

Valentine grumbled, "What is it?"

"We'll speak later of this, Uncle."

Bartholomew had followed Kang inside the coach, and things became much cozier. He greeted the others. "Jonas is growling, but he is pleased to see us, too."

The magician slammed the carriage door and knocked on the glass to get the driver's attention. "Please drive us to Hyde Park and tour the park. Take your time."

Celwyn banged the glass shut and glared at everyone. "It is possible that the greengrocer was being observed by your brother ... or Dearing's minions ... and recognized you." He demanded, "Did you see anyone?"

The big man said, "Just the telegraph clerk and a pair of elderly ladies looking for lemons. They left right before you arrived."

Valentine snarled, "We're in the middle of hunting these bastards down. They have Miss Redifer."

"I am very sorry to hear it," Kang told him.

Celwyn held up a hand. "If you were observed, they also saw Bartholomew for the first time. If not, we have a new weapon in our arsenal." He aimed a thumb at the big man. "I'd like to see Bartholomew throw Talos across a street."

"Face first into a puddle," Bartholomew added.

The magician sighed. "I need tea. I can't think."

"We could stop—" Tara started to say.

Celwyn patted her hand. "We will. But first, I want to verify if any of them are following us." With his last words, he became a gorgeous starling and sailed out the window past Bartholomew's most expressive, gasping face.

The magician flew behind their erratic driver for nearly a half-hour, noting that he made no effort at all to avoid potholes and large puddles. He seemed to speed up as they crossed through intersections where competing coaches barged through from several directions. Celwyn noticed that their coach blended well with the early evening traffic, which still seemed sparse enough; a condition most helpful to determine if anyone followed them. When he started to tire, he perched on top of the bonnet over the driver and sent him a silent suggestion to head over to Pall Mall.

The driver itched his ear and reached for his whip. The magician intervened. Instead of turning it into a snake or something more memorable, he merely made it disappear. Celwyn didn't feel playful since the automat had arrived in this pit of danger. Their driver had no idea how lucky he was as he continued forward while leering at a gaggle of women exiting a café.

After another few minutes, Celwyn re-entered the cab's interior, landing on Bartholomew's shoulder.

"Droll, Jonas," Kang said fondly.

Once again, as himself, Celwyn sat beside Tara and enjoyed the experience thoroughly.

"What did you see?" she asked.

With a most satisfied sigh, the magician said, "We are not being followed. Time for tea."

"Or wine?" Valentine raised his brows at the others.

"I want food," Kang announced.

Bartholomew chuckled. "That is code for cookies." He pulled out his watch. "It is the dinner hour. Where shall we go?"

The magician had to admit it; even with his annoyance at their arrival, he had missed these two.

"Uncle, shall we try Whitefriars?" Tara asked.

Valentine pursed his lips. "Perhaps. The chef does save venison blood for me when he is drying meat."

"It is settled then." Tara confided to Celwyn, "You will enjoy their prime rib."

A quartet of policemen holding tight to their horses raced by their carriage, followed by two of the Queen's guards.

"Have you noticed any of the Queen's men looking for you?" Valentine asked Tara.

The magician laughed, thinking of Talos's frustration. "One of my little trips yesterday was to the Palace. It seems the bogus charges originated by Talos have disappeared." Neither he nor Valentine mentioned the new ones they had averted. That reminded him; he needed to visit the castle again tomorrow to make sure Winterset's false charges against a certain Miss Tara McFein did not resurface—ever.

After Celwyn had advised the driver of their destination, he turned to the vampires. "Would you like to bring our dinner companions up to date on our enemies so we don't have to discuss it over the soup?"

Valentine nodded. "As you wish." He related everything that had occurred so far, with Tara supplying details for when he had been captive and not privy to their steps in freeing him. When the story had been told, the rain returned in force, pelting the cab so loudly it made conversation difficult. Their coach slid a bit coming out of a puddle, and everyone held on.

Kang had developed a frown during the telling of the tale. He directed it at the magician.

"It isn't *my* fault this time. He is your brother," Celwyn retorted.

Before Kang could react, Valentine asked, "What exactly are Talos and the pirate after if it isn't the flying machine?"

When Bartholomew replied, Celwyn raised his own brow in surprise.

"It's the scientific work behind the discovery of the atom, the basis of a new world of science. Xiau has been sharing the information with me."

"Ah. Because you speak science," Celwyn observed.

Bartholomew smiled. "To a point." He looked at Valentine. "Which means I can describe some of it in simple terms." He did so.

Tara asked, "And Talos and Dearing want to use it for war?"

Kang shrugged. "Possibly. They don't want to bake cookies with it. By the way, I still want cookies."

The magician said more to himself than the others, "If Pelaez was here—he would steal the information to sell it."

Tara patted his hand, and Kang sent him a concerned look as he prompted the older vampire, "Please continue?"

Valentine told them about Miss Redifer and their efforts over the last few days ending with the tea shop. "We're assuming the message has had time to reach Dearing, and we will camp out at the shop beginning early tomorrow. If possible, we will follow whoever Dearing sends with the tea."

Bartholomew grinned at Celwyn. "I thought you were kidding about the pirate liking tea as much as you."

"Of course not." Kang rolled his eyes. "It is just his luck."

The magician glared at the automat. "You cannot participate. We will fail if they capture you."

"But—"

"No!"

Bartholomew patted the air. "Xiau can stay on the *Nautilus*. Nemo will be curious. And there isn't a safer place for him."

Celwyn calmed down enough to say, "I agree. Besides, we may need Nemo." He eyed Tara. "Could you tell them how we trailed the villains to the water yesterday, please?"

After she complied, she told them of Mercury's murder. Bartholomew said, "I am sorry for your loss. We will devise a different way to get messages to the submarine."

Their coach bounced over a hole, and when Tara ended up closer to Celwyn, he sighed. They had already arrived at Whitefriars.

Chapter 47

A S THEY WERE SHOWN TO THEIR table, Celwyn admired the bowl of blood-red roses centered on the pristine tablecloth. The maître d' pulled out Tara's chair. She thanked him with a bob of her silver curls. That, and other subtle and effective changes, had been part of the magician's wholesale disguising of their party.

As for Valentine, he now sported a button nose, a bulbous chin, and a bald pate. It had not been necessary to disguise Bartholomew, since no one in London knew the large and regal black man. For the fussy Professor Xiau Kang, the magician had enjoyed himself.

The automat's constitution would not allow Celwyn's magic for wholesale changes, so he had managed with other methods. Under protest, Kang wore a silky black wig and enough cosmetics to put a dance hall performer to shame, along with plenty of jewelry to complement his evening gown and stole. Celwyn may not be able to change Kang's nose, but he most certainly could add a thick layer of rouge to his cheeks.

"Having fun, Jonas?" Kang asked dryly as he arranged his skirts. The man filling their water glasses gawked after hearing Xiau's precise tenor. The automat stared back until he moved away. Bartholomew's shoulders shook as he giggled into his sleeve.

With a studiously blank look, Valentine murmured, "I must say, Professor, you do look rather exotic." To a newly arrived waiter, he handed over a card and said, "Please deliver that to Chef Komavich."

After he departed with a bow, the wine steward addressed them while eyeing Kang. "Would you care to see the wine list?"

"Absolutely." Celwyn squinted through Dr. Tinkerton's spectacles and made his voice querulous as befitting the elderly academic. "Pardon me, but do you have trout this evening? My special friend, Miss Daisy, just adores it."

Kang kicked him under the table.

When the waiter departed, more soberly, Celwyn commented, "This is probably the only time we will be seen together in public until this is over. We are memorable, with or without disguises."

Celwyn noted Tara's fixed stare at a table a few feet away. One of the men looked precisely like the picture he had seen of Oscar Wilde. The prominent nose and full lips were distinctive. Wilde's companion would not have been remembered at all with his average face and common wool suit. Perhaps because Wilde *was* so memorable. They appeared to have been dining for a while, judging from their jocularity and volume of laughter. Nearby, the other diners displayed the careful tolerance reserved for either the notorious or the famous. The magician suspected these men represented both.

"Who are they?" Celwyn murmured in Tara's ear.

She licked her lips, blinked, and said, "Oscar Wilde and Henry James."

"What disturbs you about them?"

She nodded at another table a few feet closer to the kitchen. "At that table are two of the Crown's investigators. Not the normal ones."

The magician noted that the Queen's men had dressed to blend in with the dinner crowd, but did not speak to each other. Probably because they were too busy listening to Wilde's oration about what he considered the Queen's hypocrisy.

"Those men are assigned to matters of treason," the magician guessed.

Tara raised her brows. "How did you know?"

Kang joined the conversation in a murmur, "Because of the subversive oration we're all hearing from Mr. Wilde. He still has not lowered his voice."

She pursed her lips. "Again, I am most fortunate to be in disguise, thank you. Oscar would recognize me ... and not quietly."

Celwyn could imagine there were other underlying plots afoot here, and none of them would ensure their efforts against Talos and Dearing stayed private. Probably the opposite would result.

Kang kept his voice low. "The newspapers report Mr. Wilde's activities and gossip about him constantly. How well do you know him?" he asked Tara.

"I've known him for years and told Jonas about him." She inhaled, held her breath, and let it out slowly. "Months ago, I had some business dealings with him, which are still ongoing. And I know quite a bit about his 'activities,' as you put it. He is an interesting man. I fear for him."

"It sounds like someone with even less common sense than Jonas," Kang observed.

"Pfft." Celwyn turned to Tara. "Do you wish to talk privately with Mr. Wilde or his companion? Perhaps warn him? I could arrange a private rendezvous without the Queen's men."

"You would have them napping in the alley out back," Kang speculated.

Celwyn grinned at him. "Possibly."

Tara said, "That is a sweet offer, but not tonight." She touched the magician's wrist. "Oscar just glanced at the Crown's men. I can't tell if he knows who they are."

The magician couldn't just let the man be arrested without at least warning him. He sent a silent suggestion to Wilde that the Queen's agents watched him. Wilde shook his head violently as if to dislodge a fly that had crawled into his ear. Then he frowned and lowered his voice.

"Instead, let us talk of something more pleasant." Kang eyed the big man.

"*The Grand Duchess of Gerolstein* is playing at Covent Garden. And *Orpheus in the Underworld* just opened at Her Majesty's Theatre. Which would you choose?" Bartholomew asked the table. "I have a feeling this will be a delightful discussion. There is actually a song sung by Orpheus entitled, '*We Can Tell She's in Hell.*'"

It turned out to be so. They enjoyed a lively debate over who would give a better performance: the actress Cecily Bass or Paul Ducat. Eventually, the conversation turned more serious.

Bartholomew looked at the others and lowered his voice. "Please tell us where you have been staying? Do you consider it safe?"

Valentine said, "Miss Polly Hatcher's manor in Mayfair. Both you and the Professor would be welcome."

"However, Polly has no special security." Tara frowned. "She also has a regular parade of outsiders in the house most evenings when she is entertaining."

"True. It is an interesting place. There was a duel in her backyard a few days ago." Valentine examined the wine list and passed it to Bartholomew on his right. "Sir, if the Professor is lodged elsewhere, you would be comfortable there and be able to help us in our activities. If you accept, beware of Polly's chef." He shuddered. "I simply do not know why she employs him."

The big man nodded. "I will consider it. May I inquire where you met the chef here?" He gestured at the grand dining room where a hundred or more diners enjoyed a world of quiet elegance under twinkling chandeliers and the clinking of silver on china.

Valentine said, "I performed a service for him years ago. In return, he provides me with fresh nourishment whenever I visit."

Bartholomew frowned in puzzlement. Celwyn leaned close and murmured, "Blood."

"Oh!" The big man blinked rapidly.

The exchange served to enliven the mood of their party, including Kang, who until then could not seem to get comfortable in his restrictive undergarments. He brightened and entered the spirit of the masquerade and reunion. The automat even adopted a few feminine gestures and giggled behind his fan.

By the time their salads arrived, the magician had declared the evening priceless and began wondering where he could find a photographer at this hour. His magical version of Xiau would only last so long, and Elizabeth should have something permanent to remember her husband's evening wear by.

"Before we order our entrees, would you care to hear of our progress with the flying machine?" The big man asked.

Tara said, "I would, most definitely."

Valentine listened politely as he could to the scientists' descriptions of wind, yaw, and fuel mixtures until their waiter arrived again.

The magician put a restraining hand on Kang's arm and grinned at him. "I will order for my special friend." He winked at the waiter. "She just wants dessert, but she must eat her vegetables first."

Kang replied appropriately under his breath, and the magician rushed on, "I believe we'll start with the turtle soup."

No matter the righteousness of vegetables, they all turned to watch a cart pass by upon which assorted cakes, pies, tortes, and puddings had been artfully assembled. "You must wait. Soon Daisy, soon," the magician crooned, much to everyone's amusement.

Bartholomew turned to Tara. "I have never been to London until now. What do you suggest I see?" He frowned and added, "Providing our enemies are neutralized soon."

Hours later, they parted company. Bartholomew and Kang hopped onto a different carriage heading toward the Tilbury docks. From there, they would take another coach to an agreed-upon point where Nemo's crew would meet them. Kang needed Bartholomew's protection until he was aboard the *Nautilus* again, so he might as well stay there, too. It had been decided that the big man would meet the others across the street from Lloyd's Tea Shop early the next morning.

As their carriage drew away from the curb and merged with the others on Columbia Street, Valentine asked, "Have we a plan for tomorrow?"

Celwyn had been enjoying having Tara snuggled against him and had to concentrate on paying attention to the older vampire. He cleared his throat. "We should be positioned separately to cover the front and back of the shop so that the crewman that Dearing sends doesn't realize he is being followed."

Tara nodded. "How will we be disguised?" She pointed to her gray curls. "I assume something different?"

"You two will be dressed in different wigs and other clothing of your choosing. I won't be close enough to you to provide any of that with magic or be able to maintain it if I am distracted."

"You must have made a suggestion to Polly." Valentine rubbed his chin. "I'd wondered why she had her maid leave me some odd clothing and a few of the wigs we'd used for our performances."

"Do you have face makeup also?" she asked.

"Yes."

"All right, then what else?" Tara asked and patted a yawn.

"I hadn't thought any further than that," the magician said. "I prefer that you two stayed close enough to support each other at the rear entrance."

Tara asked, "And you?"

He smiled. "I will be in front, wearing a pair of gorgeous iridescent wings and elegant but hairy feelers." Celwyn shrugged. "Of course, I may have to change again into something swifter. We'll see."

Valentine snorted a laugh. "And Bartholomew?"

"He'll be about a block to the north, toward the water."

"Because you think that is the most likely direction Dearing's man will go. Back to the pirate ship." Tara regarded him. "And we will all follow him?"

Valentine rubbed his chin again. "Yes. Let's allow him a block or two head start and then turn in another direction when we spot Bartholomew."

Valentine seemed lost in thought and stared out the coach windows at the spire of an ancient church that reached above the trees.

Tara surmised, "As we follow him, you will be in front, and my uncle and I at the rear when he arrives at his destination."

"Yes." Celwyn frowned as he realized something else. "Please be on alert; there could be other villains accompanying the messenger Dearing sends." He directed the frown at them. "I always assume the worst so that I am not surprised."

Tara said, "I totally agree."

"The other ruffians could be automats who resemble Talos or crewmen from Dearing's ships. They will be armed." Celwyn felt his mood darken the more he thought about Talos.

"I will be also," Tara assured him. "I can outrun any of them and smell Dearing from a distance." Her eyes flared with revenge. "I won't be taken by surprise again."

"She is also an expert shot." Valentine smiled and smoothed his luxuriant whiskers. "My niece is ready for battle, and after our excellent repast, you don't want to know what I plan for our enemies."

As they turned onto Theobalds Road, a newsboy ran in front of them, holding the *Evening Standard* high. The headline shrieked:

SIR JOHN CECIL WINTERSET FOUND DEAD!!!

"Oh, my!" Tara exclaimed. I had thought today's news couldn't be more sensational." She lowered her voice, "The man I report to, in charge of the Queen's spy networks, was also found dead." A minute went by. "I suspected him of being a traitor and selling our secrets."

"That's not all," the magician told Valentine silently. *"I think you should tell her."*

The vampire growled in his throat and then, much more gently, said, "My dear, these deaths are connected." When Valentine finished the story of their earlier activities, Tara's color was high, and she looked ready to spit.

She slapped the magician's hand away when he tried to calm her down. "This was *my* problem, not yours!"

Chapter 48

Early the next morning, Polly's chef produced warm pastries and a thermos of tea. Gerald also handed them a separate one of blood.

After a silent drive through the deserted streets of Mayfair, they emerged from a hire coach a block south of the tea shop. During the ride, the magician had enough time to finish his tea because the silence in the cab lasted the entire trip. This condition could be attributed to the revelations to Tara about their meddling from yesterday.

As they descended from the carriage and stepped into the shadows, Celwyn admired their costumes. He suspected Valentine had modeled his after King Lear, considering the ornateness of his vest and ruffles around his collar. Tara had opted for the nondescript garb of a charwoman. It did not hide her beauty, but the smudge of coal she had smeared on her face attempted to do so.

As a sign of forgiveness, Tara pecked Celwyn's cheek when the tea shop came into view. The magician said, "Bartholomew is in the alley up ahead." He kissed her back.

Tara stood on her tiptoes. "I see him. The lights are on in the tea shop already."

Celwyn resisted the urge to kiss her again before bowing to Valentine. "I hope we'll meet again before noon."

Valentine kept walking toward the rear of the shop. "I do also." In the distance, the horns from the early morning boats on the Thymes echoed to them.

As a starling, Celwyn flew over them, saying, "We will." Despite his prediction of a fly initially, he had opted for the speed of a bird—it would be thoroughly tiring to beat such small wings that fast.

From his position in the alley, Bartholomew could see the front of the tea shop and have an excellent view for a good distance both east and west. When the magician reached the rooftops, he detected smoke from a few early coal fires. He perched high in the oak tree opposite the shop as the church bells in the distance rang, announcing the day.

It could not have been more than a few minutes more before the shop door opened, and a diminutive man in dark clothing walked out. *Damn.* It seemed Dearing's messenger had arrived before them.

Celwyn sent one of the mice from the bushes scurrying to the back of the shop, and as a prearranged signal, he caused it to dance in front of the vampires. Another one scurried toward Bartholomew.

It arrived, and the big man froze, probably controlling his reaction to the rodent as it spun and twirled. As they planned, he began walking at a leisurely pace down Devine Street toward the water in the direction they anticipated the man would take. Their quarry did the same, moving rapidly. The magician opened his wings and flew high, keeping above Bartholomew as he lengthened his stride.

When the big man stopped at the corner in front of Daniel's Stables, Celwyn landed on the lamppost beside him and rested. Blocks behind them, through the gloom, he saw two blurs moving so fast it was hard to distinguish what they were—then he knew; Valentine and Tara had decided to close the distance between them.

Bartholomew let the messenger cross in front of him as he pretended to pack and light his pipe. When there was a half block between them, Bartholomew started forward again, and Celwyn ascended above a nearby rooftop and hovered. When Valentine and Tara arrived, they slowed to a normal pace and continued south toward the water.

The sun rose higher, and businesses opened their shutters as the scent of many more coal fires drifted from chimneys and their mornings began. The messenger neared an intersection already alive with pedestrians, carriages, scrounging dogs, and omnibuses pulled by sleepy horses. As if Bartholomew could read the messenger's intention, he increased his steps and reached a waiting omnibus before the man. The side of the vehicle had a picture of a sun with seagulls underneath it. Sunshine Omnibuses advertised tours of the town of Southend-on-Sea.

Bartholomew casually took a seat up front on the bus while the messenger went to the rear of the open-top bus. The big man would see him if he departed. It looked doubtful the cheery red canvas stretched over the top would do much for a passenger if it rained. From his position on the roof across the street, the magician watched as the vampires caught a hire carriage and climbed in to follow the bus. Glad for a few moments to rest, Celwyn landed on top of their carriage, checking for anyone who followed. All around them, the activities seemed normal.

A string of dock workers and businessmen in top hats crossed in front of the coach. From his perch, Celwyn found the smell of bread baking a few feet away in Miss Mary's Bakery most subversive, the aroma enough to take his breath away. Only with great concentration did the magician ignore it.

The bus and carriage started forward at a moderate pace. They traveled for miles with the omnibus, gaining and disgorging passengers at various points. Signs for nearby hamlets occurred every few miles. When another coach blocked the view from the omnibus, Celwyn changed the vampires' hire carriage from black to white. To be helpful, their driver now unknowingly wore a stylish fedora and peacoat. Satisfied, Celwyn flew on ahead.

The scent of the sea enveloped them as they arrived at the Chafford terminal. As soon as the wheels stopped turning, Bartholomew swung down the steps and reached the ticket officer just after the messenger. The big man complained loudly in an accented voice about missing the scheduled coach for the town of Ashingdon. After listening to the ticket seller's explanation, Bartholomew agreed to take the next omnibus for Southend-on-Sea, for which the messenger had just purchased the ticket.

Wearing a slightly younger version of his Dr. Tinkerton disguise, complete with his nearsightedness and hickory cane, Celwyn climbed into the new bus and sat a few seats away from Bartholomew. In his new disguise, he appeared as bald as a newborn and sported a long, elaborately braided beard. A minute more and Tara walked by below. With a fingernail, he tapped the window glass until she saw him. After Valentine finished paying their coach driver, Tara tugged on his arm, and they headed toward the ticket seller's booth across the street.

I hope they hurry, the magician told Bartholomew silently as he, too, watched the street. If need be, he would arrange a slight delay with the horses. Celwyn sighed, appreciating a rest from flying. For a moment, he lost sight of the vampires until they reemerged from an alley. *They will be here soon,* he informed the big man. Bartholomew continued to watch the street, but Celwyn caught his slight nod.

The vampires approached the omnibus with a bit of fanfare. Celwyn grinned at their inventiveness. They looked like derelicts from Brixton, a most disreputable area in London. Everyone on the bus stared, and some pointed. With tattered coats, and smears of soot on their faces, they had adopted the mien of near-do-wells, and Celwyn had no problem smelling the sour stench of old hops. As they clambered onto the bus, Tara announced she needed a drink in a voice that could be heard down the street. When she pulled out a bottle from her bag, Valentine, adopting a fussy highbrow accent, complained even louder, "Not so *early*, Martha—" and threw the bottle over the open rail of the bus. Tara started a fight with him while they both ignored Dearing's messenger. The driver jiggled the reins, and they rolled forward again.

As the bus bumped and swayed eastward, Celwyn spied fewer houses and businesses near the road. Acres of nothingness stretched for miles until it met the brininess of the North Sea. The temperature grew colder, and the magician added a jacket and scarf to Bartholomew. The vampires appeared to be wearing several layers of clothing and would not feel the cold. Celwyn caught Tara's eye and sent her an unseen kiss to brush against her lips. She demanded a drink and slapped Valentine's cheek, then cursed at him for the benefit of the passengers before smiling her appreciation at the magician.

Celwyn checked the rear of the bus. Dearing's man had again positioned himself in the farthest corner near the rail. *Is he looking for someone? No,* Celwyn decided. The man faced straight ahead, not even flinching when Valentine stood and yelled profanities at 'Martha,' the drunkard.

Celwyn concluded the messenger wanted someone to see him on the bus. On the road behind them, several coaches moved along, but they seemed too far away to be interested in the bus. A lone horse rider in a scarlet jacket passed them, moving fast.

The road dipped and curved gently around a growing number of windblown row houses bleached by the sea air.

They had reached Southend-on-Sea.

Chapter 49

MINUTES LATER, THEIR BUS PULLED to a stop within feet of the churning water. The current ran strong where the Thames met the North Sea. Near the road, benches of travelers awaited the omnibus for the return trip to London, and Celwyn's stomach reminded him that it neared noon. High time for more tea.

On the north side of the road, a pristine, Edwardian-era Church of England lined with borders of delphinium and foxglove faced the bus terminal. On the waterside, a weather-beaten pub had opened its doors to air out yesterday's stench of ale and ashes and welcome the fresh sea air inside.

Still trading insults, Valentine and Tara left the bus before the other passengers and headed into the pub. Celwyn assumed they would change costumes again.

As he watched, Bartholomew swung off the bus steps and onto the cobblestones, where he bought a newspaper, pointedly ignoring the other disembarking passengers. When only Dearing's messenger remained, the magician purposely blocked the aisle of the bus while teetering from side to side on his cane. To complete the distraction, Celwyn began singing a naughty but patriotic ditty about Admiral Nelson.

The messenger shoved him aside and trotted down the steps to the street.

Behind you, ten feet, Celwyn warned Bartholomew. *He is looking around ... here comes Tara and Valentine— disguised as father and daughter. Black wigs.* The vampires strolled across a patch of grass to the water and onto the boardwalk in front of dozens of boats at tether.

The big man again nodded so slightly that it seemed he had not heard anything. Bartholomew had a future in espionage if he chose to pursue it.

Meanwhile, Dearing's man seemed to be waiting for something at the curb in front of the bus. This close, in the bright morning light, the magician noticed what he had not before in the shadows of early morning; the man's face and the elfin ears. This was Talos's man. When the glittering eyes of the automat passed over Celwyn, they lingered just long enough to give the magician pause.

It happened fast. As the omnibus pulled away, a swarm of automats descended on Bartholomew from all sides.

Bartholomew kicked and punched. As Celwyn turned toward him, another mob of automats set upon the magician. He changed back to himself, causing the chatter of the automats to escalate to a high pitch as he flung them wholesale across the road and into the trees. Celwyn again faced the big man.

By now, they had tied Bartholomew up like a large mummy and lifted him onto their shoulders as they quick-marched toward the water. Then, the magician saw something he did not want to see.

In a boat meant for a dozen tourists, double that number of automats had piled into the craft with the vampires. Valentine would not have hesitated to treat them as Celwyn had—then the magician saw why. It wasn't only automats; the witch, Ginnie, had wrapped an arm under Tara's chin and held a pistol to her head. Celwyn had not planned for this. He should have killed Ginnie the last time they saw her.

As Celwyn streaked toward them, he sent Ginnie's weapon flying with a satisfying splash into the water. When the magician landed in the boat, Valentine's long fingers wrapped around the neck of the nearest mechanical man, and the sound of metal snapping sounded most gratifying. Celwyn sent the rest of them into the water and yelled at Valentine, "Get the engine going—they have Bartholomew!" *As planned.*

Tara had wrestled Ginnie to the floor of the none-too-clean boat and sat on her. Every time she moved or tried to speak, Tara slapped her.

Valentine climbed over a pair of incapacitated automats whose glittering eyes still tracked him with the kind of eeriness that Celwyn was glad Bartholomew was not here to see. He dumped them over the side. The engine rumbled to life as Celwyn used a pole to push them away from the dock.

"Why are you here?" Tara growled at Ginnie and smacked the back of her bewigged head. The older witch's eyes remained on the boards under her chin. Celwyn caught a secretive smile from Ginnie but didn't have time to figure it out.

Their boat began chugging up and down the swells with Valentine steering and Celwyn tracking the boat with the automats and Bartholomew. The magician murmured to Tara, "She can't talk with you sitting on her."

"I don't care if she does—"

Valentine pointed. "They are drawing away from us. Our engine is smaller."

"Allow me." Celwyn waved a hand, and their craft leapt forward, skimming over the foam of the waves and keeping pace with the other boat as the water became rougher and swelled higher.

"You wanted the pirates to capture Bartholomew?" Tara surmised. "You could have easily caught up with them, but you haven't."

Celwyn admired Tara again, this time for her innate perception. He replied, "Yes. It was his idea. Even if they do not know him, they'll want to know why he followed the messenger and take him to Dearing." Tara ducked. The spray from the waves soaked them as their prow cut through the foam. "I will join them on deck if need be."

Valentine asked, "What will he do when he boards their ship?"

"He intends to find out what they've done with Miss Redifer."

Their engine sputtered, and Celwyn revived it with enough force that their bow pointed at the heavens before bottoming out and plowing forward again.

"What we did not count on was her—" The magician toed Ginnie, none too gently.

Their vessel caught a much larger wave, crested, and landed hard. The sun glinted off the waves, blinding them. When Celwyn could see again, a mile in the distance, the thick mist shifted. It revealed an enormous five-masted ship. It sat there looking as forbidding as could be. As they watched, the automats' boat bumped into its side, bobbing against it like a small toy.

"Look! They're using a pulley to hoist Bartholomew aboard," Valentine shouted.

A cannon boomed from the ship, the flash of the gunpowder clear even this far away.

"Heavens!" Tara exclaimed and crouched lower as the ball landed with a splash in front of their boat.

"The next one will be more on target—" Celwyn yelled as more concussions rumbled, and new explosions filled the sky. Plumes of seawater exploded around them as cannonballs fell like rain.

"Let me go!" Ginnie screamed.

Valentine swerved to the right. "I don't think they like you any more than they do us." He leaned close enough to use his nails to lift her chin. He showed his fangs. "Soon."

Considering her crimes, Valentine could do what he wanted with her—after they got through this. Celwyn's attention centered on the black ship. Like armies of ants, hundreds of automats swarmed across the deck of the pirate ship, some preparing more cannons.

"This isn't good," Tara commented and kicked Ginnie again. She asked Celwyn, "Are these the same automats that you froze when you met Talos the first time?"

"Probably..." More cannonballs peppered the sea within a dozen feet of them while Valentine steered an erratic path forward. "Here—" The magician lay a bank of fog between them and the pirate ship. As he turned back to ask Valentine a question, the sea on their leeward side rose, pushing water high up the side of their boat, nearly swamping them.

Encased in thousands of bubbles, the long black hull of the *Nautilus* surfaced beside them. They held on to the sides of their boat as the swells between them rolled in welcome.

Chapter 50

A S THE ECHOES OF THE GONGS SUB-sided inside the submarine, the *Nautilus* leveled off. Kang scampered up the spiral stairs, following the crew up top as they crowded onto the platform. Only feet away, a small boat floated in the rough water. Valentine sat beside Miss McFein, and Celwyn straddled the prow with his hands on his hips and wearing a most satisfied smile. He had been up to something.

"Good afternoon, Miss McFein, and Mr. Soriano," the automat called. He looked at the magician. "Where is Bartholomew?"

"How did you find us?" Valentine asked.

Celwyn pointed to the pirate ship. "He's there. We allowed them to capture him. Bartholomew's idea."

Kang backed out of a crewman's way as they secured the boat against the side of the *Nautilus*. "Nemo found Dearing's ship yesterday. Then he sent a crewman to the docks here to signal us when you arrived. Is this fog real?" He gestured at the muck as it seemed to grow thicker.

"No. Just a screen to keep them from shooting at us," the magician told him. "Where is Nemo—"

With a shriek of fury, Ginnie flung Tara nearly over the side and arose from the bottom of the boat. In one fluid motion, she pulled a knife out of her boot and flung it at Celwyn. Tara leaped between them, and the knife buried itself deep in her side.

"No!" the magician yelled as he raised Ginnie high in the sky. *"Xiau thinks I cannot kill a woman—he—is—wrong!"*

The magician hurled the witch high, sending her streaking through the sky far out to sea. Kang shielded his eyes against the sun but could not see where Ginnie fell into the water. Meanwhile, Celwyn knelt beside Tara and stopped the blood. He examined the wound as she stroked his hair, saying she would be fine. Her face could not hide the pain.

Just as Kang was about to volunteer his medical expertise, the blood completely stopped, and Celwyn lifted her in his arms. "You saved me," he whispered in her ear. They exchanged a wordless look, and the magician nodded. "If ... you are sure." He kissed her thoroughly.

"Mr. Soriano, if you will join the Professor on the platform there, I'll hand your niece over to you. Xiau will finish taking care of her wound." He kissed her again. "I love a woman who participates!"

Like a cat, the older vampire leapt between the ships and stood beside the automat. The magician floated Tara to him and turned toward the pirate ship. "Where are you going?" Kang demanded, already knowing the answer. "Damn it, Jonas!"

As a most handsome, green-eyed raven, Celwyn rose from the boat into the sky, growing larger with each beat of his wings. Kang called, "Subtle, Jonas. God dammit! Be careful!"

⟨————⟩

Bartholomew played limp as if a knock on the head had done him any damage. *Let these bastards carry me.* While they maneuvered him up the side of the ship, the big man scanned the sea and thought he saw a small boat in the distance speeding across the water, hell-bent on reaching the pirate ship. *Good old Jonas.*

The automats argued in agitated voices as they shoved him up the rope ladder, over the rail, and onto a dirty deck. He landed hard, his face on broken glass. A crust of bread with small teeth marks lay next to his hand. Bartholomew still pretended to be unconscious. While he imagined what had chewed on the bread, the jabbering continued above him like a storm of buzzing bees and loud enough to induce a headache. The deck stank of fresh vomit. Bartholomew had thought captains took pride in maintaining pristine ships. Not this one.

"Get us underway, Gaspard," came a voice as nasty as it was deep. "We don't need more than this one to trade for that fancy professor."

In addition to the chattering automats, dozens of voices in English competed with others in Spanish and Chinese. They all sounded excited. The big man caught the words *"rehén grande"* before rough hands pulled him to his feet, and a bucket of freezing water was thrown in his face. Someone punched him hard in the ribs.

Although he could not see the source, a precise, mechanical voice reached him along with the odor of cloves. From what Xiau and Jonas had said, Talos must be nearby. He opened his eyes and found a man a foot away who looked like an evil version of Kang.

"We need to question this one." Talos kicked Bartholomew hard in the back of the knee. "Black bastard."

The big man winced as he straightened to his full height and looked down on them. A herd of armed automats ringed Talos and the man Nemo had described as Captain Emilio Dearing.

Nemo had reported Dearing would be muscular and hairy. He certainly was. The pirate also had a pair of startling blue eyes under bushy brows and a full beard that a crow could have nested in if it did not mind the smell. One gold earring dangled from a none-too-clean ear, and a dozen gold chains hung from his bull neck. Bartholomew sized him up, certain he could best him in a fight—if there were no guns or knives involved.

Talos's eyes glittered with a malicious glee that Kang's never did. The cruelty came through clearly.

As if he knew of Bartholomew's assessment, the pirate caressed the hilt of the long sword that dangled from his belt to the bottom of his knee britches. Behind him, the automats shuffled closer, seeming to sense a bloody confrontation as their chatter escalated as if someone had poked a stick in a giant hive.

"Why are you here?" Talos asked Bartholomew. When he didn't answer, Dearing backhanded the big man against the rail, the only thing keeping him from a long fall into the North Sea.

"Where is the blonde woman? The vampire?" Bartholomew called out to Dearing. He wagered that of the two of them, Dearing would be more likely to brag.

"Sir?" A voice not unlike Xiau's said, "I would be honored if you would allow me to question the prisoner—" Bartholomew watched a second automat step forward. Although very much like the other mechanical men, he dressed better, like a banker, with his polished boots and tie knotted just so. He pushed through the other automats to Bartholomew and pressed a gun into his ribs.

"No, Gaspard. Back up." Dearing growled, "He is mine." The pirate smiled, revealing blackened and missing teeth.

Disappointment reigned in the curses from a half-dozen languages. The pirates and the automats had expected a gory free-for-all. When Dearing drew his sword with the kind of deliberation intended to terrorize his captive, a shadow passed overhead, blocking the sun.

Bartholomew and the others looked up, hearing the ominous thump, thump, thump of enormous wings. Just as during their direst time in the forests of Turkey, the big man saw a raven of tremendous size. He rejoiced inwardly as it circled the top of the masts, billowing the canvasses and turning for another pass by them. When one of the automats lifted his rifle, the raven swooped lower and swatted it and the automat over the side.

Dearing's crew backed up, some of them crossing themselves and others turning to run. The automats became more excited, looking to Talos and then to Gaspard.

In a thundering voice, Celwyn intoned, "Nǐ huì sǐ diào nǐ de shēnghuó fāngshì!!"

Chapter 51

TALOS FIGURED IT OUT FIRST. "IT'S the mag—"

"Who?" Dearing turned on his heel, his face a study in confusion and anger as he tracked Celwyn's flight across the upper masts. The magician's wingspan was nearly as wide as the ship, and he dipped again, sweeping most of Dearing's vermin into the sea. He flew upward for another pass by, but this time, he did not fly alone. The wyvern had appeared, almost as large as the raven, as it wove its way in and out of the masts. Bartholomew knew his mouth hung open but didn't care.

"The Hell—" Dearing shouted.

As Celwyn descended, a series of rifle shots erupted around him. Like crumbs, he brushed the remaining crew over the side and, this time, included the rest of the automats. He landed next to Bartholomew as himself. The wyvern continued its circuits through the masts, moving fast.

With an irritated look from the magician, a ring of fire surrounded Talos and Dearing. The magician lit up the canvasses behind them, and after executing a most sarcastic bow, Celwyn walked toward them. He drawled, "I promised Mr. Valentine Soriano that I would bring you with us." He flicked a hand and brought the pirate to his knees. When he would have reached for his scabbard, the magician dissolved it. "He is most annoyed with you."

Bartholomew scanned the deck, verifying that they were alone and none of the pirates were aiming a rifle in their direction. They heard pounding from the hold. It seemed the rest of the pirates couldn't get out.

"Where is Valentine's niece?" Celwyn growled, his fists clenching and unclenching. The magician kept a tight rein over his anger, trying not to think of the two of them hitting Tara and the others man-handling her. "Keeping you alive is against my better judgment." Well aware that Nemo would not wait much longer, Celwyn regarded Talos. "I thought I'd killed you once, and it should have been enough. As for you," he nodded at Dearing, "It is time you danced for your crimes."

With a roar, Dearing started toward him but found himself instead turning toward Talos, fighting to stay upright as Celwyn bent him into a polite bow. A fine waltz began, weaving its way across the deck as settees and vases of flowers solidified around a formal dance floor that gleamed in the sun. Dearing struggled as Celwyn propelled him across the deck with Talos in his arms. The automat's eyes blazed in hatred as they executed one box step, then another, and bowed to each other, three steps up and back. Dearing tried to speak but could not until the waltz faded, and the only sound was the caw of seagulls and waves lapping against the ship.

"You should know, the Professor had placed no such restrictions on Talos's fate," Celwyn told Bartholomew. "He has no affection for him. He expects that I will eliminate him again."

"You shouldn't disappoint him."

Simply killing Talos wouldn't do. The magician breathed deeply and opened his hands as a deluge began, the veil of rain so thick nothing could be seen. From across the water, forlorn violin music approached them; five notes repeated and growing into a crescendo as it surrounded the ship.

When the rain cleared, five tall men encircled Talos, all of them Celwyn. Talos remembered them from before; it showed in his eyes as he tried to run. The music became deafening, reverberating to the sky. The five Celwyns drew closer to Talos, circling faster and faster. Each moved deliberately, orchestrated to confuse—illusions designed to kill. They covered Talos, and he fought them until one cut through his shirt and removed his metal disc.

As the violins grew quiet, the four illusions faded into the gray mist, dissolving into the sea air. The magician displayed the metal disc and pocketed it.

Afraid of what he would find but realizing Tara and Valentine wouldn't rest without knowing,

Celwyn turned and entered Dearing's mind to find Miss Redifer's fate. A scant moment later, he backed out, finding worse than he had expected.

"They have her?" Bartholomew asked, his expression still anxious after Talos's violent demise.

Celwyn hadn't known the big man could read him so easily. He nodded. "It is something horrible that we will discuss later."

"Will those automats survive in the water?"

"Good question. I doubt it. We're a good fifteen miles from the coast, and they would have no way of getting back to the surface to see which direction to go." Celwyn smiled at the thought of little mechanical men wandering the seafloor forever.

The magician glanced out to sea and back again. When they were all together again with Nemo, Celwyn would tell everyone that he had found the connection between Talos and Dearing and what had happened to Miss Redifer. "At the moment, there is something more urgent about to occur. Keep an eye on the water about a mile out ... beside that abandoned boat, please."

"You could have done all of this without me," Bartholomew told him.

"Perhaps. But you and Xiau want to participate. And I promised that you would. I'm just sorry you didn't have a chance to shoot a few of them."

Celwyn turned back to Dearing, who lay still on the deck. While he trussed the pirate like a nasty rat, he asked the big man, "Do you see anything?"

"The fog is gone," Bartholomew said. He leaned over the rail and shielded his eyes. In the distance, the sea roiled, and then a flash of metal glinted at them from just below the surface. As he watched the churning water, something streaked through the sea, heading directly toward them.

Celwyn joined him.

"It appears our time aboard Dearing's ship is about to end."

"It's—it's—the *Nautilus*!" Bartholomew shouted. The realization of what was about to happen dawned upon him. He was frozen in the fascination and the horror of the moment.

"I suggest that you brace yourself." Celwyn grabbed the rail and held on.

Bartholomew did the same, his wide-eyed gaze locked on the water off their starboard side.

Like a sleek and enormous whale moving incredibly fast, the submarine grew larger as it drew close. Bartholomew pointed at the iron horn extending from the nose of the *Nautilus* as she dove below the waves.

Long seconds went by, and when the impact came, it seemed to last forever under the deafening rending that shook *Primero*. After it subsided, Bartholomew leaned over the side. Seawater flowed into the ship's hull as she began to keel over.

"I suggest that you brace yourself." Celwyn grabbed the rail and held on.

Bartholomew did so, his eyes on the water.

A second tremendous rending shook the ship, the impact seeming to last forever. When it subsided, Bartholomew leaned over the side to see where she had been hit. Immediately, the ship leaned hard to starboard.

From behind them came a loud, ominous crack and a deep groan as the ship began to keel over. The main mast tilted, only held by the ropes on it. The big man and the magician scrambled to hold on to the rail. The mast cracked again and slammed onto the deck.

"How unfortunate for you, Mr. Dearing. Annoying Captain Nemo does have consequences," Celwyn informed him with a broad smile. He tossed the pirate overboard and regarded Bartholomew.

The big man's eyes grew wider. He gulped.

"I'll keep him afloat until we join him. We've got to jump." Celwyn felt the ship shift. "This tub will sink within seconds." He slung a leg over the rail and said, "Nemo is turning around and coming back to pick us up." He patted Bartholomew's arm. "We will glide downward, and I will keep us above the waves."

"Do we have to—"

"Yes."

Bartholomew muttered an imprecation to a god and hoisted himself on top of the rail.

"*God dammit*, Jonas!"

Coda

HOURS LATER, VALENTINE LEFT the *Nautilus* to return to the coast, escorted by a pair of crewmen and Nemo's Lieutenant Granger. The vampire needed to hunt or find a butcher shop for nourishment. Their journey would begin on the morrow.

Celwyn and the others remained in the study of the *Nautilus* with their coffees and expectant faces. Kang, being the least shy, with the exception of the magician, voiced the first question.

"I believe you wanted Valentine out of the way, Jonas, at least for an hour or two?"

Celwyn paced behind the sofas, an uncharacteristic action. He felt uncomfortable with what he must say.

"Just spit it out," Bartholomew suggested.

"Captain, without yet knowing details of your interest here, can we assume it is somewhat urgent?" The magician asked.

He growled, "Yes." Then he regarded Celwyn. "But maybe not as much as what you know of Miss Redifer's predicament."

Celwyn dropped to the sofa by the automat and put his hands on his knees.

"That is true. Her situation is dire. I wanted to tell you about it before informing her uncle or Tara. We probably won't be able to control Valentine's reaction if we do not have a solution." He sighed. "When I entered Dearing's mind, I found that he had sold Miss Redifer to Sultan Sipahi. His ship carrying her sailed five days ago."

"Oh, my," Kang murmured.

"Just like what the Barbary pirates used to do." Verne frowned.

Bartholomew said, "That news alone is troubling, but I suspect there is more."

Tea would help this, the magician decided. In an instant, he inhaled a wonderful blend and offered cups around. Everyone except Kang declined with grace. The automat just rolled his eyes. When the silence grew unbearable again, the magician continued. "There is. I can't describe how I felt when I found out, knowing I couldn't rip Dearing apart. At least not yet." He indicated Nemo. "Not only had I promised to deliver the bastard here, but he may have more information buried deeper in his worm-ridden brain."

Kang patted his shoulder. "Good call. Tell us. It has to be bad for you to get Valentine off the ship and keep this from him."

With a sigh he felt all the way to his boots, Celwyn said, "The sultan intends to breed Miss Redifer to make superior, unstoppable soldiers for his army. She is one of a group of female vampires he has bought."

Silence reigned over the room. Qing's nails sounded too loud as he clicked his way across the ledge under the aquatic window.

Captain Nemo cleared his throat. "Not only is that terrible, but we must be on our way as soon as Mr. Soriano and Granger return." To Kang and Bartholomew, he asked, "Should I drop you off at Findbar or near Prague?"

"Or do we prefer to go with you?" Bartholomew asked and glanced at the Professor.

The automat pursed his lips and turned to Nemo.

"Could you dispatch another boat ashore to send a telegram for us to Prague? We will all be going with you."

Book club questions

1. After reading the book, what alternate title would you have used if you'd written the book?
2. Did the scene where Celwyn couldn't believe his brother Pelaez killed everyone at the compound resonate with you? Do you think Pelaez killed them? Why?
3. How important was the time period or the setting to the story? Did you think it was accurately portrayed?
4. Were the characters of the Wessex Club clearly drawn and historically depicted?
5. Have you read the other books in this series? How would you compare them to this selection?
6. Which character do you want to see more of? Which less of?

7. Is Celwyn evolving into a softer person? Does it suit him?
8. If you could talk to the author, what burning question would you ask about Celwyn?
9. Which character did you most relate to and why?
10. Would you like to be in Bartholomew's shoes during the ending scene on the *Primero*?

Author Bio

LOU'S EARLY WORK WAS HORROR AND suspense. Later, her work morphed into a combination of magical realism, mystery, and adventure, painted with horrific elements as needed.

Lou is one of those writers who doesn't plan a plot—no outlines, no clue, and she sometimes writes herself into a corner. Atmospheric music in the background helps, especially "Black" by Pearl Jam.

More information is available at LouKemp.com. She'd love to hear from you and what you think of Celwyn, Bartholomew, and Professor Xiau Kang.

Milestones:

2009 The anthology story Sherlock's Opera appears in Seattle Noir, edited by Curt Colbert, Akashic Books. Available through Amazon or Barnes and

Noble online. Booklist publishes a favorable review of my contribution to the anthology.

2010 The story, *In Memory of the Sibylline*, is accepted into the best-selling MWA anthology Crimes by Moonlight, edited by Charlaine Harris. The immortal magician Celwyn makes his first appearance in print.

2018 The story, *The Violins Played before Junstan*, is published in the MWA anthology Odd Partners, edited by Anne Perry. The Celwyn series begins.

2022 The partnership with 4 Horsemen Publications begins. Book 1, *The Violins Played before Junstan* is published.

2023 Book 2 of the Celwyn series, *Music Shall Untune the Sky* has been published.

2023 Book 3, *The Raven and the Pig,* has been published.

The companion book, *The Sea of the Vanities,* will be published in June 2023.

The companion book, *Farm Hall,* will be published late 2023.

Book 4, The Pirate Danced and the Automat Died will be available Fall 2023

MORE BOOKS FROM
4 HORSEMEN PUBLICATIONS

FANTASY, SCIFI, & PARANORMAL ROMANCE

AMANDA FASCIANO
Waking Up Dead
Dead Vessel
The Dead Show
Dead Revelations

BEAU LAKE
The Beast Beside Me
The Beast Within Me
Taming the Beast: Novella
The Beast After Me
Charming the Beast
The Beast Like Me
An Eye for Emeralds
Swimming in Sapphires
Pining for Pearls

CHELSEA BURTON DUNN
By Moonlight
Moonbound
Bloodthirsty

D. LAMBERT
Rydan
Celebrant
Northlander
Esparan
King

Traitor
His Last Name

DANIELLE ORSINO
Locked Out of Heaven
Thine Eyes of Mercy
From the Ashes
Kingdom Come
Fire, Ice, Acid, & Heart
A Fae is Done

J.M. PAQUETTE
Klauden's Ring
Solyn's Body
The Inbetween
Hannah's Heart
Call Me Forth
Invite Me In
Keep Me Close
Heart of Stone

KAIT DISNEY-LEUGERS
Antique Magic
Blood Magic

KYLE SORRELL
Munderworld
Potarium

CRIME, DETECTIVE, AND NOIR

FANTASY

D. LAMBERT
To Walk into the Sands
Rydan
Celebrant
Northlander
Esparan
King
Traitor
His Last Name

DANIELLE ORSINO
Locked Out of Heaven
Thine Eyes of Mercy
From the Ashes
Kingdom Come
Fire, Ice, Acid, & Heart
A Fae is Done

J.M. PAQUETTE
Klauden's Ring
Solyn's Body
The Inbetween
Hannah's Heart

LOU KEMP
The Violins Played
Before Junstan

Music Shall Untune the Sky
The Raven and the Pig
The Sea of the Vanities

R.J. YOUNG
Challenges of Tawa
The Witch of the Whirlwind

SYDNEY WILDER
Daughter of Serpents

VALERIE WILLIS
Cedric: The Demonic Knight
Romasanta: Father of
Werewolves
The Oracle: Keeper of the
Gaea's Gate
Artemis: Eye of Gaea
King Incubus: A New Reign

KYLE SORRELL
Munderworld
Potarium

DISCOVER MORE AT
4HORSEMENPUBLICATIONS.COM

www.ingramcontent.com/pod-product-compliance
Lightning Source LLC
Chambersburg PA
CBHW020001120726
47903CB00004B/1081